HIGHLAND STRENGTH
THE CLAN SINCLAIR LEGACY

CELESTE BARCLAY

A very special thank you to Patty Prather MacFarlane for sharing her original Gaelic wedding blessing adapted and recited by Thormud and Greer.
It originally appeared in His Highland Surprise and was recited by Laird Liam Sinclair.

Happy reading, y'all,
Celeste

SUBSCRIBE TO CELESTE'S NEWSLETTER

Subscribe to Celeste's bimonthly newsletter to receive exclusive insider perks.

Have you read *The Highland Ladies Guide*? This FREE first in series is available to all new subscribers to Celeste's monthly newsletter. Subscribe on her website.
Subscribe Now

THE CLAN SINCLAIR LEGACY

Highland Lion
Highland Bear
Highland Jewel
Highland Rose
Highland Strength

SINCLAIR FAMILY NAME GUIDE

Liam Sinclair m. Kyla Sutherland
  b. ***Callum Sinclair*** m. *Siùsan Mackenzie* (SH-IY-oo-san)
  b. Thormud Seamus Magnus Sinclair (TOR-mood SHAY-mus)
  b. Rose Kyla Sinclair
  b. Shona Mary Sinclair
  b. ***Alexander Sinclair*** m. *Brighde Kerr* (BREE-ju KAIR)
  b. Saoirse Sinead Sinclair (SEER-sha shi-NAYD)
  b. Nessa Elise Sinclair
  b. Mirren Louise Sinclair
  b. ***Tavish Sinclair*** m. *Ceit Eithne Comyn* (KAIT-ch En-ya CUM-in)
  b. Ailish Elizabeth Sinclair (A-lish)
  b. Tate Henry Sinclair
  b. William "Wiley" Matthew Sinclair
  b. ***Magnus Sinclair*** m. *Deirdre Fraser* (DEER-dreh FRA-zer)
  b. Maisie Blair Sinclair
  b. Blake Magnus Sinclair
  b. Torquil Lachlan Sinclair
  b. ***Mairghread Sinclair*** (Mah-GAID) m. *Tristan Mackay*
  b. "Wee" Liam Brodie Mackay
  b. Alec Daniel Mackay
  b. Hamish Kincaid Mackay
  b. Ainsley Maude Mackay

PREFACE

Welcome to *The Clan Sinclair Legacy*, a spinoff from my *The Clan Sinclair* series. As you join the second generation of this remarkable family, you may recognize heroes and heroines from the first series. For some of you, it may be a chance to become reacquainted with old friends. For those who haven't read *The Clan Sinclair*, take heart: all of my books can be read as standalones, so you don't have to read the earlier series to enjoy this one. Many readers of the original books wondered what would become of the couples from my *The Highland Ladies* series. Fear not. The children of several of those couples will have their chance to find love with the younger Sinclairs and their Sutherland relatives over the course of my next twenty books.

The Clan Sinclair Legacy takes place roughly twenty years after *The Clan Sinclair* and about ten years after the final installment of *The Highland Ladies*. In my first series, I never explicitly stated who ruled Scotland at the time; however, King Robert the Bruce and Queen Elizabeth de Burgh appear throughout *The Highland Ladies*. By the time this new series would take place, the Bruce is dead, and his son, David II, is on the throne.

PREFACE

You will discover more about King David's complicated reign in later books in this new series.

If you've read *Highland Rose*, then you met Thormud and Greer during that story. I've kept the Sinclairs and Gunns at odds through nearly thirty books, referencing the feud even in my *The Highland Ladies* series. I decided it was time to end their battles and offer a resolution. What better way to do that than a second chance and enemies to lovers story.

As is the case with all my books, I endeavor to include as much true and accurate history as I can, but there are times when I take creative license. The rivalry between the Sinclairs and Gunns dates back several centuries, as do the feuds between the Gunns and the Mackay, and the Gunns and the Keiths. An inconclusive battle against the Mackays in 1426 was the impetus for me originally creating the feud between the Mackays and Gunns. The feud between the Gunns and Keiths dates as far back as 1478 and officially ran until as recently as 1978. During one period of the Gunn-Keith feud, it's asserted that Dugald Keith coveted Helen, the daughter of a Gunn of Braemor. The young woman refused Keith's advances; however, when she learned she was to be married to another man, Dugald surrounded her father's stronghold, massacred the inhabitants, and absconded with the woman to Ackergill Castle. Unwilling to accept her fate, she leapt from the tower. This led to the Gunns' retaliation and ongoing raiding of the Keiths' land.

Unfortunately for the Gunns, they were defeated during the Battle of Tannach in 1438 or 1464 (the dates are uncertain but more likely the latter). The clans attempted to end their feud during the Battle of Champions, where they set the condition that each side would only send twelve horses. The Keiths outmaneuvered the Gunns, arriving with two warriors on each horse.

PREFACE

The Gunns remained unwilling to accept defeat, so in turn, the Gunn chief's surviving son, James, killed the Keith of Ackergill and his son at Drummroy. Peace between the two clans didn't happen officially until 1978, when the Chief of Clan Keith and the Commander of Clan Gunn signed a peace treaty at the site of the Chapel of St. Tayrs, the location of the fateful Battle of Champions.

My solution to the feuds and who I chose to name the next Laird Gunn is an entirely a product of my imagination. I won't give away more than that.

The alliance between the Macnaughtens and the MacDougalls existed during the First War of Scottish Independence. The Macnaughtens eventually sided with the Robert the Bruce and became loyal to the Scottish cause; however, the MacDougalls remained loyal to John Balliol and the English King Edward I. John MacDougall, Lord of Argyll, was exiled for the first third of the 14th century, choosing to make his home in England after his lands were stripped from him. His grandson, John Gallda MacDougall, continued his family's political machinations and eventually married Johanna Isaac, King David II of Scotland's niece. Kind David is exiled king I reference through *The Clan Sinclair Legacy* series and was the son of King Robert the Bruce.

A portion of the MacDougall land in Argyll was restored to John Gallda, but historians believe that was done, in part, to limit the growing power of their neighbors and rivals, the MacDonalds—most notably John MacDonald, Lord of the Isles, who led the Mac-Dougalls' nemeses. This desire to have the land reverted back to the MacDougalls and have John Gallda MacDougall reinstated was the foundation for this "offscreen" character's part in the story.

I fictionalized the alliance between the Gunns and

PREFACE

MacDonnells, though there is a MacDonnells of Loch Boom branch. The MacDonnells and MacDonalds share a progenitor, so it was easy to depict their alliance in this story.

Throughout this book, I reference more than one landmark such as Loch Calder, Broubster Forest, and Ben Griam mountains. These are all real places that exist in Caithness, the area the Sinclairs governed as part of their earldom. Dirlot Castle, as I described, it was little more than a three-story structure that perched on a forty- or fifty-foot-tall rock. Despite my research, I know of its existence, but I don't know how people accessed it. It did sit near a gorge, and the churning water nearby was known as the Devil's Pool. The real Sir Reginald Cheyne seemed to have built simply because he could. He spent little time there, preferring his larger and more easily accessible strongholds. Much of the landscape was as I described it with boglands and peat fields spreading nearly coast to coast, east to west. This geographic situation worked nicely as an impediment to slow the villains in parts of this tale.

I hope you fall in love with Thor and Greer as easily as I did and you enjoy their adventure to find their happily ever after.

Happy reading,
Celeste

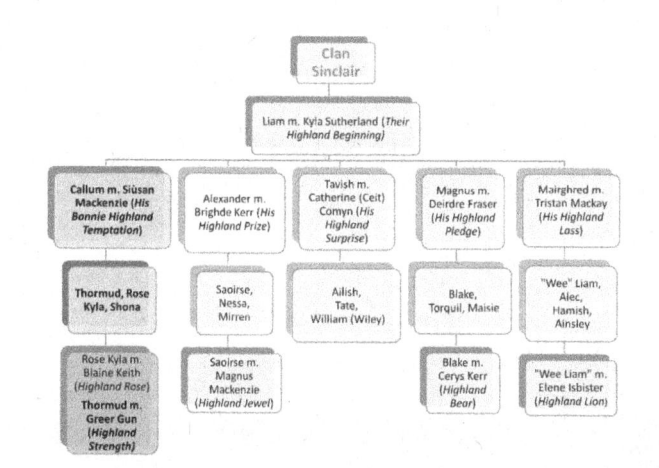

```
Clan Sinclair
└── Liam m. Kyla Sutherland (Their Highland Beginning)
     ├── Callum m. Siùsan Mackenzie (His Bonnie Highland Temptation)
     │    └── Thormud, Rose Kyla, Shona
     │         └── Rose Kyla m. Blaine Keith (Highland Rose)
     │             Thormud m. Greer Gun (Highland Strength)
     ├── Alexander m. Brighde Kerr (His Highland Prize)
     │    └── Saoirse, Nessa, Mirren
     │         └── Saoirse m. Magnus Mackenzie (Highland Jewel)
     ├── Tavish m. Catherine (Ceit) Comyn (His Highland Surprise)
     │    └── Ailish, Tate, William (Wiley)
     ├── Magnus m. Deirdre Fraser (His Highland Pledge)
     │    └── Blake, Torquil, Maisie
     │         └── Blake m. Cerys Kerr (Highland Bear)
     └── Mairghred m. Tristan Mackay (His Highland Lass)
          └── "Wee" Liam, Alec, Hamish, Ainsley
               └── "Wee Liam" m. Elene Isbister (Highland Lion)
```

CHAPTER 1

Thormud Sinclair's gaze constantly returned to the woman who sat across from him at the Keith laird's family table. From the raised dais, he could see most of the clan from his seat, but his attention wouldn't leave Greer Gunn. The words she spoke only a month ago rang in his ears. Haunted him day and night. They had a past no one knew. One he had no wish to discuss, especially since his mind had her words on loop. The few times their eyes locked, her expression softened for less than a heartbeat, then hardened to a glare that might just set him ablaze before it froze him.

He'd tried to convince himself it was purely duty and honor that had propelled him off the dais at his home and across the Great Hall to catch Greer before she collapsed. A Sinclair guard had dragged more than supported Greer when she arrived unannounced and badly beaten. He'd tried to convince himself that it was merely convenience that drove him to carry her to his chamber rather than wait for his mother to prepare a guest chamber the floor above his. And he tried to convince himself that it was common sense alone that prompted him to inform her whenever he thought she foolishly endangered her life. That last part was a constant source of contention between them.

Greer and his sister, Rose, had secretly been best friends for three-and-ten years. They'd met when the girls were only ten summers, and they'd formed a tight bond despite being from rival clans. It had shocked Thor to his core when he learned Greer was his twin's close confidante, especially since no one knew his past with Greer. The woman kept far too many secrets, and that made Thor wary.

"If you keep glowering at her, people will treat her poorly. She's done naught wrong. Be nice, Thor." Rose leaned to her left to whisper in her brother's ear.

"I'm not glowering."

"Mayhap nae if we were still at Dunbeath, but the people here at Ackergill Tower arenae accustomed to brooding Sinclairs. Ye look like ye are staring down the devil himself. Plaster a smile on yer face."

Thinking about smiling and Greer Gunn in the same sentence made him fear his face would crack. But he knew Rose was right. If he continued to express his suspicion, people would take cues from him. He didn't want them to alienate Greer. He could admit that was the last thing the young woman needed. He needed to keep his opinion to himself. With a deep breath, he forced himself to relax. He eased the tension between his shoulders and realized they'd practically been up to his ears. Another deep inhale eased the tightness in his chest. As he tilted his head down to pay attention, he took another scoop of pottage, and concentrated on smoothing his expression.

When he looked up, he felt calmer. But the moment his gaze alighted on Greer, that serenity threatened to crumble. Still, he forced himself to maintain the façade. He figured if he pretended long enough, he might convince even himself. When their eyes met yet again, he attempted a smile. It clearly surprised her, but she soon narrowed her eyes. Her suspicion only heightened by his sudden change in demeanor. He sighed and realized he'd tried a little too much, and that was even worse. He appeared a fraud and insincere.

The meal ended with them ignoring each other, not unlike all their other meals. When the servants pushed aside the tables and benches, and the musicians began the first tune, Rose nudged Thor none too gently.

"Ye owe me a dance or three."

"I owe ye? Nay, o' sister mine. 'Tis the other way around. I caught four hens for ye today."

"And I insisted Cook save an entire one for ye."

"I'm a growing lad. I have hollow legs. Mama says so."

"Ye shall grow wide nae up. And Mama isnae here to protect ye."

"Ye've always been so cruel."

Thor tugged on the kertch Rose wore now that she was married. He could no longer reach the strawberry-blonde hair they shared in common. She pinched his ribs in return. They'd done the same thing to each other since they were children.

"Come, little brother."

"Bossy since before our birth."

Never mind Thor was nearly a foot taller than Rose. She was three minutes older than Thor, and he'd always said she shoved him out of the way to enter the world first. While they were both steadfastly close with their younger sister, Shona, the bond the twins shared was unparalleled. They'd always been conscious not to exclude Shona purposely or inadvertently, but their younger sister accepted that her relationship with them would always differ from the one the twins shared. It was the same mind in two bodies.

They moved onto the dance floor and joined hands

as they took their place among the other clan members. They both enjoyed dancing and had learned together. It was a prime example of how synchronized they were in most things. But lately, one thing left them adrift, and it wasn't Rose marrying.

"Are ye ever going to tell me what's wrong? I've apologized for keeping ma friendship with Greer a secret for so long, and ye've said ye've forgiven me."

"I have. I did within minutes. Despite what people say, we are our own person. Ye can have friends who arenae mine. And I can do the same." Thor kept his tone soft despite his annoyance at discussing Greer yet again.

"But ye refuse to tell me what lies between ye and Greer. It's something more than just disliking her clan."

"Her clan is the entire reason."

It was but wrapped up with so much more. It was as much for his sake as it was Greer's that he said nothing. But he committed himself again to being better at hiding his emotions. Until they came to some type of resolution—if ever—then he would keep his reasons to himself. Rose was prepared to press the issue, but Thor's closed-off expression told her she would get nowhere. They were equally stubborn, and she knew he would only become recalcitrant if she pushed more. She wanted to enjoy the time she still had with Thor before he returned to Castle Dunbeath and their family.

"When will ye leave? Ye havenae told me a date."

"That hurried to be rid of me?"

"Nay, and ye ken it. I'm dreading it. Canna ye merely live here?"

"I'm far past the age of fostering. I'm our father's heir. I canna live anywhere but Dunbeath."

"And Grandda will outlive us all. Ye have decades

before it's yer turn. Ye're likely to be an auld mon before Da passes. Ye have time."

"Rosie, is it just because we've only lived apart when I fostered with Auntie Mairghread and Uncle Tristan? Or has something happened? Are ye scared to be here?"

"Nay. Naught like that. Everyone has been so kind to me, and I feel like this is ma home. When ye fostered with the Mackays, I kenned ye were coming back. It was easy to visit ye. But I'm nae going back to Dunbeath to live there. It's just scary to think I would live anywhere without ye."

"Ackergill is even closer than Varrich. I can ride here to visit any time. Ye can come back to visit whenever ye want."

"I ken."

Thor gave his sister a tight squeeze. "I feel the same, Rosie."

No one but Thor ever called her Rosie. Her husband, Blaine Keith, only called her Kyla. Both were special to her.

"Ye'll miss me?" It was a heartfelt question, and it saddened Thor that she doubted for even a moment how he'd pine.

"Like I would miss losing ma sword arm."

"I choose to take that as a compliment. I'd hoped to hear something like half yer heart."

"It's the ultimate compliment." Thor grinned, and Rose couldn't help but return it. "I dinna want to leave for a while. I canna make ma home here, but neither Grandda nor Da need me so desperately that I canna stay longer. Besides, we have a slew of cousins who can fill ma place for now."

There were ten cousins who now lived at Dunbeath. They had four more who were Mackays and lived at Castle Varrich, and their cousin Saoirse was married to a Mackenzie. Rose now called Ackergill Tower her home. Their parents and uncles each had three children, and their Auntie Mairghread had four. Their father, Callum, was one of five children by Laird Liam and Lady Kyla Sinclair. While their family missed them, there were plenty of hands available to fill their duties.

"Then I'm glad ye'll stay awhile longer." Rose returned his squeeze as the song ended. The next one required they change partners. Thor knew he would inevitably partner with Greer for at least one portion. When their turn came, and their arms linked for a twirl, Thor attempted another smile. Greer nearly missed her step. She would admit to no one what everyone already knew. Thor was a devastatingly handsome man with his strawberry-blond hair and deep whiskey-brown eyes.

"Lady Greer."

"Thor."

It was the most civil they'd been to each other in days. They moved on to other partners, but this time, Thor noticed Greer watched him. She was already looking at him each time he swung his gaze to her. When the music brought them back together, Thor decided it was time to clear the air at least a little. He steered them away from the others and to the main doors of the keep.

"I'm nae going outside alone with ye, Thor."

"Do ye fear me that much?"

"I fear for ma reputation. I havenae feared ye since I came to Dunbeath that night."

"Ye feared me before that."

"Can ye blame me? Ye werenae as massive as ye are now, but ye were still intimidating back then."

"Ye believed me so dishonorable that I would break ma family's creed that ye never hurt innocents." Thor's arm dropped from around Greer, and he reconsidered trying to clear the air with her.

"Ye dinna get to be insulted when I ken ye remember it all as well as I do."

"We canna discuss this here, but it's clear we must. Yer memory fails ye."

"Thor, I am nae going outside with ye. The last thing I want is to wind up married to ye."

"Ye dinna need to fear me ravishing ye."

Greer's eyes spat venom, and Thor knew he hadn't needed to add the last barb. While he didn't know all of Greer's past, he knew that comment would cut far too deep. He wished he could pull it back as it hung heavily in the air.

"Lady Greer, I apologize. That was uncalled for and unforgivably cruel. I'm sorry."

"Dinna fash." Greer's tone was the opposite of reassuring. It mocked him. His resolve to speak to her came back with force. He maneuvered her closer to the doors, even as she tried to stop him. He opened the massive wood door with the studded metal and more gently guided her to stand beneath a torch. Anyone on the battlements could see them speaking, which meant they would also see them not touching and standing apart. The key would be to keep anyone from guessing they were arguing.

"I am going back inside, Thormud."

"Nae yet."

"I will never allow a mon to make me do something I dinna want ever again. Move."

"Ye will cause a scene." Thor jerked his chin toward the guardsmen. While they faced away from the bailey, looking out for anyone who might approach, movement and raised voices would draw attention. Thor counted on few people taking notice, but if they did, being beneath the torch would protect them both from too many rumors.

"Ye dragging me out here probably already has people nashgabbing aboot us."

"Lady Greer, please. For Rose's sake, we need to come to some truce."

"Stay the bluidy hell away from me. That's our truce."

"And how am I supposed to do that with ye underfoot?"

Bluidy hell. Why canna I keep ma ruddy mouth shut? If it were anyone else, these thoughtless comments wouldnae be so bad. Why the hell canna I think before I speak? Why do words spew from me?

"Go back to Dunbeath. Then ye willna have to bear the sight of me if it's so offensive."

"Ye arenae chasing me away again." Thor practically barked his reply. It was more strident than necessary, but they were both picking at scabs on wounds that hadn't healed from nearly a decade ago.

"Yer memory is shite. I'm going inside."

"Greer—"

"Lady Greer. Remember, we arenae friends."

"Lady Greer, I'm failing at the truce I suggested seconds ago. But we must come to one. We must cease antagonizing one another."

"Dinna stare at me as though I'm muck under yer boot."

"That's nae what I think."

"Really? Because that's exactly how ye look."

Thor puffed a sigh. "Rose said I was looking unwelcoming to people who dinna ken me. Ye arenae familiar with the Sinclairs besides Rose. I dinna mean to appear so cross, and I dinna want people to think that ye're unwelcome in ma sister's home. Again, I apologize. I am sorry for nae considering how it might appear to others."

"Everyone has heard the Sinclair men brood. But it

HIGHLAND STRENGTH

isnae enjoyable to be the only one on the receiving end of those menacing stares."

"Ye think me menacing toward ye? So, we are back to ye fearing me."

"And we are back to me telling ye I dinna fear ye, Thor. But anyone looking at ye would think I should. That I've done something unforgiveable."

Thor straightened and inhaled, expanding his chest to its full breadth as his nostrils flared. He watched Greer's posture do the opposite. She appeared to retreat into herself, her shoulders rounding, and her arms going around her waist. The assertive woman from a moment ago vanished, and the haunted one who arrived at Dunbeath, battered, returned.

His tone was softer as he spoke. "Mayhap it would be best if I just keep ma distance from ye. I will do better nae to look in yer direction."

"So everyone can think I'm so below ye that ye canna deign to look at me after spending nearly a moon glowering me. Och, aye. Such an improvement. If ye willna go home or leave me in peace here, then I'll go home."

Greer made to step around Thor and truly force her way back into the keep if she had to, but he snagged her arm and dragged her into a shadow where he knew no one could see them at all.

"Ye are never going back to that fucking keep." The adamance in his voice shocked them both. "We may nae get along, Greer. But I will nae allow ye to go near that place again. Nae ever."

"Ye dinna decide that. That's *ma* clan and *ma* people and *ma* home."

"If it were as ye say, then ye wouldnae be staying here. Dinna act a fool because that is one thing I ken ye are nae. Ye canna go back."

"Why does it even matter to ye? Wouldnae life be easier if I did?"

"So I can stand beside ma sister at yer grave? So I can watch her grieve ye and ken I didna keep her from feeling such agony? Nay. Ye dinna get to do that to Rose."

"It seems ye're at least capable of thinking of yer sister rather than just yerself."

Thor knew they could keep dancing around the reason for their animosity no matter how long they remained outside. Neither was willing to discuss the events of that fateful day eight years ago. At this point, he only needed Greer to promise not to do anything rash.

"Greer, dinna threaten to go back to Gunn Castle to hurt me. And dinna do it for real. Please. That is one thing I'm willing to beg for. Our past or nae, ye canna return."

"Why do ye care even a wee?"

"Besides the fact that ye're a living and breathing person, and nay one should endure what ye must have, and besides ye being ma sister's closest friend, I canna bear the thought that someone could hurt ye enough to ever repeat what ye said that day near the cliffs."

"I shouldnae have said aught."

"But ye did. And mayhap ye let me console ye because I was the closest one there, but I dinna think that's it. I think that nay matter what we think of each other, ye ken ye are safe with me. That I will protect ye."

"As an obligation to Rose and to yer family's oath to protect those who canna protect themselves. Except I did fine protecting maself for three-and-twenty years."

Thor took another step forward, forcing Greer to step back until she bumped into the wall behind her.

He lowered his voice further and leaned to whisper in her ear.

"That is a load of shite. If ye had, ye never would have said what ye did. Ye trusted me, and mayhap it was in a moment of weakness ye now regret. But I canna stop thinking aboot what ye said. I will protect ye because ye are ye, and ye deserve it." Her death wish would never leave him. He would never forget the distraught woman he'd embraced and the rage he'd felt as the need to avenge her pulsed through him hotter than any bloodlust he'd felt before.

Greer gazed up at Thor, and even in the dark, she knew how intense his expression was. She couldn't see his face clearly, but she'd pictured it enough times over eight years to have it memorized. If only he were someone else, she could appreciate his handsomeness and his chivalry.

"Thank ye, Thor. I—" She shook her head, cutting herself off before she revealed anything else without forethought.

"What, Greer?"

"It's naught. I willna go back. I dinna want to go back." They stood staring at one another like they had on that battlefield all those years ago. Except this time, it was Greer who walked away.

CHAPTER 2

Thor and Greer kept even more distance from one another for the next sennight. Rose remained mystified, but frustration was turning into anger because she felt torn between her best friend and her brother. The deeply ingrained sense of family caused her to favor Thor, and she resented it. She didn't want to choose. She tried to mediate, but each time she brought up the topic, she felt the wedge growing between her and Greer, and between her and Thor.

"Thor, ye're acting like ye dinna want to be here anymore. Ye said ye do, but ye're keeping to yerself. Ye barely remain in the Great Hall after the evening meal. Ye dinna break yer fast with us. Ye're avoiding all of us to avoid Greer. If this is how ye're going to be, then ye may as well go back to Dunbeath."

"Are ye telling me to leave?"

"Nay. I dinna want ye to go, but ye're miserable. And people are starting to talk aboot Greer. They're already suspicious because she's a Gunn, but she's been kind and helpful since she arrived. However, yer attitude is making people question whether they're wrong to trust her. They're going to distrust me, too. That canna happen. I have to live here, and I have to run this clan alongside Blaine."

"Are ye blaming all of this on me? Are ye telling Greer the same thing?"

"Ye sound like a wean. Ye would say the same thing when Mama caught us being naughty and would separate us to find out the truth."

Thor stared at his sister as they stood together near the chicken coop. He wiped sweat from his brow, having just come from the lists. He knew she spoke the truth, at least the part about her needing her new clan to trust her. He swept his gaze over the bailey and spied Greer working in the gardens. She kneeled as she weeded. She blended in since it was still warm enough for none of the women to need an arisaid. She didn't wear her Gunn plaid, which had helped people accept her. But he knew Rose was right. His attitude toward her had only soured since their doomed conversation. He was the second in line to rule a powerful clan, and he was a renowned leader in battle already. People would believe his assessment of someone and would become suspicious of the person if they sensed he disapproved.

"I tried to do better the other night when ye asked me to at the evening meal. I tried to speak to Greer, and we didna make any progress. I've given her distance because of that."

"Why did ye need to speak to her, and why do ye need to give her distance? I'm fed up of asking why, Thor."

"Then dinna."

Rose narrowed her eyes at her twin. "Until I met Blaine, I loved ye more than anyone. But ye are still the only person to infuriate me as much as ye do. If ye dinna give me some hint of what the bluidy hell is going on, then I willna trust ye. I canna, and that pains me."

"Dinna issue me ultimatums."

"I'm nae. I'm telling ye the truth. I dinna like how I'm starting to question ye, Thor. It doesnae feel right, but I canna help it."

Thor inhaled a whistling breath as his hands fisted. This was the last thing he wanted right now. He wanted to go to the loch to bathe and escape. He'd seen Greer struggling with a basket that morning and had hurried to help. She'd snatched it back from him so hard that she nearly fell. She'd hissed at him when he tried to keep her upright. She would have rather fallen and dropped everything than accept his help or let him touch her again.

"I resent she gave useful information that's prevented plenty of battles, but the one that she didna was the one that made me lose ma best friend. Mayhap it wasna her fault, but that doesnae change the fact that Jamie isnae alive."

"And she is. Do ye resent that she was safe in the keep while ye and Jamie fought?"

Thor gritted his teeth from unleashing the full truth. He made himself wait a few more seconds to regain control of his temper before he answered. "Nay. I dinna resent that she was safe. She shouldnae have been anywhere near that battle." That was true in more than one way. "But it doesnae change the fact that what she told us led us into a trap."

"And ye blame her for that. Mayhap ye and Jamie werenae as ready as ye thought." The moment the words left Rose's mouth, she wished to suck them back in. "I didna mean ye werenae ready to protect each other. I meant…" She didn't know what she meant anymore. She'd liked Jamie, and they'd been friends too. She'd grieved alongside Thor, but not to the same depth as her brother. "Thor, I've been ashamed each time I've felt relieved it hadnae been ye who died. I blamed Grandda and Da for taking ye and letting ye ride out if ye werenae ready. I blamed them for Jamie dying and losing a friend, and for making me watch ye suffer. Do ye blame Greer for the same things I blamed them for?"

"Aye. At least part of that."

"But it wasna her fault."

Thor refused to respond to that. He knew things Rose didn't. Things that he wouldn't reveal unless he resolved the issues with Greer. That meant he likely would never tell Rose.

"Vera well. If ye canna be civil, then ye should leave."

Thor nodded. He knew she couldn't issue the same ultimatum to Greer. She couldn't go back to her clan like Thor could return to his.

"I will truly try harder. I dinna want to jeopardize yer position with yer new clan. And I dinna wish for ye to regret me being here. I ken Greer is better off here, and I dinna want her to go back to that place." He couldn't say Gunn Castle aloud. He hated even thinking the two words.

"Will ye come riding with Blaine, Greer, and me? Blaine and I can stay between ye."

Thor's lips thinned, but he nodded. He didn't look forward to an outing with only two people to separate him from Greer. They would take guards, but they wouldn't be part of the conversation. He hoped he could take part without snapping at Greer or growing sullener.

"Aye. *Gaisgeach* needs to stretch his legs. He'll grow fat from all that hay he's been guzzling without running." Warrior. He'd trained the horse since it was a colt, and that fateful battle had been the steed's first foray into fighting. He'd been perfect beneath Thor, and he'd deserved his name ever since.

"Yer horse has as much fat on his bones as ye do." Rose pinched Thor's ribs, knowing there was little to grab.

"I shall toss that hideous kertch in the fire, so I can tug yer hair. It's nay fair that ye can still get to ma ribs. Ye have a grip like a chicken's beak."

Rose laughed, and Thor wrapped his arm around her shoulders. She shoved him away, knowing he'd done that on purpose. "Disgusting. Ye did that on purpose. Bathe before Gaisgeach isnae the only one attracting flies."

"When do ye wish to go?"

"As soon as ye and Blaine are refreshed. I'll order the horses saddled and get Greer."

Thor headed toward the postern gate while Rose hurried to the stables. Once she talked to the lads there, she made her way to the gardens.

"Will ye still come riding with us?"

"Ye make it sound like it's more than just ye and Blaine."

"I asked Thor to come."

Greer stood and shook out her skirts. She kept herself from rolling her eyes. "Stop trying to get me to talk to yer brother."

"I'm nae. I want a nice day out with ma twin, ma husband, and ma best friend. I need to escape for a little while with people I dinna feel like I have to be perfect in front of. I love ma new home, and I'm getting used to being a chatelaine. But I'm scared people are judging me. Everyone speaks of Blaine's mother like she was a saint. She may well have been, but that only makes me feel like I'm doomed to never meet anyone's expectations. It's exhausting."

Greer stepped closer to Rose and kept her voice

HIGHLAND STRENGTH

low. "Has someone said something? Are there rumors aboot ye? I havenae heard aught, but then again, nay one would speak them in front of me."

"Nay. Naught like that. But I just wish to laugh and ride without seeming improper. And I want to take this ruddy kertch off ma head. I like having it because it reminds me I'm married to Blaine, and I admit I'm proud he picked me. But I hate the feel on ma head. I'm nae used to it yet, and it's annoying."

Greer laughed and nodded. She doubted she'd ever know what one felt like, but she could understand Rose's dislike. Her friend often wore a St. Birgitta's cap if she was doing work that might dirty her hair. But Rose told her she preferred it because it was lighter. Greer thought Rose would prefer the kertch since it was looser and didn't force Rose to pile all of her hair beneath it. She reminded herself that Rose now wore it anytime she wasn't in her chamber, whereas, she'd only worn the coif for certain tasks. She supposed it would take some getting used to if ever she wore one.

Greer walked to the stables with Rose, and they waited for the men to join them. Her clan council refused to allow her to take her horse when she left. They claimed it wasn't hers but the clan's. It forced her to ride with one of Rose's cousins when they came to Ackergill. Blaine hadn't hesitated to assign her a mare from his stables. She yelped when strong hands wrapped around her waist and practically flung her into the saddle. She scrambled to get herself situated astride. Thor was already mounted by the time she looked back. He paid her no attention as he spurred his warhorse forward.

The party passed beneath the portcullis, three Keith guards and two Sinclair guards joining them. The guards fanned out to make a horseshoe around the noble riders. Greer and Thor rode on the outside, while

Rose and Blaine rode beside each other. When they were clear of the village, Rose leaned forward and whistled. She spurred her horse and laid low over her horse's withers. Thor responded, squeezing his powerful thighs against his horse's flanks. The twins bolted ahead of the rest of the group, racing one another as they had since they were children. Except they didn't have their mother telling them to stop being reckless, nor their father silently cheering them on. They'd both known their entire lives Siùsan was far more of a daredevil on horseback than Callum, but she'd insisted her children be far tamer than her. Only Shona continued to push Siùsan to her limits.

Rose rode a gelding that was almost as powerful as Thor's destrier. He'd been more focused and easier to train as a colt, so for several years, he'd easily outrun Thor's horse. Now they were neck and neck, the mounts as competitive as their riders. There were few animals that could keep up with the ones the Sinclairs, Sutherlands, and Mackays bred. They'd blended the bloodlines over the past two-and-a-half decades, making them among the best in the Highlands.

The two Sinclair guards kept up, but the three Keith guards fell behind. They opted to remain around their clan's tánaiste and Greer, while the Sinclair guards chased their laird's grandchildren. Both men were used to Rose and Thor's mad gallops, and it relieved both of them to be assigned to the twins rather than Shona. They took their lives in their hands, riding with that hellion. They guided their horses across hill and dale, taking jumps the Keiths and Greer skirted. The twins finally reined in as a tie when they knew they shouldn't push their horses any further.

They dismounted and raced around their horses' heads, Rose pointing toward a tree as she hoisted her skirts and leaned down to her right boot. She whipped the dirk free as Thor grabbed his from his boot. They'd agreed upon that rule years ago since Rose didn't wear a belt with any knives attached. They flung their blades at the same time, but Rose's embedded into the trunk less than a heartbeat before Thor's.

"Huzzah!" Rose danced around Thor and laughed. He lunged forward and scooped Rose over his shoulder before darting to a pile of pine needles. He was careful, but he dumped her into them.

"Huzzah to ye too, ye wee beastie." Thor reached out his hand to help his sister up. She grabbed it and started to rise, but then she threw her weight backwards and pulled her twin to the ground. She twisted and tried to roll to her feet as she laughed at her brother.

"Ye looks fair worn out. Sit yer sen down afore ye falls down," Rose tossed over her shoulder. She scrambled away, but Thor wrapped his arm around her waist and hauled her back. He scooped an armful of pine needles and dumped them on her. "Ee, by 'eck!" Rose brushed the needles off her face before grabbing a handful and shoving them down her brother's leine.

"I'll gizza thumpin'." Thor reached for Rose again as he playfully threatened to give her a beating, but this time she was too quick. She'd already gathered her skirts and scurried to her feet. They were having so much fun that they didn't notice how their speech slipped and no longer sounded like it fit nobility.

"Ye must catch me first." She ran back toward the horses and where the others now waited. She stopped short as she took in five stunned faces. The Sinclairs were unfazed, but the trio of Keith guards, Blaine, and Greer appeared scandalized. Rose's face flushed as she hurried to brush her clothes off. She reached for her head and realized she'd lost her ketch at some point. She looked around, unsure if it flew off during her breakneck ride or while she and Thor tussled. He came to stand beside her and thrust the white, triangular cloth toward her as he pulled his leine from beneath his belt. He leaned forward to let the pine needles drop from it. She elbowed him, and he finally looked up at their companions.

"Ye walk too close to the cliffs, and ye ride too fast. Ye shall be the death of me, Kyla." Blaine's tone rebuked, but his eyes twinkled as he called Rose by her middle name, a habit that was special between the couple.

"Breed better horseflesh, and ye could keep up." Rose shrugged unrepentantly. The Sinclair guards snickered, and the Keiths' eyes almost fell out of their heads. Blaine swung down from his mount and stalked toward his wife. He slid his hand around her waist, his hand coming to rest at the top of her backside. He leaned forward to whisper.

"There's some flesh I'm certain I can keep up with."

Thor pretended to retch at the double entendre before he led his horse and Rose's to a nearby stream. Greer remained on her horse, completely dazed by the entire scene that played out before her. She'd never seen a brother and sister roughhouse and play together as she'd just witnessed Thor and Rose. Certainly not as adults. She felt like a voyeur as she watched Blaine kiss Rose in a way they didn't do within the keep's wall. At least not in public. Her eyes remained wide and riveted as Thor pulled his leine out and bent forward. The ties at his neck were loose, so she could see down his shirt to all of his rippling muscles. Her mouth had gone dry.

She nudged her horse and guided it toward the stream where all the horses now drank. The guards spread out and turned their backs to the others. She knew they were all attentive to everything, even if they appeared to ignore the newlyweds, Thor, and her. Thor looked up as her horse stopped beside his. It was the only spot available, but it trapped him between the two animals. He reached up and lifted her from the saddle without word, just as he'd done to help her mount. He put her on her feet and turned toward the water. He remained silent as he squatted to scrub his hands, then his face and neck.

"It was nice to see ye and Rose have fun together. I remember seeing ye together at the Gatherings, but ye were always with Shona and yer cousins. Ye were both playful, but I didna see just the two of ye like that. Is that how ye were as weans?"

"Aye."

Thor didn't look at Greer as he answered. His heart still pounded from the exertion and having her nearby did nothing to calm it. He rested his arms on his thighs, his hands fisting just as they had when he discussed Greer with Rose in the bailey. He reminded himself to be nice to Greer for Rose's sake. He stood and turned toward the young woman, and he caught the moment of hurt from his brusque response.

"Da has called us wee beasties since we could crawl. None of the lasses in ma family are dainty. They all give as good as they get, and they dinna mind getting filthy in the process. Auntie Mairghread was the same with Da and ma uncles. Ma grandmama didna have a good relationship with her brothers growing up. She was only close to Uncle Hamish, and even then, it wasna good. But according to Grandda, Auntie Mairghread inherited that spirit from Grandmama. All the lasses got it from her, too. Grandda says that's how we ken Grandmama is still with us."

It shocked Greer that Thor said so much to her in one conversation or that he would share such insights into his family. Rose had told her similar, and she remembered a conversation much like this with Thor many years ago. But she hadn't imagined they were in a place where he would reveal something so personal.

"I'm nae close to any of ma sisters." Greer had a slew of sisters, all of whom were illegitimate. To Edgar's eternal dismay, he'd never sired a son.

Thor nodded as he watched Greer. While her eyes and voice gave no hint to her loneliness, he could read it in her body language. He wondered if anyone else could tell because, to him, it radiated from her. He took a step closer, and her posture closed off even more. He wished to sigh in irritation, but he kept it to himself.

"I wish ye could have had that, Greer. It must have been hard to ken ye had siblings, but ye werenae raised with them."

Greer shifted her gaze to look across the stream. "It wasna as if their mothers raised them as sisters, but as children in the village, they were allowed to play together. They were friends." And they had always excluded Greer. The few times she'd tried to join their games at the beach, they'd shunned her. She'd always wondered if it was because she lived in the keep, and they lived in crofts. Had they assumed her life was easier because she was the laird's acknowledged daughter? She was certain it had been far worse since the day of her birth.

Thor already knew this. He took another step toward her, but she turned away from him. She ran her hand over her horse's flank and up its neck. It nickered and turned its massive head to rest its nose on her shoulder. She leaned against him and closed her eyes. She didn't want Thor's pity. She preferred her horse's company to that.

Thor shook his head at Greer's back. He left her by the stream's bank and went to talk to the guards. She soon heard them laughing, and tears pricked the back of her eyelids. She felt like she was eight summers all over again. She hadn't made a friend until she met Rose two years later. Then she'd had to wait twelve months between their visits for ten years. She'd eventually made some friends with the village children when they realized her life wasn't one of luxury. But she'd trusted none the way she trusted Rose.

She was still standing beside her horse, stroking between its eyes, when Rose and Blaine joined the group. It was likely only five minutes, but it had felt like an eternity. She mounted by herself when Blaine suggested they head back to the keep. While she'd enjoyed her time outside, the outing left her more miserable than before. Rose and Blaine had one another. Thor fit in among the guards. She and Thor were more at odds than ever. Never had she felt so alone. Not even when she was tied to her bed and locked in her chamber alone.

CHAPTER 3

Thor blew out a sigh as he headed into the lists. It had been two days since he'd ridden out with the others and talked to Greer beside the stream. She'd retreated into herself as much as Thor had. She smiled at Rose and other people, and she laughed while she danced at night, but the good humor that had been there before that excursion disappeared. She appeared more guarded than before. It made Thor wonder if it was merely their conversation that changed her or if something more had happened.

He forced the subject from his mind as he did every time he entered the lists. He didn't wish to lose an ear or an arm from inattentiveness while training. He'd taken a nasty blow to his ribs the first day in the Ackergill lists because thinking about living under the same roof as Greer had distracted him. He didn't wish for any more bruises that took a fortnight to heal. He approached a group of Keith guardsmen who didn't see him.

"Is she going to live here for good now?" A blond man asked the others. Thor believed his name was Tim.

"Looks like it." Thor watched Blaine's second, his cousin Marcus, shrug as he answered.

"Ye ken what yer da said aboot her. She used to spread her legs for the Gunn warriors. Mayhap she'd like to earn her keep here." A man Thor knew was named Drew grinned as he spoke.

With a roar, Thor ran the last few feet and launched himself at Drew, knocking them both to the ground. He grabbed a fistful of Drew's hair and pulled his head up before slamming him cheek-first into the ground.

"Dinna ever speak of a lady like that again. Douglan was a piece of shite traitor to yer clan. He spewed filth as he tried to undermine Blaine's position as yer clan's tánaiste and *de facto* laird. Would ye speak that way if he could hear ye? If Lady Rose could? Are ye the type of mon Laird Keith trusted to guard his clan when he followed King David to France? Ye're disgraceful." Thor brought his fist down to Drew's nose, where it pressed against the dirt. Blood sprayed from it. He leaped to his feet before kicking Drew in the kidneys. "Get up."

The man was doubled over and yelped when Thor grabbed his leine and easily pulled him to his feet with one arm.

"If ye or any other mon here ever spews such filth again, I will challenge ye, and I will kill ye. Ye dinna ken aught aboot Lady Greer's past but what Douglan told people. She is Lady Rose's closest friend and companion. I will defend her as a lady, as ma sister's friend, and as a guest of the laird's family. Ye would do well to think twice before ye open yer gob again."

Thor shoved Drew away before he swung to face Marcus, who'd watched without intervening. Now he stood to his full height, almost as large as Thor but nowhere near as intimidating, despite being a warrior many men cowered before. Thor stood with his feet hip-width apart and his arms crossed. While he hadn't inherited the Sinclair men's dark hair, he had inherited the deep whisky-brown eyes that could nail a man to the cross with one look. His chest flexed with each breath. He'd adopted the Sinclair Stance, a posture people knew only boded poorly for whomever received it.

"Ye arenae yer father, and I ken that. But Blaine trusts ye to lead yer men. If they speak this way before ye, it's because they ken ye will allow it. I dinna give a shite who ye are in this clan. *I* will nae tolerate it. Fix yerself and yer men before they wind up in single combat and dead. Ye can explain that to yer laird and yer tánaiste because it'll be yer fault." Thor spat beside Drew's feet before he spun on his heels, his plaid swishing against the back of his tree trunk thighs. He passed Blaine on his way to his men. "Ye need to speak to Marcus. Yer men are vile and speaking ill of Greer. Marcus did naught to stop it. She willna be safe if they continue to repeat what Douglan claimed. Rose trusts ye. Dinna disappoint ma sister."

Thor stormed off, continuing to make his way to his men. They recognized the tornado approaching and braced themselves for hours of rigorous training. Thor didn't disappoint. He worked himself and his men until they could barely stand. They sparred through the midday meal and didn't break until the bells rang for the evening meal. He hadn't kept the reason for his anger a secret because he knew his men would understand. A menacing aura settled over the Sinclairs that kept the Keiths away. Not a Sinclair among them would have reacted differently from Thor.

Liam never tolerated any abuse—physical or verbal—to the women in their clan. Any man who raised a hand to beat a woman or child received a swift, unrelenting, and memorable punishment. It rarely happened. Kyla had arrived to marry Liam with bruises remaining from the beatings she'd received from her father. While Liam's father never ignored abuse to women, Liam had been even more adamant and wrathful with his judgments when he became laird. It had only taken three men's public lashing to make every man understand that Liam turned a blind eye to none of it. He'd raised his sons to believe the same, and in turn, they'd raised their sons as they had been. It would have been a personal failure on Thor's part and a disgrace to his family to ignore the slight against Greer. It mattered not that they didn't get along.

By the time he dunked his head in the water trough set aside for the men to clean themselves and ran a bar of soap over his torso, he'd spent his physical anger. But his mind wasn't at rest. He donned a clean leine in the barracks that one of his men lent him since he didn't have time to go abovestairs to his chamber. He tried to settle himself as he took his seat on the dais, but his chair placed him at an angle to see the men he'd interrupted. Marcus sat farther down the table to Blaine's right. Rose sat to Blaine's left, and Thor sat to her left. His sister leaned toward him after the priest blessed the food.

"What happened? Marcus told Blaine ye got in a fight."

"I dealt with something."

"Thor, they arenae yer men to deal with. Ye humiliated Marcus."

"Good. Mayhap he'll find his bollocks and deal with his men, so I dinna have to."

"It's nae yer place to—"

"They repeated something aboot Greer they shouldnae have. Ye would have had ma bollocks if I didna do something."

Rose glanced at the men sitting below the salt, then to Greer, before turning her gaze to Thor. "What did they say?"

"Ye heard aboot the lies Douglan spread aboot

Greer. They suggested they would make that the truth here."

"What?" Rose's voice rang out, and people turned to face her. She looked at her husband, fury clear. Blaine peered over her head at Thor, who wore a matching expression. So much for his physical anger ending. Her gaze didn't waver from her husband's. "Who?"

"Thor dealt with it, and so did I."

"Who, Blaine?"

Blaine leaned to whisper to Rose. "Kyla, dinna. At least, nae right now. It'll only draw attention to Greer, and that's the last thing she needs. Please let it be for now. If ye wish to have words with them or even geld them, fine. But dinna fash in front of everyone. Only Greer will suffer."

Rose's chest heaved as she nodded. She turned back to Thor, and their expressions matched. With synchronicity they'd had since their birth, they shifted their gaze to the Keiths dining at the trestle tables in front of the dais. Their gazes swept the crowd before they settled on the men in question. Rose didn't need to know who. She could guess from the brief time she'd met a few of the warriors. Drew's face was battered, and he only had soft food in his trencher. Tim looked as though he would pish himself when his gaze locked with Rose's. If she'd been able to hear their conversation, she would know Tim confessed she terrified him far more than any man in the room. After all, she was a Sinclair woman. They were fiercer than any of the men in the renowned warrior clan.

When she finished staring down the men, her gaze swept the dais until it landed on Greer, who sat with her back to the other diners. She'd pushed her trencher away and leaned back in her chair. She'd watched Thor and Rose and marveled at their similarities. She'd wondered what caused the shift in their tempers. When

Rose met her gaze, she knew whatever happened was because of her. Her stomach knotted, and she wished to excuse herself from the table. But that would only draw attention to her. At least, only people at the dais could see her face. Her eyes darted to Thor, who watched her. His expression was shuttered now, and she couldn't be certain what he thought. But he nodded to her, the movement so small that she almost missed it.

Why did he acknowledge her like that? What happened earlier? She knew it wasn't something that happened during the meal. She'd heard people marvel at the Sinclairs' training that day. As she watched Thor, she realized he'd been working off anger that now returned. She wanted to know why, but she didn't want to ask him. She waited for the meal to end, and for once looked forward to meeting Thor on the dance floor.

"What happened in the lists?" She blurted her question the moment they partnered. Thor wouldn't have time to answer if they continued to dance because he had only a few notes before the dance would force him to someone else. He guided Greer away from the other clan members.

"Lies. A mon repeated rumors, and I made certain he understood it wasna acceptable."

"Rumors and lies aboot me." It wasn't a question. She already knew the answer.

"Aye." Thor wouldn't lie. He wouldn't repeat what he heard, but he wouldn't diminish the event either.

"And ye fought him over it?"

"There was nay fight. I made ma point vera clear. Nay mon says such things aboot any woman."

Greer nodded, but her eyes no longer met Thor's. He'd done it out of his inherent sense of honor and duty. It had nothing to do with it being about her. She didn't want to examine why that hurt so much.

"Greer, nay matter what, I will always protect ye. I've told ye that before. Ye deserve a champion, someone who willna allow anyone to mistreat ye ever again. For now, I will be that person."

"Because ye're a Sinclair? Because ye're ma friend's brother?"

"For those reasons and because ye are ye. I would even if I wasna a Sinclair, and ye werenae ma sister's friend. We dinna get along, and we dinna trust each other. But that doesnae mean I think ye are worthless."

Greer stepped back. "That's exactly what ye've thought for years. I dinna need yer chivalry. Let people talk. It's better than drawing more attention to me than I already have."

"If they said they didna like yer gown, then I would let it go. I willna ignore aught that puts ye at danger."

"Danger? Did they name me a spy?"

"Nay." Thor really didn't want to tell her, but he knew her next statement before she opened her mouth.

"They called me a whore."

"Aye."

"So ye really did defend me because of yer name and Rose."

"*Greer*," Thor snapped. He looked around to be sure no one overheard them. "I have never believed that."

"Dinna lie."

"I have plenty of faults, but I dinna lie. I dinna care what anyone says or what I think may have happened. Ye are nae that filthy word. I dinna want to hear anyone —certainly nae ye—say that aboot ye."

"I dinna need ye defending whatever honor I might have left after being a Gunn ma entire life. Yer attention only causes me naught but trouble. Leave me alone, Thor."

"Gladly. But that doesnae mean I'll leave anyone alone who slights ye."

"What part of *I* dinna need ye dinna ye understand?"

"Ye shall prove yerself a fool to be so stubborn and refuse help."

"Ye've already done a fine job of proving me a fool. Ye dinna need to do it again."

"Greer."

"Thormud."

They glared at one another until they both remembered they didn't argue in private. They turned away from one another, nothing resolved any more than it had been since the day Greer turned up at Dunbeath. The wounds on her body weren't the only ones that had opened.

Greer spent her night just as she always did: restless and frustrated. Nightmares plagued the few moments when she would drift off. But it was the waking moments that were the worst. She was accustomed to the nightmares. They no longer terrified her to the same degree as they had for years. It was the recurring thoughts about a certain strawberry-blond haired man who seemed to exist only to be the bane of hers. She woke as exhausted as she always did, but as she dressed, she forced herself into the role she played daily. Someone who had no visible or invisible scars. Someone who functioned like everyone else around her. Someone normal.

She'd spent the morning with Rose in the gardens, picking the last of the late summer vegetables and readying the storerooms for the major autumn harvest that would arrive in only a few weeks. If they waited, the food would be ready, and they wouldn't. Now she accompanied Rose, Blaine, and Thor to the loch for a picnic. The newlyweds remained in their blissful bubble, but she knew they hoped that removing Thor and her from the rest of the clan's prying eyes might give them a chance to resolve their hostilities. She also knew they would divide and conquer and attempt to learn from Thor and her why they were the way they were. Blessedly, she knew Thor was as unlikely to share as she was.

"Shall we swim?" Rose grinned at Greer as she picked up her pace the last yard of the path to the loch's edge.

"Aye. Dinna cheat this time!" Greer picked up her skirts and hurried after her friend. The men carried the baskets and plaids, so neither had anything to slow them. Greer came alongside Rose and bumped her with her hip before disappearing behind a massive willow tree. Its overhanging branches would protect the women from anyone seeing them as they stripped to their skin. They both hopped from one foot to the other as they kicked off their slippers and tugged down their stockings. They flung their clothes in a pile and raced one another into the water. While Rose was a far stronger swimmer in the North Sea's open water, withstanding the cold and currents better than anyone in her family except her aunt Mairghread, Greer was stronger in the still water, able to hold her breath close to three minutes.

She emerged halfway across the loch and laughed as Rose swam to catch her. They splashed each other as they had since they were girls, rendezvousing at the loch that separated Sinclair and Gunn land. They'd met at a Highland Gathering when they were young girls, neither bothered by the other's clan name. They'd become fast friends, but for many years, they'd only shared one another's company at the Gatherings. But a few years ago, they risked meeting in person at that loch. After that, they met covertly once a month. It wasn't long before Greer become an informant for the Sinclairs. No one asked her. She did it to protect her people. She did it so the Sinclairs knew when her father would strike and to prevent a violent retaliation.

It came to head when her father attacked the Keiths while Blaine visited Rose's Sutherland family. Blaine had ridden to seek help from Laird Sutherland's son-by-marriage Laird Hardwin Cameron about another clan. Love drew Blaine and Rose to one another immediately, and their romance soon flourished. But during a battle, Greer's father, Laird Edgar Gunn, took Blaine captive. He died for that decision, and she held not a moment's regret. But her clan's council refused to consider making her their laird outright, even though she'd silently run the clan while her father spent his time as a warmonger. She'd traveled to Ackergill when Blaine brought Rose to her new home. She and Thor had been guests ever since.

"I swear ye are more fish than woman," Rose teased.

"And ye're a bluidy selkie the way ye swim in the sea. It's nae natural."

"I'm just like Auntie Mairghread and ma grandmama before her. We're made of sterner stuff than the rest of ye." Rose grinned as she splashed Greer, sending a spray of water into her friend's mouth and up her nose.

"I shall get ye back for that."

CHAPTER 4

Greer watched Blaine and Thor set up the picnic on the shore before they both took off their boots. They propped their swords near the loch's edge, then unfastened their belts and plaids. Greer twirled away as Rose laughed. She was already looking away from the men, but they could hear as they both splashed into the water. It only a took a moment before the men joined the women. While Blaine swam directly to Rose, Thor kept a respectful distance. Greer gave the couple more space. The water was clear for several feet, so it hid little.

Greer watched Thor's shoulder muscles bunch and relax as he drifted his arms back and forth to tread water. He attempted to keep his attention diverted, but she caught him glancing toward the waterline that barely covered her submerged breasts.

"I'm going for a swim." Greer and Thor spoke simultaneously, both wishing for an escape. Blaine and Rose barely noticed them, and Greer was certain they would prefer to be alone. She swam away from Thor, enjoying the solitude for a little while. But their paths crossed, and both considered avoiding the other. However, Thor kicked hard until he was in front of Greer. He kept his gaze locked with hers.

"Aboot the other evening. I shouldnae have forced ye to go outside with me or to have a conversation ye didna want. I regret that, but I dinna regret telling ye how I feel aboot ye going back to Gunn Castle. I was serious, Greer. Please dinna do it."

"I dinna lie, despite what ye insist upon believing. I told ye I wouldnae, so I willna."

"Ye've spent most of yer life lying. That's how ye collected secrets to share with Rose."

Greer's temper spiked. If she thought she were strong enough, she would rise out of the water and press Thor's head under. "I have never lied to ye, and ye ken why I did what I did."

"For a clan that's never appreciated ye."

"We dinna all get to be perfect Sinclairs. Some of us live in reality nae some tale a bard spun."

"Do the Keiths seem the same frauds ye claim we are? They seem like a happy enough clan. Mayhap it was yers that was a pile of shite and nae everyone else's."

"I didna say ye were frauds. I dinna think there is aught ye fake in yer family. But we dinna all get to be cherished in this life or the next."

"Greer—"

"Lady Greer."

Thor swam closer, testing the boundaries of propriety. He prayed no one across the loch from them thought they were any closer than they were. It would look incriminating, and he didn't want either of them forced into marriage.

"Greer, we dinna get along. But that doesnae mean ye dinna deserve to be cherished."

"Ye spew shite like it comes from a hog's arse. Ye detest me. Ye dinna think I deserve aught but the life I've had."

"Be glad I canna drag ye out of this water like I did the keep's steps. I dinna detest ye. I dinna trust ye. But I have never wished ye harm, and I dinna wish ye a miserable life."

"Really? Ye certainly made sure that's what I had."

Greer dove under the surface, giving Thor a brief glimpse of the most perfect female backside he'd ever seen. Then she was gone. He knew she could hold her breath for several minutes. But so could he. He dove beneath the surface, his eyes open as he searched for her. Her hair floated around her bare shoulders as her skin glimmered beneath the sun's refracted light. He swam hard to catch her, grasping her ankle and dragging her back to him.

Her head popped out of the water at the same time as his. She tried to turn to face him, but his arm slid around her waist. Thor was careful not to make their bodies touch, and he kept his arm far below her breasts. The last thing he needed was for her to scream bloody murder when she discovered what she always did to him. His reaction was still visceral to the wee firebrand.

"Cease, Greer. I'm nae letting go until ye explain what ye meant."

"Nay."

"Greer." Thor infused the authority into his voice that he used with his men. She laughed. "*Greer.*"

"I shall hate ma name if I must hear ye keep saying it."

"Ye owe me an explanation if I've made yer life worse."

"I dinna owe ye aught. Ye dinna believe when I explain things, anyway. Let go, Thor, or ye shall never sire an heir."

He sucked in a breath, and his arm reflexively tightened around her waist. He moved her a dangerous inch closer. She stilled before she looked over her shoulder.

"Ye dinna care for that threat. Well, I dinna like them anymore than ye do. Let go."

"Will ye ever stop running and just tell the truth?"

"I'm nae the one who walked away."

"Ye lied to me."

"That was easier to believe than the truth. I'm sick of justifying maself to ye. Stay away from me." Greer pushed down and against Thor's arm, but it was a steel band around her.

"Mayhap ye dinna owe me an explanation, but I'm asking for one. I need to ken what happened. I saw yer chamber that day, Greer. Did I cause that?"

"Aye."

Greer made her body go limp and dropped beneath the water's surface before pulling her legs up and kicking backward to make Thor's taut stomach a springboard. She dove deeper until the water became murky, and she knew he would have a hard time spotting her. She swam as hard and as fast as she could until she no longer had breath to hold. She emerged from the water, gulped a lungful of air before diving again. She swam until the shore rose to meet her. She didn't expect Thor to be so close. She glanced at Rose and Blaine, but they hid beneath the drooping willow branches, out of sight. Greer could guess what they were doing. She wouldn't interrupt, but she also wanted her clothes.

"Stay here." Thor barked his order, then stalked out of the water. Greer couldn't turn away. She watched as the muscles moved in his calves, thighs, and buttocks with each step. It was mesmerizing in its masculinity. She whipped her head away when he donned his leine, snatched his plaid, and returned to the water's edge. He snapped his plaid open and swung it around his shoulders like a cape before he turned on his heel. He held his arms out, extending the plaid to nearly its full length. Greer squatted, agog, where the water was just deep enough to cover her. She realized he was offering her privacy and protecting her modesty from anyone who might see. He wouldn't ogle her as she had him. She rushed to yank the great plaid from him and wrap herself in it from head to toe. It practically drowned her.

Thor turned back to her, and his nostrils flared as his gaze swept over her wearing his clan's pattern. She looked far too fetching with her unique violet eyes peering at him from beneath the blue wool. She recognized the look in his eyes because she'd seen it too many times from too many men. Except, Thor didn't make her want to run, screaming, into the mountains. Or better yet, off a cliff into the sea.

Thor clenched his jaw to keep from speaking. The last thing he needed was to admit his thoughts. The very ones that had plagued him since they were five-and-ten. When Greer looked down at the plaid, she held it tighter. Her gaze rose to meet his, but he didn't expect the regret that shone in her luminous eyes. If they could have read each other's mind, they would have known they thought the same thing.

This is how it should have been.

"Greer, are ye ready to get dressed? I'm famished." Rose's voice shattered the moment. Greer backed away, almost tripping on the hem that tucked under her foot. Thor's hands shot out to steady her, which only made her rear back like a scalded cat. She started to fall, so Thor pulled her back toward him. He didn't realize how much weight Greer had lost since she arrived at Dunbeath seeking shelter and an audience with Laird Liam Sinclair. She'd already verged on thin. Now she collided with him, their bodies pressed together. Her eyes jumped up to Thor's, huge from her surprise as she felt his reaction to her.

"Some things may change, but others remain." Thor's voice was barely loud enough for Greer to hear. She didn't fight him this time. She didn't want to. She was too shocked to do anything more than watch him.

"Greer?" Rose's voice roused them from their stupor, and Greer gathered the material until she wouldn't trip again. Thor let go, and she hurried to Rose's side. Once she had her chemise on, she stuck her hand out and shook it with Thor's plaid. She didn't see him approach, but he took it from her. Rose observed her best friend as they dressed. Finally, she tired of waiting for Greer to offer an explanation. "What was all that?"

"Naught."

"Dinna tell me falsehoods, Greer. We've never done that. What is going on with ye and Thor? Ye have a past together, and ye've kept it from me. Now I ken how miserable Thor must have felt to learn I'd been friends with ye and never told him."

"I dinna ken every moment of yer life, and ye dinna ken all of mine."

"Ye practically do. If ye kenned Thor, why didna ye ever tell me?"

"Why didna he ever tell ye that he kenned me? Ye canna fault me from keeping this from ye and hold him blameless."

"I dinna hold him blameless. Ye and I admitted our friendship and that we'd mutually lied to hide it. But ye continue to keep secrets, and now so does Thor."

"Now? He's been keeping it from ye for years, and so have I."

"Why?" Rose's voice demanded an answer. It was the harshest she'd ever used toward her friend. They'd never been cross with one another before, but the situation was rapidly moving from frustrating to infuriating.

"None of yer fucking business, Rose. Leave off." Greer swiped her slippers and stockings from the ground before hurrying out from beneath the branches. She raised her skirts above her ankles and ran toward the keep. Thor glanced at his sister as he finished pulling up his second stocking. He watched Greer run past, tears streaming from her eyes. He abandoned his boots and chased after Greer. He looked farther down the path than she was. His arms wrapped around her, lifting her off her feet and pulling her off the path. But it was too late. He didn't reach her in time. The infuriated adder lunged, its fangs latching onto Greer's toe. Thor ripped a dirk from his belt and sliced the head from the animal. He pried its mouth open to release Greer and flung the head several yards.

"Greer?" Thor's voice cracked with fear.

"Thor, it hurts."

"I ken. Let me look."

He was careful as he eased Greer to the ground with him. But rather than have her sit beside him, he positioned her on his lap. He yanked at her skirts until he could see her feet. She drew her legs in, and Thor leaned to look. The site was already red, and Thor was certain was very painful. It troubled him that Greer barely reacted to what would have hobbled most people. He glanced at her other foot before moving to push down her skirts, but his hand whipped out and twisted her uninjured foot so he could see her sole. Greer hurried to push her skirts down as Rose and Blaine ran toward them. Greer shot Thor a warning glare.

"What happened?" Rose's stricken face appeared before them as she kneeled in front of Greer.

"An adder. Thor must have seen it because he killed it before it sank its fangs all the way into me." Greer twisted to look at Thor again. "How did ye see it before me?"

"A guard mentioned seeing a few the other day on his way back from bathing at the loch. Normally, they dinna bother people. I noticed ye were barefoot. That put ye at risk of stepping on aught that might hurt ye. But running toward one would threaten it, even if ye didna mean to. I was looking along the path just in case. I just wish I'd gotten to ye a moment sooner. Let me get ye to the keep. The healer needs to see that. It may have gotten more venom into ye than ye think. Ye may nae feel poorly now, but ye could soon."

Greer's arms shot out and wrapped around Thor's neck, unprepared for how smoothly he rose with her still in his arms. Their picnic forgotten, Rose and Blaine hurried ahead to open the postern gate. Rose ran to find the healer as Thor carried Greer in through a side door that wasn't frequently used. He took the servants' stairs to reach her guest chamber. He placed her on the bed and made to stand up, but her hand shot out and clutched his leine.

"Dinna go. It hurts more than I wanted Rose to ken. I'm scared."

Thor glanced toward the open door before he sat on the edge of the bed. He eased her grip on his shirt before holding her hand in both of his. He leaned forward and moved hair that nearly covered her eyes. He found the same trust in her eyes as he'd seen the last time he carried her, injured, to a chamber. It was the expression he remembered from years ago.

"I ken, wee one." Thor's hand cupped her cheek, and Greer's eyes watered as she nodded. "I miss calling ye that."

"I miss hearing it. I dinna want to die now."

"Ye willna."

"Ye always believe ye can decide fate. Ye dinna ken

that. I dinna want to die with ye hating me, Thor. Ye may nae detest me, but ye canna stand me."

"I've never hated ye, wee one. I havenae trusted ye, but ye ken the truth." Thor's heart raced. He didn't want to make a deathbed confession, even if he wasn't the one who might die. Greer face crumpled as she shook her head. "Greer, ye ken I still love ye."

"I still love ye. But that doesnae mean ye like me, and it doesnae mean ye'll ever forgive me."

Rose and Una, the healer, cut their conversation short when they rushed into the chamber. Thor released Greer's hand and stood from the bed. He glanced at Rose before he watched Una walk to Greer's feet. He moved aside and gestured for Rose to take his spot. He positioned himself so Rose couldn't see past him to what Una was doing. He knew the moment the older woman spied what he had. Her head jerked up, her gaze dashing from Greer to Thor when he waved his index finger in front of him. He shot her a warning glare before tilting his head toward his twin.

Una nodded before pushing Greer's skirts back, so she could properly inspect the bite. She feathered her hands over Greer's foot and up her calf, seemingly pleased with what she saw, or rather what she didn't find.

"Lady Greer, I dinna think it got much poison in ye. How do ye feel?"

"Hot, nauseous, and lightheaded."

Una's expression tightened. That wasn't what the experienced healer wanted to hear. She opened her cloth sack and rummaged in it. She pulled out two jars, one clearly honey, and the other something none of them recognized.

"Lady Rose, can ye have someone fetch a mug of wine, please?"

Rose hurried to fulfill the healer's request. Una

looked at Greer once Rose left. "The wine and honey will help the theriac go down. Ye are vera fortunate that Laird Keith traveled so frequently to Europe. He brought this anecdote back with him the last time he returned before following Our Majesty to France. He brought this a great many years ago, and it is stronger for having fermented." Una pushed Greer's skirts up farther until both of her feet rested, exposed, on the coverlet. "Ma lady?"

"They're fine." Thor answered for Greer, not looking away from Una. His gaze warned her not to press the issue. When Una nodded, he turned to look at Greer. Her appreciation was clear. She didn't want to explain to anyone, but that didn't mean Thor wouldn't press harder than Una. He would know the truth to the scars across the bottom of her feet. It was clear someone had lashed her many times.

Rose ran back into the room and thrust a chalice at Una, nearly sloshing the liquid. The younger woman returned to her friend's side as the older woman mixed the herbal concoction, honey, and wine.

"What's in it?" Thor had a moment's trepidation about allowing Greer to ingest something he didn't know. He'd never heard of the medicinal, and he didn't know the woman's history as the clan's healer.

"A great many things, lad. But none that will hurt our lady. Alone, each ingredient is fairly mild. Together, with ground snake flesh, it's a powerful remedy for the ills of wild animal bites." Thor narrowed his eyes, not liking the idea of Greer ingesting snake flesh if that was the very thing making her ill. "Lad, snake's dinna die from biting one another. They have their own natural way of curing venom. They've been using this since the ancients in the land of our Lord."

Thor relaxed enough to nod, but he observed every movement the woman made and stared at her as she offered the chalice to Greer. In turn, Greer watched Thor. Rose looked back and forth, still mystified by the pair. She hadn't expected to find them holding hands amid what appeared to be an intensely private conversation. When Thor carried Greer to his chamber at Dunbeath, he'd carefully lowered her to his bed then hurried across the chamber to stand by the fireplace. Now he looked like he wouldn't budge an inch.

"May I sleep?"

Thor wanted to refuse Greer's request, fearing she would slumber and never wake, but Una said yes. The healer packed her belongings as Rose pressed a cool, wet cloth to Greer's forehead. She drew the Gunn plaid that sat at the foot of the bed over Greer. Thor's face darkened to a thundercloud. Greer offered him a reassuring smile before Rose pushed her brother toward the door. When they were in the passageway alone, having thanked Una, Rose turned on Thor.

"When the devil are ye going to tell me what's going on? Greer refuses to. I confessed ma only secret to ye. But ye seem content to keep yers."

"Ye kept it for three-and-ten years, Rose. I've only kept mine for eight. I'll tell ye in five years."

"Eight yea—That was when—"

"Aye. I dinna ask what goes on between ye and Blaine."

"But ye kenned from the start how we both felt aboot each other. Ye encouraged us to be together. I didna keep that from ye."

"Rosie, can ye let us sort out what lies between us before either of us has to explain what we dinna ken?"

"What lies between ye is hate. That isnae hard to understand. This has to do with Jamie."

Thor's chin notched up, but his expression closed off. Rose rolled her eyes. No one else might understand that shuttered mien, but she'd known him since the moment of their conception.

"Ye can make yer face go blank for as long as ye want. But I ken this has to do with that battle and losing him. Ye blame Greer. We were five-and-ten back then, and she wasna even at Gunn Castle that day."

"Aye, she was."

"Nay—"

"Rose, she was there. I willna say more until I sort this out with Greer. I canna promise we ever will. Ye must accept this, or I'll go home."

"Nay. That isnae what I want. I want ma twin and ma best friend to get along, so I dinna have to see ye hurt each other."

Thor wrapped his arms around his sister. Jamie Sinclair had been the closest friend he had besides Rose. He knew now that Greer was Rose's Jamie. But no friend would ever be closer to them than they were to each other. He understood Rose's relationship with Blaine was entirely different. However, when it came to friendship, Rose and Thor would always put each other first.

"Rosie, I ken ye're caught in the middle, and I wish that werenae the case. I canna promise ye that things will ever be well between Greer and me. But I will try harder to nae put ye in the middle. I'm sorry for hurting ye."

"I ken ye are and thank ye. But ye and Greer are hurting each other. I just wish I understood."

"Mayhap one day. But ye must find a way to live with possibly never kenning. That or I have to go home."

"I dinna want that at all. I told ye the other night that I'm nae ready for ye to go. I'll figure it out."

"I love ye, ye wee beastie." Thor kissed his sister's cheek.

"I love ye, too, ye wee beastie." Rose stretched to kiss his cheek.

"Ye wee beastie" was what their father had called them since they were old enough to crawl and get into everything. They'd overturned bowls of flour, spilled buttermilk, and strewn ash across the Great Hall floor and themselves when they were barely toddlers. They'd been getting into trouble together since then.

CHAPTER 5

Thor claimed to go to his chamber to change since his plaid was damp from Greer wrapping it around her. It was, but he could live with it. He went halfway up the stairs until Rose disappeared at the bottom of them, entering the Great Hall. He hurried back down and along the passageway until he reached Greer's door. He knocked once, but he didn't wait for an invitation to enter. He froze.

Greer spun toward the door, grabbing her chemise and holding it in front of her. Her eyes bulged as she observed Thor gauping at her. He snapped out of the trance before her and pushed the door closed, having enough sense to lock it. They didn't need anyone to barge in on them as he'd done to Greer.

He crossed the chamber and ran his hand over her back, feeling a multitude of scars. He saw a brief glimpse before she turned toward him, but he would never forget. His hand trailed gently over her ribs before both hands gripped her shoulders.

"Did I cause this?"

Greer kept her gaze locked with his, but she wouldn't answer. At least, not aloud. Her silence was her answer.

"Please help me understand." He cupped her cheek so gently that her eyes filled with tears. "Wee one, I saw the restraints on yer bed. I think I ken—"

"Whatever ye think ye ken, ye can stop." Greer snapped her interjection. She pressed her lips between her teeth, not meaning to sound so hostile when he was being so gentle.

Thor stepped away and turned toward the door. "Put yer chemise on. Then we are going to talk. Mayhap ye willna tell me all of it, but ye will tell me some of it. Ye will tell me how I caused men to—" He couldn't finish. He feared he'd be ill.

"I told ye, whatever ye think ye ken—"

"Greer." Anguish filled his voice as he spun back around. She still held the chemise in front of her, but he wrapped his arms around her and pulled her against him. He kept his hold loose this time. "I wish to kiss ye again, but things are so different now. If ye dinna want me to touch ye, then I willna. I dinna want to take that choice from ye."

She struggled to slide her hands up between them, their bodies keeping them and the chemise in place. When they were free, she eased them over his chest until her arms wrapped around his neck.

"Ye never have." Greer lifted her chin and parted her lips. Thor's mouth descended to hers, pressing his lips to hers lightly at first. Then the kiss erupted. They clung to one another as eight years dropped away, yet their eight years of longing and hunger exploded into a scrambling need to hold one and to gain more with each passing heartbeat. Thor kept his hands at her lower back not wanting her to feel threatened if he moved them elsewhere. Her moan as she pressed harder against him, arching her back, nearly snapped his resolve. "Thor."

Her breathy whisper went straight to his aching cock. He'd missed the sound of need that matched his.

"Greer, put some clothes on. Ye're still as tempting as ye were back then. If ye dinna, I'll be hefting ye over ma shoulder and searching for the priest."

She bit her bottom lip, tempted to drop the chemise instead. She nodded, and Thor released her. He turned away once more, and Greer's lips twitched at his own modesty. She realized he wouldn't touch her much more than he had unless they were married. She shook her head before she donned the white linen gown that covered her to her toes.

"I'm covered."

Thor turned around as Greer reached for her Gunn plaid. He snatched it and stormed over to the fireplace. He barely caught himself before he tossed it into the flames. He had no right, but a mere glance at the plaid's color and pattern threatened to push him into a rage that would terrify Greer. She would never trust him if she saw the ferocity of his feelings toward her clan. Most of his enmity over the years had been from his friend's death and a little from his past with Greer. Now, nearly all of his abhorrence came from what he suspected had happened to her.

"I willna. That's nae ma decision."

Greer joined him at the fireplace and took her plaid back. She stared at it before shifting her gaze to the flickering flames. It tempted her just as much.

"Thor, I canna change who ma people are. Ma father and the lairds before him may have been despicable, but ma people are just like everyone else. They wish to live in peace and security. They arenae to blame for ma family. That's why I still have ma plaid. But I dinna want to wear it anymore. I dinna feel like one of them the way I used to."

"Because they wouldnae let ye be laird in yer own right?"

"That was to be expected, even if it is frustrating and insulting. I dinna want to be forced into marriage with a mon I dinna ken just to have the right to eat at ma own table or sleep in ma own bed."

"Ye will never sleep in that bed, Greer. I'll burn the fucking thing before ye touch it again."

"Ye are vera adamant aboot something ye dinna ken aught aboot."

"Then explain it to me, Greer. Explain to me why I saw those restraints, why ye said what ye did that day on the bluffs. Tell me the truth, so ma imagination can stop running wild."

"Because the truth is so much worse. I can promise ye that."

Thor pulled her back against his broad chest. He wanted to devour her all over again, but this wasn't the time, despite how his cock tried to convince him otherwise. He wanted to carry her back to the bed, strip the chemise from her, then kiss each and every inch of her. Kiss away the painful memories from each scar until all she could remember was how much he cared about her.

"I've already told ye. I need to ken what I did, even if it wasna intentional. I hurt ye even when I wasna with ye."

Greer inhaled, filling her lungs, before she slowly exhaled and pulled away from him. She nodded and turned the chair closer to her toward the other one. Thor did the same. She dropped her plaid to the floor as she perched on the end of hers, while Thor filled his. He leaned forward and took her hands in his.

"Greer, I meant what I said. I still love ye. I always have. I didna think we could have a future, so I was prepared to love again and marry someone else. But I can never give ma whole heart to a wife like the men in ma family do when they wed. Too much of it still belongs to ye."

"I felt the same. Except, I never expected to love the mon I married. I hoped for a good one who might treat me well and even love me. That's so selfish, but I canna move beyond our past. But, Thor, do we love the person we once knew? The person we thought the other would become? We dinna like each other now."

"Do ye really dislike me? I told ye, I dinna trust ye. That's mostly true. That's what makes this hard. I admire the woman I ken now. Ye were always strong, wee one. But I dinna ken anyone braver than ye. I still see all the goodness in ye that I did when we were younger. I'm scared ye'll betray me again."

Greer's gaze hardened as she snatched her hands away. "I didna betray ye. Ye betrayed me. Ye immediately thought the worst of me and turned yer back on me. Ye refused to listen, so certain ye kenned everything. Ye abandoned me, and the mon I called Father raped me for eight years because he kenned I'd been with ye. He let his men have me. So ye wish to ken why there were restraints on the bed, it was so I wouldnae kill maself or the men. It was so I couldnae fight back. That was ma future after ye rode away, leaving me branded a whore and carrying yer bairn."

Greer was breathless by the time she revealed only a portion of the nightmare her life had been. Thor didn't appear to move, not even to breathe. She'd never seen the energetic man so still.

"We were going to have a bairn?"

"Until Edgar beat me till I lost it."

Tears filled Thor's eyes, and she had a moment where she wished to console him. But anger and resentment coiled around her. Why should she make him feel better?

"Why didna ye tell me? Did ye ken that day?"

"Nay. Nae until I was miscarrying."

"Ye were still ma—"

"Nay, I wasna. Ye repudiated me the moment ye got on that horse and rode to yer men. Ye told me ye never wanted to see me again. Ye told me ye hoped I had the life I deserved. I certainly did."

"Do nae ever say that again, Greer." Thor's voice was a hoarse whisper. "I would dig him out of his grave to kill him all over again."

"Edgar—now that I'm free of him, and ma real father is nay longer a secret, I dinna ever want to call him Father again—kenned I wasna truly his since I was a wean. He saw naught unnatural aboot what he did. He loathed me because he was forced to acknowledge me as his own, but he had nay male heir."

"Did anyone ken what he did to ye?"

"Nay. They kenned what he allowed others to do. But nay one kenned that."

"Greer, I—" Thor's head fell as he shook it. His ragged breathing filled the chamber, and Greer was certain he cried. When he looked up at her, she recognized all the misery she'd ever felt. It was agonizing to see Thor, a man she'd always believed the strongest and bravest in the land, reduced to guilt and shame. "Will ye let me hold ye?"

She rose, and he sat back. She slid onto his lap, and his arms wrapped around her. They held each other as he sobbed. Her tears had long since run out, except for a trickle here and there. She stroked his hair and cheek, but he snatched her hand away.

"I dinna deserve ye consoling me. Ye are the one who suffered."

"We both did, Thor. I didna ken ye still cared at all, let alone this deeply. I thought I suffered alone, but it's obvious now that I didna."

"Greer, I can never make this right. I can never be good enough for ye after what I did."

"I dinna agree with that. But why did ye? Why couldnae ye believe me if ye said ye loved me as much as ye claimed?"

"Because I needed a reason why. I needed ma grief to be justified, and someone to blame for what happened that day. I couldnae think straight after being in ma first battle and what happened to Jamie. I didna ken how to deal with all the emotions of battle as well as the emotions of losing someone so close to me. It seemed so clear that ye were to blame for all I thought I lost that day, including losing ye."

"Ye didna have to lose me."

"I thought I had because I was so certain ye betrayed me. Until an hour ago, I still thought ye had. Neither of us kens all that happened that day. We have to talk aboot this. We have to ken what we each believed happened."

Greer rested her head against Thor's chest as she had years ago. His brawny arms were larger and heavier now than they were when they were still adolescents. But she still felt shielded from the world in his embrace. Even more so now that he was so much larger. She closed her eyes as she recalled those days leading up to the battle.

"Edgar met with Laird Oliphant because both of our clans were feuding with yers. I ken they and the Gunns were the causes, and I ken yer grandfather did what he had to because yer clan is his responsibility. Albert—Da—got a message to Henry, and I arranged to meet Rose. I told her everything I kenned. I told her how Edgar intended to ally with the Oliphants, and they would lead raids on the same night. I told her when it would happen. I kenned Laird Oliphant's widowed sister was Edgar's mistress back then. I didna ken that he lied to the clan council every time they met. I hid in the tunnel and listened to his meetings in his solar. He was telling Lady Meredith something entirely different. He was telling her the truth. He suspected a spy in the clan and a traitor on the council. He didna ken I was the one."

"Ye truly didna ken his battle plan." Thor winced, remembering how she kept repeating that she hadn't known.

"Nae until an hour before the raid was to happen. I tried to find ye. I sneaked out of the keep and tried to reach ye in time to tell ye things had changed. I kenned where ye and yer clan camped. It would have been ideal if the plan was as I thought. Instead, it put ye in a net surrounded by Oliphants and Gunns. There were more patrols than I expected, so I couldnae get to ye in time. I had to keep hiding."

"That's why ye were outside the walls when yer—when Edgar—launched his attack."

"I wasna spying on ye, Thor. I was trying to find ye."

"I couldnae understand how ye werenae safe in the keep unless ye were up to something nefarious. With how fast things happened, I couldnae accept that the seemingly nefarious reasons were to actually help us. It seemed the other way around."

"I ken. That's why I tried to explain, but ye wouldnae listen."

"I didna ken to look for ye, so I had nay idea ye werenae where I thought ye'd be safe. We didna intend to besiege yer keep or even enter it. I believed ye safe in the keep, in yer chamber. We discovered they surrounded us just before dawn. We were trying to move into a new formation when Gunn warriors rode toward us. The battle started so much sooner than I could have imagined. One moment, Grandda, Da, and ma uncles were shouting orders to their men. The next I was trying to keep ma head on ma shoulders. Jamie and I fought near Da and Uncle Alex. We were back-to-back on our steeds, just the way we'd always trained. I could tell Da kept looking at us to be sure we were together and where he could reach us."

Thor sighed as his eyes closed after staring into the fire. His brow furrowed as his memory transported him back to that day. He felt the fear coursing through him. No matter how he'd trained, how his family warned him about the sounds, smells, and sights of battle, nothing could have prepared him for how much *more* it was. Everything was more. Everything compounded until it threatened to overwhelm him. The scent of blood, sweat, pish, and human and horse excrement filled his nose, just as it did on every battlefield. He no longer sat with Greer on his lap in his sister's peaceful home.

"I remember having to dismount, and so did Jamie. We would have been unseated if we tried to stay on horseback. We slapped our horses' rumps, and they took off for safety. Now we truly were back-to-back. We brushed against each other every time we swung our swords. Kenning he was there gave me the confidence to keep going. I ken it was the same for him. We were both so terrified, but duty to each other and to our clan kept us fighting. I kenned if I gave up, he would die. Yet I did ma damnedest, and he still died."

Greer kissed his cheek, and this time, he didn't stop her from grazing her thumb over his cheek. He turned his head and kissed her forehead, returning her affection.

"Yer father's—Edgar's—second charged toward us. We tried to shift without breaking apart, but he just steered his horse toward us. We stayed together, calling out to each other, trying to maneuver away from him, but the mon was determined. We had nay choice but to separate lest he trampled us both. He watched me, our eyes locking for a brief second before ma gaze shifted to his sword as it swung from his shoulder down, nearly cleaving Jamie in half. He laughed at me. He pointed his sword at me and laughed. He could have killed me just as easily, but he made me watch."

"Mitchell was a sick bastard. It's why he and Edgar had been friends, nay just brothers. They shared the same mother, but nae the same father."

"I killed him three days later."

"I ken."

She felt Thor tense beneath her. She leaned away to look at him.

"Was he one of them?"

Greer waited a long moment before she answered. "Does it really matter who they were if they're already dead?"

"Yes."

"He kenned aboot us. He's the one who told Edgar. He targeted Jamie on purpose because he kenned he was yer best friend, and he kenned aboot our handfast. That's what I tried to explain when I found ye that night."

"How'd he ken aboot us?"

Greer rubbed her hand over her eye and cheek before she sank back against Thor. "Every piece of jewelry I had came from ma mother. When she died, he went through it for Edgar. He took everything of any value and left me with things that had nay value but sentimental, and that was only to me. He noticed ma ring on ma thumb."

"The one I moved from yer finger to yer thumb after the first time we made love, after we pledged ourselves. Aye. Ye understood, like I did, that ye couldnae wear it on the correct finger."

Greer reached into the small pocket she'd sewn within the bigger one, her thumb slipping inside. She pulled her hand back and held it up for Thor to see. He took it and brought it to his lips, kissing the ring on her thumb.

"Ye kept it."

"Of course, I did. The day Mitchell found out, I sewed a tiny pocket inside every larger one in each of ma gowns. I kenned I could never wear it in public again, and I couldnae leave it anywhere someone might find it. But I also couldnae live without having it near me."

Thor shifted Greer to sit on one knee, so he could reach inside his sporran. When he pulled his hand out, the ring she'd given him was on the finger she'd placed it.

"Ye kept yers."

"I will never give this up."

"Even when ye wed someone else?" If Greer didn't know Thor would never intentionally physically hurt her, she would have run when she saw his reaction.

"If ye think after all of this—all that we're finally explaining—that I'm marrying someone else, ye are a bluidy bampot. The only person I'm marrying is ye."

Greer's mouth dropped open. There was no hint of a question or even a mere suggestion. It was an edict. It was the decision of a man who'd been trained to lead not just a clan but an earldom from the day of his birth. It sent a shiver along her spine. Trepidation and excitement warred with her.

"And if ye arenae the person I wish to marry?"

"Then ye have finally lied to me. Ye wouldnae have kept that ring *and shown me* if ye planned to marry someone else."

"Ye were so furious with me that night when I found ye after the battle. Ye drew a dirk on me."

"Aye, and nay matter how things stood, that is ma greatest regret in life. At least, it had been until now.

Nae listening to ye, nae having this conversation that night, is ma greatest regret."

"Ye believe I intended to kill ye. Ye thought I was a spy, and that since ye hadnae died in battle, I planned to do it then."

"When ye speak it aloud, it sounds so ridiculous. But it made so much sense that night, and I've told maself over and over that it still made sense, even when I questioned maself."

"I came to see if they hurt ye. I couldnae tell from the distance where I stood. I kenned ye were grieving for Jamie. I saw how ye fell to yer knees and held him, and how yer father and Alexander tried to help him."

"He was already dead by the time they got to us."

"I wanted to hold ye and try to ease yer pain."

Thor looked away. "Instead, I rejected ye and abandoned ye. I threatened to turn ye over to ma grandda if I ever saw ye again. I betrayed ye in the worst way. I didna listen to ye. It was ma fault."

"I could have tried harder, but I was too hurt. I was also too scared of what yer family would do next since the battle ended in a stalemate. I had to slip ma missive to yer grandda. I prayed he would believe it since it wasna written by the same hand—Rose's hand—that shared all the previous secrets. I prayed that if he thought that person nay longer reliable, then he might believe the new source was."

"He did. Ye saved ma life and most of our men's by sneaking that missive to Grandda. I realized it was ye when I learned what Rose was doing. Once I kenned she'd been the messenger, leaving the missives for Grandda and Da in their saddles, I kenned it had been ye that night. I thought ye'd done it out of guilt, mayhap even to manipulate yer way back into ma good graces. Then I didna see or hear from ye, so I figured ye did it purely for yerself because ye feared us sacking and burning yer home."

"I feared that. But I did it because ye wouldnae listen to me and let me tell ye what was in the missive. I couldnae keep that information to maself and ken ye'd undoubtedly die if yer grandda and da didna ken."

"Ye protected me even after I rode away."

"I understood. I'd already lost ma mother, and I ken Edgar did it. Albert confirmed it, but I kenned all those years ago. I recognized yer grief. But I thought I would have a chance to speak to ye again once the bloodlust wore off. I didna imagine ye would avoid me and ride away without me."

"I thought ye'd given up on us when I saw ye near the battlefield. I thought ye were spying on us to tell the mon I thought was yer father. I couldnae imagine bringing ye into ma family's home."

"We werenae too young to be in love, but we were far too young for the weight of marriage. We were too naïve and too inexperienced to understand how to trust." Greer looked at her lap. "We were too young to be parents, even if there are plenty of women who are mothers younger than I was. We wouldnae have been the type of parents we wanted to be."

"That doesnae mean I wouldnae have done ma best by ye and our bairn. I would have learned and tried until I got it right." Thor's dark chocolate eyes filled with such sorrow and remorse that Greer regretted for the umpteenth time that she didn't contact Thor, but she continued to believe she'd done the right thing to protect him.

"I ken that now, but I couldnae be sure back then. I never had the chance to imagine it."

"Will ye tell me what happened after the battle?"

CHAPTER 6

Greer shifted to look Thor in the eyes without straining. She cupped his cheeks and titled his head up, so their gazes remained locked.

"All of them are dead now, Thor. They died in the last battle or when they refused to renounce Edgar. None are left. Ye dinna have to track them and avenge me."

"Then what do I do with this rage, Greer? What do I do with this feeling of failure and disgust that I wasna the mon ye thought I was?"

"Ye love me instead."

She leaned forward and brought their mouths together. Thor cupped her face just as she did his.

"Always, Greer. Can ye do the same for me?"

"I already do."

This was a tender declaration of what was still so fragile. Their truce. Their rediscovery of each other and their enduring love. The declaration of their need to repair their relationship. When they pulled apart, they rested their foreheads together.

"After Mitchell noticed ma ring, and he told Edgar, everything changed. Edgar had the midwife examine me.

She kenned I wasna a virgin anymore, but she didna ken I was carrying. At least, she didna tell me. He'd seen ye on the battlefield, and he kenned we'd talked after. I didna ken someone followed me when I sneaked out. The guard told Edgar that things ended badly between us. That night was the first time he forced himself on me."

Thor thought he was going to be ill. He looked around for the chamber pot. He picked Greer up and practically dumped her onto the chair she'd first sat in before he rushed across the room. He barely made it to the massive bowl in time. He heaved until there was nothing left to come up but bile. He wiped his perspiring brow on his sleeve, unprepared for a sprig of mint to appear beneath his nose.

"Was it every night for eight years?"

Greer shook her head.

"Was it other men every night for eight years?"

"Nay, Thor. I dinna ken if I can ever tell ye all of it. I dinna want—"

"Wee one, I willna turn away from ye again. Naught that ye tell me will ever push me to make the same mistake twice."

"It will disgust ye."

"Was there a mon ye cared aboot?"

Greer's face blanched before it flushed red. Thor could have kicked himself.

"Nay. Are ye jealous?"

"Nay. Good God, nay. I hoped there might have been someone who was kind to ye, who might have cared enough to—I dinna ken. Someone ye cared enough aboot that it wasna all Hell on Earth."

"Ye wished me to love someone else?"

"Nay." Thor's answer was immediate. "But ye deserved it. Ye should have had someone to protect ye, to take care of ye at least a little. Some time of solace. If I'd kenned, Greer, naught would have kept me from coming to ye."

"And ye would have died for it. Albert could have gotten word to ye. I could have told Rose. But I could endure as long as ye were safe."

"Nay... Nay, Greer... Nay." Thor shook his head as he fought for each word. "Yer scars. Who did that?"

"I wish ye hadnae seen those."

Thor chewed a sprig of mint quickly before dropping it into the chamber pot. He led Greer back to the fireplace. He thought about his words more than he ever had in his life, and he still feared he would misstep.

"A few minutes ago, I told ye that I'm marrying ye. I didna ask if that's what ye want, and I should have. But I still mean ma intentions. I want to marry ye, Greer. I only have sisters, and Uncle Alex only had lasses. But Blake already has a son. He's Uncle Magnus's auldest son. Uncle Tavish is aulder than Uncle Magnus, and he has two lads. Tate and Wiley may have sons one day too. I dinna have to have an heir, Greer. If ye dinna want me to see ye, touch ye, like that, then we can have a marriage in name only."

Greer's chin fell forward as she tried to weed through the brief family tree and understand what Thor told her.

"Ye wish to marry me, but ye dinna really want me as yer wife?"

"That isnae what I said. I said, if *ye* dinna want me to see ye or touch ye, that wouldnae stop me from making ye ma wife. I will never force ye to do aught intimate with me. I wouldnae regardless of yer past, but I will nae expect aught from ye."

"Ye'd marry me, and then what? Be miserable? Sinclairs dinna have lemans. Never. Ye would never touch another woman once we wed. If I turned ye away, ye would live the rest of yer life as a monk."

"I hope ye'd grow comfortable enough for us to share a chamber and a bed. I'd like to hold ye while we sleep just as ye let me hold ye while we sat together. But if that isnae what ye want, but ye'd spend yer time with me when our duties dinna keep us apart, then, aye. If ye'd help me lead our clan one day and be ma confidante like ye once were, then, aye."

"Is this really aboot me?"

"Wee one, there isnae another woman alive who I could desire as much as I do ye. I've chastised maself so many times for still wanting ye in ma bed when I ken something like this happened to ye. For wanting ye when I was so certain ye were ma enemy. For loving ma enemy. I want ye, Greer. I will always want ye. But if that isnae what ye can give, then I willna forsake ye over it."

"Thor, I desire ye too. I always have, and naught has changed that. But, truthfully, I dinna ken if I can. I dinna ken if I can share a bed with ye and be intimate without remembering all the times I was forced. I dinna ken if I can couple with ye and enjoy the act. I dinna want to reject ye, but I'm scared I'll panic and scream. I dinna want anyone to think ye're hurting me. And I never want to humiliate ye by people thinking ye have to force me or that I'm rejecting ye."

"Nay one would ever believe I'm forcing ye. But I dinna want to embarrass ye in front of anyone."

Greer's shoulders drooped. "If I married ye, I dinna want a marriage in name only. But I fear I'm too broken to be the wife ye deserve." Her brow furrowed as she swallowed and looked at the rushes covering the floor. Then she met his gaze again. "I dinna ken how ye arenae disgusted with me. I dinna understand how ye could want me after so many—"

"Wee one, I will never be dismissive aboot yer past. I will never pretend like it didna happen. But, if we're nae keeping aught to ourselves, then I will put it this way. I dinna give a fuck who's touched ye in the past as long as I'm the only one who ever touches ye again. If that's burying maself in ye every night for the rest of our lives or holding yer hand until I breathe ma last, I want ye to be mine as much as I want to be yers."

"Most men—"

"Arenae Sinclairs. I dinna lie, Greer, and ye ken that. If I pledge maself to ye in front of a priest—just like we planned—then it's absolute. I would never marry ye under false pretenses, and I wouldnae marry ye if I couldnae love ye as ma wife. If ye will marry me, then I'd have us set the date the Monday after they read the banns the third time. I would have them read the first time tomorrow."

"Ye say ye dinna need an heir, but yer family isnae going to agree with that."

"Yes, they would. There isnae a doubt in ma mind that ma da would have married ma mama if she were barren."

"They were arranged. She went to Dunbeath because there was a contract to marry. They wouldnae have met otherwise."

"Her father never consulted a midwife. He didna ken one way or another, and he wished to be rid of her. He looked for an excuse to send her away. If she'd told Da she couldnae have any bairns, he still would have married her. They fell in love before they married. They handfasted first. They'd be as happy as they are today, even if they hadnae had three weans. Ma da has three brothers. He wasna worried aboot heirs when he married Mama. What if Uncle Alex had been the auldest? He has three lasses. He has never loved them less for nay being sons, and he wouldnae if he were

Grandda's heir instead of Da. I'm more worried that ye willna like living in a keep with so many people. It's crowded."

Greer's expression softened as she smiled. "That's what Rose says. It's why ye two and Shona were at Dunrobin when Blaine showed up. Ye wished to escape to yer Sutherland family for the space."

"Aye. One day—God willing nae for scores—I will be laird and will have to live in the keep. But if ye wish for privacy that ye havenae had, then we can live in a croft until then."

Greer rested her hands on his waist. "Thor, ye're making a lot of concessions to me that ye havenae had time to consider."

"Aye, I have. I've had years to think aboot this. I've wondered what life would be like if we did ever reconcile. It's all I've thought aboot since ye arrived at Dunbeath and since we've come here."

"I have, too. But now that the chance is here, I dinna ken if I can. I want to, Thor. Please dinna doubt that. I just dinna ken if I can. I'm scared."

"Wheest, *mo ghaol*." My love. "We dinna have to wed in three sennights. We can move much slower."

"It's nae the wedding or the thought of marrying. It's the act of being married."

"Then we wait, and we see how things progress. If ye wish for me to touch ye, to try things with me, then we can. It doesnae have to happen all at once."

Greer studied him for so long Thor forced himself not to shift nervously. "If ye hadnae barged in here, we might never have cleared this mess between us."

"Aye, we would have. I couldnae live with this tenuous balance we had. Ma need to ken why ye did what I believed ye had was becoming too strong. It's why I wanted to speak to ye the other evening, but that conversation didna go well. I was too heavy-handed, insisting that ye talk to me because that's what I wanted."

"However this came aboot, I'm glad it did. I wanted to sort this out too, but I wasna sure I could tell ye what happened that day and after. I should have had more faith in ye. Ye arenae that different from the mon I kenned back then. I think that's why this has all been so hard. It's why I still love ye. Would ye still kiss me?"

"Aye, wee one. Anytime ye wish." Thor threaded his fingers with hers as their mouths once more fused together. She opened to him, welcoming his questing tongue as it swept the inside of her cheek before dueling with hers. When she sucked lightly, he nearly lost his resolve to keep this exchange tame. There was an uncertainty to her action that made Thor realize it wasn't the act of a woman who'd been with anyone other than him. He didn't want to think the word many, even though he suspected that was the case. It didn't disgust him. It infuriated him. He didn't want his anger to take hold again because he didn't want Greer to think he directed any of it at her.

"How do we move forward?" Greer prayed he didn't say they keep their distance in public.

"We are going to have to tell Rose at least some of our past. She deserves to ken, and we're hurting her by refusing to confide in her. I will never ask her to keep aught from Blaine. Are ye all right with him learning at least a little of our past?"

"He was in ma chamber, wasna he? He saw what ye did."

"Aye."

"Then he must have some idea."

"He and Rose believe Edgar restrained ye as a punishment. I dinna think either of them ken it was worse than that."

"Would ye have kenned if I hadnae hinted?"

"Aye. I think I would have. When ye arrived so badly beaten, I feared Edgar wasna the only one to attack ye. I thought he might have turned a blind eye to his men. I never imagined he would have nae only allowed it but encouraged it."

"I dinna want Rose to ever find out aboot that. She will blame herself for nae guessing, especially if she ever learns ye did. She will never forgive herself for letting me go back there after every time we met at the loch."

"I ken."

"That's another secret I'm asking ye to keep from yer twin."

"This isnae a secret she needs to ken. This is something between a mon and his wife. The entire world doesnae need to ken what happens between married people."

"We arenae married—anymore."

"Do ye still believe that we were, Greer?"

"Vera much." She held up her hand, reminding him she wore her ring once more. "Do ye?"

He held up his hand. "Aye. We may nae be right now, but ye ken I wish us to be again. And nae just a handfast."

"Can we consider starting with that? I dinna want ye bound to me and then realize ye made a mistake if I canna be a true wife to ye. A year and a day or until one of us repudiates it. That is long enough to discover what we want."

Thor pulled her against him, and for a moment, he worried he should be far gentler. But when she pressed her body against his, he wondered if her body already knew what her mind struggled to accept.

"If ye love me and say I do, then ye are a true wife to me. Dinna ever doubt that. As far as I'm concerned, the moment ye decide ye wish to marry, then we're betrothed. If we're betrothed, then we're as good as married. I willna ask to make love to ye until we marry, but ye will be ma wife in every other way."

Until. He sounds so certain. I hope ma mind doesnae forsake me. I want to believe we'll marry, and we'll be a regular couple that finds joy with each other through intimacy. But what if I canna?

"Dinna fash aboot it until there's a reason to."

"Hmm?" Greer's brow furrowed.

"I ken what ye are thinking. Dinna fash aboot whether ye're ready or nae for more. I've told ye more than once where I stand. I think ye ken how I feel aboot ye and our future. We dinna have to rush."

She nodded before glancing at the door. "What aboot in front of everyone else?"

"What do ye wish? That we've been courting but thought we needed to pretend otherwise? That we resolved our differences and realized we're more alike than we thought?"

"Both? We resolved them a while ago, but then we thought that because of our clans' pasts we needed to pretend."

"And why are we now willing to let others ken?"

"Ye came back here to talk, but I also saw how worried ye were for me. People will ken a snake bit me, so why nay say we're tired of pretending? That we dinna want to hide our concern for each other anymore and that we dinna want to waste any more time keeping our distance. It's all true, even if nae directly."

"Vera well. Will ye let me court ye properly?"

Greer beamed and nodded. She went onto her toes but winced. Thor swept her into his arms and sat in the chair he'd occupied before. He pulled her chemise up and looked at her feet. Her toe was a little swollen, but it wasn't red. The rest of her foot and leg appeared fine.

"Whatever was in the tincture worked. By the time

ye returned, I felt better. I wasna scared I was going to die, and I didna feel so poorly as I did when we first came up here. It's just sore, *mo ghràidh*." My darling.

"Shall we go belowstairs and meet the world as a couple?"

"Aye."

Thor lowered her feet to the floor before she donned her stockings. He helped her lace her gown, bringing back another flood of memories. She slipped her shoes on, wincing once more. She abandoned them, knowing there would be other clanswomen who would be in stockings or barefoot. They exchanged a brief kiss at the top of the stairs before they descended hand-in-hand. They expected stares. They didn't expect a retinue of Gunns standing in front of Blaine.

CHAPTER 7

Thor instinctively pushed Greer behind him, wishing he had his sword. But he'd trusted Blaine to pick it up from where he left his beside his friend's when they entered the loch. He rested his hands on his belt next to the hilt of two dirks. He pressed his shoulders back, expanding his chest to its full breadth, knowing it hid Greer entirely. It didn't change that the Gunn men already saw her, but they couldn't spy her now.

"Go abovestairs, Greer." Thor spoke from the side of his mouth, keeping his lips from moving, and his voice low.

"Nay. I need to ken what they want."

"Naught good. Please let me find out what this is aboot before they speak to ye. I dinna trust them."

"Neither do I, but I've kenned them ma whole life."

"That makes it all worse. Greer, if ye are where I can see ye, I will kill them before they say a word. They might live if I dinna have a reminder right in front of me of what I learned today."

"Ye canna slay every mon who ever—"

"Aye, I can."

"Lady Greer." Matthew, the newly appointed leader

of the Clan Gunn council, stepped forward, cutting off their conversation. Thor felt Greer shift to step around him. His arm wrapped around his back, snaring her against it. It held her in place.

"Dinna speak to her," Thor snarled.

"And ye dinna speak for her."

"Aye, he does. He's ma betrothed." Greer felt Thor go rigid before his body relaxed more than he'd been since he held her against him in the water. She felt his relief, and speaking the words aloud eased all the tension she'd felt since seeing him again after eight years. However, it didn't do away with the fear these men's arrival caused.

"Impossible, Lady Greer. We've chosen yer husband, and he sure as hell isnae a Sinclair. Now come away from him and stop hiding like a naughty wean. It's time ye acted like a woman."

Greer's hands fisted the back of Thor's leine to keep from flying at the man like a woman possessed. She'd told Thor the truth just not the entire truth.

"Make him leave, Thor." They both heard the tremble in her voice, and Thor's body tensed again, ready to launch an attack. He took a step forward, but Greer still clung to his leine. "Dinna leave me."

"Go abovestairs right now. None of them will make it to the laird's family chambers alive. None of the guards will allow it. I will come to ye as soon as they are gone. Go."

"I'm too scared, Thor."

"Wee one, I ken. But ye're braver than anyone I ken. Go up there, and I will come as soon as I can. Then I willna leave until ye tell me to."

"I canna."

Thor realized fear paralyzed her. His fury nearly boiled over. He could guess the one reason to make Greer so terrified.

"I dinna want ye to see me kill another mon. Ye did that day on the battlefield, but I ken ye were far enough away to nae see the true gore. Go, wee one. They canna harm ye again."

Greer didn't respond. She couldn't. The thought of letting go of Thor was more terrifying than seeing Matthew and the others in the Ackergill Great Hall. From the way Thor's arm rested akimbo, his hand still next to the dirk handle, she could spy the men. His other arm remained wrapped around her, and it was all that kept her from collapsing. When Matthew took a step forward, and the other men followed him, she pressed her face against Thor's back and trembled. She feared she might wet herself. How could she have imagined ever going back to Gunn Castle? She couldn't manage these men away from her former home. How would she have dealt with them there alone?

Thor's gaze met Blaine's before it darted to Rose's terrified one where she stood beside her husband. Their eyes met, and Rose released Blaine's arm, that she held onto with both hands. She hurried to Thor's side and tried to ease Greer from her position behind Thor. Greer whimpered and pressed herself tighter against Thor.

"Greer, come with me," Rose whispered. "We'll go to ma chamber and lock ourselves in. Blaine and Thor willna let them come near ye."

Greer couldn't hear Rose or anyone else. She'd slipped back into her memories. Matthew had been the one to follow her that fateful day. He'd told Mitchell what he'd seen, and Mitchell told Edgar what he knew, plus what Matthew shared. They'd been the reason Edgar beat her so badly that she lost her bairn. She truly didn't know if she could carry a bairn even if she could bring herself to be intimate with Thor.

"Lady Greer, cease this nonsense. Ye will gather yer

belongings and return to Gunn Castle. Yer betrothed will be there tomorrow. The wedding is after the midday meal."

She wished she'd said she and Thor were handfasted. She'd been unsure about their future until the moment the words tumbled out of her mouth. She'd not been so certain of anything since the day she and Thor pledged themselves to each other next to the loch that separated Sinclair and Gunn lands. The same place where she'd met Rose so many times. The same place she'd met Thor when he was out hunting with Jamie, the only person who'd known about her and Thor.

Thor continued to look forward, but he spoke to Greer once more. "Do ye truly wish to marry? Nae just handfast?"

"Aye." She didn't have to think of the answer. She knew without hesitation. She didn't know what would happen after they married. She didn't know what kind of marriage they could have. But she knew she wanted to find out. She wanted to try. It was all she'd wanted for eight years. When Thor spoke next, he made sure everyone in the Great Hall could hear him.

"Lady Greer, do ye wish to marry me?"

Greer answered just as loudly. "Aye."

"Are ye sure ye wish to marry me?"

"Aye, I wish to marry ye, Thormud."

"Do ye wish to marry me now?"

"Aye. I wish to marry ye now before all these witnesses present."

Edgar's surviving older but illegitimate brother, Samuel, pushed forward. "Greer, cease this moment before I beat ye maself. There's a priest standing across the chamber from ye. This nonsense willna stand. Ye canna marry by consent with a priest available to conduct the ceremony. Now bring yer whoring self away from that mon before I kill him and lash ye."

CELESTE BARCLAY

"Rose, take ma wife. *Now*."

"Shite," Rose muttered before she tugged Greer's arm. It did nothing to get her to let go of Thor. She twisted and wrapped her arms around Greer, using her greater weight to push her friend until she couldn't hold on to Thor any longer.

"*THOR!*"

Greer's panic-stricken cry tempted Thor to look at the floor to see if someone had ripped his heart out the way it felt. But he didn't allow himself to look back at Greer as she continued to cry out to him as her voice grew farther away. He trusted Rose to get her abovestairs and safe. He didn't trust his sister not to come back down and kill the man who slighted Greer.

"Leave before ma sister returns. There's naught I can do that can compare to what she'll do. I willna stop her either."

"Ye still need someone to hold yer bollocks, do ye? I hear Greer did a fine job of that every time she spread her legs for ye."

"She was ma wife. Say another word, Samuel, and I will figure out how to be more heinous than ma sister will be." Thor stalked forward, a dirk in each hand now that Greer wasn't attached to him. "I ken ye learned we married."

"Bah. Ye handfasted, so ye could swive. Yer da and grandda would never accept a Gunn into yer clan. She was yer whore. She was even going to bear yer bastard."

"Ye are going to die." Thor had no patience to follow through with his threat to allow Rose to kill the man or to carry out his own torture. He hurled the dirk in his right hand and imbedded it in the man's left eye. His other dirk flew from his left hand and landed in the man's jugular, killing Samuel instantly.

The Gunn entourage surged forward, causing the Keith and Sinclair guards present to draw their weapons. None carried their swords inside to prevent a slaughter, but that didn't prevent the melee that began. Women screamed as they ran for shelter. They swept up children as they fled. Thor drew two more dirks from his belt as he rushed forward.

"CEASE!" Blaine roared. His thunderous voice filled the Great Hall, even over the sound of metal clashing, bodies hurtling into one another, and furniture skidding. Blaine's sword tip pressed against Matthew's sternum.

Thor glowered at Blaine. But the tánaiste wouldn't allow a bloodbath in his home, certainly not when his wife was within the keep.

"Matthew, ye lied aboot the reason for yer arrival. Ye insult ma guest, and ye besmirch a mon's wife. Ye are lucky that I stopped these men from slaughtering ye all. I certainly wouldnae miss the lot of ye. But I have a duty to ma people to nay endanger them nor make them clean yer blood off the floors ma wife keeps immaculate. Ye remain within the keep. The rest of the Gunns leave through the front gate or accept accommodations in ma dungeon. Decide."

"Kill another one of us, and all the MacDonnells near and far will descend on ye," Matthew responded. "They wait outside yer walls. Ye canna winge to the Sinclairs and their fucking kin in time to save yerselves. Ye will return Lady Greer to us, or we will slaughter yer clan."

Thor and Blaine looked at one another and laughed. Thor already knew what Blaine would say. If Thor weren't so focused on the continuing argument over Greer, he might have considered how unsettling it was to have a dead man lying before him as though he didn't exist. The conversation carried on as though Thor hadn't just killed a member of the Gunn clan council.

"Ye daft bugger. Ye dinna have anyone outside these gates. Ye said they dinna arrive until tomorrow. I kenned ye approached an hour ago. Ma patrols havenae reported anyone within leagues of the keep."

"We killed them."

"Nay, ye didna. Ma patrols overlap their areas. The dead men would have already been found, and someone would have already ridden to the keep. Ye canna tell me the MacDonnells hide, waiting to launch an attack because ye canna get to ma land without crossing the Sinclairs' and Mackays' first. Now that I've married into their family, our alliance is stronger than ever. We expected trouble from ye. Laird Sinclair and Laird Mackay have quadrupled their patrols along our borders to support us. Ye'd be dead if ye came with a force large enough to be a threat."

"We made it past yer patrols and the Sinclairs'."

That was true and something Blaine would have to address, but he wouldn't admit that now. "Only because it's clear ye arenae a threat to aught but a gnat." Blaine laughed at the men still standing with knives pointed at them. Only Blaine, as the man acting as laird in his father's stead, carried a sword inside the keep. "Go home, and we will pretend ye never stepped foot on ma land."

"We dinna leave until we have Lady Greer. She isnae married to Sinclair, but she is betrothed to Laird Arthur MacDonell. Edgar didna marry the laird's daughter to secure the alliance to the MacDonnells of Loch Boom, so Greer will wed the mon himself. Ye willna be so mighty once the Gunns ally with the MacDonnells and MacDonalds. The Sinclairs, Sutherlands, and Mackays are naught compared to the MacDonalds."

Matthew's final comment caused uproarious laughter throughout the Great Hall during a time that warranted no hilarity. But his statement was patently false. While there were more MacDonald branches combined than tentacles on an octopus, they didn't equal the mighty family alliance among the Sinclairs, Mackays, Sutherlands, MacLeods of both Assynt and of Lewis, Camerons, Rosses, and Mackenzies. They were the Highlands. Indirect family ties also allied them with the Campbells of Glenorchy and the MacKinnons of Skye, and the Kennedys in the Lowlands.

The MacDonalds and MacDonnells were welcome to try, but they would die for their efforts.

Matthew redoubled his efforts rather than back down. "Ye defiled Lady Greer when she was merely a lass. Ye got her with child and abandoned her. Now ye claim ye will marry her. Ye just want yer whore beneath ye again. Or on top, as we ken that's how she likes it."

Thor saw red. No one expected how fast he could move. Not even the men who saw him attack Drew in the lists. He launched himself at Matthew, his arm going around the older man's throat as they collided. His free hand went to the back of Matthew's head, grabbing a handful of hair. He was about to snap the man's neck when Blaine and five Sinclair guards struggled to pull him free. Thor was beyond reason. He thrashed, head butting one of his men and thrusting an elbow in another Sinclair's nose. He swung one man holding onto his arm like a rag doll. Only Blaine and one Sinclair guard kept their grip long enough to restrain him. Three more Sinclairs rushed forward to stand between Matthew and him. He tried to plow through them, but the men locked arms behind each other's backs and made a wall.

"Move or I'll kill ye, too." Thor cared not that he threatened his own clansmen. He wouldn't let anyone speak ill of Greer because he understood the threat it posed. Not only was she going to be his wife, she would one day be Lady Sinclair, Countess of Caithness. He would defend her honor and protect her name.

"Thor, stop." Blaine positioned himself next to Thor and placed his hand on his brother-by-marriage's shoulder, but he whipped it away when Thor released a feral snarl and glared at Blaine. "Cease or I will have ye confined to yer chamber. Then how will ye protect Greer?"

"Separate me from ma wife, and yer wife will be a widow." He didn't care that he'd just threatened to kill his twin sister's husband. He didn't care that it would be a long time before she forgave him for that. The only thing that made any sense in his mind was protecting Greer. He had eight years of penance to do. It clearly started today.

Blaine lowered his voice so only the Sinclair men could hear him. "Take him to his chamber and guard the door. Two of ye escort Lady Greer there. Neither is to leave until Lady Rose or I come for them. If ye dinna wish to tell Laird Sinclair and Callum that he's dead, do nae move from outside that chamber. Thor, if ye dinna want us to knock ye out, go with them."

It took a total of seven Sinclair warriors to get Thor finally up the stairs. He ceased struggling against them, but they didn't trust leaving an inch between them lest he break through their wall. When they reached the landing, he looked toward the laird and lady's chamber.

"Neither she nor Lady Rose will come out unless it's Blaine or me who knocks. I want ma wife." He turned toward the chamber, and the men were wise enough to move with him. They'd never seen Thor in such a state, but they'd been Sinclairs their entire lives. They knew what the men in that family were capable of when it came to their wives and children. None of them wished to die that day. Thor pounded on the door. "Greer, it's me."

It shocked the men how calm he sounded after fighting like a taunted bull. Thor took a step back as they heard something scraping on the floor as it moved away from the door. Then the bar lifted, and the door unlocked. Rose opened it, but Thor could see Greer behind her. Rose was quick to move out of the way, so Greer could fling herself into Thor's open arms. He held her tight as he kissed her temple.

"We heard everything," Rose mouthed.

"I'm sorry I threatened yer husband, Rosie. But naught is separating ma wife from me ever again. I ken now how Uncle Magnus must have felt when Auntie Deirdre's father took her from him."

When Magnus and Deirdre were barely adolescents, they'd fallen in love. After years of courting from a distance, they handfasted. The moment Deirdre's parents learned of it, they took Deirdre and hid her for nearly eight years. Magnus and Deirdre only reconnected when he discovered her at Robert the Bruce's court, days before she was supposed to marry someone else. Neither of them had broken their handfast vows, and to this day, they both considered themselves still married the moment they handfasted. They always insisted that a Highland pledge like theirs could never be broken.

Thor tucked Greer against his side as they turned toward the stairs leading to the third floor. Thor looked back at his sister. "Thank ye. Stay locked in yer chamber until Blaine comes for ye."

"I'll stay," Antony, a Sinclair warrior, offered. He knew Blaine wouldn't fault him for leaving Thor's detail to guard Rose. Thor nodded. He fought no one as he led Greer to the stairs. He swept her into his arms, fearful she was too overwhelmed not to fall. He also couldn't bear another moment without holding her. She burrowed against his chest as she had so many times while they courted. They entered his chamber, and a guard pulled the door closed. He knew they would remain there until it was safe for Greer to leave. Ostensibly, they were there to keep Thor locked in, but he knew they'd keep anyone but Blaine and Rose out.

"Thor?"

"Wheest, wee one. Let's sit by the fire, and we can talk if ye wish."

He walked to the bed and leaned forward to grab the pillows. Still in his arms, Greer did it for him before snagging the Sinclair plaid from the foot of the bed. He carried her to the hearth and set her on her feet. They silently spread the plaid and pillows in front of the fireplace. He wasn't certain how she wished to sit, so he waited for her to move toward him. He sighed when she wrapped her arm around his waist but laid down. She inched closer once his arm draped heavily over her waist. His arms encircled her, and she finally felt her racing heart calm. She'd feared she was dying from how it had continued to beat so fast once she was in Rose's chamber.

"Please dinna send me away again, Thor. I canna do this alone again."

"It's a good thing ye werenae there, *mo ghaol*. I dinna want ye to see me like that. I was the mon I become in battle."

"I'd rather see that than nae ken if ye were alive and coming back for me."

"Greer, I will always come for ye. We broke each other's hearts all those years ago, and we made ourselves miserable for too long. But there will never be a repeat of that. Unless ye tell me ye wish for me to put ye aside, I will nae let aught come between us. Even then, I dinna think I can oblige that wish. I dinna think I can survive being apart from ye again."

"I still dinna ken if I can be a proper wife to ye,

Thor. This only made those fears far worse. But I have nay doubts that I want to be whatever kind of wife I can be. I want us to marry in truth."

"That last bit is all I need to hear."

They held each other as Greer stroked Thor's back, and he stroked her hair. Neither knew what continued to happen in the Great Hall, and for a brief time, neither cared. They were holding one another again. The moment was surreal for them both. Memories and dreams collided and coalesced into their private retreat. The world disappeared, and time no longer had meaning. At least, not until someone pounded on the door. Blaine's voice passed through the thick wooden portal as though it weren't there.

"Thor, ye'd better come out. King Edward's men are here."

CHAPTER 8

Greer's terror-stricken eyes met Thor's. He was fed up with seeing his wife so fearful that day. They'd laid their hearts bare, and they'd resolved their past as best they could for now. It should have been a joyous time for them. Instead, they faced people who wished to tear them apart. It made Thor wonder what would have happened if they hadn't reconciled that day. The Gunns would have shown up, and he still wouldn't have agreed to her leaving with them. But would she have considered marrying him to prevent them taking her? Would he have watched her walk away? No. He wouldn't have allowed that. He would have ridden off with her before that happened.

"Thor?" Greer pressed her hand against his chest.

"We'll be down in a moment, Blaine." Thor called out to his friend before pulling Greer closer. "We canna avoid going back down there, but we must make some decisions vera quickly. Samuel wasna wrong that a marriage by consent willna easily stand since there's a priest here to marry us. We can claim we handfasted recently, but we kept our distance because of our clans' pasts. That doesnae change the fact that people have seen us argue, even if they havenae heard us."

"We say we couldnae agree on when to tell people. We wished to make it kenned, but we never agreed on the right moment."

"Mayhap, but I dinna ken how many would believe that."

"Would the Keiths turn me over to them? Would they accept what they ken is a falsehood if it helped a Sinclair?"

"I dinna ken. We canna pretend to have a sheet either, so we canna say that we've lain together and consummated a handfast."

"Because too many people ken I'm so far from being a virgin that—"

"Greer, shh." Thor stroked her cheek, wiping away the tears that streamed down them. She'd thought she had so few left to cry, but apparently, that day released a geyser that had sat under too much pressure for too long. His heart ached to see the pain in Greer's eyes. If only he could take her away for a while. Somewhere they could learn to be a couple again without prying eyes watching them.

"Do ye think Una would lie for us?"

Thor shrugged. "Mayhap. Do ye wish her to say ye're carrying ma bairn?"

"Aye."

"And when they realize ye arenae?"

"Then we need to make it so that I am."

"Nay. I am nae bedding ye just to get ye with child. Ye dinna want that."

"I want to stay with ma husband, and I do want a family with ye, Thor. There's only one way to do that. And if it means nay one can deny our marriage, then I'll do whatever I must."

"That isnae how I want ye to see making love with me. Something that ye must do."

"I dinna ken if I can enjoy it like I once did with ye. I

dinna ken if I can even manage to couple long enough for ye to plant yer seed. But regardless of who's belowstairs, I already kenned I want to try to get to a point where I can. This just makes me want to try sooner and faster."

"I dinna want to agree to something that will hurt ye." Thor glanced toward the door before returning his gaze to Greer. "It's been eight years. Do ye have other bairns?"

Thor feared he'd be sick again, but he needed to know. He'd wondered that question throughout their conversation, but since Greer didn't offer the information, he couldn't bring himself to ask before now.

"Nay. I drank penny royal tea to keep from getting with child. Naught ever took root. I fear Edgar beat me badly enough that I canna get with child or canna bear one. But I willna ken until I try."

Thor considered what Greer suggested. "We could say we handfasted before we arrived here. We've been here more than a moon, so we can say ye're with child. We married by consent today to ensure we were bound by more than a handfast. That can be repudiated, but a marriage by consent canna."

"If we say we've already handfasted, and people heard us marry by consent, could a priest marry us without posting the banns? Could he marry us tonight?"

"Ye're certain ye wish to make it permanent so soon? Is it to protect ye from going back with them?"

"Aye to both. But, Thor, I ken what I want. This is happening fast, but it's also making ma priorities so clear. All the things that seemed gray for so long are now so obvious. I've kenned all along that if ye ever asked me to marry ye again, I would say aye. I felt a fool for it, but I couldnae help it. I admit for many years it was because ye would have been ma escape from Edgar and the others. But since being around ye again, it's because of ye."

"Then we agree to say we handfasted before we arrived here but thought we needed to hide it because of everything that's happened recently and all the bad blood between our clans. We argued because we couldnae agree on when to tell people. We say that ye're with child, and that's why we made sure everyone heard us marry by consent today."

"And we pray Una will either lie for us, or I can convince her nae to examine me. We also pray the priest will marry us without reading the banns."

"That's right." Thor reached for her hand and moved the ring from her thumb to the right finger. She watched him, and she stole his breath when she looked up at with a beaming expression.

"Thor!" Blaine pounded on the door again. "Either open it, or I'll break it down."

Thor raised his eyebrows to Greer, and she nodded. He called out, "It's nae locked." He'd known no one would get past the guards, and they wouldn't enter uninvited.

Blaine pushed open the portal and stepped inside, taking in the couple sitting before the fire. He glanced at the bed, but it was still made except for the pillows now in front of the hearth. He pushed the door closed and approached Thor and Greer.

Thor kept his voice low as he filled Blaine in. "I ken we've already been up here too long, and I dinna want to explain everything to ye and nae have Rose with us. But when we get belowstairs, we will say we handfasted before we came here. We've argued aboot when to tell people. And Greer is with child. That's why we married by consent today since we feared a handfast wouldnae be enough."

Blaine nodded along with what Thor said until the

part about Greer being pregnant. His eyes darted to her belly before he scowled at Thor.

"Dinna look at Thor that way. It was ma idea to say it. I'm nae, so we need ye and Rose to keep anyone from insisting Una examine me. Or we need her to lie."

"We can protect ye, Greer. Ye dinna have to claim ye married Thor, and we can agree the marriage by consent was an attempt to keep ye here."

Greer stepped in front of Thor, as protective as he had been in the Great Hall. "Blaine, there is plenty we need to explain to ye and Rose. But ye need to ken the one thing we arenae pretending aboot is wanting to be married. We've wanted it for eight years, but life has been cruel."

Thor slid his arm around Greer's waist as he stepped forward to press his body against hers. "Did ye catch Samuel said Greer and I handfasted in the past? It's true. We married when we were five-and-ten. She was ma wife, and she is again."

"Ye're right. We need to wait for Rose before ye explain all this. She's still in our chamber."

"I want Greer to go back in there, and I want guards posted outside and at the stairs. I dinna want her anywhere near someone who can snatch her." Thor tightened his hold around Greer before releasing her and slipping his hand into hers. Noise in the passageway made them all turn toward the door. Blaine hurried forward and yanked open the door.

"Stand aside," a nasal English voice commanded. Blaine took a menacing step forward.

"Ye dinna command me in ma home. I warned ye once. I willna warn ye again. I have enough men to bury ye and yers, and nay one would ever be the wiser. Move."

The man not only didn't comply, he signaled for other men to rush forward. They tried to push their way past Blaine and into the chamber. Blaine and the Sinclair guards still at the door formed a barrier. The Sinclairs knew they had to step aside for the king's man, but it now trapped him between Blaine and them. They scuffled with the other three Englishmen who tried to help their leader. When Thor and Greer entered the chamber earlier, he'd immediately noticed someone placed his sword to rest against the bedside table. He assumed Blaine did it while he was in Greer's chamber.

"Get into the far corner." Thor turned Greer toward it, then rushed forward to grab his sword. The Keiths hadn't forced the English king's men to surrender their weapons at the gate like most visitors—like the Gunns had. Blaine unsheathed his as Thor did the same. Working together and with the Sinclair guards, they pushed the English guards away from the door. "Lock and bar it, Greer."

The moment they were far enough from the door that she didn't fear someone reaching in, she bolted across the chamber. She slammed the door shut, locked it, barred it, and inched the bedside table against it. She looked around and followed that by adding both chairs to the blockade. She only had one dirk, so she withdrew it from her skirt's pocket before she huddled in the corner where Thor ordered her to go.

Her hands shook as she drew her knees up to her chest. Then she thought better of it. That position wouldn't allow her to rise to her feet with ease and fight back if she needed. She moved to crouch in the corner; her knife clutched in her hand the way Thor had taught her. That memory surged forward, and it allowed her mind to escape her current situation. Recalling how he taught her to defend herself calmed her racing heart. She strained to hear anything coming from belowstairs, but she was on the third floor. Anything she could have heard would have been soft and muffled. Nothing floated up to her. No matter how many times she'd been cuffed to her bed or locked in her chamber, nothing had seemed longer than the infernal wait she endured now.

Thor shoved one of the Englishmen hard enough that he stumbled backward and would have gone over the third-floor landing's railing if he hadn't grabbed the man's doublet and yanked him back only to drive his fist into the man's throat. He almost crushed his opponent's windpipe, but he made certain the force behind his punch wasn't that significant. It made the delegate crumple to the ground, gasping and clutching his throat.

"Dinna come near ma wife, and I willna hurt ye." Thor roared his statement, and every man in the scuffle knew he spoke to each Englishman. Blaine and the others corralled the king's representatives toward the stairs and away from Greer. None of the Highlanders cared if the other men tumbled to their death, but the men King Edward III sent survived. Just barely.

"Ye didna have ma permission to come abovestairs." Blaine crossed his arms and glowered at the leader.

"We represent King Edward. We do not need your permission to enter anywhere. You will hand over the woman."

"Nay." Blaine and Thor answered at once. Blaine wished to turn his scowl on Thor, but he wouldn't make them look like anything less than a united front, even if Blaine wished to remind the new arrivals that he was laird while his father was away.

"You have no say. Your father is a traitor to the crown. You are lucky we don't seize your keep and your lands before throwing you in the oubliette." The

HIGHLAND STRENGTH

forgotten. A pit with no way out unless someone tossed down a rope or ladder. It had no windows and no door, except for a hatch eight to ten feet above. Once inside, most prisoners never left.

"Ye represent the usurper. He may wear a crown in England, but he isnae the King of Scotland. Ye're lucky ye made it this far into the Highlands with yer heads still attached." The Keiths lived even farther north than the Sinclairs, occupying the most northern tip of Scotland. There was nothing but the North Sea beyond their land. If these men rode from King Edward's court, they'd likely ridden the entire length of Britannia, from London to Ackergill. None of the Highlanders recognized the English King Edward as the rightful head of their country. Their sovereign, Robert the Bruce's son David, was their king, even in exile.

Thor listened as Blaine articulated what everyone present thought. It made no sense to him why the English king's men arrived at Ackergill. What concern did they have with Greer and her supposed betrothal to the laird of a MacDonnell branch? Not even a large branch at that. Sharing progenitors closely tied the MacDonnells to the MacDonalds. The MacDonalds were fiercely loyal to Robert the Bruce and would never join sides with the English. It was simply impossible. It would not—could not—happen. Yet, here stood these men.

Thor shifted his gaze to the Gunns, settling into the Sinclair Stance. For all their foul choices and their baseless claims against the Sinclairs, Sutherlands, and Mackays, they'd been loyal to the Bruce too. Why would they invite the English to meddle? He recognized smugness on several faces, but just as many of the Gunn representatives appeared shocked.

Thor recalled the English leader merely told Blaine to stand aside and to hand over the woman. He hadn't said why, and he said nothing about giving her to the Gunns or the MacDonnells. Could they be there for another reason? What interest could they have in Greer?

"What are ye called besides a piece of shite under ma boot?" Blaine demanded.

"Sir Richard Fitz-Simon, member of Our Majesty's Order of the Garter."

"Never heard of ye or that. Another one of that bastard's pretentious brotherhoods."

"The Order of the Garter is the king's finest knights—"

"Who prance around in yer noisy metal buckets. We ken all aboot ye knights. Would ye like to ken how we kill ye? Besides letting ye sweat to death in those death suits."

"Heathenish savage. King Edward prevailed and now rules all of Britannia. Our noisy buckets soundly defeated you. Now bend the knee." Sir Richard thrust out his hand with a signet ring. Blaine withdrew a dirk and made a downward swiping motion that the knight barely avoided.

"Try that again in ma home, and ye will come away minus a finger or five." Being called a heathen or a savage was nothing new to Highlanders. They'd heard it from their Lowland neighbors as well as the English. But they didn't care since they were victorious more often than not. Blaine intended to distract the knights long enough for his men to scout whether more men accompanied those standing before him. He needed to ensure no one could besiege his castle before he made his next move.

"Why do ye want Lady Greer?" Thor understood Blaine's tactic without having it explained, but he wanted to know why anyone in England wished to take Greer. He wanted to know how anyone had even heard of her.

"Our Majesty sent us on behest of John Gallda MacDougall."

Teeth gritted, lips thinned, and eyes narrowed throughout the Great Hall. The MacDougall name wasn't well received in the Highlands. John Gallda's grandfather, John MacDougall, Lord of Argyll, sided with Edward I and was forced from Scotland for his betrayal to his countrymen. John Gallda grew up in England, and as far as anyone in the Highlands was concerned, he was not Scottish of any sort.

Thor's heart raced. Greer's mother was a Macnaughten before she married Edgar Gunn. The Macnaughtens allied with the MacDougalls and fought against the Bruce during the First War of Scottish Independence. They eventually came around to the Scottish king's cause, but never entirely severed their ties to the MacDougalls. As best Thor knew, John Gallda MacDougall was unwed. Thor's stomach dropped. Did John intend to marry Greer and return to Scotland to reclaim his land? Did he think he could inherit Macnaughten land through Greer? Why else would he take interest in her? Thor knew little about the Macnaughtens beyond what Greer told him nearly a decade ago. Back then, her mother was the only daughter, and Greer was the only granddaughter. He knew nothing about the male lineage.

Matthew Gunn pushed forward. "Nay. Absolutely nae. Lady Greer is nae going to that English bastard. She's a Gunn nae a Macnaughten."

Thor fought to keep from sneering. Now the man would claim her as a respected Gunn. Only when he stood to lose the alliance he wanted. Allying with the MacDougalls would worsen their stance in the Highlands. Greer was a Gunn through her birth father, Albert. He was a Gunn warrior and sided against Edgar in the last battle. Greer's illegitimacy had been a secret until recently.

"Lady Greer is already married." Thor watched Sir Richard's reaction before darting his gaze to the Gunns. "We handfasted eight years ago, but it ended. We handfasted again a moon ago, just before we arrived here. We married by consent an hour ago."

"So, you never married in a church. Not surprising given your heretical practices in this godforsaken land." Sir Richard looked down his nose at Thor.

"Lady Greer has been a wife in truth twice." Thor hoped Greer's lack of virginity would send Sir Richard and his men away. He doubted John knew about their first handfast since only a handful of Gunns did, and no one in any other clan did. The one person who did —Jamie—had been dead for years. He counted on none of the Gunns revealing Greer's life for the past eight years since they wouldn't want Laird MacDonnell to learn of it. Unless—had he been one of the men?

"All the better," Sir Richard responded. "Sir John likes a woman who knows what she's doing. I've heard she—"

"How have ye heard aught all the way in England? Ye must be a spy. Ye ken what happens to them." Thor watched as the Sinclair and Keith guards moved their hands closer to their dirk handles, ready to withdraw them and punish the man Thor accused of espionage.

Blaine would gladly allow his men to run the royal guards through, but he needed to be more prudent about this. If there were more Englishmen waiting outside his gates, then they would question where their leader and the other men went. If there were none, then he could easily claim no one made it to his keep. He could leave them somewhere miles away from the keep or even cross onto Gunn land and dump them there. The sea would swallow them whole. He needed Thor not to incite a riot.

"Ye have delivered yer message, but ye will nae leave with a Clan Keith guest. She has sanctuary here from them," Blaine jerked his chin toward the Gunns, "so she remains."

"You are not a church. You cannot grant anyone sanctuary."

"But I am a priest. I'm Father Bennett." A man in his early forties stepped forward. His hands were steepled before him as he strode toward the unwanted guests. "Lady Greer sought sanctuary with me, and I granted it. She is in the keep because something injured her earlier. She will return to her place within the kirk forthwith. She is under the protection of our Lord Almighty. Would ye violate the sanctity of our Holy Church?"

"She cannot be under your protection if she has a husband." Sir Richard tried to assert himself, but the priest shot him a pitying mien.

"Of course, she can. Do nae be ridiculous. One doesnae negate the other. By the by, ye are in the Diocese of Caithness. Ma brother, Fearchar Belegaumbe, is the bishop. We began our service to our Lord in the parish of Dunbeath. Mayhap ye ken of the Sinclairs? We are a most devout family. Should ye violate Lady Greer's right to sanctuary, then I will ride to ma brother. He will excommunicate ye before ye can leave Keith land. His writ is binding even in England. Do ye have children, Sir Richard? They will have a right time trying to marry with an excommunicated father. Such a shame to a family. And such a shame ye will have to support them."

"I have no issue. You do not scare me, priest."

Father Bennett came to stand before Sir Richard with his hands clasped before him, his shoulders rolled forward. Now he dropped his hands and stood to his full height. He'd been born and bred in the Highlands. He stood four inches taller than Sir Richard, and his broad shoulders were more reminiscent of a warrior than a meek man of the cloth.

"Have ye ever heard of Odo of Bayeux? He was King William the Conqueror's half-brother and both the Bishop of Bayeux and the Earl of Kent. He was a mon of the cloth who carried a club into the Battle of Hastings. We all ken who won that war, but did ye ken he served as regent when his brother was away? I ask ye this because it isnae uncommon to find warrior monks in history. We canna wield a sword, but we can wield a club. Come near Lady Greer, and ye shall learn what it means to meet a Highland priest." Father Bennett stared, unblinking, at the Englishman. "I didna come out of ma mother's womb a monk, Sir Richard. I had a great many years of training both in the lists and in the church before I took ma vows."

Thor watched the man. He hadn't realized the Bishop of Caithness, who made his home near Dunbeath, and Father Bennett were related. Now that he looked, he could see the similarities. The bishop was a strapping man who also wielded a club. Thor recalled seeing him train in the lists with it when he was merely the Dunbeath parish priest. He'd met other men who'd trained to be warriors before being called to the priesthood. While none carried a sword, none forgot their skills either.

"You will not convince me that Lady Greer is under your protection or that of the church. You will not convince me she is married to this heathen. You will not convince me of anything because I am leaving with the woman now. Move aside." Sir Richard attempted to step around Father Bennett, but not only did the priest shift to block him, all the guards surged forward. Thor held up his hand and moved to stand beside the monk.

"Leave with yer life. Insist, and ye will be responsible for yer men's deaths. We have entertained yer presence long enough. Lady Greer *Sinclair* is ma wife. She canna marry anyone else because she is already carrying ma bairn. Ye willna make ma wife a bigamist, nor will ye make the future heir to the Clan Sinclair illegitimate. Choose: yer life or yer death."

"Sir John will not back down so easily. We will return with more men. You will have no choice but to acquiesce unless you wish this pile of rock turned to rubble." Sir Richard spun on his heel, motioning for his men to follow him. No one in the Great Hall doubted he would return with more men, but now they knew to be ready. Once the main doors shut, the Gunns wasted no time focusing on Thor.

"Ye may have made him go away, but ye canna make us leave so easily." Matthew crossed his arms. Thor laughed. He stalked toward the man and stood with his legs hip-width apart, his arms crossed. Despite being at least two decades older than Thor, Matthew looked like the child next to Thor's enormous frame. The muscles in Thor's forearms rippled as he flexed his hands beneath his elbows. He tilted his head from side to side, the corded muscles straining in his neck. He'd left the neckline of his leine untied, so the division between his pectorals was visible, each side chiseled.

"There is little that I canna do, Gunn. Do ye wish to test me? Ye lead yer men, and I lead mine. We go against each other as equals and see who comes out the winner. That mon decides what happens next." Thor cocked an arrogant brow. He didn't question Matthew's experience, having seen the man on more than one battlefield. But he knew the older warrior was no match for Thor's strength, and Matthew's agility wasn't what it was when Thor was an adolescent. He felt confident in his likely triumph.

Matthew maintained his impassive expression, but Thor knew he was racing to conceive an excuse not to fight Thor in a single combat. It didn't have to be to the death. Thor was content to fight to Matthew's disgrace.

"Ye are overly confident, and that shall be yer downfall, Sinclair."

"That isnae a nay."

"Ye are nae the woman's husband. Ye have nay claim to her. She is still a Gunn, and she will return to her home. Her betrothed will nae take kindly to being kept waiting."

"Ye were to receive the MacDonnell lass's dowry. Now ye must pay one to them. How is that beneficial to ye?"

"The dowry was never consequential. Ye ken that as well as anyone. It'll be a small price to pay for the alliance. One that even yer family canna defeat."

Thor shook his head. "Daft as a spring lamb. Ye shall follow a wolf and call him Father. Then he'll eat ye alive. Ye willna come out the winner with an alliance with the MacDonnells or MacDonalds. Ye shall give and get naught in return. The Macnaughtens arenae anyone ye should rely on either. Ye broke ties with them when Lady Greer's mother died. Ye'd do well to keep the sniveling English bastards far from here. King David already doesnae like ye. He'll brand ye traitors if Lady Greer marries a MacDougall. It's nae like any of yer neighbors will come to yer aid. We shall all fiddle while ye burn."

"Dinna ye worry aboot our relationship with the MacDonnells and how it serves us just fine."

"Ye truly are daft. Ye should thank the Almighty that I married Lady Greer. Allowing her to marry Sir John Gallda MacDougall will ensure yer downfall, and nae a clan in Scotland other than the Macnaughtens will fight alongside ye. If she marries him, ye get nay alliance with the MacDonnells and MacDonalds. If ye force her to marry the MacDonnell, ye shall have the English so far up yer arses that it's their tongue ye're sticking out. They willna let it go that ye married her to a MacDonnell. The only people none of them will come near are ma family."

Thor unfolded his arms and held up his hands, ticking off his fingers as he named his extensive family tree that was nearly impossible for anyone to remember if they weren't one of the leaves.

"Ma grandda is the Earl of Caithness, which is the Earldom of Sinclair *and* the Earldom of Orkney. Ma great-uncle is the Earl of Sutherland, and ma great-aunt-by-marriage is the Earl of Ross's great-aunt. Between the Sinclairs and Sutherlands, we've married into all the most northern Highland clans but ye and the Oliphants. We have half the Lowlands too. We're allied by marriage and blood to the MacLeods of Lewis and of Assynt, the Camerons, the Mackenzies, and the Mackays. Through the MacLeods of Lewis, we're allied with the MacKinnons of Skye and the Grants. Through the MacLeods of Assynt, we're allied to the Dunbars. Through the Rosses and the MacLeods of Assynt, we're allied to the Campbells of Glenorchy. They alone will make the MacDonalds shite. In the Lowlands, Laird Innes Kennedy is ma uncle Tristan Mackay's godfather. Laird Kennedy's daughter Lady Cairren is married to Laird Padraig Munro. His other daughter, Lady Caitlyn, is married to a Lowlander, Alexander Armstrong. Ma father's cousin, Lachlan Sutherland, is married to the Lowlander Laird Johnstone's sister. And ma aunt Deirdre is Laird Fraser of Lovat's cousin. And dinna forget ma grandda was friends with the Black Douglas, and ma da is friends with Andrew Murray. So please,

CELESTE BARCLAY

tell me how I should fear the MacDonalds and MacDonnells."

Thor crossed his arms once more and rested his weight back on his heels as though he were in no rush to end the conversation. He tilted his head to his left and raised both eyebrows. He knew he'd backed Matthew into a corner. The man wasn't foolish enough to raise his sword to Thor if his men couldn't help him, and Matthew knew the younger man spoke the truth when he rattled off the spider web the Sinclairs created when Laird Liam Sinclair married Lady Kyla Sutherland nearly five decades ago.

"I'll be as wrinkled as ye if ye dinna explain soon," Thor taunted. Blaine walked to Thor's right and towered over Matthew just as Thor did. Even though he weighed a stone less than Thor, he was an imposing figure. Father Bennett remained a silent force not to be underestimated.

"Ye leave ma land now, and ye leave alive. Make me wait another minute, and ye are all dead men." Blaine placed his hands on his hips, making him appear even broader. Matthew looked between the two young men and nodded. He retreated, and much like Sir Richard had, he signaled for his men to follow. The door slammed behind them, but no one moved until they were all certain none of the Gunns would return.

The moment Thor felt certain they were gone, he whirled on his heel, his plaid splaying out around him. "I want ma wife."

CHAPTER 9

Greer allowed Rose into Thor's chamber only minutes after the disturbance in the passageway ended. She'd scrambled to move the barricades away from the door and admitted Rose. They worked together to put everything back. The women even considered an attempt to move the bed. Now Rose stood beside the window embrasure looking out as the sun finally dipped below the horizon, wondering how many men lurked beyond her home's gates.

Before she started pacing, Greer told her that King Edward's men had arrived. The minutes felt interminable as she waited for some sign that Thor was safe, and no one would force her to leave. She could hardly believe that it was still the same day. A snake bit her; she reconciled with Thor; her clansmen arrived; and now, the English forced their way into Ackergill.

"What's taking so long?" Greer bit at her thumb's cuticle as her right elbow rested on the back of her left hand. She walked around the room with her left arm across her middle as though she might protect the bairn she'd only made up. Fear that she would return to her hellacious existence at Gunn Castle made her heart race. Terror that some new form of torture awaited her with the English king made her worry that she would retch. Both made her protective of where she prayed one day Thor's seed would take root again.

"I dinna ken." Rose didn't turn away from the window as she watched the royal guard prepare to leave in the waning light. She pointed outside, and Greer hurried to join her.

"They're just leaving?"

"It looks that way. Why would they come, then leave so easily?"

"It makes nay sense to me, but it's better than a battle."

Rose turned her head toward Greer. "Do ye fear for Thor's life?"

"Of course. But I fear more what will happen to him when he kills the English bastard's men." Greer stood beside Rose as they watched the men mount and ride away. They were tiny dots when they finally faded from view. A moment later, the Gunn contingency stormed out of the keep. She couldn't hear Matthew, but she could guess the curses he spewed as he gestured toward the keep. "How could I have ever imagined remaining there? What possessed me to think that I could lead a clan with men like him and Samuel?"

"Ye wished life could finally be fair."

"And it's proven once more that it isnae."

"Greer!" Thor pounded on the door as he called out to her again. "Greer!"

"Aye!" The two women darted to the door and began pulling things away.

"Greer!" Thor's voice became more panicked each time he said her name.

"Thor! I'm here!" Greer pushed a chest away as Rose inched the bedside table far enough that Greer could unlock the door. "He canna hear me because he's caterwauling so loudly."

She lifted the bar and barely moved out of the way before Thor swung the door open with enough force for it to slam against the wall and bounce back toward him. He yanked the bar from Greer's hands and tossed it aside as though it weighed nothing. He pulled Greer to his chest so hard that she stumbled.

"Leave, Rosie." Thor didn't wait for his sister to respond. His mouth crashed down to Greer's before he kicked the door shut. He spun Greer and pressed her against the portal. Their hands roamed over each other as she returned his hungry kiss. It was only when he lifted her arms above her head and captured her hands in his left while his right cupped her breast that he realized what he'd done. He released her immediately and stumbled backward. Greer nearly fell forward, unprepared for Thor to no longer be there to support her. She blinked like an owl as she tried to form a coherent thought. She feared she'd done something wrong. Humiliation from her lust and fear that he was rejecting her made her tremble.

"Thor?"

"I'm sorry. I'm so, so sorry. I willna do that again. I'm so sorry." Thor's horrified expression mystified Greer. She'd enjoyed their kiss, and she'd certainly enjoyed exploring Thor's body. She realized she wished to become fully reacquainted with the masterpiece. But shame even more grave than when she'd told him what happened after they parted ways filled his eyes.

"I dinna understand. What are ye sorry for?"

"Yer hands. Touching ye."

"Ma hands?" She looked at them, her brow furrowed.

"I restrained yer hands above yer head, and I touched ye when I promised I wouldnae without ye saying that's what ye want. I shouldnae have kissed ye if that wasna what ye wanted. I'm sorry."

"Och, *mo ghaol*. Ye did naught wrong. I hadnae even noticed what ye were doing with ma hands. I was as eager to kiss ye as ye were to kiss me. I've been pacing since ye left. I thought Blaine was going to tell me ye were dead. Kissing ye reassured me ye are still vera much alive. And as for touching me, I ken what ye offered, but I never said I dinna want ye to touch me. I said I dinna ken what I can manage. I liked that, so I ken I can manage ye touching ma breasts. I'd hoped ye'd keep doing it."

"I should have asked, Greer."

She watched his stricken expression as she drew closer. She placed her hand over his heart as the other went to his waist. "I dinna want ye to be afraid to show me any affection. I need it more than aught, Thor. And I dinna want ye to hide yer desire. I need that too. I need to ken ye arenae repulsed by me, and I need to feel a mon's desire that isnae meant to hurt me."

"I will never intentionally hurt ye, *leannan*." Sweetheart.

"I missed hearing ye call me that, too. Thor, ye dinna scare me. Mayhap certain things will, but nae ye. If I dinna like something or I canna do it, I'll tell ye. I ken ye'll never make me feel badly for it. I dinna want ye to fear me." Greer bit her bottom lip as she gazed up at the man who was doing his best to muddle his way through something he knew nothing about. His pained mien spoke to his noisy conscience. He wasn't convinced.

"Mayhap I can just hold ye again."

"I'd like that."

Thor wrapped his arms around her, and she felt his sigh as her head rested against his chest. His heart still raced, but he already felt calmer. After a couple minutes of standing in silence, Greer slid her hand from his heart to his shoulder and around the back of his neck.

She leaned back and lifted her chin, her eyes searching his. This kiss was gentler but infused just as much emotion. She returned her head to his chest when they pulled apart, their lungs finally screaming for air.

"What happened?" Greer needed to know, but she didn't want to know.

"What do ye ken aboot yer mother's people?"

"Vera little. Apparently, Edgar despised ma mother from the start. He was cruel to her, and she found solace with Albert, ma real father. Ma father said he and ma mother began an affair nae long after she arrived. They fell in love almost immediately. Until I was born, neither kenned if I was ma father's or Edgar's bairn. Ma birthmark made it obvious."

Greer pushed back her sleeve to what looked like a cluster of freckles.

"Da has one exactly like it in the exact same place. I didna ken why Mama always insisted I keep it covered. I thought she feared someone would claim it was the mark of the devil or a witch. I saw Da without his leine on one day when I was four-and-ten. I kenned for certain what I'd suspected for a while. I was so happy to ken he was ma da and nae Edgar. I was also certain Edgar murdered ma mother for the affair. Since she died when I was only eight summers, I didna have much chance to learn aught aboot her people. Edgar slapped me when I was eleven summers and asked aboot them. I decided never to ask that again. Why?"

"The Macnaughtens allied with the MacDougalls and supported John Balliol against Robert the Bruce. Eventually, the Macnaughtens came around to the Bruce's cause, but the MacDougalls didna. The Bruce stripped them of their lands, and John MacDougall, Lord of Argyll, fled to England. The Macnaughtens didna sever their ties to the MacDougalls, even once they supported King Robert. The MacDougalls supported Edward Balliol and now King Edward of England. The king's messengers came for ye. Their leader said King Edward sent them at John Gallda MacDougall's behest. He was the Lord of Argyll's grandson."

"Came for me at his behest? Why does he want me?"

"He's unwed with nay issue. Ma guess is he wishes to return to Scotland through a Scottish bride. He thinks he might have his lands restored to him since King David is in exile. I assume he thinks that as the only daughter of the auld laird's only daughter, ye must have substantial dower lands through the Macnaughtens."

"I dinna. At least, nae that I ken of." Greer brow furrowed deeply enough to create two grooves between her eyebrows. "Why me? There has to be a better woman to rely upon than the illegitimate daughter of a disgraced lady who came from a relatively small clan."

"I believe he thinks he can summon the Macnaughtens to his side to help defend the MacDougalls, nae only because of their auld alliance, but because he will renew it by marrying ye."

"He's basically an Englishmon, right?"

"Aye. I dinna ken much aboot him, but I've had to learn a little aboot all the clans' leaders." Thor despised the monotonous lessons with his grandfather. It was the only time he loathed being with Liam. The older man seemed to drone on and on about who begat who after marrying so-and-so. Thor considered it as boring as lessons from Deuteronomy, which he thought of as God's Ragman Rolls. The list of two thousand signatures demanded by King Edward I surely wasn't as long as all the names listed in the early book of the Bible. Now, though, he appreciated his grandfather's unceasing insistence that he memorize the lairdships and the families.

"And ye sent the Englishmen and the Gunns away? I saw them riding out."

"Aye." Thor looked around before taking Greer's hand and leading her to the bed. "Will ye sit with me?"

"Of course. Thor, are ye still shaken by earlier? Are ye still scared to touch me?"

"A wee."

"Sweet mon." Thor sat, but Greer stepped between his legs and cupped his cheeks. "I told ye what I need. What do ye need?"

"To make ye happy." He didn't think. The words poured forth, but he meant them.

"That's vera kind. But what do ye need to make ye happy?"

"Kenning ye are safe and kenning I will see ye every day."

Greer wrapped her arms over his shoulders as she stepped a little closer. His head rested against her belly as his arms went around her thighs. She stroked his hair as they once again basked in being in one another's company, with no enmity. They found comfort in their embrace. She gazed down at Thor, and love filled her heart to near busting. She kicked off her slippers and stepped back. Thor immediately released her, but his eyes showed his confusion.

"Will ye help me unlace ma dress, Husband?"

"Greer, ye dinna—"

"I ken I dinna have to. I want to. Mayhap all I can do for today is lie on the bed in yer arms. Mayhap more. I dinna ken yet. But I want to be closer to ye. I need ye curled around me to feel safe again."

Thor tugged her laces free, watching as she shrugged out of the kirtle. He pulled off his boots, but he left the rest of his clothes as they were. He would assume nothing. While she'd waited, Greer put the pillows back and returned the Sinclair plaid to the foot of the bed. She climbed onto the massive piece of furniture and thought Thor would walk around to the other side.

"Scoot over, wee one. Ye will never sleep closer to the door. I dinna want ye to be the first anyone can reach, and I dinna want to hurt ye by scrambling over ye." Thor propped his sword against the bedside table, which was nearly in its place. He climbed onto the bed after Greer moved to the other side. He slid his right arm beneath her neck while his left arm wrapped around her. He spooned her, and her eyes drifted shut. Her hands covered his forearm as they laid in silence.

A few minutes later, she covered Thor's left hand with hers and moved it to rest his palm on her belly. The heat seeped through her chemise and radiated out to her limbs. Thor kissed her cheek and neck before pressing soft ones to her shoulder. She remained facing away from him as she spoke.

"While ye were belowstairs, I kept thinking aboot how certain I am that ye wouldnae let anyone steal our future from us again. I kept thinking aboot how much I want our family to be more than just the two of us. Thor, I could see maself with child." Greer released his hand and grasped her chemise, pulling it up her thigh until it revealed her hip. Thor's calloused palm barely grazed her skin as he ran it along her thigh up to her hip and over it before cupping her bottom with the lightest touch. When Greer didn't flinch or push him away, his hand slid back over her hip and around to her bare belly. He returned his hand to where it had been, and it held the softest skin he'd ever felt. "Can I ask ye something that might ruin this moment?"

Thor suspected he knew her question. "Do ye wish to ken aboot when we were apart?"

"Aye."

"There have been others, Greer. Nae many. Da and

ma uncles have put the fear of God into all of us lads. We dinna want what happened to Da, Uncle Tristan, and Uncle Tavish to happen to us. Or more importantly, nae have what happened to Mama, Auntie Mairghread, and Auntie Ceit to happen to our wives. We dinna want to embarrass our future wives, and we dinna want to disgrace ourselves. Ye ken I'd never been with a woman before ye, but I have been with a few since."

"Good."

That wasn't what Thor expected to hear. "Good?"

"Aye. Was it more than ten?"

"Greer."

"Was it?"

"I dinna want to tell ye this. I dinna see how any answer will do aught but hurt ye."

"So, it was."

"Nay. I didna say that. But giving ye any number canna be what ye want. I dinna want to make ye think of me sharing this with someone else."

"But ye ken I have."

"Nay." Thor pushed up on his elbow. "What happened to ye is nae the same. It wasna for mutual pleasure like the women in ma past. And it wasna for love like it was with ye."

"If ye'd been with nay other women, while I'd been with other men, I would feel like even more of a whore. Was it more than ten, Thor?"

He didn't want to answer, but he knew she wouldn't relent. She watched him over her shoulder. With a sigh and his eyes squeezed shut, he shook his head.

"Are ye embarrassed that it wasna more than that?"

Thor's eyes flew open, and he tugged Greer's shoulder until she laid on her back, and he could see her face properly. "Nay. I dinna like admitting that it was even one. It feels like I betrayed ye all over again. Nay one forced me. I chose to bed those women."

"I wasna yer wife anymore."

"I ken, but it just doesnae feel right now."

"There's nay point to regret, Thor. Neither of us imagined we'd lie together on a bed again anywhere but in our dreams. It wasna every mon in ma clan who came to ma chamber. It was the same handful, but they came back more than once. I dinna want ye thinking that it was scores of them."

"Wee one, I dinna care if it was scores. I dinna hold any number against ye. I am nae going anywhere unless ye tell me to leave."

Greer nodded because she couldn't speak around the lump in her throat. Knowing he'd been with other women should have hurt her. Or at least, she thought it should. But she felt a little less of a whore knowing he'd been with women besides her. She reached for him, and he lowered himself, careful not to rest any of his weight on her. But she pulled him closer. When they were chest to chest, she cupped his cheek before their mouths met for another gentle kiss. But it soon turned into a blaze that heated them from the tips of their ears to the tips of their toes.

As the kiss continued, Greer yanked at Thor's leine until she could slide her hands along his scorching skin. She marveled at the taut muscles she felt beneath his smooth skin. She recalled the way he felt each time they'd come together when they were younger. They'd met while Thor and Jamie hunted near the loch. She'd been alone, swimming. Thor had offered to hold out his plaid to shield her as she came out of the water. He'd warned her that more Sinclair men were in the area. He'd wanted none of them to spy the gorgeous water nymph who wore nothing but her skin.

He'd held his plaid across his back, just as he'd done

when they swam that morning. She still couldn't believe that was only a few hours earlier. Once she'd dressed that day eight years ago, they'd talked while Jamie continued to hunt. It alarmed Thor that Greer didn't have a guard. He knew who she was because he'd recognized her from the Highland Gatherings. She'd thanked him for his concern but insisted no one from another clan would ever come near her. None would see any value in her as a Gunn. Thor's face had turned to a thundercloud, and she'd nearly tripped trying to back away. He'd pulled her close and admonished her for saying something so negative about herself. He warned her not to do it again. She truly believed him and didn't wish to learn the consequences if she did.

"Do ye remember the first time I kissed ye?" Thor asked as his whisky-brown eyes met her violet ones.

"Of course, I do. Ye came back to hunt at the loch every day for a sennight. I never went to the loch so many days in a row, but I hoped each time that I would see ye. On that seventh day, ye told me yer hunting party was returning to Dunbeath, and ye wouldnae be able to come back again."

"And I asked if I might have something to remember ye by. I was so nervous. I'd never kissed a lass before, even if plenty of lads ma age had done far more than just kiss. But I'd never seen someone as bonnie as ye. I didna want to walk away and never ken what it was like."

"I felt the same way. There's never been a mon brawer than ye, *mo ghràidh*. I thought I would surely melt into a puddle. I felt so overheated as ye wrapped yer arms around me and gave me the sweetest peck. Then I feared that was all ye would do."

"I couldnae stop. I wanted to taste ye, so I did."

"Aye, ye did." Greer grinned, and Thor swooped in for another kiss.

"I couldnae leave ye alone after that. I couldnae stay away. We were so foolish with all that we risked sneaking out to that loch. Bless Jamie because he lied for me so many times, so I could visit ye."

"I dinna ken how we werenae caught during those nine moons."

"Now that I think aboot it, I think mayhap ma mama kenned. She kenned ye and Rose were friends. She said she always kens where her weans are. When I remember some looks she gave me when ye were with us at Dunbeath, I think mayhap she was questioning why we werenae the same as we once were."

"Does that mean other people in yer family kenned?"

"Nay. Grandda's brother, Daniel, fell in love with Edgar's great-aunt. Edgar's grandfather, Tomas, killed Daniel because he learned of Daniel's relationship with Ceana. She was with child when it happened. He beat her badly enough that several moons later, her bairn was stillborn. Now I ken Grandda would have understood if he'd learned aboot us. I didna realize that soon enough."

"Thor, I never want to live apart from ye again."

"We never have to. I hated kenning ye were ma wife for three of those nine moons, yet I couldnae see ye every day. We never had enough time. Even when we spent hours together, and even when I arranged hunting trips and patrols, so I could go to the loch. It was never long enough."

"At least one of those times after we handfasted was long enough to get me with child."

They looked down between them at Greer's belly. Balancing on one forearm, Thor laid his hand over her belly.

"There is so much I regret, but I regret ye believing ye couldnae come to me."

"Thor, I kenned I could come to ye. I didna because I feared ye'd die too. I couldnae live with losing ye and our bairn."

"I should have protected ye, nae the other way around."

"Why? Because ye're the mon? I refuse to believe that. I love ye, and I will always protect ye. Ye canna convince me otherwise. Ye do that for people ye love. Would yer mama nae protect yer da because she's a woman?"

Thor chuckled. "Nay one is more protective of ma da than Mama."

"I've heard." Greer grinned.

"Ye are so bonnie, wee one. I could look at ye all day."

"Can we try a little more than just kissing?" Greer prayed she didn't panic and start screaming like a banshee. But nothing about being with Thor reminded her of what she had endured. The way they were now reminded her of how they'd once been.

"Tell me to stop the moment ye dinna like it."

"I promise." She pulled him back down to be chest to chest. He slid his hand up her thigh and beneath her chemise. He eased his hand beneath her backside and cupped the soft flesh. They continued to kiss, and when she made no move to stop him, he withdrew his hand. He swept it over her belly before inching it upward. He expected her to stop him, but she arched her back into his hand when he cupped her breast. He did nothing but hold it.

When she pulled away from their kiss, he moved his hand, but she covered it above her chemise. She pressed him to squeeze then knead the mound. She lifted her head and brought their lips together again. The kiss grew more heated, but Thor was determined not to take anything further than they already had. He didn't want to rush Greer and ruin the moment.

Greer found herself far less patient than Thor. She twisted to bring her body closer to his, so she could pull his plaid to his waist. She moaned as her hand gripped his chiseled arse. It was as she remembered it. She found the groove on the side where her hand fit perfectly.

"Thor, can ye take yer belt and sporran off, so they arenae poking me?"

Thor's mind warred with him because part of him screamed of course he could, but the other still feared ruining the moment. "If I take off the belt and sporran, ye will ken how badly I wish to make love to ye. And without a belt, ma *breacan feile* willna stay in place. It'll unravel." He didn't have to explain further since she'd see the outline of his rod, which pulsed against him at the idea of finally being close to Greer's sheath.

"I ken. I want to see if I can be that close to ye."

Thor drew back and kneeled as he unfastened the belt. He pushed it to the far side of the bed, keeping it away from Greer's bare legs. He didn't want to risk anything scratching her if he wasn't paying attention. He settled back on his side, no longer hovering over her. She frowned at him, but he pressed his hips forward, his cock now touching the outside of her hip. She waited for the panic she'd felt so many times before. None came. He repeated what he'd done before, skimming his hand up her side beneath her chemise until he could knead her breast. She arched her back into his hand again.

"That feels good," Greer whispered. Once more, she twisted toward him, so she could reach him. Her hand dipped under his leine and spread across his back before she inched it beneath the waist of his plaid. She watched Thor as he gazed down at her. Her heart ached with how careful he was being. No one since him had cared at all about her. Never. It was like they were five-and-ten again, discovering the wonders of coupling with someone they loved. She bent her right leg and pressed it against his thigh.

"Do ye wish me to slide mine between yers?"

"Aye."

"Are ye all right with—"

"Thor, I love ye. I trust ye. Ye dinna have to ask for each thing."

He kissed her again as he slid his thigh between hers. He stopped before it touched her sheath, but she raised her hips and squeezed his thigh. He took it as a sign that he could do more as they continued to kiss. He pressed his firm leg against her mound as he shifted to hover over her again. Her hands flew to his chest and pushed. He reared back, sitting and putting his hands up.

"I'm sorry. I—"

"Ye trapped ma hair. I couldnae tell ye that it felt like ye were going to rip it from ma head."

"I—What?"

"Ye moved somehow, and ye caught ma hair under yer arm. It felt like ye might scalp me." She lifted her head and moved her hair out of the way before she reached for him. He was slow to move, but when he did, he slid both arms beneath her and moved his thigh back between hers. She pressed on his back and brought their bodies together. She could feel his cock against her hip again, and it didn't repulse her. Just the opposite. She rocked her hips, wanting the friction against her pearl. Her chemise and his plaid kept them from being skin-to-skin, and neither moved to change that. She could feel her passion stirring, but the barrier kept her from panicking.

She grasped the back of his thigh and pulled him

closer as she ground her mons on him. She recognized the sensations from so long ago. Thor moved along with her, his rod rubbing along her hip.

"Wee one, I love ye."

"Dinna stop. Kiss."

Their mouths fused as they increased their pace. Greer clutched his leine as pleasure erupted through her. Thor squeezed her tighter against him as his sword pulsed under his plaid. They clung to one another until the need for affection blended with passion led them to smatter kisses across each other's faces.

"I thought ye were perfect when we met, Thor. Then there were many years I didna ken what to think. For the past moon, I've thought ye were perfectly awful. I should have kenned I was right the first time. Ye're a good mon, Thor. I understand now that ye've always done the best ye could."

"I thought the same thing aboot ye. When I thought ye betrayed me, I would ask God why ye couldnae be so perfect for me. Why would some other mon marry ye, and he would have what I thought I was going to? Even when I thought ye conspired against me, I still thought everything else aboot ye was perfect. I think that's why it hurt so much."

"We ken our faults now, and we realize neither of us is truly perfect. But I believe we are perfect for each other."

"I believe the same. Will ye let me hold ye?"

Greer's smile was soft as she gazed up at the perfectly flawed man beside her. "Ye've asked me that three times today. I havenae said nay. I willna. Ye dinna have to ask, Husband."

"If that's how ye feel, then I willna let go, Wife."

"Good."

Thor rolled onto his back, and Greer followed. Her head settled on his chest where she could hear his steady heartbeat. She placed her hand beside his cheek, and he covered it with his. If they did nothing more intimate, Thor would die a happy man. Greer remained still, but she was restless. She wondered when Thor would be ready for another interlude.

"*Leannan*, give me five minutes to catch ma breath." They laughed together as Thor's hand once more cupped her backside.

"Can we skip the evening meal and hide in here?" Greer didn't jest.

CHAPTER 10

Thor and Greer laid together in silence, neither sleeping because neither wanted to miss a moment of bliss. They'd spent hours gazing up at the clouds as they got to know each other. Losing that was one of the most painful parts of her separation from Thor and her basic captivity in her own home. Edgar allowed her to come and go from her chamber when no one demanded she be available to them. She'd even left the keep once a month to meet Rose. But she had little freedom in reality. Other people's wants and demands dictated days at a time.

While she recovered at Dunbeath, she'd been bedridden for several days, but she felt free. At Ackergill, roaming around the keep and bailey as she wished had done much to heal her wounded soul. But lying in the safe harbor of Thor's arms felt like he'd brought her back from the dead. Life finally had color again. It had purpose rather than a mere existence. She would allow nothing to ruin it. Not the Gunn clan council. Not some foreign Englishman. Not her own fears. As she cuddled closer to her husband's side, she tried to imagine what it would be like if it were another man she could have freely chosen who laid next to her.

HIGHLAND STRENGTH

Greer had met Thor's cousins, Wiley, Tate, Blake, and Tor. She'd met their friend Kirk Hartley. They were all handsome men who caught any woman's eye. She'd ridden to Dunbeath with Tate because she and Thor couldn't be near each other without arguing. She imagined getting to know them and perhaps growing smitten with them. Then she tried to picture herself in bed with any of them. Her stomach caved, and her heart raced. Her fingers curled to cling to Thor's leine.

"Greer?"

"Aye. I'm all right." She relaxed at the sound of Thor's voice and the reminder that he shared the bed with her, not someone else.

"Ye tensed and grabbed ma leine. Ye arenae all right."

"I dinna want to say what I was thinking because it willna sound good. I dinna want to anger ye or hurt ye." Greer slid her hand from over his heart to around his waist, holding on to him as though he might try to leave. Thor stroked her hair.

"Wee one, yer thoughts are yer own. I wish ye'd share them with me, but I willna force ye. I'm curious, and I want to help if I can."

Greer couldn't look at him as she spoke. He'd been so open and accepting of her that day. She didn't want him to think she was growing closed off again. And while the first half wouldn't sound very good, she wanted him to know how special he was to her.

"I wondered if feeling this at peace was because I'm with ye or because I am nae in that chamber at Gunn Castle." She refused to say her chamber. "I tried to picture being here with another mon and whether I would feel the same. The moment I pictured one, I panicked. I dinna panic around ye."

Thor's morbid curiosity wanted to know who'd she'd pictured. Was it someone from her own clan, and that's why she'd panicked? If she thought of someone else, would she react differently?

"Who was it?"

"I willna tell ye that. It'll hurt ye and make ye angry."

"One of ma cousins," Thor deduced. "I ken it's unusual for a family to have so many good-looking people. We're blessed many times over. Ye also dinna ken that many people outside yer clan. Ye were around ma cousins most recently. It doesnae surprise me they came to mind. Ye rode to Dunbeath with Tate. Was it him?"

"Dinna ask. Naught good can come of me answering."

"I'm nae jealous. Ye arenae out there trying to bed someone besides me. It isnae wrong to wonder if this is merely comfort from already kenning me, or if it's something real."

"Do ye think it's just familiarity for ye?"

"I enjoy that it feels like I've finally come home. But I dinna want to spend ma life with ye just because I already ken how much I enjoyed bedding ye. I like the idea of discovering who we are together now that we're eight years aulder and wiser."

"I dinna have a way to explain why ye're the only one in yer family that's attractive to me when I can admit all the men are braw. I thought aboot lying beside another mon, and a few faces flashed through ma mind. I settled on Tor, and it felt wrong. It felt scary. It made me want to get back to being by yer side, even though I kenned I never left it."

"Thor and Tor. Makes sense. We're also the most alike in personality. It made us unholy terrors when we were weans."

"Thormud and Torquil arenae that similar, but Thor and Tor must be quite confusing."

"The hair helps."

Greer looked up at Thor's grinning face, and he tugged a lock of his strawberry-blond hair. The rest of the men in his family possessed heads of deep chestnut hair. She couldn't help but return his infectious expression. She shifted and pushed upward on her elbow until she could kiss him.

"I willna picture anyone else. I dinna want ye to wonder if I am when we're together like this."

"Greer, I am nae worried. I told ye I understand."

"Is that because ye're picturing someone else?"

"Nae right now, but I admit I have. When I've laid in bed at Dunbeath, I've imagined a lass beside me. I've never brought one to ma chamber, and I willna until ye return with me. Our chambers are only for married couples. Single men dinna bring women there. The bed is a sacred place for a mon and his wife. I've pictured other lasses I ken who I could marry, but none felt right. Ma mind always came back to ye. I believed I would one day find someone I loved, and I would marry her. But every time I imagined falling asleep or waking up next to a woman, it was ye."

"I want to try more."

"It doesnae have to all be in one day." Thor chuckled.

"I ken, but I feel brave right now."

Thor drew Greer's right leg over his right thigh, then his hands guided her to straddle his leg. Greer reached between them to push her chemise and his plaid out of the way. Her netherlips met bare skin. With the undergown around her waist, both of Thor's hands rested on her uncovered backside.

"We enjoyed this many times before we handfasted and made love. I want to make ye climax like I used to." Thor recalled those early days when they began to explore how to pleasure one another.

"Can I—can we—I want—" Greer stumbled over her

words until she gave up and in a moment of impulse, she kneeled and whipped her chemise over her head. Thor surged upward and wrapped his arms around her waist. She moaned as their chests collided. His hands pulled her hips closer. "Take yer leine off."

Thor hesitated before he nodded. He unpinned the extra length of plaid from his shoulder and pushed it around his back. He tossed the brooch toward his belt and sporran before his leine followed it. Greer reveled in the sight of each honed muscle. She was certain her mouth watered as her fingertips grazed over his chest and belly. He was exactly as he had been, only so much bigger. His entire torso was broader and more solid.

Thor gazed at the firm breasts before him, and he wanted nothing more than to alternate suckling them. Greer's body was thinner than he remembered, and it worried him she wasn't eating enough. But his hands itched to touch her. He moved slowly, starting at her waist, and moving upward, ensuring she could predict what he would do.

"Are ye trying to tease me?" Greer whispered. Thor could only shake his head. He moved his hands a little faster until they slid over her breasts. He cupped them and brought them together, looking up at Greer, waiting for her permission to do more. She nodded, and he groaned as he licked one nipple then the next. He wrapped his lips around one, then opened his mouth to take as much as he could into it. She pressed the back of his head closer as her other hand gripped his shoulder. She watched every moment, not wanting to miss the most erotic thing she'd ever seen. He moved to the other one, not wanting to ignore either. He repeated his actions, switching between the two.

Need made her core ache, wanting to move against him. But the moment his hands slid from her shoulders down, she pulled back. She pushed his shoulders away, and once more he surrendered, his hands in the air.

"Dinna touch them." She'd hated him seeing her scars when he entered her chamber earlier. She'd been so badly bruised when she arrived at Dunbeath that only the healer noticed when they started to heal. She knew she couldn't hide the long one across her chest because Thor had seen the wound.

"Do they pain ye?"

"Nay. I dinna want ye to…" She could only shrug.

"Do ye nae want me to remember what happened to ye? Or does touching them make ye remember?"

"Both. And I dinna want ye to feel…" She trailed off again. She didn't want him to feel her imperfections. Edgar had lashed her many times if she hesitated to follow his commands or if any of the men claimed she'd been unwelcoming. Tears welled in her eyes and spilled down her cheeks. This intimacy was more overwhelming than the acts they'd already engaged in. Once more humiliation and shame for how much she desired Thor weighed on her like a crushing boulder. Knowing he'd seen and could now feel her scars made her wish to shy away. Emotions surged to the surface that she didn't know how to tame. The tears fell faster until they were broaching on sobs.

"Are ye fearful that I willna love ye because of them? That I willna want to touch ye, look at ye, because of them?"

"Aye." She could no longer control the deluge, and she sobbed her answer.

Thor swallowed before he took a deep inhale. "Greer, one thing I hope we can build up to is me taking ye from behind. St. Columba's bones, ye have the finest arse I've ever seen. I want to watch as ma cock slides into ye over and over. I want to see ye stretched before me as ye hold the bedcovers. I admit I pictured that when I found ma release earlier. I didna get a clear view, but I ken they cover yer back, *leannan*. I still want to couple with ye that way."

Greer's memory flashed back to a late evening rendezvous where they'd coupled upon a Gunn plaid. They'd tried that and found they both enjoyed the position. She'd long suspected that was the day she got with child. But she felt so different from that girl.

"Ye ken I have scars too. Some are worse than others. Some are from wounds that nearly killed me. A few have faded, but most will never go away. I dinna like them or how they look. I dinna want them to make ye think aboot what happens to me when I ride out. But I crave yer touch more. I dinna care aboot yers. All I want is to make love to ma wife. I want to touch and kiss all of ye. I willna lie and say discovering them didna tempt me to kill every mon in yer clan. I willna say ma heart doesnae break for ye, kenning how ye got them or that they bother ye. I understand why they do. All I want is ye as ye are. All of ye."

"Yers dinna cover ye and arenae hideous." Flashbacks surged unbidden.

"Do they pain ye when they're touched?" Thor ensured his hands were nowhere near her back now. Instead, he wiped her tears as quickly as they fell. She willed herself to stop crying before she tried to answer. She reminded herself that she was with Thor, a man she'd never planned to keep secrets from. As she gazed into his whisky-brown eyes with the gold around the pupils, she calmed. His steady presence was the balm she needed to push away the fear.

"Nay. Some parts are just numb."

"And ye fear how I will react to them?"

"Aye."

"Wee one, ye fear me rejecting ye, but I've told ye all I want is ye. I'm nae rejecting ye at all."

Greer swallowed her fear, even as tears threatened again. She nodded and grasped Thor's wrists. She raised his hands to the middle of her back. He groaned before pressing her closer, so his mouth could capture her breast. One arm wrapped around her waist while the other hand slid up her back, between her shoulder blades, and grasped the top of her shoulder. The arm wrapped around her waist soon released her, and his fingertips ran over her lower back before his hand grasped her backside. He squeezed as he guided her to rock against his thigh. His hand slid between her buttocks until his fingers glided through the dew coating her netherlips. He did nothing more than leave them there; he didn't press into her entrance.

"More, *mo ghaol*. Aye." Greer's head fell back, her dark hair wafting over his knees.

"Tell me what ye want. I'll do whatever it is."

"Yer fingers in me."

Thor rolled them, so Greer laid stretched beneath him. His fingers went to her mons, and one circled her pearl. She rocked her hips up to meet his hand as their gazes locked. He slipped one finger inside her, and her head pressed back against the pillow. When a second finger entered her, she grasped his wrist and pressed harder. These were things she remembered from so long ago but hadn't experienced since. His thumb rubbed the nub, and she writhed.

"Wheest. I'll make it better."

"I need ye."

"I ken. Let me pleasure ye."

"Ye are." She cried out when he moved, and she feared he was pulling away. But he eased down the bed until he laid between her legs. He kissed the inside of her thighs as he moved toward her sheath. He licked from stem to stern. "Thor, nay mon has ever…"

He smiled at her wolfishly before he moved to devour her. His tongue flicked her pearl before delving into her entrance. His fingers and tongue worked in tandem as he pushed her to her limits, then he pushed her over the edge. Her body tightened as her core spasmed. She fisted the bedcovers as her hips rose to press her mons against his mouth.

"Thor." She moaned his name as she settled back against the sheets. Her eyes didn't want to remain open, but she didn't want to miss a moment of watching her husband. He'd started to pleasure her that way once, but she'd grown too embarrassed and made him stop. Now she chided herself for not only refusing to let him taste her, but not encouraging him to do so. She wouldn't miss that opportunity again.

"How do ye feel?"

"Replete. But—" She rolled to face him as he moved up the bed. "—I want to touch ye."

"Ye dinna have to do that. I didna do any of this because I expect aught in return."

"Do ye nae want me to touch ye?" He was pushing her hand away as she asked, and the rejection stung. Had her offer made him think of her past? Made him think she was a whore to be so forthright?

"I canna stop thinking aboot ye touching me. But I want ye to ken I give ma love and affection freely. I dinna do it just so ye'll return the favor."

"I ken that. I never thought ye did." It shocked Greer that she had rejected nothing Thor had done so far. She welcomed it. But her mind also understood the circumstances were entirely different. Everything about their time together felt different. Some acts were the same, but the effect couldn't be more opposite. "I want to do these things with ye. I dinna want it to be done to me or for me. I want us to be equals."

Thor understood how significant that was for her. She'd had no control over what happened at Gunn Castle, and they had done everything to her. She also didn't want him to only pleasure her because she wanted a say in what they shared. She wanted what she desired to matter as much as what he did. She wanted a partner.

"Touch me, please," he croaked. He guided her hand beneath his plaid, and she cupped his bollocks. He squeezed his eyes shut.

"Thor?"

"I'm trying nae to finish. I want to last more than a few seconds."

She rolled them in her palm before moving her hand up his rod. She remembered the way he felt as though eight years ago was only that morning. His sword was honed of the strongest steel, and she marveled at how hard he was for her. She stroked him as he kissed her. She explored his mouth with her tongue, their mutual excitement building. She savored the feel of being in control of her own actions and being with someone she cared about. She understood his pride wished for him to last longer, and she imagined he wished to prolong her ministrations just as she'd wished for his to never end. But she wanted to bring him to climax and offer him the same surreal satisfaction she'd experienced.

"Wee one, slow down. I need—"

"I ken what ye need, and I want to give ye that release." She redoubled her efforts, stroking him with varying speeds and tightness until his kiss became savage, and his hips thrust in her hand. He yanked his plaid out of the way and pushed up on his elbow as his seed shot forth, covering her belly and breasts. Other men had done that as though it marked her as theirs. It had always revolted her and made her more resentful. Now that it was Thor's essence that covered her, she loved how it made her feel like his.

He settled beside her as they lay facing each other

again after he used his leine to clean her. She leaned in to kiss him, and it was tender after their burst of passion. He drew her closer, so she once more rested her head on his chest when he rolled onto his back. Thor wouldn't press for anything else that day. He was content to share the quiet with his bride after exploring and pleasuring each other.

"Thank ye," Greer whispered.

"I can say the same to ye. Thank ye, lass."

"But nae just for the pleasure. Thank ye for going slowly with me. I dinna feel as scared as I did before."

"Good. I want to share these moments with ye, especially since there is so much uncertainty now. Whatever happens, I will be by yer side for all of it."

"I ken. And I willna cower behind ye again. I want us to truly be partners."

"There is naught wrong with seeking shelter from those who might harm ye. They are a threat to ye, and I dinna blame ye for yer reaction. I hated sending ye away. Hearing ye call to me was the worst thing I've ever endured. But ye were safer abovestairs, and I'm glad ye didna see what happened to Samuel."

"Samuel? What happened to him?"

"He's nae alive anymore." Thor tucked his chin to watch Greer, but he couldn't see her face clearly. She nodded but said nothing. "Are ye all right with that?"

"Vera. He wasna any better than Edgar, and I told ye how he got between us. I'm glad he canna do that again. Did ye kill him?"

Thor hesitated, making Greer lift her head to look up at him. "Aye. Blaine must have had his body removed before I went back belowstairs. I didna see him when the Sassenachs were there."

"Will aught happen because ye slayed him?"

"They should ken nae to come back for ye, and nay one should speak ill of ye."

"Ye ken what I mean."

"Mayhap something will happen because of it. But I think me refusing to let ye go is more likely the cause than Samuel dying. He's a reminder of Edgar, and the council would do well to be rid of anyone related to him."

"Am I a reminder of Edgar that they wish to be rid of?"

"Nay. Ye are but a pawn to them. They think an alliance with the MacDonnells and MacDonalds will allow them to exert more power against us. The MacDonalds may be a huge clan, but they dinna outnumber us when we summon our allies to our side."

"Are we safe to stay here?"

Thor kissed her forehead before she settled back against his chest. "Right now, I believe staying here is the safest place we can be. But we shall see, wee one. We may need to run."

CHAPTER 11

Rose rapped on her brother's chamber door, uncertain whether she should intrude on the couple. Curiosity and concern drove her up to the third floor. She wished to learn how the supposed enemies resolved their conflict and wound up married in the space of an hour. She wondered how Greer fared after the confrontations, and she wondered whether they wished for a tray to be sent up to them.

"Who is it?" Thor barked.

"It's me," Rose called through the door. She heard the bed creak, but little else, until her brother spoke again.

"Give us a moment."

Now that she was married, she understood what that meant. Her cheeks flushed as she considered her twin brother coupling with her best friend. Not only did the idea seem outrageous, it embarrassed her. She wished to think of neither of them in that context. She stepped back from the door and waited until Thor opened it. He wore his leine, but he hadn't pleated his plaid, merely wrapped it around his waist. Greer wore her chemise with a Sinclair plaid wrapped around her shoulders. The couple didn't appear like they'd recently been locked in the throes of passion, but it was almost too intimate for Rose. She certainly wouldn't want either of them to arrive at her chamber door if she and Blaine were in such a state of undress.

"Rose?" Greer came to stand beside Thor as he opened the door wider.

"Aye. I came to make sure ye were all right after everything that happened, including the adder bite."

"I'm well. Whatever Una gave me cured me almost immediately." Greer observed Rose and noticed her friend's flushed cheeks and how she looked anywhere but at Greer or Thor. "Perhaps you should come inside, so we can explain."

Rose looked around, realizing there were only two chairs and the bed upon which to sit. She didn't consider herself a prude now that she was married and barely able to keep her hands off her husband—and he was no better with her—but it felt like she intruded.

"Mayhap ye could dress and join me in Blaine's solar. That way he can be part of this."

"Nay, Rosie. I dinna want Greer where people can stare after what happened. I wish for things to blow over, and we'd prefer our privacy."

"Ye may want the latter, but I dinna think hiding is the way to make sure gossip doesnae begin. It looks like ye're too embarrassed to be seen in public or that ye're avoiding explaining what the devil is going on between ye."

Thor crossed his arms. "Does the clan wish to ken or do ye wish to ken?"

Rose stepped closer to her brother and rolled her eyes. "Ye ken it's both. Ye need to look like a married couple, and nae just by remaining locked in yer chamber."

"I recall ye remaining locked in yer chamber for a sennight after ye and Blaine wed."

"After our kirking. We didna do that after we handfasted. It wasna an option. I dinna think it is for ye either."

Greer rested her hand on Thor's arm and gazed up at him. She silently wished for him to agree to them appearing belowstairs. She didn't want to leave their cocoon, but she saw the prudence in what Rose suggested.

"Nay. I dinna want people to have aught to pass along to someone outside this clan. The less they see, the less there is to talk aboot." Thor wouldn't budge.

"The less they see, the more for them to make up." Greer tugged on Thor's forearm. He released them immediately and wrapped one around her waist. He gazed into her violet eyes, and he could deny her nothing. He nodded, and his heart stuttered when she smiled her appreciation. Without looking at Rose, she spoke to her friend. "Can ye give us five minutes before we meet ye in Blaine's solar?"

"Aye. Will ye join us for the evening meal?"

Greer suspected that might ask too much of Thor, but she was quick to respond. "We'll be there." She expected the scowl that settled on Thor's face, but she placed her hand over his heart as the other arm wrapped around his waist.

"If there is even a moment where I dinna think ye are safe or ye feel uncomfortable, we leave. I willna waver on that, *mo ghràidh*."

"I wouldnae expect ye to. Let's get ready."

Rose slipped out of the chamber, and the couple hurried to don their clothes. Thor helped Greer with her gown, and she tried not to think about how he was so adept at the task. She knew it was hypocritical to have even a moment's jealousy about anything Thor did in the past.

"Wee one, I have two sisters. Ye ken we swim often and have traveled many times."

Greer nodded, feeling foolish. Thor cupped her shoulders and eased her back against his chest. He kissed her cheek before sliding his hands down her arms and wrapping them around her waist. She leaned against him and closed her eyes. Did they really have to leave their chamber? She already thought of it as theirs, but they hadn't discussed it.

"Thor, do ye wish for me to return to ma chamber after the evening meal?"

"Aye." He felt her tense. "Because I'm coming in here with ye."

"Here?"

"Unless ye dinna wish to sleep beside me, I thought we'd share a chamber. Would ye prefer we use the chamber ye have been using?"

"Nay. I prefer being up here away from everyone else. I just wasna sure what would happen."

"I told ye I wish to hold ye in ma arms every night and wake to ye there. That hasnae changed. Do ye fear sleeping beside me?"

"Nae at all. I was more scared ye'd changed yer mind." She turned in his embrace and wrapped her arms around his neck, one hand tunneling into his hair. "I dinna want to be out of arm's reach of ye."

"Are ye scared something will come between us?"

"I dinna want to stop touching ye."

Thor's mouth lowered to hers in a tender kiss that ended far too soon. "I love ye, wee one."

"I love ye, *mo dhuine.*"

"I am yer mon, and I always will be."

They clasped hands and made their way down to Blaine's solar. The people they passed stared. Greer's smile was less forced than Thor's, but they were both wary. Thor knocked on the door, and Blaine bid them enter. Greer stepped into the chamber once Thor pushed it open and he closed it behind them. Blaine and Rose sat before the fireplace even though there was no blaze. Rose sat on Blaine's lap, leaving the other chair facing the hearth free. Still holding hands, Thor and Greer made their way to the chair. He was uncertain whether she would want such a public display of affection, even in front of their family.

They stared at each other expectantly. Thor gestured to the chair, and Greer's disappointment flashed momentarily in her gaze. It was all he needed. He sat and pulled her onto his lap with enough force that she more fell than sat. She nestled against his chest and closed her eyes. She hoped he could tell their story, and she could merely listen. She was too comfortable and felt too protected to want to delve into what happened all that time ago.

Rose observed Greer and Thor, and she could see her friend trusted her brother in the same way Rose trusted Blaine. She recognized the sentiment and affection. "I guessed something happened between ye years ago, and I thought it might have been romantic. But ye've been so frigid to one another that I decided it wasna possible. Clearly, there was because ye are far too comfortable with each other for just one afternoon in a locked chamber."

Thor rested one hand on Greer's hip while the other stroked her hair. "We met eight years ago while Jamie and I were hunting near the loch. Much like ye two must have arranged to meet, we did the same for nearly nine moons. I rode patrols and went hunting near the loch to have an excuse to be there. After six moons, we handfasted and spent three moons married before that battle. Losing Jamie and being in such chaos for the first time made me unreasonable and unable to make sense of what happened. I believed Greer betrayed me.

I didna ken at the time she was the one giving information to Da and Grandda, but I thought she'd sneaked to the battlefield to spy on us. I thought when I didna die alongside Jamie, she'd come to finish me off. I thought so vera many wrong things. I walked away—rode away—that day believing I was the slighted one."

"I didna fight hard enough to make him see the truth." Greer opened her eyes to look at Rose, but her hand slid beneath Thor's arm that rested on her lap. She wrapped hers around it and rested her hand on top of his. He splayed his fingers, and they entwined them. "I went to warn him aboot the change in Edgar's strategy. I couldnae get to him because of the patrols. I went to him after the battle ended to see if he was hurt and to console him aboot Jamie. When he rejected me, I felt I was the one who'd been betrayed. A lot's happened in those years, and we've changed as much as we've remained the same."

Thor picked up the story. "We've been angry with one another for what we were certain happened. But we've also been hurt because we didna ken we still feel the same as we did when we were five-and-ten. I kenned I still loved Greer, but I couldnae resolve that with how certain I was that she'd betrayed me. And I was certain she didna still love me because she had betrayed me."

"I felt the same. We needed to talk, but I refused every time Thor tried. I didna want to hear excuses, which is what I was sure he would give. I didna want him to press me to confess I still love him."

"And I couldnae live with how things were any longer. So, after ye left Greer's chamber and went belowstairs, I didna change ma plaid. I went back to her. We finally really talked. We learned things aboot each other, and we decided we're done with what's kept us apart too long. We want the life we planned together."

Blaine observed as Greer and Thor offered an abbreviated version of their history. He wondered what more they discussed to come to such a sound resolution after a contentious month. "Did ye handfast again?"

"Nay." Thor tightened his hold around Greer as though Blaine's question was really a threat to separate them. "We didna get to talk aboot that before we had to go belowstairs. When we realized how serious Matthew was aboot taking Greer, we both kenned we needed to do something quickly. That's why I had us marry by consent."

Rose frowned. "But Matthew wasna wrong that a marriage by consent doesnae really work if there's a priest to marry ye. Do ye consider yerselves married?"

"Aye." Thor and Greer answered together.

"What aboot what ye said, Thor?" Rose shifted her gaze from Greer to her brother.

"What did ye say?" Greer leaned forward to twist and look at Thor.

"I said ye carried ma bairn."

Even though they'd discussed making that claim, realizing Thor had spoken it aloud brought back a wave of agonizing memories. Greer's face drained of color, and Thor pulled her back against him. She burrowed her face against his chest. Rose's eyes widened, unsure what just happened. Thor kept his voice low.

"I didna ken until today that we lost a bairn. Edgar beat Greer after he learned aboot us after that battle. She didna ken she was carrying until she miscarried."

Rose and Blaine sat dumbfounded, both shifting their focus to Greer's belly. Thor shook his head, warning them not to say anything about her current condition. His heart ached for the petite woman on his lap. It reinforced his commitment to do anything to protect her. He refused to imagine a future without her.

"I dinna ken if I can have more bairns after that." Greer lifted her head and peered at Rose and Blaine. "I hope I can."

"And if yer clan contests yer marriage? If ye conceive now—" Rose snapped her mouth shut at her brother's glare.

"She's a Sinclair, and our clan willna contest our marriage," Thor barked. He would skirt whether Greer would conceive since he wouldn't humiliate her by saying they might never couple.

"If I conceive, then the bairn is a Sinclair because Thor and I consider ourselves married." Greer looked at Thor again. She knew he was trying to save her the embarrassment of discussing this, but they sat with family. She didn't want to hide more than she had to. "I want to handfast, so we can ask Father Bennett to wave reading the banns if we handfasted and married by consent."

"If that's what ye want, wee one," Thor whispered, and Greer nodded.

"I'd like to marry ye all three ways. That way nay one can say we arenae married before God and the law."

"I'll marry ye any and every way under the sun." Thor relished the same smile Greer shot him before they left their chamber. It made everything right in the world, even if only for a few moments.

"I thought we should have a feast tomorrow eve to celebrate. It will make it feel more official to everyone. Are ye all right with that?" Rose reached out for Greer's hand, and they clasped them like they had when they were girls.

"I think that is a good idea. And I wish to celebrate. I'm proud to be Thor's wife, and I'm happy that we're finally together again."

"Since people ken ye've already been handfasted,

nay one should insist upon a bedding ceremony." Blaine thought he offered reassurance, but at the terror on Greer's face, he darted his eyes to Thor, who swept Greer into his arms.

"We may nae come back down."

Rose jumped off her husband's lap and raced to the door to open it before Thor reached it. Greer's pallor was worse than a moment ago, and she trembled so hard that it was easy to see. Thor went to the servants' stairs rather than the main staircase in the Great Hall. He took the stairs by twos and threes until they reached the third floor. He rushed down the passageway until he fumbled, then shouldered the door open. Greer lurched from his arms and nearly fell to the floor. He barely steadied her before she darted to the chamber pot and heaved. The best he could do was hold her hair out of the way and rub her back.

"I'm sorry." Greer's voice croaked, her throat sore. She stood and looked around. Thor grabbed a linen square from beside the ewer and bowl. He poured water into the bowl and dunked the cloth. He kept the cloth out of Greer's reach when she put her hand out. He gently smoothed it over her face and neck before he handed her a sprig of mint like she had done for him when they talked in her chamber.

"Ye dinna have to apologize. Even if ye were a virgin, there isnae a chance I would allow anyone to watch me make love to ma wife. We dinna believe in them in ma family. What a mon and his wife do is private. It isnae an event for people to watch. We arenae horses trying to breed."

"What if people insist?"

"What mon is daft enough to think a Sinclair would allow that? And what mon is large enough to force me?"

"The women can be just as bad as the men. I dinna want them to see ye. I dinna like that at all."

"Wheest. I'm nay showing maself off to any woman but ye, and nay mon is looking at ye and keeping his eyes. It willna happen."

"But—"

"Greer, it willna happen."

Tears streamed down her cheeks as she nodded. "I dinna want to fear things like this. I want to believe ye when ye say all will be well. I want to be normal."

"I canna think of any woman who's excited for a bedding ceremony. It isnae abnormal to fear that. We dinna ken yet if all will be well or how we can make it well. But I willna give up on our future, even if people interfere. I ken ye have scars I canna see. I ken ye dinna feel like Rose or other women. But that doesnae mean ye arenae normal. Ye eat, drink, sleep, pish, and shite like everyone else. I'd say that makes ye perfectly normal."

"Thor, ye're disgusting." Greer offered him a watery smile. He shrugged unrepentantly. "Thank ye."

"Do ye feel better?"

"Aye." Greer looked at the bed, and her shoulders slumped. "I really dinna want to go back down there. I'm suddenly so tired."

"Ye dinna have to. We'll take a tray up here like we planned. There are plenty of nights ahead of us to dine with the others. I'm tired too, Wife. Ye wore me out."

"Good." Greer chortled as Thor went to the door and turned to her.

"I'll be right back. I'll tell Rose and the cook that we're retiring early. Nay one will blame us after what's happened today."

Greer inhaled and nodded. That was little consolation, but she knew Thor was right. He shut the door behind him and made his way down the stairs and to

Blaine's solar. He wondered if his sister and brother-by-marriage were still there. He knocked and heard Blaine's voice. Rose swiped tears from her cheeks and rushed to Thor.

"Is she all right? Blaine didna mean aught."

"We ken."

"Thor, something happened to her, didna it? Someone did more than just beat her." Rose's deep brown eyes bore into his matching ones. His sister was an avenging angel for those who were wronged. She would lead Blaine's men into battle if she thought she could punish anyone who hurt her closest friend. But Greer specifically said she didn't want Rose to know.

"She wasna treated right while she lived with her clan."

Rose's left eye narrowed, and she cast him a mulish expression. She wouldn't be satisfied with such a vague answer. She took another step forward. "I have never seen ye so angry as when ye ripped that restraint from Greer's bed. They werenae there just to keep her from trying to leave her chamber or to punish her. They were there because men—"

"Dinna ye let her ken ye figured it out, Rosie. It will upset her."

"She'd be ashamed in front of me?"

"That too. That—" Thor pointed at his twin's face. "—expression of guilt and pity is why she didna want ye to ken. She doesnae want ye to believe ye could have done more. Ye couldnae have."

"But I could have. If I'd kenned, I would have told ye. Ye would have gone. Da or Grandda—any mon in any part of our family—would have gone to save her. She didna need to endure that."

"Rosie, to her mind she did. By staying, she gathered information to give to ye. She wanted to protect her people. She couldnae have done that—or at least, she didna think she could have done that—if she left. Edgar wouldnae have stopped, but we wouldnae have had any warning. More Sinclairs and Gunns would have died."

"That wasna her cross to bear. Did she tell ye all this? Did she tell ye that's how she felt?" Rose demanded answers she knew she couldn't ask Greer to give. Thor would have to suffice.

"Nay. I figured it out while we were there. But she told me she doesnae want ye to ken because she doesnae want ye to feel guilty."

"More secrets," Rose hissed.

"She's ma wife now, Rosie. Ye dinna tell me all that goes on between ye and Blaine. Ye canna expect me to tell ye all that goes on between Greer and me."

"Ye married today. Ye could have told me all of this well before now. Ye kept far more from me than I kept from ye. I kept a friendship from ye. Ye kept a wife, a life ye planned, a bairn—"

"I didna ken aboot the bairn. Do ye think I would have left her there if I'd kenned? I'm tired of ye assuming the worst aboot ma intentions with Greer. I love ye and have since long before we kenned what that meant. Dinna judge me lest ye be judged."

Blaine came to stand between them, but they shot him matching glares that would have been funny if the siblings weren't in the midst of a heated fight.

"I dinna just blame ye. I blame Greer too. Even if ye hadnae wanted to tell me, she had plenty of chances to share this."

"To what avail? We were together for nine moons, then apart for eight years. Did ye wish for each of us to harp at ye aboot what a horrible person we thought the other was?"

"Nay, ye daft sod. I would have fixed it. Ye could have been happy together."

Thor exhaled through his nose, his head tilting to

the right before shaking it. He wrapped his arms around his sister and pulled her close. "Ye wanting to fix it is something Greer and I both love ye for. But she feared what would happen if ye got involved. She didna slight ye. She's as fiercely protective of ye as ye are of her. This wasna yer mess to fix, even if ye are ma bossy aulder sister."

Rose didn't wear her ketch in the solar, but she'd pinned her hair up that morning. Thor grasped the rolled knot and tugged lightly. She pinched his ribs much harder than usual.

"Ye deserve far more, little brother."

"Three bluidy minutes."

"And dinna ye forget it. I'm sorry for getting upset with ye. I dinna like kenning I canna make this better for either of ye."

"I love ye nae just because ye're ma sister. Ye have a kind heart, and ye're loyal as the day is long."

"Ye make me sound like ye're favorite hound." Rose pinched him again, but this was playful.

"I dinna like being at odds with ye. I'm glad it never lasts long."

"It only happens when we want the best for each other." Rose squeezed Thor's waist before she released him and stepped back. She looked up at her husband and saw his relief. It was disconcerting for him to see the twins argue. When they did, it grew heated quickly, but they resolved it just as fast.

"I came down to ask for a tray for the evening meal. Today has been a lot for us both. We are tired and dinna want to have people staring while we eat."

"I dinna blame ye. I'll have one sent to ye. Do ye think Greer would want that feast tomorrow eve after all?"

"Aye. I hope she has fun, and we want people to see

us as a truly married couple. Celebrating our wedding does that. Thank ye, Rosie. Goodnight."

"Goodnight, Thorny." Rose winked.

"*Rose.*"

"Thorny?" Blaine asked.

"I shall remember this, Sister. Aye. She would call me that when I got bad tempered as a wean."

"And ye got bad tempered because I was better than ye at plenty of things."

"I'd check ma shoes for snails if I were ye." Thor waggled his brow before stepping out of the solar. His heart felt a little lighter for knowing he didn't have to keep at least one secret from Rose. But he prayed Greer wouldn't be upset again by the time he made it to their chamber. He felt overwhelmed by the day. He couldn't imagine how she felt. He entered the chamber but stopped short. Greer lay fully clothed on the bed in her spot, her hand outstretched to where he would lie. She was sound asleep. Thor kicked off his boots and climbed onto the bed, drawing the plaid over them once again. He slid his arms around her and kissed her forehead.

"I love ye, wee one."

A moment later, he barely heard her. "As much as I love ye."

They'd said the same thing the day he asked her to handfast with him beside the loch.

CHAPTER 12

Morning came, and Greer's eyes fluttered open. She'd never felt so comfortable and content. Thor slumbered beside her; his body wrapped around hers. He radiated heat, and it was like sleeping beside a cheery fire. They'd woken for the food a maid brought to them, and they'd taken turns bathing. They knew they'd both considered sharing a bath, but they settled for only the intimacies they'd already shared. While Greer soaked, Thor had hurried down to her chamber and gathered her few belongings into the trunk at the foot of her bed. He carried it up to the chamber they now shared. She'd sat before the fire, brushing her hair as it dried while he bathed. Now she wore a fresh chemise, and he had on a fresh leine.

"Did ye sleep well, *mo ghaol*?" Thor's chest rumbled behind her back. She turned to look at him.

"Have ye been awake long?"

"Nay. I woke when ye did." He drew her closer as they embraced. "Did ye sleep well?"

"Better than I have in years. Did ye?"

"Aye. I usually dinna sleep as deeply as I did."

"Are ye a light sleeper all the time?"

"Always, except for last night," Thor said. "I still

woke each time ye stirred and then when ye woke just now. But I feel more rested than I have in ages."

"Did I disturb ye? I'm sorry."

"Ye dinna have to apologize. All warriors are light sleepers, and all people move in their sleep. I didna mind. It let me savor holding ye all over again."

"Ye are a sweet mon." Greer pressed a brief kiss to his lips before sighing. "I really dinna want to get up."

"Then dinna. There's nay rush. We can go belowstairs when ye're ready."

"Ye need to be in the lists soon, and I told Rose I'd help her in the storerooms again."

"I got married yesterday. I'm nae going to the lists, and ma bride isnae going to any storerooms. We can go to the beach or the loch. I'll take ye riding, or we can sit in the gardens. We can stay here and talk or read. I'm spending the day with ye."

"Is that so?" Greer cocked an eyebrow, but she shot him a sympathetic look when his face fell. She cupped his cheek. "I want to spend the day with ye, too."

"What would ye like to do?"

"All of it?" Greer wiggled her nose playfully. Thor tickled her and followed her as she rolled onto her back to get away. He was careful to hover above her and not rest his weight on her. He continued to tickle her when all he wished to do was kiss her before ripping the chemise off to worship her breasts as he'd done the day before.

"Cheeky, wee one. Which would ye like to do first?"

"Mmm. Can we go swimming again? This time I willna kick ye or swim away from ye."

"I will only chase ye if ye do. Aye. We can do that." He dropped a smacking kiss on her lips before pulling away, but she wrapped her arms around him and pressed him closer. She lifted her chin and parted her lips. He accepted the invitation, far hungrier for her than the porridge that awaited them. When the kiss drew to an end, he shifted away from her. He feared her seeing his arousal and assuming he expected more. He'd been hard every time he'd woken during the night. He hadn't told the entire truth. It was her arse rubbing against his cock that woke him, and he'd been in sweet agony when they came awake at the same time that morning.

Greer didn't miss how Thor's sword tented his leine as he tried to climb discreetly off the bed and gather the plaid he would wear. He hurried to pleat it as Greer straightened the covers and folded the plaid that would remain on the bed. They completed their morning ablutions before Thor positioned himself to wrap his *breacan feile* around him and over his shoulder. He once again tied Greer's laces before they donned their shoes and made their way belowstairs. They drew stares from everyone they passed. He wondered if he should make an announcement or wait for Blaine to say something at the feast that night.

They joined Rose and Blaine at the dais, and he nodded to Marcus. He still wasn't on good terms with the man after the incident in the lists, and Blaine's second-in-command appeared uneasy when he spied Thor and Greer walking up the dais's steps, holding hands. Thor helped Greer into her chair, and without a word they passed each other the milk and honey. Greer poured the milk into Thor's porridge, then her own, before he poured honey into hers but skipped his. They didn't notice how people stared at them preparing each other's food.

"Be careful it isnae too hot," Greer warned.

"I need the loch to cool off anyway," Thor whispered in her ear. She blushed at his wolfish expression, the same he'd worn the day before as he slid down the bed to pleasure her with his mouth. He squeezed her thigh before he gestured to one of the Sinclairs sitting at the tables below the raised platform. The man hurried over.

"Lady Greer and I are going to the loch. I want all the men to come."

Greer's hand clutched his plaid as she stared up at him, terrified. She shook her head, but Thor covered her hand, easing her fingers open. "Please, nay."

"*Leannan*, they will spread out over the path and around the loch. Unless they hear us screaming aboot a monster in the water, they will be looking away from us. They're guarding us from anyone who might approach. I'm nae comfortable taking ye outside the gates without that many guards."

"Then mayhap we shouldnae go out."

"I willna make ye a prisoner in this keep. We can enjoy ourselves, but we must take reasonable precautions. If they bother ye too much once we get to the loch, we'll come straight back."

Greer nodded, then looked at the Sinclair men sitting among the Keiths. She willed her heart to stop racing. She wasn't comfortable around men she didn't know and couldn't predict. But she knew Thor would never put in harm's way, and he would allow no one near her who might hurt her.

"Finish that bowl, and I'll give ye another." Thor jutted his chin toward her food.

"I canna eat that much, Thor. That's a serving for ye nae me."

"Ye've lost weight."

"How would ye ken?"

Thor peered down at her before he leaned over to whisper again. "Because I ken every inch of yer body, and I dinna like that there are less of them to love. Ye were lighter at Dunbeath than I remembered, and ye're even lighter than when ye arrived. I've carried ye several times, Greer. I ken the differences."

"Ye dinna like how I look?" Greer murmured.

"I didna say that. I said I dinna like that there is less of ye to love. Ye're still the most desirable woman alive. But I worry aboot ye. I call ye wee one because ye're smaller than me, nae because ye're tiny. I dinna want ye to fall ill."

"Ye think I'll become ill because I dinna weigh enough?"

"I dinna want ye to be underfed."

"I'm nae a cow."

"I'm making a right mess of this. Greer, I just want ye to be healthy and well. I will always like how ye look regardless of yer size. I fear hurting ye."

"Ye would never hurt me on purpose, and I ken how careful ye are nae to do it on accident. I'm sorry I panicked."

"*Mo ghaol*, ye dinna have to keep apologizing for how ye feel. There's naught wrong with these emotions."

"I've spent most of ma life apologizing, praying to appease whoever was around me. It's going to take me a little while to unlearn those lessons."

"I understand. Let's eat before it grows too cold. Mayhap nay second bowl, but we could take a small repast with us."

"I'd like that."

Greer and Thor finished their meal, and Greer went to the kitchens to see what she could gather. Thor met with his men and explained their assignment. They all congratulated him since they had no opportunity to the day before, and they all swore to protect Greer as the future Lady Sinclair. By the time Thor and Greer made it into the water, and both stripped to their skin, Greer felt more comfortable with so many men around. Just as Thor predicted, the men spread out and faced away from the water. They were unobtrusive, and the couple enjoyed their time together. They chased one another and splashed until their need to hold each other brought them together. They exchanged several heated kisses before they silently decided they should head to the shore before things went further.

"Thor, who's that?" Greer jerked her chin to the south of the barmekin.

"I saw them while we were in the water. I dinna ken. They're watching us, but they dinna pose a threat at that distance. They merely want us to ken they're there."

"Gunns? The English?"

"Mayhap. If Blaine doesnae already ken, then I'll tell him. He can send a scout if he wishes.

Greer hung back before they stepped entirely out of the privacy the willow tree offered. She grasped Thor's arm, and he turned toward to her. "Are ye sure it's safe to return? Can they ride to us faster than we can run to the gate?"

"Nay. They canna cover that much ground, and even if they did, there's two-and-ten of them to our score."

"But what if there are more we canna see?"

Thor whistled, and the men hurried to gather near them. "Surround Lady Greer until we're inside the bailey."

The men drew their swords, sensing what Thor didn't have to say. They encircled the couple and escorted them back to the keep. The path was nearly half a mile, which made it about a five-minute walk for them. Thor held her hand the entire way as he walked on the side closer to the possible threat. When they reached the bailey, he sheathed his sword.

"I'm going to see Blaine and let him ken aboot those men. Do ye wish to rest more?"

"Nay. I'll find Rose and see if she needs me to do aught for tonight's feast."

"It's our wedding. Ye dinna have to do aught."

"I ken, but it'll keep me occupied for now."

"Vera well. I'll look for ye, and we can decide what ye wish to do next." Thor and Greer exchanged a brief kiss before he watched her take the steps up to the keep's main doors.

"Thor!"

He turned toward the voice calling him, glad to see Blaine making his way toward him. "Did ye see them?"

"Aye. One of ma men alerted me. We couldnae tell who they are, even from the battlements."

"Greer spotted them too. It unnerved her. Do ye think it's more likely the Gunns or the bluidy Sassenachs?"

"I truly dinna ken. Naught reflected off them like they're wearing chain mail, but the men didna come into the bailey yesterday in more than hose and doublets. Mayhap they willna wear their armor if they arenae attacking. It would certainly make it harder to tell if it's them approaching. They ken that'll keep them alive a few more minutes."

"I'm trying to make this a nice day for ma bride, but I'm concerned aboot staying here much longer. I need to get her to Dunbeath. I dinna want a threat near Rose, and ma clan is larger than yers. We're better equipped to ward off an English attack, and I dinna want us to create more problems between ye and the Gunns. We're barely in a truce with them. This is likely to end it. I dinna want to bring the battle to yer gates."

"I appreciate that. But I dinna think it's safe enough to travel with Greer right now. Even with yer full score and with some of ma men accompanying ye. We dinna ken what lurks beyond what we can see. Ma patrols ken to keep an eye open for more Englishmen."

"We could have some of the Sinclair men riding our border come here and help escort Greer and me home."

"That might be wisest."

"If there are any signs we need to leave, I'll send word to Grandda that Greer and I wish to return, but we need more to our retinue. I hate telling him I wed through a missive, but I may have to. If we can wait three days, then we'll have men from Dunbeath to travel with. If we canna wait that long—if aught happens—then we'll rely on ma men here and yers, then pick up more Sinclairs when we reach the border. Blessedly, that's closer to Ackergill than Dunbeath."

"If it comes to it, where will ye flee?"

"Either the mountains or toward Varrich."

"That's most likely to keep ye safe. Do ye wish me to send a messenger to Varrich now and warn them that ye might head there?"

"Nay. I dinna want ye to send any men farther afield than yer border. I dinna want them intercepted or to rouse any suspicions."

"All right. We have something of an idea what to do. Until we need to do otherwise, we carry on."

"Aye. I promised to spend the day with Greer. I want to go back and find her."

"I'm happy for ye, Thor. Ye've been a good friend to me since I met yer sister. I dinna take that for granted. I hope ye ken I will support ye just as ye did me."

"I ken ye will if for nay other reason than ye dinna want ma sister to take yer bollocks." At Blaine's shameless grin, Thor pretended to retch.

"Ye brought it up, little brother." Blaine was a few years older than Thor and Rose. He elbowed his brother-by-marriage.

"If ye wish to keep that elbow attached to yer arm,

ye'll remember who's bigger." They matched in height and had similar builds, but Thor had at least a stone on Blaine, whose body wasn't as bulky.

"Go find yer wife while I go pester mine."

"Trying to make me an uncle already?"

"Working on it."

Thor grimaced, but he was happy for Blaine and Rose. They'd had a rocky start, but it hadn't taken them long to realize how well suited they were to each other. They had a marriage that reminded Thor of his parents. He hoped Blaine and Rose found as much happiness in their marriage as his mother and father had in theirs.

He entered the keep to a group of women surrounding Greer. It was immediately clear that they were not congratulating her on her nuptials. His wife's expression spoke of a woman used to being in charge of an entire keep. It appeared reserved, but self-assured. The other women appeared nothing less than hostile. He approached, but none noticed him.

"We didna believe the rumors when we first heard them, but now we ken ye're the whore Douglan claimed. Ye got with child on purpose and trapped Thor into marrying ye." A young woman pointed her finger at Greer. "He may have tupped ye, but he wanted me. Now he's stuck with ye."

"Ye are a shite liar. He hasnae looked in yer direction. Do ye ken how I ken? Because ma husband watches me wherever I go and whatever I do. Even if he didna love me and I wasna here, he wouldnae have ye. The Sinclairs dinna have lemans, whether they're married or nae. And he wouldnae marry a villager from a clan his sister helps lead. The Sinclairs may choose who they marry, but they've all married fellow nobles. Do ye think ye could be Lady Sinclair one day? Have ye spent yer life training to be a chatelaine? Have ye learned yer sums or to read? Have ye learned how to plan a year's inventory of food? He's second in line to an earldom. Even if he hadnae married me, he would have chosen someone who is prepared to run a keep as enormous as Dunbeath. So dinna try to tell me what ma husband wanted when I ken it's only me."

"Ye bitch." Another woman hissed at Greer. "Ye think ye're better than all of us, but ye're naught more than a whore."

"And ye arenae? I ken which men ye're bedding, and nay a one of them is yer husband. He's been on patrol for what? A moon? Yet ye have love bites peeking out from beneath yer kirtle. They dinna last that long."

A third woman spoke, her malice the worst of them all. "Ye will regret the day ye came here, ye traitor. Thor, Blaine, and Lady Rose canna be with ye every minute of every day. There are ways to get ye out of this keep if we want. We'll turn ye over to the Gunns, so ye can rut with those pigs. Or mayhap, it'll be a Sassenach who finally breaks ye. We dinna care."

"Ye're a right bampot if ye think Thor would let anyone take me. And ye dinna have a healthy fear for yer life if ye think Lady Rose wouldnae put ye in yer grave for touching me. Then again, she might just put ye in the sea. Save her having to dig. Ye can snarl and hiss at me all ye want, but I matter to the people who lead this clan. If ye dinna like that, it's too bluidy bad."

The first woman lunged at Greer, her hand raised to slap her. Greer's fist shot out and landed in the center of the woman's throat.

"Do ye ken who taught me to defend maself? Ma husband eight years ago. He is mine, and he's been mine." She turned to face him, and he realized she'd known he'd stood there the entire time. He wondered if it angered her that he hadn't stepped in. He would have if the woman struck Greer, but he wanted them to see she wouldn't cower again. He walked over to her, and the women took a collective step back. He lifted Greer off her feet and gave her a passionate kiss that should have remained private.

"Wife, I love ye best when ye're fierce. Let me show ye just how much." Thor swept her into his arms and made his way toward the stairs, but he stopped at the bottom. He turned to the women all standing agog. "I heard what ye all said. She wasna wrong aboot ma sister or me. But Lady Greer doesnae need Lady Rose or me to defend her. I would fear her in her own right if I were ye. I kenned when we were five-and-ten that Lady Greer should be Lady Sinclair one day. I love her even more than I did then, and there isnae a doubt that she'll be as great a chatelaine and partner for me as ma grandmama was for ma grandda and ma mama is for ma da."

Thor placed Greer on her feet but wrapped his arm around her waist. They would walk up the stairs as equals for all to see. But once they reached the stairs up to the third floor, he hoisted her over his shoulder, making her giggle, and ran up the rest of them. When they reached their chamber, he put her down.

"Are ye all right? Should I have intervened?"

"Nay. They need to ken they canna intimidate me like they believe. Like ye said, one day I will be Lady Sinclair. I dinna want anyone to believe ye've picked a weak woman to marry. I dinna want anyone to think that once I take that role, they can target our clan when ye ride out."

"Our clan? I love hearing ye say that. Say it again."

"Our clan." Greer loved seeing how happy it made him as much as he loved hearing it. But she grew serious. "Should we be worried aboot what they threatened? Could they go to the Gunns or the English?"

"I dinna ken any of them. Rose probably doesnae

ken them well enough to say. I'll talk to Blaine aboot that too."

"What did he say when ye talked to him aboot those riders?"

"We agreed that for now, it's best we stay. If it becomes too dangerous, then we take Sinclair and Keith men and ride for Dunbeath. If there's time, I'll ask Grandda to send more guards. If there isnae, we have the Sinclair patrols we pass join us."

"That's assuming we can ride south. What if we canna get that far?"

"We head to Uncle Tristan and Auntie Mairghread."

"Will they welcome me?" Greer already worried that the Sinclairs wouldn't welcome her as warmly as a new family member as they did when she sought refuge.

"Of course. Kenning ma aunt, she probably already figured out everything aboot us just from when she was here for Rose and Blaine's wedding. She'll scold me for taking so long to get ma head out of ma arse when I should have proposed a moon ago."

"She's really that perceptive?"

"Lass, if she wasna a woman, she'd have kicked Andrew Murray out of his position and already led our men to victory against the English. And every mon would follow her without a doubt. Uncle Tristan has never feared being away from Varrich. He kens people are more afraid of her than him if their weans are there. Auntie Mairghread grew up with four aulder brothers who all became warriors. She's a wee more bloodthirsty than Mama and ma other aunts."

"I wouldnae have kenned from the woman I met here."

"Havenae ye ever seen her compete at the Gatherings? She's even better at knife throwing than Da—which he hates admitting every year."

CELESTE BARCLAY

"I thought that was just for sport."

"It is. And Mama is just as skilled with a blade. But Auntie Mairghread was meant to be a warrior. Uncle Tristan says that it was destiny they should marry because there was once a clanswoman, Lorna Mackay, who married a Norseman, Rangvald Thorsson, who fell in love with her. Lorna trained with her aulder brothers at Varrich before the Norse killed her family. Despite being from the Highlands, she became one of the most feared and famous shieldmaidens. Uncle Tristan says Auntie Mairghread has the same spirit as Lorna Mackay and the Lord always intended her to become a Mackay."

"I dinna ken that I'm brave enough to be a shieldmaiden, but I want to be brave enough to make ye proud."

"I'll always be proud of ye. I dinna need a warrior for a wife, but ye have the heart of one. Ye havenae given up any fight, and ye survive by yer wits. That's why I ken ye'll be the perfect partner for me and an excellent lady of our clan."

"Thor, do ye give me all these compliments because ye believe I need them? Do ye really think me fragile?"

"There are some parts of ye that are fragile. But the Lord forged most of ye from iron. I give ye the compliments because I believe each one, but I also ken nay one has been kind to ye in a long time. Ye deserve to hear the good in ye now. I dinna do it because I think ye're weak and need me to bolster ye. I do it because I'm proud."

"Thank ye. That means everything to me, Thor. Far more than I can express with words or actions. I will survive, but ye're right. There are parts of me that are fragile. I dinna like it, but it's a fact. Despite revealing so much that I've kept hidden, I feel better today and yesterday than I have since we parted ways." Greer bit

HIGHLAND STRENGTH

the corner of her bottom lip as she considered what she wanted to ask. "Can ye teach me more aboot how to defend maself? It's nae that I think ye would ever leave me unprotected. I would feel better kenning nay one can easily force me to do aught ever again."

"Of course. We can do it in here if ye prefer the privacy."

"For now. Besides, I wouldnae want to give away how well ye teach me to fight. That secret may be ma best weapon."

Thor didn't want to consider how right Greer might be one day. The visits from the Gunns and King Edward's men, along with the distant threat from the horseback riders and the women in the Great Hall, made Thor worry she might need these skills. He would never let his wife be a victim again, but he dreaded the looming sense they would both soon be tested.

CHAPTER 13

For the next three days, Thor spent his mornings with Greer, encouraging her to sleep late. When she woke, they laid in bed and talked more about their time apart. They skirted the one topic that neither wished to discuss. Thor learned more about why Greer spied on Edgar and how she accomplished it. She told him about the code she and Rose developed when they needed to get information to one another. She also reminded him about how she'd known Albert was her birth father since her childhood. She'd insisted that he be her guard whenever she rode out. She wanted the time with him, and she knew he was more dedicated to her safety than anyone else.

Thor wondered how she'd slipped away to the loch if Albert guarded her. She'd always told him she came alone. She explained she had. She learned how to sneak out of the keep with no one knowing, not even Albert. She and Thor formed their relationship before her abuse began, so she hadn't believed she needed a guard as much then. It was the closest they came to Thor asking questions or Greer admitting anything. She told him she would answer any he had, but he insisted he only wanted to know what she was ready to volunteer.

Their intimacy didn't progress beyond what they'd shared the first day. Neither realized how the other hid their physical frustration. Greer wished to explore more, but she recognized how fearful Thor was that he'd hurt her. In turn, Thor didn't want Greer to feel pressured into giving more of herself than she was ready to. So, they settled for exploring one another with their hands and Thor's mouth.

In the afternoons, they ventured away from their chamber. The first day, Greer was too apprehensive to leave the keep's walls. They went to the garden instead. They spent more time talking about their roles during a typical day among their clan. Thor deduced Greer ran the clan almost entirely on her own. The clan council was only interested in discussing clan politics and scheming with Edgar. She maintained all the ledgers, both the ones the lady and the laird would keep. She oversaw the kitchens, often helping there. She managed all the maids and laundresses who were often at odds with one another. She adjudicated all disputes between women, and most often heard the complaints between men.

Edgar ceded that role to her because he claimed it drove him barmy to listen to people whine. She met with the farmers to plan their crops every spring. She ordered repairs to crofts and controlled the budgets for those. She knew every project on which the blacksmith worked and how many sacks a day the miller filled. She'd started taking over these responsibilities when she was three-and-ten. By the time she was six-and-ten, she led the clan in all things apart from battle.

Thor described how he'd earned his position as the captain of the guard, inheriting the position from his uncle Alex, and how it had been the proudest moment of his life since he and Greer parted ways. While his father was still the clan's tánaiste, he'd taken over many of Liam's duties since the laird was well into his sixth decade. Until Liam and Callum decided Thor was mature enough to take over leading the clan's warriors, Alex had served as Callum's second-in-command.

He spoke of his long hours in clan council meetings with his grandfather, father, and uncles along with the other members. He'd been a silent observer for many years, absorbing the lessons his family taught. But over the past three years, they'd begun asking his opinion as though he were a true member of the council. The men who made up the rest of the council weren't family, so he'd feared they wouldn't take him seriously. But they'd all seen him grow into the role.

Greer asked about his training as a warrior and the specifics of what happened in the lists. She wanted to know more than that they fought. He'd explained much of what the men did when they sparred and how he now directed groups just like his father and uncles. He shared how people still stopped to watch when the four brothers sparred together and Liam joined as a pretend foe or to call out scenarios and corrections. He told Greer how he prayed one day he and his cousins would be as respected and renowned as their fathers.

The second afternoon, they met with Father Bennett and discussed their choices for marrying within the church. The priest agreed he saw no reason to post the banns since they were already married in the eyes of the Keiths, and he knew the Sinclairs wouldn't contest it. The Gunns had tried, but it didn't change the fact that they were living as man and wife.

They rode out with Blaine and Greer on the third afternoon and enjoyed a picnic with the other couple. The air between Greer and Thor couldn't have been more different from their first excursion. Rather than being more frigid than the blusteriest day during a Highland winter, the heat between threatened to send them up in flames. Their desire mounted with each moment spent together, and they couldn't be close enough. If they weren't lying in bed together, Greer spent most of her time seated on Thor's lap. That day, Greer sat astride before Thor on his horse. He'd hesitated to share the mount because he knew it would be harder to swing his sword if someone attacked. It also meant he couldn't order Greer to ride to safety. But he convinced himself that riding together would keep them from getting separated. The truth was neither wanted to go without touching the other even for an hour's ride.

"Do ye wish to go for another swim, *leannan?*" Thor whispered in Greer's ear as they cantered back toward the keep. His arm rested beneath her breasts, his thumb daring to sweep over her nipple from time to time. She'd pressed her hips back each time, but his sporran kept her from feeling what she was certain was an erect cock. Now she shifted restlessly. His hand slid up her ribs until it rested beneath her breast, the weight of the mound pressing against it.

"Aye." Greer could barely form the sound. When they approached the loch, Thor announced they would split off. The half a score of Sinclair guards fanned out around the loch and turned to face away from the water after letting their horses drink. While the mounts recovered from their ride, Thor and Greer slipped beneath the tree's branches.

"I love riding with ye in ma arms, Wife."

Greer's mind flashed to something she'd rather ride. She turned to Thor after he loosened her laces. She didn't want her voice to carry to the men standing closest to them. "I hope to ride something else soon."

Thor froze. He gazed down at Greer's upturned face. He cupped it in one hand. "Whenever ye are ready."

It surprised Greer how easily she'd accepted Thor's touch and how much she enjoyed it. Everything felt so different from what she'd endured. She would never forget those years, and she bore the scars on her feet and back from them. But with the hours she and Thor had spent in each other's company over the past five days, she found herself inching past those memories and visceral fears. It was like she returned to the moments she'd shared with Thor when they were adolescents. The other experiences moved from the forefront of her mind. They still occupied more space than she wanted, but her need for more connection with Thor intensified.

She wondered if she dared offer something more intimate for him. If they lingered beneath the tree much longer, the men would guess what they were doing. Her stomach knotted with a moment of embarrassment and shame, then she shoved it aside. They were married. She would feel no regret for sharing private time with her husband. She reached for his belt and released it as he unfastened the brooch at his shoulder. She unraveled the *breacan feile* while Thor removed his leine. They'd both already shed their shoes and stockings. Greer remained fully dressed, but Thor stood before her naked. They'd slept with a layer of clothing on, and they'd been discreet while each of them bathed. It was the first time in years that Greer saw Thor fully naked. He was magnificent. She trailed her hands over his chest and shoulders before wrapping them around him to glide down his back to his hips. Then one hand wrapped around his length.

She sank to her knees, her head tilted back to watch Thor. She feared she might disgust him with her offer, but his hungry eyes told her she should have offered sooner.

"Wee one, ye dinna have to do this because I've already given ye the same."

"I want to, Thor. It has scared me that ye would disapprove, but I want more between us."

"Only do what ye are comfortable with. Dinna try for aught else." Thor thought his eyes might roll into the back of his head when Greer's tongue swept over the tip of his cock. She continued to stroke him as she swirled warm, wet heat over the entire head. She flicked the underside of his rod, making him twitch and swallow a groan. He watched her as her lips slid down his length. He pushed aside thoughts that attempted to creep in. He didn't want to think about how she'd gained such skill or the number of times she'd likely performed this act. He knew it was different for her, so he wouldn't spoil the moment by thinking about something neither of them could change.

He'd been with other women since his time with Greer when they were younger. He'd received the same attention as he did now, and he'd enjoyed it. But nothing compared to the attention she lavished on him now. Her gentle touch when she cupped his bollocks made them tighten. Her head bobbed as she inched farther down his shaft until Thor's hands fisted to keep from thrusting. He was racing to his release too fast, so he pulled back a little.

"Nae yet unless ye canna keep going." Thor's voice was a hoarse whisper as the back of his fingers caressed her cheek. She slowed her speed, but she didn't ease the suction. His groans signaled he wouldn't last much longer. "Dinna take it if ye dinna want to."

Greer released him and looked up at him. "Make me yers, Thor."

He grasped his rod and stroked, but she shook her head as she stood.

"Make me yers."

She placed her hand over his as she pressed her body against his. He tore at her clothes as they kissed. She shimmied to drop her kirtle and chemise rather than pull apart to lift them over her head.

"Ye are already mine, and I am yers."

"Ye ken I'm nae truly yer wife yet. I want to be. Right now, *mo dhuine*."

"If ye change yer mind—"

"I willna. It feels right. Please." She wouldn't change her mind, but she feared she might lose her nerve. Self-doubt reached its fingers toward her, but she pushed them aside when Thor lifted her and guided her legs around his waist.

"Ye are already ma wife whether we couple or nay. But I wish to share this with ye."

"I ken, and I've wanted this all along. I want to feel the same way I used to."

Thor waded into the water, holding Greer in place as each step made his sword rub against her sheath. He didn't stop until the water submerged their shoulders. He lifted her high enough for him to find her entrance. He took his time as he lowered her onto his cock.

"More. I willna break. This is torture moving so slowly."

With only a couple inches left, he thrust into her, seating himself to the hilt. Greer's kiss was demanding as they fused their bodies into one. She'd never experienced this need before. When they were adolescents, they'd both been shy and uncertain, even during their most vigorous couplings. But her hunger became insatiable as she rocked her hips against him. She sucked his tongue into her mouth, mimicking what she'd done only minutes ago. Thor's fingers dug into her hips as he increased their pace.

"Good God, Thor. I didna ken I could be this—this —lusty."

"I'm so much stronger than ye. I fear being too rough, but I canna slow down. What are ye doing to me, Greer? I have nay control left. I need more, too."

"I'm telling ye, I willna break."

"Is it because—" Thor winced, fearing he'd destroyed the moment.

"It has naught to do with what I'm used to or what's been done to me before. It's ye. I feel out of control just like ye. I canna get close enough to ye."

"It's like I need to make up for all those years in this one moment."

"Do ye fear I willna want this again?"

"Mayhap a little. But I just need ma wife."

"Ye have—Thor... I'm close... Dinna stop."

"I canna unless ye tell me to."

"Never." Greer cupped his face as she spoke the truth. Making love to Thor once wouldn't overcome the damage done, but she suspected a lifetime with him would. "*Thor.*"

"Me too, *mo ghràidh*."

They clung to each other as their bodies shuddered and couldn't calm. Their kisses remained as hungry as before they'd climaxed together. Greer's core continued to flex around Thor's shaft, refusing to let it go. He didn't want to end her pleasure, so he continued to thrust and move her along his rod. One arm rested beneath her backside as his free hand moved to knead her breast.

"Ye feel so bluidy right, wee one. I want to bring ye another release. I'd do it as many times as ye can manage."

"I want the same."

It surprised Thor that he remained hard while he brought Greer to a second release. He hadn't been this starving for release when they'd been five-and-ten or afterward. It'd taken him a year-and-a-half before he could bring himself to couple with another woman. He'd pictured Greer every time he'd been with someone else. He'd even said her name more than once, leading a couple women to claim he was married. But he'd meant none of his interludes to develop into relationships, so mutual satisfaction overcame the blunder.

When they were finally too fatigued to continue, they remained in the water, enjoying the erotic feel of it lapping around them. Greer hadn't panicked, and she considered that an accomplishment. Once more, she wondered if she would have reached this point with another man. She didn't think she would love another the way she did Thor, so she didn't think she'd ever be as physically attracted to one. But she could admit when she saw a handsome one and knew they could make her curious. However, she could never picture coupling with them. Something made her shy away in every musing. She'd imagined Thor so many times. It was what sustained her. She was certain that influenced her eagerness now and the ease with which she accepted joining with him. They made love. He hadn't rutted on her.

Will I ever get to where this isnae always on ma mind? I dinna want to live in those memories. I dinna want them to own any more of ma heart or mind. I want to fill those spaces with Thor and the life we'll have together. But can I merely push them aside and demand they cease?

Greer, ye survived for eight years. It hasnae even been two moons since it ended. Ye arenae wrong for this to still consume ye.

But I dinna want it to. Nay more wondering if it's Thor or whether I could do this with another mon. Nay more fearing I disgust him or waiting for him to reject me. All that's doing is forcing him to prove himself over and over and making him repeat himself. That's what he's most likely to get fed up with. He doesnae need to prove aught to me. I'm the one who needs to accept that he loves me. That if he believes I'm worthy of his love, then I must be. Mayhap one day I will believe that on ma own, but for now, that's enough.

"Greer?"

"Sorry. I was lost in thought."

"I ken. Is everything all right?"

"Vera." Greer pecked his lips. "I love ye."

"I love ye more than aught. The only people I could love as much as ye are any bairns we have together. If that never happens, then ye will have ma entire heart to yerself."

"Ye can keep a part for yer family." Greer chuckled.

"Ye're giving me an order?" Thor tickled her ribs.

"Aye." She gasped as Thor pulled them beneath the surface, then pushed them out. Greer spluttered as she swiped her hair from her face. "What was that for?"

"Ye can order me to do aught ye want, and I'll do ma best to comply. But dinna forget I dinna always follow directions well. They can have a sliver. The rest is yers."

"Daft mon."

"Ye drive me to distraction, lass."

"If these are yer distractions, then I'll happily drive ye to them all day and night."

"Promise?"

"Aye, Husband. I promise."

"Ye are the best wife ever." Thor twisted and floated on his back before kicking his legs, moving them farther across the loch. He didn't expect Greer to release her legs and force her body out of the water. Her hand landed on his head and shoved him down before she kicked to get away. Hands wrapped around her waist and yanked her back. She splashed water in Thor's face before her body collided with his. She pushed sopping hair from his forehead.

"Am I still the best?"

"Even better than before. I like how we can be playful together again. I missed that."

"I did too. The last time we rode out with Blaine and Rose, I felt horrible because I was so jealous of the way ye and Rose teased. I wanted that to be me again."

"It will be. I'll dump pine needles on ye anytime."

"It's a good thing I love ye."

"Aye, ye do. As much as I love ye." Thor kissed her before they frolicked. He couldn't remember the last time he'd done that. But they raced each other, saw who could dive the deepest, splashed more water at one another, and made love twice more before they were too tired to continue, and Thor noted their fingers were more wrinkled than an old man's bollocks.

"I canna remember enjoying a day more than this. Thank ye, Thor."

"I ken we canna do it every day, even though that's what I wish. But we can enjoy it whenever we have the chance."

They waded out of the water, and Thor used his plaid to dry them before they dressed. Greer realized she'd entirely forgotten about the guards, who'd stood watch the entire time. However, her brow furrowed when they stepped back onto the path.

"We were gone long enough that the ones at the keep kenned to come and relieve them. They took their horses back with them."

"We were really out there that long?"

Thor peered up at the sky. "At least two-and-a-half, mayhap three, hours."

"I dinna believe that."

"I told ye, ye were the best distraction. Mayhap I'm the same." Thor tapped her on the backside, pushing her a step ahead of him. She gathered her skirts in one hand as she waited for him to catch up. Then she reached behind him and pinched his arse. She took off running back to the keep. She squealed when he snagged her around the waist and hoisted her over his shoulder. He landed three playful smacks on her backside. "What shall I do with ye wife?"

"I can think of plenty." Greer waited until they were in their chamber, then they tested each of her suggestions. They arrived halfway through the evening meal.

CHAPTER 14

Every day they spent together made it easier for Greer to accept her new life as Thor's recognized wife in public and his lover in private. She flourished, no longer trapped by her fears, relishing the independence the decision not to doubt Thor gave her. Thor spoke to Blaine about the women who accosted Greer before she had the chance to address it with Rose. She knew Rose called the women into Blaine's solar, and he sat beside her, holding her hand, as Rose made it clear she had no tolerance for that kind of behavior toward anyone. If the women wished to remain employed within the keep, they would keep a civil tongue in their head lest Rose cut it out.

After a sennight spent together, Greer returned to helping Rose with the chatelaine duties. Thor returned to the lists and his men's teasing. They made no comments about Greer or hinted at her past. But they made plenty of jests at his expense, questioning whether he was man enough to keep such a beautiful woman's attention. He took the jokes about his prowess in stride since it was a reminder that he and Greer not only reconciled but found happiness and fulfillment together.

However, their good cheer didn't negate the lingering worry about the Gunns and the English. After a sennight and a half, Thor could no longer ignore the question why nothing more had happened. He didn't believe either party gave up. It made him anxious about what they plotted. He didn't want the Keiths to face two separate enemies or an attack from both sides combined.

"Thor, we havenae talked aboot what we'll do if the English or men from ma clan return." Greer worried about the same thing as they sat together in the garden. She frowned after she spoke. "Nae ma clan. The Sinclairs are ma clan. Men from the Gunns."

"Do ye say it that way because ye dinna want to hurt ma feelings or because ye dinna feel like a Gunn anymore at all?"

"Nae at all. Just like it was easy to stop referring to Edgar as ma father, I find it easy to nae speak of them as though they're still ma people. I ken they arenae all bad, and nae all of them have forsaken me. But as a whole, they have. If the clan council hadnae been as bad as Edgar, they would have removed him and found someone else. They could have ended that family line and began a new one. They kenned what he allowed, and they supported his efforts to harass other clans. I'm nae ready to forgive that. I want to one day, so I dinna live with this anger, but I'm nae there yet."

"I'm worried aboot the same thing. It makes me suspicious aboot why naught has happened. Besides seeing the riders once, there hasnae been any disturbance. Blaine's patrols along the Sinclair and Mackay borders havenae seen aught. The patrols along the Gunn border havenae seen anyone coming or going from Gunn Castle since the battle nearly two moons ago. Mayhap a messenger got past, but nay party has."

"What are they waiting for? For us to be complacent?"

"Mayhap. Or they're waiting for us to venture back to Dunbeath."

"Do we have to ride? Couldnae we take birlinns?"

"I thought aboot that. Blaine's offered to let us borrow one. It may come to that."

"How much longer can we stay here? I ken ye canna stay for forever. Ye have duties, and I'm eager to begin mine. I want to go to ma new home. I'd rather learn how people will treat me now than continue to worry aboot it."

"Are ye scared they will reject ye because ye were a Gunn?" He was careful to use the past tense.

"Aye. Do they ken I helped yer clan?"

"I think everyone in the keep and village probably does by now."

"I told those women that ye wouldnae have married anyone but a noblewoman, but is there someone at Dunbeath who willna be pleased ye married?"

"Are ye asking if I was involved with someone?"

"Aye, or someone who thinks they deserve to be yer wife."

"There's nay one serious. There are women at the tavern, but that's their business. There's a widow I've been with a few times, but I made it clear from the beginning that if she even hinted at something permanent, then I would walk away."

"Do ye have any weans? Ye ken how I dinna, but I dinna think I ever asked."

"Nay. I've always been careful. Do ye ken there are ways to couple without risking that?" Thor swore to himself that he wouldn't ask such questions, and now he had.

"Aye. I ken." Greer's voice was soft as she responded. At the guilt in Thor's eyes, she shook her head, realizing what he thought. She didn't want to speak aloud anything to do with a man violating her back channel. "I never have. I dinna ken how I escaped that. I often wished that had been the preference. I wouldnae have feared the pox or getting with child."

"That's why I—"

"It's all right to admit ye have a past and what ye did. I dinna hold it against ye."

"But ye're moving to a place where ye will meet these women. I dinna want ye to feel uncomfortable."

"I ken ye arenae going back to any of them. I ken ye love me. It might be a wee awkward, but I feared someone begrudging me marrying ye. I didna want a woman thinking I stole ye from her or thinking she might steal ye from me."

"There's nay one like that." Thor grinned. "Ma mama wouldnae allow it. She'd have ma cods if I led a woman to believe that, and she would skelp them if they claimed any lies."

"I like yer mother." Greer waggled her eyebrows.

"Greer, she likes ye too. I ken she does. Before we left Dunbeath, I saw her face when Rose said she was riding with me to the Gunns, and ye insisted on going too. It pained her, and she feared for ye if there were a battle, and there was. I also saw her relief when she arrived and found ye hale. I ken she suspects something between us, so I think it will relieve her to ken we've nae only come to peace, but we're married."

"Willna it hurt yer family's feelings that we didna include them?"

"They willna love it, but they'll understand."

"Father Bennett said we can marry when we're ready. But I havenae brought it up because I want yer family to be there. I dinna want to take that from them."

"Ye're nae taking aught, but I appreciate ye considering them. I admit I'd like them to be there too. I want to marry ye right this minute, but I havenae pushed for the kirking for that reason."

"I suspected as much." Greer looked toward the bailey wall as though she might see through it. "That still doesnae resolve when we can leave here."

"I wish I kenned more aboot where they are and what they want. I dinna think either is far. Mayhap the Gunns returned to their keep, but I dinna believe the bluidy Sassenachs rode all the way back to London. But nay one has seen hide nor hair of them. It makes me wonder if they're hiding on Gunn land. If they are, do Matthew and the others ken? I canna see them condoning it since they're a threat to their plans for ye."

"I've been thinking the same things." Greer's cheeks filled as she exhaled a slow breath. "I dinna like it being so unresolved. I also dinna want to leave Rose and Blaine. They've been so kind and generous, but we canna stay here much longer. I ken they willna ask us to leave, but this isnae our home. I'm ready to leave when ye say we should."

"I'm glad ye told me. I didna want to ask or insist."

"I ken."

"Let's talk to Blaine and Rose together and ask Marcus to join us."

"Ye really dinna like him, do ye?"

"I think he's an excellent warrior, and he trains his men well. But I dinna agree with some things he lets his men discuss."

"Have ye heard some of them talking aboot me again?"

"There hasnae been a death in the clan, so nay. They just arenae respectful of women in general. Mayhap I'm sensitive because I have two sisters and a passel of cousins who are lasses. But ma cousins and I would never say those things where people could hear us."

"Ye'd say them in private?"

"I admit we would say some of it. At least, I would have before I married ye. They've spoken aboot other men's daughters and sisters, and naught's done aboot it, except for when Blaine hears it. But he was away so much recently that the men think they can continue. Marcus never should have allowed it to start."

"That's a pity. That makes more work for Blaine."

"Aye. But I can tolerate Marcus as a warrior, and I trust him to arrange our guard. If for nay other reason than he's devoted to Blaine. They're nay just cousins. They're best friends, and I understand why. Blaine's responsibilities as acting laird made him mature faster than some men. Even though Marcus has acted as tánaiste while that's still technically Blaine's title, he hasnae had the same burden to represent Clan Keith that Blaine has."

"I can understand that. It makes sense. Are ye more mature than yer cousins because ye're second in line?"

"Nay. At least, I dinna think so. Our family has given us all a great deal of responsibility from a young age, and we all wish to keep our parents', aunts', uncles', and Grandda's respect. We dinna want to jeopardize that."

"I'm glad I'm joining yer family, *mo ghràidh*."

"Me too, *mo ghaol*. There are Marcus and Blaine. Do ye wish to be there when I speak to them?"

"I do. I'll look for Rose."

The couple rose from the garden bench, and Greer went in search of her friend. She wasn't hard to find since she carried two ledgers toward Blaine's solar. Greer knew they often worked together in the chamber. Rose didn't have a lady's solar, and the lady's chamber would one day become a nursery.

"Rose, Thor's asking Blaine and Marcus to join us in here. We'd like to talk aboot our plans for returning to Dunbeath."

"I dinna wish ye to leave yet. Ye just got here." Rose knew Greer would finally find happiness by being surrounded by Sinclairs, but she selfishly didn't want to end the time she spent with her best friend. And she feared she would grow lonely. The altercation she heard about in the Great Hall remained nothing like the welcome she'd experienced. No one had accosted her, but neither had anyone warmed to her enough to call them a friend. She feared she'd be adrift without Greer and Thor, and she didn't want to cling to Blaine either.

"We've been here more than a moon. Thor has duties, and I'd like to make a permanent home somewhere with him."

"Ye have plenty of time for that, and Thor and I have enough cousins that he isnae missed when it comes to duties."

"Rose, are ye scared aboot when we arenae here?"

"Nae scared, but I ken I'll be lonely. I'm trying to make friends, but there doesnae seem to be room in anyone's life for another one. I'm busy enough during the day, but I'd like to ken I have someone to talk to, someone to join me with some of the chores."

"We're nay that far apart. We can visit each other."

"Until we both get too busy to have the time."

"I will make the time for ye. Always."

"I will too." Rose looked up as three massive shadows fell upon Greer and her. Thor wrapped his arm around Greer's waist, and Rose enjoyed seeing them happy together rather than at odds. Now that they were reconciled, it was easy to see how deeply they'd loved one another, and she couldn't fathom the pain they'd suffered while apart.

"Let's go inside," Blaine offered. Rather than moving to sit beside the empty fireplace, Blaine pulled out a chair next to his for Rose at the massive oblong table.

He held his clan council meetings in his solar, and they sat around the table. Thor helped Greer with hers before taking her hand as he sat. Marcus watched the two couples, wary of Thor. The man told Blaine and him he wished to plan for his departure with Greer, but Marcus worried he was in the Sinclair warrior's crosshairs.

"Greer and I ken we need to travel to Dunbeath soon. We canna remain here indefinitely. Nay one kens what's become of the English bastards, but they canna be that far away. The Gunns have been quiet, but they've proven to be patient when they hold a grudge. We have those two enemies looming and nay army to travel with. I have a score of men with me, and I would ask for a score to travel with. When we reach the border, I'll have the Sinclair patrol join us."

"When do ye plan to leave?" Rose leaned forward, one arm resting on the table, and her other hand's fingers biting into the back of Blaine's hands.

"Within a sennight." Thor watched as Rose's lip trembled, and it broke his heart. Reasonably, he knew he and Greer couldn't remain much longer, but he knew Rose was still adjusting to her new home. He didn't want to abandon her. He still struggled with his guilt over doing that to Greer. He didn't want to commit the same crime twice. Rose tucked her lips between her teeth and nodded. "As soon as we settle this, we will come back to visit. Mayhap Mama and Da can come with us."

"Just dinna send Shona without Mama. I had a hard enough time keeping ye from throttling her at Dunrobin. I dinna need to hear ye carping at her again."

"Mama can deal with her until she finds a husband barmy enough to love the wee hellion." Thor had threatened to lock their younger sister in her chamber while the siblings visited their Sutherland family.

Shona got away with far more with Great-Aunt Amelia than she did with Siùsan, and everyone considered Amelia strict. Her antics terrified Thor, and he'd been riding into battle for years. Marcus and Greer met Shona at Blaine and Rose's wedding, so they knew exactly what the twins meant, and Greer had heard about her for years.

"I feel better kenning ye plan to visit sooner rather than later." Rose sat back in her chair and eased her hold on Blaine's throbbing hand. She glanced down and realized what she'd done before offering a sheepish expression and a peck on the cheek.

Thor turned his attention to Marcus. "I'd like to ken which men ye'll send. I trust ye and them. It isnae a test or for me to approve or deny. I just want to ken who will travel with ma wife."

"I can understand yer concern. I dinna think ye wish to hear this, though. Drew is one of our best scouts. I ken ye dinna like him, but he's good to have with ye. I can promise ye, he will nae speak as he did again."

Greer remembered the man who'd appeared at the evening meal with a battered face. She never learned what he'd said, but Thor told her the gist. She gazed up at her husband and watched the muscle in his jaw tick. There was a heavy silence in the room before Thor nodded. She knew he didn't like agreeing, but she could tell he would put aside any dislike for her safety. She prayed for their sake and Drew's that he didn't step afoul of Thor again. He wouldn't forgive a second time.

"If there are two score men riding out, then I need to plan provisions for that. I ken it's only a day's ride each way, but the Keith men will need food for the way back. And ye ken Mama taught us to always have enough for at least one extra day, just in case."

No one there wished to think about any "just in cases."

"Today is Monday. I'd like to travel on Friday." Thor shifted his focus to Greer. They had set no days, but she liked the idea. It gave them three more full days with Blaine and Rose, but it satisfied her eagerness to reach home. She turned her attention to Rose, and she knew her friend fought back tears. She didn't want to appear happy at Rose's expense.

"I'll send Drew and a few others out to scout Wednesday and Thursday, and he can set off an hour before everyone else," Marcus offered.

"I appreciate that." Thor stood and thrust out his arm to Marcus. The Keith's second-in-command grasped Thor's forearm. Thor squeezed mercilessly. "I ken all yer men will do their vera best to protect ma wife. It's good to ken I dinna need to worry."

Marcus fought not to squirm or flinch. He resented Thor more by the minute, but he understood the man's position. He'd married only a fortnight ago, and he felt just as protective of his own bride. He wouldn't volunteer himself for the mission because he didn't wish to be away from his wife. At least Thor hadn't chastised him in front of his men after that disastrous encounter in the lists. He'd been cordial to Marcus, but neither man trusted the other off a battlefield.

"I'll help ye, Rose." Greer would make the most of her last few days, and since she was certain Thor would do the same to spend time with his twin, Greer didn't worry that they would be far apart.

"I'd like that. Thank ye." The women left the solar, both thinking the men were right behind them. They turned when the door closed, but the men weren't with them. They looked at each other, both knowing Thor must have far more to say to Marcus. Or the threat was worse than they'd told the women. Greer and Rose feared it might be both.

Once the women left the solar, Thor turned back to Marcus. "Ye are Blaine's best friend, and I ken he's a good judge of character. I willna hold a grudge, but I am wary. I ken ye've trained yer men well, but I need to be sure none of them will do aught to harm ma wife. Do they believe what yer father said?"

"Some do, aye. I've spoken to all of them, and they ken nae to speak of her the way Tim and Drew did. But people trusted and respected ma father. Blaine and I lost that faith in him, but others didna, even when they learned that he'd betrayed Blaine. They believed the things he would say, and they didna see aught wrong with him because he always said aught he did, he did for the clan. Some will go to their grave saying he didna really wrong anyone because he thought he was protecting our interests and strengthening us. I'm assigning men I ken dinna think like that. Ones who dinna believe the rumors aboot Lady Greer."

"Do many other clan members still believe them?" Thor looked between Marcus and Blaine.

"Nae that I ken of," Marcus replied. "It was odd to see ye go from being at each other's throats to saying ye were married. But it hasnae been hard to see ye have vera deep feelings for one another. Love and hate are actually closer together than people think. Hate is often just wounded love. I think that was the case with ye and yer lady wife. It's obvious she only has eyes for ye, and it's genuine. She's happier now, and we can tell it's because ye're married. So, nay, I dinna think most people would agree with any of the rumors ma father spread."

Marcus looked at Blaine before taking a deep inhale and looking at Thor as he continued. "I ken what happened to Lady Greer. I found out just before ma father died. He admitted he kenned, and he'd been a part of it. I hoped to never have to tell either of ye that I kenned. It makes me far guiltier that I didna step in during that conversation and stop the men. But I feared making a fuss would only make their tongues wag more. I willna ask what yer wife has told ye because that isnae ma business, but from what ma father told me, I dinna ken a stronger person than Lady Greer."

Thor stood stunned. His heart raced as Marcus spoke, and it didn't slow despite the man's compliment. He looked at Blaine and shot him such a menacing stare that Blaine almost took a step back. "If aught of this leaves this chamber, I will kill ye both. I dinna care if ye are ma sister's husband. I will protect ma wife before aught else. What exactly did yer father tell ye?"

"Thor—"

"What the fuck did he tell ye?" Thor lunged forward, but he kept his hands to his side. It was enough to make Marcus put up his hands to defend himself.

"Thor, they're all dead now. It will only hurt ye if ye dinna already ken this."

"Tell me."

Marcus scrubbed his hands over his face. "They would restrain her on the bed for days at a time. Edgar enjoyed lashing her before he…The other men watched each other sometimes, but mostly, they were alone with yer wife. They could stay as long as they wanted, so sometimes it was two and three days at a time before someone else… If she wouldnae cooperate, Edgar wouldnae allow her any food or drink. She—she—she tried to end her life several times. Despite how badly Edgar beat her or how he encouraged the men to be harsher with her, she still tried."

Thor's heart would surely beat out of his chest. Rage heated him so much that his ears felt aflame. He ripped open the solar door and sprinted toward the Great

Hall. "Greer! ... *Greer!* Where the bluidy hell is ma wife? ... *Greer!*"

"Thormud, I'm right here." Greer stepped out of the kitchen, shocked by the shade of fuchsia Thor's face was. He was far gentler when he pulled her into his embrace than she expected. His kiss was the gentlest he'd ever offered her. He rested his forehead against hers.

"What happened after we left?" She ran her hand up and down his arm, hoping to comfort her clearly distraught husband. It alarmed her when he didn't speak. She saw tears in his eyes, and he could only shake his head. She looked to her right and found Blaine and Marcus watching. She knew Rose now stood behind her, and other people stared. "What did ye say to him?"

Neither Blaine nor Marcus spoke. Thor pulled her back into his embrace, nearly smothering her. He whispered, "I need to be alone with ye."

She nodded and took his hand, then led him toward the stairs. They didn't speak until they entered their chamber. He once more clung to her, and all she could do was rub his back. "Thor?"

"Marcus's father was one of them, wasna he?"

"Aye. Did he tell ye that?"

"He found out just before his father died. I suspect it was part of what made him so angry that he didna realize how hard he pulled to get his father off his mount."

"What did he tell ye, Thor?"

"That ye were lashed. That ye were starved. That there were days at a time. Witnesses."

"He had nay right to say any of that. He shouldnae have ever kenned."

"But he did. Part of me is glad he told me because it's been eating at me to nae ken. But I never wanted to ask ye. I need to ken something, though."

"What?" Greer wasn't eager to answer questions

about things from her past that she hadn't already shared with Thor.

"He said ye tried to end yer life more than once."

Greer went rigid. She pulled away from Thor, defiance radiating from her. "I ken it's a mortal sin. I dinna care."

"*Leannan*, I wasna faulting ye for that. I didna when ye said ye wished ye werenae alive that day on the cliffs. I'm nae now. How—how—close—"

"I willna answer that. Nay matter what I answer, ye willna forgive yerself for this. I willna make it worse."

"Dear God. Ye almost succeeded, didna ye?" Anguish etched Thor's face and rang in his voice. "If I had only listened to ye. If I'd believed ye like I should have. None of this would have happened. I did this to ye as much as if I held the lash or ordered the men…allowed them…"

"Stop." Greer's forceful tone made Thor snap his mouth shut. "Listen to me when I say this, Thormud. Ye are the only reason I didna succeed. The tiniest speck within me held onto hope that one day we would be together. I couldnae let that wish go, and so I couldnae kill maself because then there would never have been a chance. Ye didna do any of this to me. Ye kept me alive."

Thor didn't wipe away the tears that dripped from his chin. He could only nod.

"I decided a few days ago that I wouldnae ask ye to keep proving yerself to me. That I wouldnae make every moment of every day aboot what happened to me. I dinna want ye to do that either. Ye dinna have to prove yerself. We are together because we want a future. We dinna need to live in the past. Ye ken the worst of it now."

"I love ye so much, wee one. I'll do aught for ye."

"I ken. And I love ye too. I'll do aught for ye, *mo*

ghaol. And that has to be we move past this, or it will consume us both."

"Can I hold ye?"

"Daft sweet mon. Ye never have to ask." Greer led Thor to the bed and kicked off her shoes. He toed off his boots and climbed onto the bed. He leaned against the headboard, and she shifted onto his lap. They sat in silene for several minutes as they held each other. "Do ye feel better? I dinna like that someone else told ye, but it made it easier. It's a relief ye finally ken."

"I do for finally learning it all. And having ye in ma arms makes life right again."

They remained in their chamber until the bells rang for the evening meal when their peaceful bubble burst.

CHAPTER 15

Greer and Thor's heads jerked up in unison as English warriors stormed into the Great Hall. Keith guards flanked and followed them. Blaine came to his feet immediately, putting his hand out to stay Rose. He walked to the front of the dais but didn't descend.

"Why are ye here? I certainly didna invite ye back?" Blaine's voice boomed throughout the cavernous gathering space.

"You knew we would return. You will surrender Lady Greer forthwith. I remand Thormud Sinclair into the king's custody."

"Ye're arresting Thormud?" Blaine questioned. He heard Rose murmur the same question.

"The Sinclair man has impeded the king's decree. We have the men to ensure neither Lady Greer nor Thormud cause trouble."

Father Bennett stood from his seat on the dais and stepped beside Blaine. "I fail to see how ye dinna understand that Lady Greer sought sanctuary with me. She is under ma protection as God's representative on Earth. Last I kenned, our Holy King reigns over yer king. Ye canna deny the sanctity of the Holy Church.

Beyond that, Lady Greer canna marry any mon since I've already wed the lady to Thormud. Ye may check the parish register if ye so choose."

No one moved since every Keith and Sinclair knew the priest just spoke one of the boldest lies he could. He'd not only lied before the English delegates and his people, he'd lied before God about a sacrament. But the Keiths trusted him and knew him to be a good man, and they sided with the Sinclairs, even if some were still wary of Greer because she was a Gunn. Eyes darted back and forth between the brazen priest and the invading English.

"Bring the register to me," Sir Richard demanded, flapping his fingers to his upturned palm. Father Bennett cast him a glare that made the Englishman cease and drop his arm. Father Bennett nodded and left the Great Hall with his hands tucked into the sleeves of his monk's tunic.

Greer's hand gripped Thor's beneath the tablecloth. She didn't know what to make of the exchange. She feared Father Bennett would take too long to create the entry or that other events had transpired, making it difficult to backdate the supposed wedding. Her stomach was in her throat when three English warriors accompanied Father Bennett. How would he enter anything now?

"Dinna fash, wee one. He wouldnae have said aught if he didna ken it would work. Have faith," Thor whispered, his lips barely moving.

"Ma faith is all I have right now, but I dinna trust these men."

"Neither do I. They will nae take ye from me, and we arenae leaving with them. We need to ride at a moment's notice. If that's the case, we head for Varrich. They will expect us to ride to Dunbeath. There are Mackays at the border with the Gunns, which we'll have to pass. They can accompany us. If we push the horses, we can be there in two-and-a-half days. If we canna make it there, then we go into the Ben Griam mountains. There are places we can hide that they willna ever find."

"But how will we even get out of the keep? Assuming we could slip out, we canna get horses out. We canna do this on foot."

"I ken. We have to find a way to get our mounts out before us."

"They must have men posted at both gates. Nay one is going to lead a horse out, let alone two."

Thor had no chance to say more since Father Bennett returned with his escorts. He held open the register and thrust it out for Sir Richard to examine. He tapped the page and cocked an eyebrow. Sir Richard seemed to scan the page, but Thor narrowed his eyes as he wondered if Sir Richard could actually read. It was as though the man stared at a blank page for all he seemed to understand what was before him. Had Father Bennett somehow realized that?

"As ye can see, I entered the marriage between Thormud Seamus Magnus Sinclair and Lady Greer Adelaide Gunn. Ye can also see I have registered three births and a death since that date. The ink is fully dried, and I didna have time to falsify aught. Ask yer men." Father Bennett turned toward them. "Did I write aught in this book while ye followed me?"

"My lord, the priest touched no quill, nor did he open the book until he entered the keep." The guard who stepped forward clearly wore a hauberk beneath his doublet. Sir Richard appeared more prepared for a battle than the last time he arrived. While none of the men who entered the Great Hall wore their full suit of armor, Thor didn't doubt there were now fully armored mounted knights nearby. This complicated matters even beyond Greer's observations.

"When were the banns posted? I would see record of that."

"The couple already handfasted, which by the laws of Scotland is a binding marriage for a year and a day, and they married by consent before the same witnesses present today. There was nay need to read the banns since they already married. I performed the ceremony because they wish to seal their marriage before God. The law already recognized them as wed."

"And when we were last here, both the men from Clan Gunn and I objected to any union between Lady Greer and this mongrel. The marriage does not stand without the posting of the banns and the opportunity for concerned parties to object. Two objections were already presented."

"The couple has been living as mon and wife by mutual consent. That is all that is required. Even the Church recognizes this as an irregular but acceptable marriage in Scotland. The banns are a tradition, but Rome hasnae made it an incontrovertible decree. They'd already handfasted when ye attempted to object. That doesnae negate the marriage."

Greer and Thor watched the priest argue with the English king's delegate. Blaine stood silently next to the man of the cloth, who'd returned to his place on the dais. Rose clutched Thor's sleeve beneath the table, grateful that she was already sitting beside her twin. Greer's fingers ached from how tightly she clung to Thor's hand. She feared she would be ill. The longer the exchange carried on, the more she feared casting up her accounts in front of everyone. When she could no longer deny her nausea, she pushed back her chair, her hand covering her mouth as she rushed to the dais stairs.

"Greer!" Thor rushed to help her, gathering her skirts in his hand as she descended the stairs. Sir Richard made the grave mistake of stepping in front of her, attempting to block her from reaching the main stairs to the bedchambers. Greer had no control of what happened next, but she felt a smug satisfaction when it did. She removed her hand and vomited across the front of the knight's doublet, spraying some up to his neck and much of it landing on his boots. Thor caught her as she feigned unconsciousness. "I warned ye the other day that ma wife is with child. Ye have made her distraught in her fragile condition. If aught happens to ma bairn, I shall name ye the cause."

Thor swept Greer into his arms, stepping around the mess she made and the stunned man whose nose curled. Thor didn't wait for anyone to agree or disagree, making his way directly to the stairs. He climbed them to the second floor with Greer motionless in his arms. When they reached the second-floor landing, her eyes popped open, and her hand covered her mouth.

"Do ye fear being ill again?"

"Nay. I can smell maself. It's wretched. It canna be pleasant for ye." Greer grimaced.

"I dinna give a damn. What I care aboot is getting ma poorly wife away from that mon before he does more to upset ye and before he can do aught to separate us. I willna have it."

"I feel much better now. I didna make maself ill, but neither did I try hard to move past him when he blocked ma way. He deserved it." Her unrepentant grin eased Thor's worry, and he couldn't help but join in.

"I agree. Let's get ye to our chamber where ye can rinse yer mouth and wipe yer face. Then we must ready the few things we can carry. Rose will sort out sending the rest to Dunbeath. I also dinna want the chamber to appear like we left for good."

"Where are we going to go? This keep doesnae have tunnels, and there arenae any caves that we can hide in that they couldnae search." She assumed it had no tunnels. She imagined if it had, Blaine and Rose would have told them after the first time both the English and the Gunns arrived. They understood how beneficial those would be if they existed and could provide Thor and Greer with a safe escape.

"We have the servants' stairs, and they end near the passageway out to the gardens. If we can make it to the gardens, then we stand a better chance of skirting the Sassenachs. We need a way out of the bailey. If we can find that, then we can flee by foot or by horse. We may nae have a choice for a while."

"Where will we find mounts?"

"I have the coin to buy at least one. If we canna buy any, then we borrow them."

"Borrow?" Greer's chin tucked as she looked up at Thor, an eyebrow raised.

"I'll send them back to their owner once we reach Varrich or Dunbeath. Uncle Tristan has plenty of horses he can lend us. He can send someone back with the ones we borrow along the way."

"That is a vera sound way to excuse theft. But I canna think of aught better, so I willna complain."

"Our choices are vera limited, so we will have to take whatever opportunities appear." They reached their chamber door, so Thor lowered Greer to her feet. They entered, and Thor locked and barred the door. Greer poured water into a mug and rinsed her mouth before chewing a few mint leaves. She soaked a linen square and wiped it across her face and along the back of her neck. She felt better for it, but she still didn't feel herself. She wished she could claim a bairn was the reason, but they'd only made love for the first time that day. While she understood she might already carry their child, she doubted she would experience any symptoms this quickly. She assumed it was her frazzled nerves and fear that caused it. She didn't want to imagine having the ague while making a mad dash.

"Gather what ye need and we can place it in a plaid. Only pick what can fit into a saddlebag once we get a horse."

"I dinna need aught but a plaid for the nights."

"I'll keep ye warm, lass." Thor winked. They both knew they still needed the extra layers. Even though it remained warm enough that Greer didn't need an arisaid while the sun was out, at night, she would freeze. She tossed a fresh chemise and two pairs of stockings onto the Sinclair plaid Thor unfolded. He added his own stockings and a leine. Once he refolded the yards of material, it was impossible to tell they'd hid anything within. "We need to make our way out before anyone comes to check on ye."

"We have to tell Rose and Blaine. They'll panic if they dinna find us."

"I ken. That's to our advantage. It'll be obvious to the Sassenachs that they didna help us if they are anxious to find us too. They ken which direction we'll head."

"And if we dinna find a way out when we get to the gardens?"

"Then we come back up here. The sooner we try, the easier it'll be to sneak back up here if we canna leave. We must do it before anyone can check on us." Thor gathered the folded plaid, but Greer thought better of it and took it. She quickly refolded it into an arisaid. She could hide the items within the billowing lengths of the shawl since there was far more material than she needed for her height and size.

"Nay one will ask why I'm wearing one, but they may ask why ye carry a spare plaid." Greer's explanation made sense to Thor, so he moved to the door. He put his ear to it, but only silence met him. He lifted the bar soundlessly and eased the lock open. He waited again, but no noise came from the passageway. The door opened without a creak, but Thor paused after every inch. He peered down the passageway toward the main stairs, but there was no one there. He looked in the opposite direction, and the passageway was still empty.

They crept to the back stairway and descended. Both prayed no servants crossed their path, and they only breathed easier once they stepped outside. The stars shone brilliantly that night, and they cursed them. An overcast night would have made their flight far easier. Thor's eyes swept the bailey, noticing the knights and foot soldiers milling about the enclosed area. Walking through the front or postern gates were impossibilities. Their options appeared so slim that he considered having them return to their chamber.

Greer pointed across the bailey. "Canna we hide in a storeroom? Some of them have dugouts as cellars, but ye ken women and children hide in them during raids. Rose is smart enough to guess that might be where we'd hide. She would never let them search any."

"We dinna have a way to cover the hatches, so if they insist upon searching the storage buildings, they'll see the rings on the ground. They'll use them to lift the door before anyone can stop them."

"We need to have faith that Blaine or Rose would be certain to stand on top, so the English wouldnae see them. Do we have any other choice?"

"Nay. We hide down there for the night, then we try to make our way out at dawn. There's a market tomorrow two villages over. It isnae in the right direction, but there are bound to be wagons and carts with sacks of grain, hay, and animals. Mayhap we can hide on one until we can get away."

"Arenae those two of yer men?"

"Aye." Thor released an owl's hoot. Both men drifted toward them, neither acknowledging what they heard. But they'd recognized Thor's call and came to investigate. "What's happening?"

Alasdair, a black-haired man a couple years older than Thor, opened the garden gate. He and David, his younger brother, entered as though they didn't hear Thor's question. The group of four moved in the far depths of the garden where no one could hear or see them. Alasdair glanced over his shoulder before answering.

"The priest and the Sassenach argued until Father Bennett threatened to have them all imprisoned and carried off to see his brother, the bishop, which made the bastard bluster and screech like a rooster. Blaine's guards still outnumber our unwanted visitors, so they settled quickly when the Keiths stepped forward, a dirk in both of each mon's hands. The bluidy turd insists Lady Rose and Blaine offer them chambers for the night. It's obvious they wish to poke around once everyone retires. They're daft to think they can shut even one eye if they remain inside the keep."

"What has Blaine said?"

David grinned. "He suggested they make their beds in the dungeon and refused to entertain the idea of them as guests. Sir Richard what's-his-face warned Blaine that he had to agree since the piece of shite represents the king. Everyone laughed. Even men who arenae warriors drew dirks at that threat. The English were still tossing worthless threats when we stepped out."

"Why'd ye come out here?" Greer asked. "Are ye

headed to the barracks? Is that where the other Sinclairs are?"

"Nay, ma lady," David answered. "We all ken Thor. We figured he'd be in the gardens or a storage building by now if he wasna with ye in a storeroom within the keep. We kenned he wouldnae remain with ye in yer chamber. Harris and Keenan slipped away to look inside while we came out here."

"If Lady Greer and I can hide in the cellar of one of the storage buildings, then we can try to escape in the morning." Thor looked in the front gate's direction. "We canna cross the bailey with so many knights standing aboot."

David looked in the same direction. "We can distract them and get them to face away while ye sprint across. Ye'll need someone to cover the hatches in case any of them get a hair up their arse to search. Henry is on watch tonight. He can come to let ye out just before dawn."

"Give us three minutes," Alasdair offered. The two warriors slipped out of the shadows and hurried toward the garden gate. Thor and Greer followed at a far slower pace. They remained in the dark and watched. They couldn't hear what the Sinclair men said, but it was clearly antagonistic to the English. The Sinclair warriors shifted, so the knights had to turn their backs to most of the bailey to keep their eyes on the Highlanders.

Thor grasped Greer's hand and bolted. She'd already gathered her skirts well above her ankles. While anyone could tell there were two people running, no one could tell it was Greer since Thor's bulky frame completely hid her in profile. Greer tugged his hand and steered him toward a building where she knew there was a dugout. He hurried to slide barrels out of the way, and she lifted the trapdoor. Thor jumped down, then raised his hands to help lower Greer. She hadn't realized how deep the dugout was until she waited for her feet to touch the dirt floor. It also made her appreciate Thor's unusual height. She'd grabbed the inside ring and pulled the door shut as Thor pulled her down. They held their breath when they heard people moving inside the building.

"Thor, we're covering ye now. Henry will fetch ye in the morning. Are ye all right there for the night?"

"Aye." Thor prayed Greer wouldn't freeze. They would have to huddle and make do. It was the best he could offer.

CHAPTER 16

Thor kneeled and felt around in the dark, barely having had a chance to see what surrounded them in the darkened space. He led Greer as they inched away from the trap door, his hand outstretched to prevent himself from slamming into any of the sacks of grain stored in the cool crawl space. There was enough room that Greer might have navigated the area while crouching, but it wasn't nearly deep enough for either of them to stand. Thor didn't wish to bang his head into anything, so he opted to inch forward on his hands and knees. When they reached the far wall, Thor pushed aside a bag of what he guessed was seed.

"Come here, *mo ghaol.*" Thor guided Greer to sit on his lap. Once she was situated, he pulled her arisaid's extra lengths of wool over her head and around her shoulders. He unpinned the extra plaid on his *breacan feile* and draped that around both of them.

"Ye shall suffocate me. Between the wool, the clothes I have stuffed against ma back, and yer body heat, it's like stepping into a bluidy fire." Greer nestled closer despite her complaints. Waves of exhaustion crashed over her, so she shut her eyes and tried to relax.

"How do ye feel?"

"Better than before, but I'm tired."

"I ken. Sleep. Ye need it. It's been a long day, and tomorrow likely willna be any better."

"Ye willna sleep will ye?"

"Nay."

Greer knew Thor wouldn't let his guard down long enough to sleep. He would be alert to any sounds or even a shift in the air. She appreciated her husband's dedication to her safety, but she felt badly that he would get no rest. It had been a long day for them both, and he would grow exhausted from lack of sleep. Until they reached Varrich or Dunbeath, she doubted Thor would do more than catch forty winks here and there.

"Wake me in a couple hours, and I'll keep watch while ye sleep."

Thor's hand glided up Greer's arm until it reached her cheek. He nudged her head toward his and silenced her with a kiss. Greer's sleepiness fled as their passion sparked blue like the hottest part of a flame. His hand moved from her face down to her breast, which he kneaded until Greer moaned in frustration. She arched her back, pressing herself closer to Thor. Each of them feared it might be their last night together, and that thought spurred them. His hand continued down over her ribs and hip until it skimmed her leg and found her kirtle's hem.

"Are ye too sore?"

"Nay. I ache for ye, *mo dhuine.*" Greer shifted and let her legs fall open. "I willna accept that aught will keep us apart again, but I ken we may nae have control of that. I havenae had enough time with ye. I dinna want to miss what might be ma last opportunity to make love to ma husband."

"I dinna want to think aboot being separated from ye again. I willna accept that either, but I fear letting ye go. I want to join with ye again before anyone interferes. We've claimed that we handfasted, but we've never exchanged those vows. I would do it now. I want ye to hear that I swear never to forsake ye again, and that I will love ye until ma last breath."

"I want that too. But ye dinna have to say aught for me to ken that's the truth. I believe ye, and I ken it in ma bones."

"I need ye to hear it, Greer. I need to speak it aloud, so I'm certain ye ken. I dinna want to keep any of how I feel to maself anymore. If I hadnae feared what might have happened all those years ago, I would have told ma family. I should have had more faith in them, and I should have declared maself before the world. If I had, none of this would have happened. Ye would have made yer home with me at Dunbeath, and ye wouldnae have been anywhere near that field. One of these days, I will have the chance to do that, and we'll stand on the steps of Dunbeath's kirk. Until then, I make ma pledge to just ye."

"I want to say ma vows, too. I want ye to hear the sincerity in ma voice, and I want ye to never doubt ma love ever again."

"Greer, I'm—"

"Dinna apologize. I didna say that to make ye feeling guilty aboot any of our past. I'm explaining how certain I am of our feelings for each other."

Thor unwrapped the part of his great plaid that draped around Greer, and they clasped hands. They worked together to bind their wrists with the Sinclair plaid. The only thing Thor regretted was being unable to watch Greer. It was too dark to see even a hint of her shadow. Over the years, Thor had heard the stories about how each of the older generation's couples handfasted or married by consent before reaching a kirk. He knew the various handfast vows they'd spoken, and he'd always loved the ones Uncle Tavish and Aunt Ceit shared. He recited them now.

"I take ye to be ma wife and ma spouse, and I pledge to ye the faith of ma body, that I will be faithful to ye and loyal with ma body and ma goods, and that I will keep ye in sickness and in health and in whatever condition it will please the Lord to place ye, and that I shall nae exchange ye for better or worse until the end. To ye, I doth plight thee ma troth."

Greer was familiar with the ancient vows and responded, "As our hands are bound, so are our lives now bound with all our hopes for a new life together. With these vows, we tie all the desires, dreams, love, and happiness wished here in this place to our lives for as long as love shall last. I pledge to bind ma life with yers, to love and honor ye with ma body, mind, and soul, to remain ever faithful and forever by yer side nay matter what the future holds. I shall cleave to ye and nae exchange ye for better or worse until the end. To ye, I doth plight thee ma troth."

"I love ye, wee one."

"I love ye, *mo dhuine*."

The kiss they shared began with tenderness and a sense that the world was finally right again, but within minutes, their unsated need roared to life. They unbound their hands, and one of Thor's slipped beneath her skirts. His fingers pressed against the back of her calf, then up her thigh until he walked them across the front of her leg to the juncture with her hip. His fingertips found the dew between her legs, coating them before he pressed inside her sheath. He loved the feel of Greer's breath hitching as she practically squirmed.

"Wheest. I'll make it better."

"Only ye can. Ye make everything better, Thor. Can we—" Greer wished she could see his face to judge how he'd receive her request. "Can we just get on with it?"

"Are ye in a hurry for this to be over?"

"Nay. I'm impatient to begin. What ye're doing feels amazing." It did. His fingers thrust into her over and over, stroking a spot that only drove her mad with need. He kissed her again, but she mewled her frustration as she yanked at her skirts. She didn't recognize the woman she'd become. It was the opposite of who she feared she would remain. But making love to Thor brought back all the memories they'd once shared and redeemed an act she'd once reviled. It was more than just pleasure she sought. It was the closeness of their bodies joining. No alpha and no omega. They were just one.

Careful not to bang her head, Greer crouched as she readjusted her skirts, and Thor moved his plaid aside. With his hands on her hips, she eased onto his rod before they moved together. They cupped each other's jaw, making it easier to find their partner's mouth. Thor pulled at the belt that kept her arisaid in place before wrenching on the end of her kirtle's laces. Only a vague memory that this was the only gown Greer had, kept him from rending the fabric as he grasped it at her shoulders and tugged.

"Are we addlepated to make love while hidden down here? Is it right to be finding pleasure while in so much danger?" Greer wouldn't stop them, but she was curious.

"Mayhap. But I canna think of a better way to pass the time with ma bonnie wife. And I can keep ye warmer this way."

"Ye're more chivalrous than those Sassenach knights," Greer said with a hint of humor to lighten her own worry.

"Aught to make ma wife happy." Thor laughed as he once more encircled her waist with his hands, moving her on his rod, helping Greer to find the rhythm and movement that maddened her with need. She dove back in for another kiss but missed his mouth. They chuckled until they could only focus on how their tongues dueled and the pleasure from caressing the silky skin of their inner cheeks. Greer remembered as clearly as if it were yesterday how insatiable Thor became when she sucked on his tongue lightly.

"Lass, I willna last long if ye continue with that."

"Whether we go slowly, and this lasts a long time, or we go quickly and do it many times, I want to spend the night joined with ye."

"Ye dinna feel rushed?" Thor worried he shouldn't have interrupted the moment by forcing them both to recall the past, but he feared some of Greer's eagerness stemmed from her wish to please him, not herself.

"I feel like ye arenae moving fast enough. Thor, this isnae the same as those times. They did that to control me. We're doing this because we're deeply committed to each other, and I want to show ye how I feel. This is us as we once were. I can separate them and recognize that we're making love."

She appreciated his patience, and she was relieved they could talk so openly. But she didn't want to keep having these conversations now that she'd compartmentalized as much as she could. But she realized Thor hadn't done the same. He had his own shame, humiliation, and guilt to move past. As much as she needed to feel his love to grow stronger, she understood he needed the same from her. She couldn't underestimate the depth of his pain simply because he was a hardened warrior. She'd known since they first met that he was sensitive and felt his emotions deeply. It was part of why she fell in love with him with such ease.

Except for their heavy breathing, they remained quiet as they moved together. Neither wanted to talk any more, and their focus was on giving and receiving pleasure. She clutched the front of his leine and burrowed her head against the crook of his neck as her core spasmed, pushing her into bliss that cleansed her soul. She redoubled her efforts, and when Thor thrust into her and held her pelvis pinned to him their bodies rewarded them. She knew he pulsed within her, and the friction on her pearl brought her to release a second time. She collapsed onto him as he leaned back against the wall, both spent.

Once more, Thor wrapped them in the extra material once his body no longer cooperated with his wish to remain joined with Greer. Fatigue threatened to make him shut his eyes. But with every rise and fall of Greer's shoulders as she slumbered against him, he recalled why they were in the dank space. He wouldn't relax his guard since he was Greer's only protection. His arms rested loosely around her, but as his mind wandered to their future, he found himself squeezing her tightly against his chest. It surprised him she didn't wake. He worried not only about the immediate danger that loomed, but he worried how his clan would react if they ever learned the truth. He wanted to believe they would never shun Greer, and that it would never interfere with her position when she one day became Lady Sinclair, but he couldn't be certain. The unknown created a knot in his belly that ached.

Thor knew his great-uncle Daniel once loved a Gunn woman. They'd met similarly to how he and Greer had. They'd rendezvoused on their lands' borders for many months. Eventually, they'd began having picnics together, taking turns crossing the border to sit beside each other. When the Gunn patrols started to report her actions to her older brother, Tomas, they'd moved their clandestine liaisons to the beach.

When Tomas learned Ceana was with child, he beat her and locked her in her chamber. Then he led a raid and killed his grandfather's younger brother. A warrior and his wife smuggled Ceana out of Gunn Castle and to Dunbeath. She'd arrived in much the same condition as Greer had. Thor's great-grandfather and great-grandmother offered her a home at Dunbeath, but Ceana couldn't reconcile living in the keep and sleeping in the bed she and Daniel once planned to share. She opted to retire to Inchcailleoch Priory, or the Island of Old Women, where her son was stillborn, but she found her calling as a nun. She eventually became the abbess there.

Thor prayed his clan accepted Greer as easily as they'd accepted Ceana. But he recognized the situations were different. Possibly disastrous scenarios played out in his mind. His instinct told him to forego his family and his clan and put Greer above everyone and everything. But he knew she wouldn't agree to him giving up the life his family trained him to inherit. She had already believed he was prepared to make too great a sacrifice when they weren't sure Greer would ever be ready to couple. He also knew that, as willing as he was, duty would always come before his own wants. It meant the only option he could accept was ensuring Greer made a place for herself among the Sinclairs.

"Thor, close yer eyes for a while. I'm awake. I'll listen for aught. I ken ye're a light sleeper. If anyone comes within a league of this building, ye'll be alert. But ye need the rest. Ye may be used to riding on patrol or going into battle and nae sleeping for days, but why put yerself in that position if ye dinna have to? Rest, *mo ghaol.*"

"I ken the soundness of what ye suggest, but I canna settle enough to even doze. I canna imagine aught happening to ye because I fell asleep during ma watch."

"And yer watches always have shifts. Please, Thor. If ye canna fall asleep, then vera well. But at least try."

"All right." They shifted so Thor could rest his head against the front of Greer's shoulder while her head rested on top of his. She stroked his hair, and it wasn't long before she felt his breathing slow. She knew he wasn't asleep, but he was more at ease. They passed the next six hours in two-hour intervals. Greer slept when Thor kept watch, and he rested while she listened for any disturbance. When someone moved the barrels above the trapdoor, they shrank into the darkest corner. Barely any light shone in, so they knew it was still very early.

"Thor?" A deep voice murmured.

"Aye, Henry."

"Ye can come out. There's nearly nay one in the bailey. The English forced us out of the barracks, but we didna mind. It meant we found places around the keep to rest. Naught happened that we didna ken aboot. A farmer arrived with a wagon loaded with hay. He's only delivering half here. He's taking the rest to the market. If ye hurry, ye can climb on and hide. If ye wait any longer, then more people shall stir. We risk those pieces of hog shite waking."

Thor and Greer crawled back to the hatch. She reached toward Henry's hands while Thor hoisted her upward. He did so with more force than Greer or Henry expected, making her collide with Henry. She screamed and recoiled, but Henry caught her before she fell backward in the cellar. She scrambled away from him as Thor rushed to pull himself out. Greer cowered in a corner, and Henry appeared stunned.

"It's all right," Thor whispered to Henry. "Wait for us outside."

The guard didn't need telling twice, and Thor inched across the room to Greer, who appeared petrified. He kept his hands where she could see them and raised his arms slowly. She launched herself at him, making him stumble back a step as he caught her. She trembled as she kept trying to get closer to him, but short of sharing his skin, there was no way for her to lessen a gap that didn't exist.

"I'm sorry. I panicked because I wasna prepared for him to pull me closer. Ye lifted me, and he wasna ready to step back. When I collided with him, I—"

"Ye dinna have to explain. I understand. Can ye reason that he didna mean ye any harm?"

"Aye. I ken that, but it was the feel of ma body hitting another mon's. It wasna the same as touching ye. I didna mean to scream. Do ye think anyone heard me?"

"Nay one's come rushing in here, and I dinna hear Henry turning anyone away. I think it was only loud in here."

"I hope so. I havenae embraced any mon but ye since arriving here. Yer da gave me one, and I didna feel scared with him. But I dinna ken how I'll react to any other mon. I think I was only all right with yer da because he reminds me so much of ye, and I kenned he would never hurt me."

"Nay one in ma family will, but they'll understand if ye dinna wish for embraces from the men. They'll think ye modest as ma wife. They willna take offense."

"I hope so. I havenae asked ye this, but I need to ken before we leave here. Will ye tell yer parents and grandfather the truth aboot what happened to me?"

"I will give them only what they need to ken unless ye give me permission to tell them more."

"I'm nae sure what I can manage."

"Then we willna rush that. But we must rush leaving before it's too late." Thor adjusted his *breacan feile*, and Greer pulled her arisaid over her head and shoulders. Thor knocked on the door once. A return knock echoed in the storage building. He opened the door and found Henry standing to his left. The guard canted his head to the right.

"Over there. He has a tarp over the bundles because he swears it's going to rain. It's the Highlands. Of course, it's going to rain. But it'll keep ye dry and hidden. Keenan and Dominic already got two horses through the front gate the moment the Keiths raised it. They're on the other side of the village. But I must warn ye. There are more knights camped just outside the barmekin. Dinna uncover yerselves until ye reach the far side of all the crofts."

"We're riding to Varrich. The English will likely force ye to stay here. Or at least, they'll try. If ye can get yer horses out, ride to Dunbeath. If ye canna, ask Blaine for the birlinn and sail home."

"But—"

"Nay. If ye join us, then we attract too much attention. If they chase us, the moment they see a party of riders, they'll ken it's us. Ma hope is we can keep our distance, and Lady Greer doesnae have to wear an arisaid."

"I took a pair of those bluidy hose the English prance around in. I figured ye might need to avoid wearing yer plaid."

"Aye. I'll stick out for nae wearing one, but at least nay one will ken who we are by our plaids."

Greer reached up and tugged a lock of hair. "It's a fine thing there are so many red-headed people in Scotland."

Thor and Henry exchanged a few more words before the warrior guarded them while they crept to the wagon.

"Does he ken he'll have passengers?"

"Aye. We slipped him some coin."

"Thank ye." Thor's gaze swept the bailey. He noticed a few Keiths watching them, and a couple nodded their

HIGHLAND STRENGTH

encouragement. He felt uneasy that anyone saw them, but he had to have faith none would betray them. Their people respected and liked Blaine and Rose, so he didn't think anyone would hurt them by turning Thor and Greer over to the English or the Gunns.

Greer climbed on first, pushing aside a few bundles to make space. When Thor sat beside her, she covered them with the scratchy plants. Once they laid flat, covered almost entirely in hay, Henry pulled the tarp over them. It felt like an eternity, but it was likely just more than an hour before the wagon tilted and jostled them as the driver climbed onto the seat. The wagon lurched forward, and Greer's hand shot out to find Thor's arm lest she slide. Thor braced her before she could disturb the tarp. He braced himself for whatever awaited them on the other side of the portcullis.

CHAPTER 17

Greer held her breath when she was certain they passed beneath the raised gate. She pictured the spikes that could skewer them falling toward the ground and trapping them. She waited for someone to raise the alarm and for hands to rip her from the wagon and Thor. But everything remained quiet until she felt the wagon hit the first rut on the path to the village. She turned her head to look at Thor, who already watched her. She gave him a jerky nod before looking up at the canvas tarp. She prayed more fervently than she ever had when sneaking out of Gunn Castle or when she made her perilous flight to Dunbeath after Edgar attacked her.

Before lying down, Thor had removed his sword from his back, so it rested beneath his right hand. He'd taken it out of the sheath, so it was ready for him to swing the moment he perceived a threat to Greer. He tried to keep his breathing calm, using all the tactics he utilized before riding into battle. But his heart raced, and his chest rose and fell far faster than it should. He hadn't been this anxious since that first time he'd ridden out with Jamie. He didn't want Greer to suspect

HIGHLAND STRENGTH

his unease, but she slid her hand into his and curled her fingers between his.

They knew they passed the village as the sounds of people and animals met their ears. They waited for them to quieten, indicating they would draw closer to their waiting horses, but the wagon slowed well before then.

"You there. You've just come from the castle. What is in your wagon?" An English voice demanded.

"Hay for the market."

"There's no market today." The Englishman's tone rang with condescension.

"Nae in this village, but there's one two over from here. I must go, or there'll be nay one to buy from me."

"We will inspect your wagon."

"By what authority?"

"The king's."

"I didna realize ye kenned King David all the way in France." The driver chuckled, and Thor and Greer heard the reins slap the horse's back. The wagon lurched forward.

"I said stop. I will run you through."

Thor prepared to leap up, his hand raised to grasp the canvas and pull it out of his way. The wagon picked up speed as the driver encouraged the steed to run. It was hardly a gallop, but it moved the wagon faster. More voices called out to them, but the driver ignored them. Thor felt certain the English would give chase, so he didn't know how they would move from the wagon to horseback with people pursuing them.

"Whoa, mon. Stop yer wagon."

Thor breathed easier, recognizing the voice. It was Keenan. He'd never been happier to hear it. The wagon slowed, and Thor wasted no time removing the tarp. He rose to his feet in one lithe move, thrusting his hand out to Greer to help her to her feet. As he re-sheathed his sword and put it on his back again, Keenan reached for Greer. She hesitated for only a moment before accepting the warrior's help. He lifted her from the wagon and pivoted to help her onto her mount. Thor stepped onto the raised side before swinging onto Gaisgeach's back.

"There's food for ye in the saddlebags. Lady Rose guessed ye would need it and smuggled it to us. Blaine is arranging for birlinns to take us home if ye didna want us to ride with ye. At least the two of us could come with ye."

Thor glanced at Greer, then at his friend. He'd planned for them to ride alone, hoping they could remain inconspicuous. But with only him to protect Greer, she remained vulnerable. Two more men could guard her other side and her back. He nodded his head. Dominic handed the reins to Keenan's horse to him before mounting his own. Thor wheeled his horse to head west, and the others followed him.

"Thank ye." Thor looked at the driver, who appeared ready to drive away without a word. The man gave him a single nod before encouraging his horse to continue along the path. Mounted knights without armor clattered toward them, and their warhorses had the endurance to carry the men when they wore their heavy battle armor. Without all the extra weight, the horses could ride for far longer. Thor relied on Sinclair horseflesh being superior to anything the English had. It was the only chance they had. Greer rode a gelding Thor recognized. It was Rose's horse. He would thank his sister later, but he prayed Greer could remain astride. He didn't know what type of mount she'd been riding on the last few years. The one he knew from eight years earlier couldn't have kept up.

Thor spurred Gaisgeach forward, and the other horses followed its lead. Keenan fell behind to follow Greer, while Dominic rode to her right. She glanced at Thor, wondering what would happen if he had to draw his sword and she was stuck beside his sword arm. She feared he was more likely to decapitate her than defend her.

"Dinna fash, I fight with ma left hand as well as ma right. Da taught me, and Uncle Tavish loves naught more than to send ma cousins and me to run laps around the lists if we forget how. I havenae dropped it in years." Thor saw her skeptical look as her eyes darted from his right hand to his back. She nodded and turned her attention forward.

"Thor, we need to push. They're gaining on us." Keenan called out as he kept checking over his shoulder.

"We ken this land. They dinna. We ride for Dirlot Castle near Loch More and the River Thurso. I hope we dinna need to seek shelter from Reginald Cheyne, but I believe he would grant it if we asked. He's on good terms with the Mackays and Sutherlands right now since they've kept the Gunns from harrying him. Ma wife is Lady Adelaide Sinclair nae Lady Greer Gunn." He reasoned they should use her middle name rather something so recognizable as her real one.

"Dirlot?" Greer's eyes widened. "That's barely a keep, and it sits in the middle of the river. Albert said there's a gorge, and the water below is called the Devil's Pool. That doesnae sound inviting. The rock it sits upon is massive. How do we even get to it, let alone climb it?"

Dirlot Castle sat upon a rock that soared forty or fifty feet out of the water. While it had three floors, it was tiny and could hardly be considered a castle despite its name. It was more like a tall stone croft. Greer wasn't certain Sir Reginald was in residence since he had other strongholds that he frequented more. She'd passed it one year on the way to a Highland Gathering at the Mackays. She'd thought it more a folly than a home. But perhaps Thor knew somewhere along the river or loch, even in the gorge, where they could hide.

"Ye ken I fostered with Uncle Tristan. I ken the area since he would bring Wee Liam, Alec, Hamish, and me on patrol near there. It was a time when the Mackays and Cheynes didna get along, so he wished for his lads to ken the land if ever there were a fight."

"I trust ye." Greer had never meant those words more.

The group fell silent as they charged over hill and dale. The only one to talk was Keenan as he called out distances between them and their pursuers. Thor pulled ahead just enough for the others to see where he led. After they'd ridden for nearly twenty minutes, they came to a crag they all considered a blessing. Their Highland horses could navigate the uneven and precarious terrain far better than the English horses that likely weren't raised in such countryside. None of the voices that had called to them as they left the village sounded like they were from northern England. It was a relief to Thor, since he supposed only mounts familiar with the moorlands of Northumbria would pose a threat to them.

They slowed their horses to a trot, then a walk, as shale skidded from beneath the hooves. But with direction from the riders, the horses picked their own path as they climbed along the rocky hillside.

"They'll be at the base in a couple minutes. I canna tell if they have bows," Keenan updated.

"We must assume they do. We keep Lady Greer in the middle as best we can. We never leave her back unprotected." Thor knew his two warriors understood that implicitly, but he felt better for offering the reminder. They reached a point where it was too narrow for even two horses to ride abreast. Thor took the lead with Greer sandwiched between him and Dominic. Keenan continued to bring up the rear.

"Their horses are balking at the uneven ground. They're climbing now too, but they're having a hard time controlling some of them." Just as Keenan announced the English's predicament, a horse whinnied loudly in anger. Frustrated voice carried on the wind as the knights attempted to coerce then force their steeds to continue along the crags. It tempted Greer to look back, but she feared twisting in her saddle would spook her mount or that she wouldn't keep her seat. She told herself to put as much faith in Keenan as Thor clearly did.

"Over there. Past the outcropping. It drops off a foot past it. But if ye ken that, ye can turn to the left just after the rocks. From a distance ye canna tell that the path shifts. They'll still see us moving."

"Can we slow down when we get to it?" Greer knew her horse would follow Thor's especially since the horse was from the Sinclairs' stables too. But she didn't feel confident in her skills to maneuver the beast in such a foreign environment.

"Aye. We must. The moment yer horse's chest gets past the last boulder, ye must steer him to the left. Guide him before his tail passes the end." Thor spoke clearly, but low. He didn't want his voice to carry to their enemy, and he hoped it would calm Greer's nerves. He understood why she sounded fearful. They were in one of the most dangerous situations in which Thor had ever found himself. He wouldn't have willingly chosen to lead Greer on this path as a day's excursion. If they weren't fleeing, he would have kept them miles away.

Thor was certain Gaisgeach remembered where they were because he barely had to use his thighs at all to guide the horse. The steed turned before Thor even had a chance to move the rein. He hazarded a glance over his shoulder and noticed Greer's teeth dug into her lower lip so deeply he expected to find dents when they stopped. But she and her mount did well.

They followed the path as it curved before straightening. The ground proved smoother along this strip, so they nudged their horses into a faster walk. They reached flat terrain and spurred their horses into a trot. They heard orders for the men to increase their pace, then they heard a horse scream as it fell. More horses whinnied and neighed as the English halted, their horses rearing and rebelling.

"They're dismounting and trying to lead their mounts, but the wee beasties arenae having it. I suppose our Highlands arenae as gentle as all their English flower gardens," Keenan scoffed.

"They'll get some of them to settle, then they'll be after us again." Thor might agree with Keenan's assessment, but he kept their pace sedate until he was certain they were out of such imminent danger. "This only buys us a few more minutes. We need to get to the bogland where they're likely to get stuck. We ken what to look for. They likely dinna and will think they can cut across to catch us. If they're mired in the mud, at least a couple horses are likely to go lame. I'll take aught that slows them."

He scanned the terrain they approached, knowing that it had likely changed since the last time he'd ridden anywhere near the area. He spied the difference in plants first. The grass grew taller where he knew small ponds lay. But it was the scent from the peat that confirmed it. The spongy texture could fool someone into believing it was sturdy enough to walk across, but a man's weight would be enough for him to sink knee-deep into the muddy water that rest beneath the plant. He counted on the knights assuming the peat was solid enough for their horses to tread across.

Thor gave Gaisgeach his head and allowed the horse to pick the best path, only correcting him a handful of times. Greer's horse followed Gaisgeach and stepped where the lead horse had. They continued the same way as they rode through the muck that sat alongside the bogs. They were nearly across the marshland when a thunderclap filled the air. The storm lay to the south, which was the direction Thor intended to turn them. He looked north instead and found the skies clearer.

"We dinna head to Dirlot Castle. We ride for Broubster Forest. It's away from the storm and likely closer. We can lose them amongst the trees and find shelter for the night." Thor estimated they'd already ridden for two hours, and their horses would need rest and water soon. They couldn't afford for their own animals to go lame. They changed their course and hurried north.

Dominic still rode to Greer's right as they changed their course. He was the first to spot the body of water. "Isnae that Loch Calder?"

"Aye. We can let the horses rest there." Thor wanted Greer to have an opportunity to stretch. She wasn't used to the long hours in the saddle like the men, so he worried that not only would she be stiff, but that the inside of her legs would chafe. When they arrived at the loch, Thor handed off the reins to his horse and Greer's before helping her from the saddle. She gripped his biceps as she steadied herself. She looked around and spied a bush where she could have a moment of privacy.

"I'm just going to the other side of yon bush." She pointed, and Thor drew his sword. Her brow furrowed.

"I dinna need ye getting bitten by a snake again. Let me be sure it's safe, then ye can do what ye need." Thor took her hand as they walked away from the other men. When they reached the spot, he used his sword to shake the branches. When nothing hissed or scurried away, he felt confident about giving Greer her space. "Wee one, how do ye fare? Are yer legs chafed?"

"A little but naught that will keep me from riding."

"We all keep a salve in our saddlebags for just that. If yer skin is irritated, tell me, and I will give ye some. Dinna wait until it's raw."

"I'll let ye ken."

Thor bent down and dropped a kiss on her cheek. "I'm happy to examine ye."

"Off with ye. I dinna need a nursemaid for that or to mind me while I relieve maself. Turn away." Greer swatted at him with a chuckle. Thor playfully harrumphed before taking ten steps away and kept his back to her. She wasted no time, appreciating the moment's reprieve. When she was through, she did her best to look at the inside of her thighs. She believed she could manage a few more hours before she needed the salve, but she didn't want to overestimate her endurance or her skin. "Thor, I think it might be best if I use some of that salve. Naught's wrong, but I'd like to keep it that way."

"Are ye decent?"

"Aye."

"Dom, bring me the salve from ma saddlebag, please." Thor met his guardsman halfway before taking the jar to Greer. "Hold up yer skirts. It's hard enough to see with a plaid. Ye'll have the devil of a time trying to hold up yer skirts and seeing around them."

Greer laughed, then covered her mouth. She pictured Thor grappling with his *breacan feile*, trying to hold it out of the way without getting ointment all over it while getting the medicinal in the right place. "Thor, I'm a woman. Believe me when I tell ye that I can manage doing what I need in that area, even with ma gown on."

Thor's cheeks burned almost the same shade as his hair. Now Greer really laughed. "I ken I have a wife who I will share a chamber with, but I must get used to that. I barged in on Rose once when we were two-and-ten. I nearly passed out. I have never entered either of ma sister's or any of ma female cousins' chambers without knocking and waiting to be asked in ever since. It's nae natural for a woman to survive that every moon. If a mon did that, he'd be dead on a battlefield."

"Aye. And that's why we survive to have more generations. Men couldnae endure what we do, and they certainly wouldnae survive all the blood during childbirth."

"There's blood?" Thor thought he might swoon as he considered Greer one day delivering their child in a pool of blood.

"Of course."

"Greer, I havenae seen a bairn being born. There isnae that much blood when a foal, lamb, or calf is born. If there is, it's a sign something is wrong. I didna ken." Thor stared at Greer's belly.

"Are ye regretting that ye might have gotten me with child? Do ye fear me giving birth? Ye dinna have to watch."

"There isnae a chance in hell I'm being anywhere but beside ye if that's the case. I dinna want ye out of ma sight. I would see for maself that ye're well."

"Ye'll be giving the midwife instructions." Greer rolled her eyes as she took the jar from her now pasty and clammy husband. He watched as she easily moved her skirts aside and applied the ointment. She handed back the container in half the time it would have taken him. She went up on her toes and brushed her lips across his. "Yer mama had two bairns at the same time, and then Shona. Yer grandmama on yer da's side had five children. Giving birth and having yer courses is completely natural for women."

"They arenae ma wife."

Greer's shoulders lowered before she wrapped her arms around Thor's waist. "For such a vera large and intimidating mon, ye are the sweetest one alive. I love ye."

"I love ye too. I canna stomach the idea of aught hurting ye."

"Then ye definitely canna be in the room when I'm laboring."

"Nay. I ken there's some pain involved, but—"

"Some? Sweet, but daft. Some." Greer snorted as she released him. She muttered "some" as she walked back to their horses, shaking her head as she went. She gathered her reins and slid her foot in the stirrup, but she should have expected the hands that wrapped around her waist and lifted her like a feather. She arranged her skirts, making sure her chemise offered a modicum of protection from the leather saddle.

Dominic sat forward to see Thor around Greer after they set off. "Do ye think they ken aught aboot the land up here? If they saw us turn north but couldnae catch up, would they ken to water their horses at the loch or that we're headed to the forest?"

"I dinna think so. If they find the forest, it's purely because it's so large. But I dinna think they'd ken aboot the loch. We must be vigilant from now until we reach the forest and make sure we cover our tracks. I dinna ken how good their scouts are." Thor couldn't afford to send Dominic ahead of them if he wanted Greer to be protected fully. While Dominic might warn them of an approaching enemy, he could only do that if their foe traveled along the same route as them. If they came from another direction, Greer would be vulnerable. He'd rather have both warriors with him. They kept their horses away from anywhere that would leave obvious hoofprints or would trample the grass too much.

When they were within an hour of the forest, Thor called them to a halt. Greer watched as he climbed a pine tree with his dirk handle between his teeth. Keenan did the same in another tree. Before Greer understood what was happening, four large branches fell, two from each tree. The men dropped to the ground and dragged the severed pieces with them.

"The path is still dry, and it doesnae look like we're getting rain soon. We need to wipe away our tracks. This is heavy, but I need ye to hold on to it while we ride." Thor explained as he handed one limb to Greer. "Is it too heavy? If it is, I'll tie it to yer saddle."

"That might be better. I dinna ken what to do with it."

"Yer horse will drag it behind him, and it will work like a broom to sweep away his hoofprints."

"These are heavy, Thor. It would be better if we all tied them to our saddle. That way none of us drop them." Dominic's suggestion made sense, and he'd considered making it. But he hadn't wanted to insult either man by implying they weren't strong enough.

"It'll make it easier to control our horses if we arenae half hanging off to drag this behind us." Thor pulled rope from his saddle and used it to attach the branch to Greer's horse. He cut the extra with his dirk, then did the same thing with his horse while his men mimicked him with their own mounts. She turned to watch the makeshift brooms sweep over their horses' hoofprints, making them disappear. She wondered if all warriors knew to do this or if it was one reason the Sinclairs remained superior to everyone not related to them. They would know how well camouflaging their tracks had worked if no one stumbled upon them once they were in the woods. She prayed they would have a quiet night.

CHAPTER 18

*G*reer watched as the men moved around the camp on silent feet. Dominic tended to the horses while Keenan built a fire. Thor slipped away and brought back a brace of rabbits in less than an hour. They cooked and ate before the sun set, then they extinguished the flames, so no smoke could rise into the night air. They didn't need to offer their pursuers a beacon by which to find them. They'd ridden several miles into the forest, hoping it would keep them well hidden.

Greer knew she couldn't offer to stand watch. Even if she were alert to an encroaching threat, she could do little but wake the others. She couldn't defend them. She'd tried to do her part by preparing and cooking the rabbits, but she still felt guilty that she couldn't contribute equally.

"I need ye to sleep more than I need aught else." Thor drew her close when he returned from his two hours of watch. Greer dozed while he was gone, but she hadn't relaxed enough to fall asleep. Without Thor near her, she didn't trust her surroundings well enough to be as ease. "If ye really feel ye must do more, ye can make us bannocks in the morning."

Greer's mouth twisted from side to side before she scrunched her nose. "I suppose."

"We both need what sleep we can get. Come closer, so ye can keep me warm."

"Me keep ye warm? Ye're a bluidy roasting pit to sleep next to." She adjusted the extra plaids they had. Each man always had one in his saddlebags, and they had the extra one from their chamber. They were soon curled together beneath their layers. She couldn't stifle her yawn once she was comfortable. Her eyes drifted closed before she knew what was happening. She didn't stir until Thor shook her shoulder. As she came awake, she realized he wasn't gently nudging her to come round in the morning. His movements told her it was urgent.

"Dinna say aught," Thor whispered beside her ear. "We heard wolves circling. I need ye to stay right here. Dom's going to light the fire while Keenan and I get the horses. If aught happens, go with Dom."

Greer's eyes swept around their campsite, but she froze when she heard the howl. She nodded before Thor slipped into the darkness. She knew he was no more than ten yards from her, but she couldn't see him. She spun around when the fire sparked. She grabbed pieces of wood and helped Dominic feed it. They didn't make it too large, but it should have been enough to deter the wolves. At least, she prayed it was large enough to frighten the feral animals more than the horses tempted them.

She clung to the plaid she'd wrapped around her, relief coursing through her when Thor and Keenan stepped into the firelight. Her head whipped around to the right when she caught movement in her peripheral vision. She knew the wolves circled their camp. Each man had his sword drawn, and she wielded her own dirk that she'd pulled from her boot.

"They may remain all night," Thor explained in a hushed voice. "If I put ye on yer horse and tell ye to ride, ye do it. Ye dinna wait for any of us, and ye dinna look back or slow down. Do ye understand me, Greer? I dinna jest. Dinna do aught ye think is noble. If I tell ye to go, then go."

"I understand." *I dinna like it. But I understand.* Greer knew she would only be in the way if she remained. The only reason Thor would send her off was if he believed she had a greater chance to survive that way. If she didn't listen to him, he was more likely to die trying to protect her. She accepted the makeshift torch Dominic handed her. The men held theirs and swept them in front of them as they each faced a different direction.

Eyes glowed in the dark, and when Greer held hers out, she watched one beast snarl. They appeared to fear the people and horses not at all. When the one Greer assumed was the leader of the pack stepped toward them, then pushed his front paws forward while shifting his weight back, she feared it would pounce. The animal was closest to her, and Thor must have feared the same thing. He pushed Greer aside before pulling a stick from the fire and hurling it at the animal. It landed across the wolf's muzzle, making it whimper. It snarled but backed up. Another wolf tried to approach closest to Keenan. He did the same thing as Thor, striking the animal between the ears. This one howled with pain, and no more stepped forward. But they continued to pace circles around the camp. The horses nickered and shifted restlessly, stomping their hooves and their eyes rolling.

Eventually, Thor decided it was safe enough for Greer to sit. The men remained on their feet until the early rays of sun drove the wolves back to their den. As soon as Thor stepped away from the fire, Greer hurried to gather their extra plaid and shoved it into Thor's bags. She'd shoved their spare clothes into her saddlebag before they'd settled for the night. She helped by saddling her own mount. She gladly accepted his assistance to mount, and she was ready to leave when the men were.

"We travel east through the forest. We need to hide because we dinna ken how long the English tracked us," Thor explained to Greer. "It's likely two more days to Varrich if we have to travel slowly in the woods. If we can ride in the open, it's still a day-and-a-half."

"If I can keep using the salve as I need it, then I'll be all right. Dinna fash, Thor. I can keep up."

He knew sheer tenacity and resilience would drive her to keep up, even if she struggled physically. He knew no braver person than the woman riding beside him. He wished they were in their chamber at Dunbeath, tucked away for a sennight of newly wedded bliss. They'd spent much time together the week following their reconciliation, but once they reached their home, he intended to shut the world out morning, noon, and night, only opening the door for food.

"What are ye thinking?" Greer asked when she glanced at Thor, otherwise keeping her attention on not smashing into a tree. She felt heat rise in her cheeks when she looked back and found Thor's eyes devouring her. She canted her head toward Dominic and shot Thor a disapproving mien. He grinned and licked his lips. She glanced back at Keenan, who she knew pretended to see nothing. When Dominic choked on his chuckle, Greer threw up her hand and huffed.

"Ye are nay better than lads."

"We ken," three deep voices responded.

"It's a bluidy good thing I love ye, Thormud."

"Ye ken ye like ma cheeky side."

"Aye. All four."

Thor blinked at her before he grinned. He reached out and plucked her from her horse, settling her sideways on his mount. "Ye ride with me, Wife." He kissed behind her ear before she sank against him.

"I ken ye did that as much to give me a break from riding astride as aught else, but I willna complain, Husband."

"Good. I wouldnae have listened anyway."

"I ken." Greer pressed a quick kiss to his jaw before settling back against him. She found herself more tired than she could ignore. She closed her eyes and let herself drift off.

It was midafternoon before Thor and his two warriors agreed it was likely safe enough to test leaving the forest. It would soon end, so they would have little choice, anyway. Keenan set off to scout, and he soon disappeared as he rode south to the edge of the trees. Thor, Greer, and Dominic remained silent, the only sound coming from the horses' hooves striking the ground. There was enough room between the trees for the horses to trot, but they could go little faster than that without having to weave and risk their mounts stumbling.

Thor glanced at Dominic over Greer's head several times as the minutes ticked by. Dominic returned his gaze, his expression grim. Greer sensed something was amiss. She knew Thor and Dominic continued to exchange looks, and it seemed as though Keenan should have returned by then. Movement to Thor's left made them all look, praying it was Keenan. Instead, they found a buck darting to safety from a perceived threat.

"This isnae right," Thor whispered. "I canna send ye alone, Dom. But we also canna remain without kenning. We ride toward the forest's edge and wait. We dinna reveal ourselves until we ken what surrounds us. If naught appears, then ye can ride back to find him."

"And if we spy anyone? It isnae easy riding around here. There's little more than bogland. We ken how to navigate, but if we're pushed to gallop, it'll be hard to pick our paths."

The massive expanse of peatland stretched twice the size of Orkney and made up much of the areas of Caithness and Sutherland. It was land that belonged to the earldoms to which Thor's family claimed. The areas where he'd never ventured, he knew from maps he'd studied as a child. There were vast expanses of Caithness and Sutherland that were inhospitable to people and remained uninhabited by anything but wildlife. When Thor traveled between Dunbeath and Varrich, they usually followed a coastal route to avoid this landscape. He debated turning them toward the sea, but if their pursuers guessed they headed to Varrich, he feared they would assume that was the path he would take. He wanted to remain unpredictable to them.

"If we truly must, then we travel the way we normally would." Thor prayed it wouldn't come to that, but if no one suspected their destination, then it would be the safest course to traverse.

When the tree line was visible, they slowed their pace. With only ten yards of trees left, Dominic nudged his mount forward while Thor and Greer hung back. Greer returned to her horse, and now both men had their swords drawn. Dominic rode with his arm poised to swing while Thor waited with his weapon resting across his lap. Greer focused on not fidgeting as her horse swayed, sensing its rider's tension. They watched Dominic's horse step past the last tree. Immediately, men swarmed him, encircling his mount, pulling him from it.

"Fucking hell," Greer cursed.

The men all wore plaid. Greer recognized the pattern as the one she'd seen far too many times in her life. Men on foot and on horseback charged toward them. She and Thor turned their horses, ready to retreat farther into the woods, but men appeared to their left and right.

"They have a full war band. There must be at least two score," Thor estimated. If they tried to outrun the Gunns, they would still likely become captives. But he feared racing through the forest was more likely to injure Greer than protect her. He didn't doubt they would beat him, but he prayed surrendering would keep him alive. Fleeing would only embolden them after angering them further. "We dinna have a choice."

"I ken. I'll go along with what they want for now. I ken ye willna let them do aught to me or take me anywhere without ye. But I dinna want to make it worse. Ye must accept how they treat me, Thor. Ye canna fight that many of them."

"If a mon touches ye, naught will keep me from ye. I'll die protecting ye."

"And where will that leave me? Completely at their mercy for the rest of ma life. We accept what we have for now, kenning that it's a short sacrifice for a life together."

"I canna accept ye making that sacrifice again."

"Ye dinna own me, Thor. Ye can do what ye can to protect us, and I will do the same. It's ma decision to make."

"We canna argue now, but we shall have words aboot this later. I'm nae in agreement."

"I didna think ye would be." Greer squeezed her thighs and straightened her back. She wouldn't appear before her former clan as anything less than confident and proud. Her shoulders went back, and her chin notched up. She'd spent a lifetime pretending, so this was a role for which she was prepared. She guided her horse forward, forcing men who'd once intimidated her to move aside. She cared not if her horse trod on their feet. They shouldn't have been in the way.

As Thor and Greer joined Dominic, the sunlight nearly blinded them momentarily. But once their eyes adjusted from the forest's dimness, they spied Keenan. The man barely remained atop his horse. The Gunns had beaten him, leaving him with a black eye, a bloodied nose, and a gash to his sword arm. The arm wound still bled, red blossoming along his sleeve to his wrist, but it didn't appear serious enough that he might lose it. He appeared dazed, and Thor wondered how many punches or kicks he took to his head. Thor's gaze moved to the other assembled men, recognizing most of the Gunns from various raids and battles. But his heart raced when he recognized MacDonnell and Mac-Donald plaids in the midst. Things became exponentially more complicated with Laird Wallace MacDonnell of Loch Broom sitting beside Matthew Gunn. Thor wished to pummel the smugness from Matthew's face. He'd leave it unrecognizable.

"Sinclair, yer friend isnae so bonnie anymore." Matthew jerked his head in Keenan's direction. Thor'd noticed they'd bound Keenan's wrists, but they hadn't taken the warrior's sword. Fools. Keenan's eyes met Thor's, and he winked. He might not look well, but even with his hands restrained, he could still reach and swing his double-handed broadsword. Blacksmiths forged the claymores for warriors to hold it with both hands, but many warriors possessed the strength to wield it with one hand. It was a requirement for Sinclairs.

"Ye're too far from home. Ye ken ye're on Sinclair land." Thor's weapon continued to rest on his thighs.

He leaned forward as though he sat at ease in the saddle, but it fooled no one. Everyone knew he would be ready to wage war the moment the air changed.

"So?"

"Ye ken ye're trespassing. Whether we report ye to King David or King Edward, it's uncontestable that ye have crossed into our territory. Ye canna say this is a disagreement aboot borders." Thor turned his attention to Wallace. "Ye have ridden a long way on a fool's errand. Ye have nay bride to claim, and ye've laid yer head on the wrong clan's bed."

"There are only three of ye, whelp." Wallace's white, bushy beard and missing or chipped teeth might intimidate some on the battlefield, but to Thor, it spoke of a man who was growing old and had already lost too many fights.

"Here, aye. In ma family to avenge me? Hardly. Ye ken ma family is all the Highlands except ye. Uncle Tristan kens we're on our way. If we dinna show up, he will let Auntie Mairghread decide what to do with yer carcasses after she slays ye. Dinna tell ma cousins, but I'm her favorite." Thor winked. He'd realized they were closer to the end of the forest than he'd suspected, which meant they were almost to the border. If Keenan or Dominic could break away, they could find Sinclair and Mackay patrols within twenty minutes.

"Enough," Wallace snapped. His gaze bore into Greer's. "I willna tolerate this any longer. Ye are mine. I've paid the bride price and accepted the dowry. The betrothal documents are signed, so ye belong to me. I dinna give a shite where ye left yer maidenhead. I prefer ye broken in, and I ken plenty have made sure ye are."

Thor didn't dare shift his attention to Dominic or Keenan to see their reactions. But he sensed both men were even angrier than they were a moment ago. Disgust poured from them as their posture grew more defensive. They were only slight changes to how Keenan sat astride his mount and Dominic stood, but it was enough for their enemies to tell. Several horses sashayed sideways, their owner's nervousness increasing.

Good. There are more than ten times us, but three Sinclairs are enough to worry them. They must ken how close we are to the border.

"Lady Greer, it would be best for the Sinclairs if ye come with us without a fuss." Emmanuel, the second-most senior member of the Gunns' council, stated. "We will leave Thormud alive, but if ye wish him to remain in one piece, ye get off yer horse and walk over here."

"Father Bennett of Ackergill Tower has our marriage recorded in the parish register. Ye should have returned there rather than chase us for naught. Ye canna force me to marry lest ye make me a bigamist. Any child conceived after today would be illegitimate. Ma husband's red hair will prove the bairn I carry now is his. Neither will get Laird MacDonnell what he desires. Neither will be an heir. Moving forward with any of this is pointless. Return each other's coin or keep it. Marriage to Laird MacDonnell is impossible." Greer raised her hand to stay anyone's objection. "Ye ken ye canna kill Thormud and survive the outcome, so dinna threaten to make me a widow. Laird MacDonnell, even if ye forced me to live as I did before, dinna think for a moment that I canna kill ye. I endured what I did to protect ma people. Without that as ma purpose, I have nay reason to remain chained like an animal. I will kill ye the first night ye come to ma bed."

"Such bravery from a woman half ma size. Ye willna do aught, lass. I've survived this long for a reason. Ye willna be the one to end ma life."

"Yer daughter is a hen-wit. Ye need a wife to bear ye

HIGHLAND STRENGTH

a son and to run yer keep. Ye dinna want her to continue as chatelaine, so ye will have nay choice but to give me the keys. Ye ken as well as I do that the lady of the clan keeps various things that can kill a mon. I could poison ye with nightshade or lye. I could pour wax and tar on ye, then set ye aflame. I could hide a meat cleaver and butcher ye. There are plenty of ways to do away with a tiresome husband. Men arenae the only ones who can be rid of an unwanted spouse. Touch Thormud or take me from him, and ye can pick the day of yer death. But dinna make it one too far from now because ye willna have long to wait."

"Lass—"

"Bitch, be silent." Wallace interrupted Matthew and nudged his horse to walk until its nose nearly brushed the nose of Greer's horse as he lunged for her throat. However, he was unprepared for the dirk she hid in her skirts' folds. She thrust the *sgian dubh* upwards, piercing his palm through to the back of his hand. She twisted and withdrew before anyone understood what she planned.

"I dinna belong to ye or any mon. Ye have nay right to touch me. Try it again, and I will leave ye with a hole in yer throat rather than yer hand. I tell ye all now. Ye thought I couldnae fight back. Ye thought me weak and subservient. I endured far more than any of ye could. That I can promise. I did it because ye and Edgar led the clan to ruin. I kept the ledgers. I paid the servants, merchants, and laborers. I resolved disputes. I did it because it was ma duty, and the Gunns dinna deserve to suffer for the likes of ye. But I am nay longer a Gunn. I am a Sinclair. I bear ma husband's name, and I wear his ring and his plaid. I have nay loyalty left for ye. Ye dinna ken me at all, but I will be yer angel of death if ye try to take me from ma husband."

"Such a pretty speech," Wallace sneered. His uninjured hand swept back in a fist and swung toward her head. Thor's sword swished through the air, severing the limb at mid-forearm.

"Ma wife said dinna touch her."

Men surged forward as Wallace stared dumbfounded at his amputated limb before howling in agony. Amid Dominic and Thor maneuvering to protect Greer, Keenan pulled his horse away from the group and spurred it into a gallop, racing toward the border. Thor knew his friend would understand Thor's intentions by reacting so extremely. He was several furlongs away from the group before anyone noticed Keenan's escape. A dozen men charged after him, but he navigated the bogs better than most.

Men pulled Thor from his horse, shoving him between them as others did the same to Dominic. Greer knew what Thor wanted her to do, but she hesitated to flee. But she caught him looking back at her, and she knew he would die if she remained. He would fight these men, and they would kill him. She whirled her horse around and laid low over its withers as they charged back into the forest. She heard men bellowing and horses pursuing her. But she trusted Rose's steed since she knew what a daredevil the beast's owner was. If Rose had trained it, and it survived its mistress, then it would carry Greer with ease.

She pressed her chest to the horse's neck, ensuring her head was lower than the animal's. If she didn't, a low-hanging branch would sweep her from the saddle. She fisted hanks of its mane to help her remain atop him during their breakneck dash among the trees. She couldn't afford to look back, so she trusted they remained ahead of their enemy since no one yanked her from the saddle. She veered and weaved until she was at least three miles into the dense forest. Then she turned left and headed west. The shift in direction gave her a chance to spy her would-be captors.

There were easily ten riders chasing her, and when she changed course, the last three thought to get ahead of her by turning before reaching where she had. When those men pulled ahead, she yanked on the horse's reins unexpectedly. The stalwart beast neighed but followed the command. They cut between the main group of warriors and the three that broke off. She swerved again to head west once more.

CHAPTER 19

"Lady Greer!"

She heard her name, but it didn't come from any of the Gunn warriors she evaded. As she charged on, the voice that kept calling her name grew louder. It wasn't threatening. Instead, it sounded as though the owner searched for her. She recognized the bird call as one Thor taught her years ago. Altering her path once more, she burst out of the trees and into a group of Sinclair and Mackay warriors.

"They have Thor and Dominic. They pulled them from their horses. Ye have to go to them."

There was no opportunity for anyone to reassure her that men were already on their way. The Gunns emerged from the trees, and the Sinclairs and Mackays surrounded Greer. A man with hair as dark as a raven's wing and eyes the same shade of emerald as Highland grass after a thunderstorm rose in his stirrup.

"Ye trespass on ma father-by-marriage's land. Ye pursue ma nephew and niece. Ye can turn back now, and I willna kill ye. Or ye can continue with this fool's errand and die for it. Are ye that keen to meet our Lord? Because if ye arenae and are just following orders, I give ye the chance to live."

HIGHLAND STRENGTH

Greer realized she watched Laird Tristan Mackay speak to men she'd known since she was a child. Men who'd once ignored her when they were weans and she wished for friends. Men who'd grown into adolescents who leered at her. Men who'd turned their back on her when their counterparts assaulted her.

The man who walked his mount forward to place himself in front of the Mackay warriors he led was massive. He was easily the same size as Thor's father and uncles, but they were related by marriage, not by blood. She hadn't missed how he addressed her. There was no niece-by-marriage or his nephew's wife. He claimed her as his family.

Her eyes darted to three men who were Tristan's replicas. She gazed at Wee Liam—who no longer fit his name but was still called that to distinguish him from his grandfather—and his brothers Alec and Hamish. They all rivaled their father in size. She had a passing thought that the Sinclairs were known for the whisky they distilled, and they shared it with their Sutherland and Mackay relatives. She wondered if that's what made them grow so large. Then she realized Tristan was likely this size before he married his wife, and she knew Laird Hamish Sutherland—Hamish Mackay's namesake—was a bear too. She forced herself to focus.

"There are a dozen of us and seven of ye," Colin Gunn called out. He was her second cousin through Albert. It stung that he would side with the council now that he knew they were related. But she expected nothing better.

"I can count, lad. That's why I made ye the offer. Ye arenae so daft that ye dinna ken seven Mackays and Sinclairs will trounce yer dozen." Tristan nudged his horse forward a few more steps. "Will yer mama miss ye? Do ye have a wife and bairns depending on ye?"

When Colin didn't respond, Greer did. "Ma cousin

has a mother and father who live with him, his wife, and four weans. His parents are auld and in poor health. His weans are too young to do aught to support their family. If he dies, they'll have naught."

Greer pointed her dirk at another man, then another and another as she listed their family situations. There were only four bachelors in the group. The men looked at each other before they sheathed their swords. Greer breathed a little easier. She didn't care that it proved she wasn't worth a fight to any of them. She preferred it that way since they wouldn't have battled to protect her but to hand her over to more men who would harm her.

"We ride for ma nephew. Ye either ride ahead of us and return to the rest of yer party, or ye choose the wiser option and enter the forest again. Ride due north, and ye will come to the road that can take ye back to yer land. The men ye rode with arenae likely to live, so nay one will tell that ye didna return to the others."

"Smug bastard." Colin sneered at Tristan and licked his lips as he stared at Greer. "There are a score and a half of men waiting for us to return. Ye number seven. There couldnae be that many on their way to Thormud. We'll ride back just to watch ye die. How are ye so certain of yerself?"

"I'm Laird Tristan Mackay." He spoke as though merely stating his name made the answer obvious. He shook his head, and Greer pictured him rolling his eyes. "I married Lady Mackay and ended a long-standing feud with the Sinclairs. Before our marriage, I met all four of her brothers on the battlefield and lived to tell the tale. So, I think that ought to explain why I'm so bluidy certain that I will kill all of ye and sleep like a bairn in ma wife's arms tonight."

Tristan jerked a thumb over his shoulder and chuckled.

"Ye can see the three lads who look just like me. I made half of them. The other half is made of the finest Sinclair steel. Ma wife isnae just the bonniest woman in Scotland. She's also fiercer than any mon alive. They may have inherited ma size and strength, but they inherited their mother's cunning and precision. Ye willna survive them. And if any of us return with a hair out of place, ma wife will find ye, kill ye, and dump yer bodies at yer families' doors with her fondest regards. She's a wee protective of her weans and me. I ken ye've all seen her compete each year at the Gatherings." Tristan shook his head and shrugged. "I'm giving ye a choice. She willna."

Greer shifted her gaze to the three younger versions of Tristan. Their expressions beamed pride as they listened to their father. Anyone could see they thought as highly of their mother as Tristan did. None of the Sinclairs or Mackays with them looked any different. These men clearly respected Mairghread, and they knew Tristan didn't exaggerate. She looked back at her cousin and could tell he considered Tristan's offer.

"Colin, Aggie needs ye. Ye ken she canna manage yer ma and da along with yer weans." Greer prayed guilt would stir the man into action. Their gazes met, and she knew it worked. He nodded and signaled for the men to turn around. The Gunns rode ahead of the Sinclairs and Mackays, who continued to encircle Greer. She hadn't realized she had progressed as far west as she imagined. Weaving through the trees distorted her sense of distance.

They spotted more Sinclairs and Mackays waiting for them. When they joined the other men who'd been on patrol, Greer's brow furrowed. There were far more men than she expected. There were at least thirty between the two clans. Tristan ordered the Gunns to continue on into the woods, and the Sinclairs and Mackays fanned out to make a horseshoe around those who already encircled her. Keenan rode with the group they joined.

"Lady Greer, I'm Alec." The man was clearly a few years younger than Greer, but he had the hardened expression of a warrior who'd already ridden into battle many times. "Wee Liam, Hamish, and I will remain with ye. We're going to stay here. The rest of our men will ride with our father. They'll get Thor and his mon. Yer husband willna forgive us if ye get any closer."

"I understand. Thank ye, but ye should lead alongside yer father."

"I'm Wee Liam." A second younger version of Tristan stopped his horse alongside her. "He willna forgive us if we arenae the ones who stay with ye. He willna trust anyone as much as us, and it would hurt him far more if we didna protect ye ourselves."

Greer inhaled deeply before she sighed. She knew Wee Liam spoke the truth. Thor wouldn't overlook his cousins leaving her safety to someone else. The three warriors and Greer watched as the others continued riding. They remained too far away for her to make out what was happening. She strained to spot Thor, but the riders gathered tightly, so she couldn't tell one man from another.

"How are there so many of ye?" Greer continued to look forward, so she spoke to any of her protectors.

"We were with Da visiting a village on the border," Hamish responded. "There'd been a storm that damaged several crofts. We spent last night with one of our patrols. Men arrived to relieve the current patrol this morning, and the current patrol was giving them an update. The same was the case for the Sinclairs. Their camp wasna far from us. Keenan had already passed them when he reached us. He'd told them to prepare to ride, so they joined us as we went past. He explained once we were all together."

"Do ye think they've already killed him?" Greer's voice was steadier than she expected. It didn't match her racing heart, sweaty palms, or nausea that crept up her throat.

"They willna kill him," Alec assured her. "Nae with Da there, and they wouldnae have done it yet. He's an heir to the Sinclair legacy of warriors and leaders. Nay one is that daft."

"That's what I thought too, but now I am nae so certain. Do the MacDonalds have the might to defeat the Sinclairs if the Gunns and MacDonnells join them?"

"Nae unless the MacDonalds from several branches rode together," Alec explained. "They're too spread out to rally easily now. I dinna think there are that many lairds and chieftains who would have already agreed to attack the Sinclairs. This isnae the MacDonalds as a clan but a branch or sept that thinks they can win because they are nay where near Dunbeath. It's a greedy MacDonnell laird of a lesser branch who thinks too much of himself. He shouldnae even carry the title of laird. He's more a chieftain than a true laird. Yer father thought he could influence the MacDonnells and really make his alliance with the MacDonalds. He kenned nay MacDonald laird would marry their daughter to him. The MacDonalds thought they could gain an ally in the northern Highlands for free."

Greer's stomach caved as though Alec's fist rammed into her belly rather than just his words. Obviously, word hadn't reached the Mackays that Edgar wasn't her real father. It reassured her they likely had heard no rumors about her, but neither did she want to listen to anyone call Edgar her father ever again. She knew the truth would come out eventually since they were

Thor's family. She could concede some things without giving away her entire history.

"Edgar wasna ma real father. Ma mother was involved with a guardsman named Albert. He's ma father."

"Then we dinna have to pretend to care aboot yer loss." Wee Liam shrugged a shoulder without turning his focus away from what happened in the distance.

"Dinna mind him." Hamish chuckled at his brother's abruptness. "He has a six-moon auld bairn who willna let him sleep. He thought he might get some rest by coming with us, but it's chucked it down every day since we left Varrich. He'd rather be tucked away with his wife, Elene."

"Can ye blame me? She smells far finer than either of ye."

"Yer lad didna when he shite down yer arm the other day." Alec elbowed his brother. Greer marveled at the banter among the brothers. It was so similar to the Sinclairs. She knew all three men were aware of every movement around them, both near and afar. She knew they were prepared to defend her without a moment's hesitation. But just like Thor and Rose, they could make light of a situation and keep the heaviness from growing oppressive. It calmed her without being a distraction.

"What's yer lad's name?"

"Thome. It's Orcadian and ma wife's father's name."

"She's from Orkney?" Greer tried to recall Rose telling her about the woman, but nothing came to mind. She remembered hearing Wee Liam married a couple years ago, but she knew none of the details.

"Aye. From a fishing village where I stopped while representing Grandda when the king granted him the Earldom of Orkney."

Greer knew of no other man who held the title

twice over. The earldoms of Sinclair and Orkney merged and became the Earldom of Caithness, which rivaled in size to the Earldom of Sutherland. These men's great-uncle held that title. It was moments like this when she recalled just how powerful the family she'd married into was. It reassured her that the MacDonalds and MacDonnells couldn't be as reckless as the Gunns. They had to realize the folly in their plan.

She continued to watch but grew confused when she recognized Tristan turning back toward them. Two more horsemen didn't join them. It meant neither Thor nor Dominic was with the Mackays and Sinclairs. The Gunns, MacDonnells, and MacDonalds turned east and spurred their horses.

"Where's Thor?" Greer demanded even though she recognized her companions knew nothing more than she did.

"They must have already taken him," Alec admitted. "Da's coming back because they must have dispatched men with Thor and Dom. I just dinna ken if they intend to ride to Gunn Castle or skirt the bogs then head south to Loch Broom."

Greer feared her heart might stop. Her ears rang, and panic danced at the edges of her mind. "What are ye going to do? He canna go anywhere with them."

"We arenae far from where Mackay, Sinclair, and Gunn territories meet. There are other patrols along the borders. We will follow them, but at a distance. We'll gather men as we pass them. Now that they arenae chasing ye, they'll turn north once they reach the end of the forest. If they continue as they are, they'll have to cross the bogs to get to more reliable terrain before they continue much farther east. They'll take the road along the coast instead. Even though it's predictable, it's faster for a party that size. However, it's still quicker to navigate the peatlands for individual riders. Da will send men to gather the patrols."

"But we're going to watch them go?"

"This isnae the time for a battle when what we wish to gain isnae here. We could kill all of them, but that wouldnae change that we must still go after Thor. We could risk losing men, but then they wouldnae be with us when we reach ma cousin. Da's thinking beyond right this moment."

"It doesnae make me feel any better, but I understand." Greer struggled to keep a tight rein on her emotions. She was too tired and scared to add more frustration to the mix. She refused to cry in front of them, but when Tristan's distressed expression came into view, she couldn't choke back her sob. She squeezed her thighs and rode to meet Tristan. "Where is he?"

"They're taking him to Gunn Castle. They have a writ from Andrew Murray giving the MacDonnell the right to challenge Thor to single combat over bride thieving."

"Thor didna steal me," Greer blurted.

"We all ken that. Lass, Andrew Murray didna become the Guardian of Scotland by being an eejit. He kens Thor will kill Wallace, and it will be a gift to most of Scotland. Wallace is a lesser laird, but it'll be a reminder to the MacDonnells and MacDonalds nae to antagonize Murray's friends. It's obvious he's confident in Thor. Otherwise, he wouldnae ever sanction putting Callum's son in that type of danger. He kens Callum would track him and kill him if he condoned Thor's death."

"Nay, Da." Alec shook his head. "Murray kens Uncle Callum wouldnae stop Auntie Siùsan from torturing him. I ken ye believe there is nay woman alive like

Mama, but even ye ken our aunts are as protective as Mama."

"Aye. I warned them I wouldnae keep this from yer mama, and once yer aunts Siùsan, Deirdre, Brighde, and Ceit learn of it, then there'll be nay where safe for them to hide."

Greer recalled the maternal women she'd met during her brief stay at Dunbeath. They'd been kind to her, and she'd felt safe with them. She hadn't had a mother in more than ten years, so she welcomed their nurturing. When she recalled the group as she'd known them, she didn't envision warrior women. But as she gave it more thought, she realized the very maternal nature she'd reveled in was what would make them fiercer than any man Greer knew. They might not have the size or training of their husbands and sons, but they were mothers. That was all the explanation Greer needed to accept the men who took Thor should assume their lives were over.

"What do we do next? We canna stay here." Greer looked at Tristan, but she didn't like what she saw in his eyes. "Nay. Ye arenae sending me to Varrich or somewhere else. I'm going where ma husband is. If ye refuse me that, then I go to Ackergill or Dunbeath. Varrich is in the wrong direction. I willna go."

"Wheest, lass. I ken ye willna go to Varrich. I'd rather nae have to chase ye, which I ken is what will happen if I try to send ye there. Ma lads will take ye to Dunbeath once we cross these bogs. The rest of ma men and I will continue to Gunn Castle. I'll send a mon to Ackergill to alert Blaine and Rose. God help them. I didna think of how Rose is going to react to this. Blaine may have to get her three sheets to the wind to keep her from storming the gates. She's a right wee beastie when it comes to her twin. They can hiss at each other like cats in a sack one moment then be a bluidy two-headed monster the next if anyone comes too close."

"The women in yer family—are—unusual," Greer surmised.

"Ye canna be that different if Thor loves ye." Alec grinned.

"Ye just got the highest praise from ma little brother, lass." Wee Liam smirked at Alec since they could be a set of twins for how similar they were. It was a challenge to guess who was older just from their appearance. When she turned toward Hamish, who laughed, she decided they were more like triplets.

"Ye must all be vera close in age."

"Alec is a year younger than me, and Hamish is three. We have a sister, Ainsley, who's five years younger than me. If ye think we look like Da, ye should see how much Ainsley looks like Mama now. It's bluidy uncanny because she can sound just like Mama. She scolds us from a distance, and we think it's Mama. The little hellion thinks it's hilarious to make us run to do her bidding." Wee Liam grimaced, and Alec and Hamish matched his expression. Tristan merely laughed.

"We've waited long enough. Our men have likely caught up to the men who have Thor and Dominic. We keep our distance, but we follow." Tristan led the group, riding directly in front of Greer. Alec maneuvered to be on her left while Hamish was on her right. Wee Liam followed behind her. The rest of the Sinclairs and Mackays fell into a formation that looked well-rehearsed despite the warriors being from two clans. Greer realized they must have trained and fought together many times for them to be so natural with one another.

"How long will it take for them to get to Gunn Castle?" Greer asked anyone who would answer.

"A day and a half like it did from Ackergill," Tristan responded over his shoulder. "It'll take ye at least two, mayhap three, to get to Dunbeath. Once we're past the bogs, we can ride harder."

Greer closed her eyes, careful not to lose her balance and fall from her horse while she prayed.

Holy Father, Mother Mary, shed Yer grace on Thor and protect him from the evil that threatens. He's a good mon who should have so many more years to serve his family and his clan. I canna imagine how his mama and da or Rose and Shona or Laird Sinclair would survive losing him. I dinna ken that I can. Guide him, Lord. Hail Mary. Watch over him in this hour of need. Strengthen his resolve and give him peace to ken he isnae alone. His family and I will never forsake him. I willna make the same mistake twice.

I will fight till ma last breath for him, but I am nae Ye, Lord. I canna do what Ye can. I pray ma intercessions to Ye and Mary, Mother of God. I pray to anyone listening. Please send down the Holy Spirit as Yer divine messenger to shield Thor and to assure him that Ye hear ma prayers. I ask this for him and for me. I ask it for his mama and da and sisters. I ask it for his grandda. I ask this for his family. I ask it for his clansmen who depend on him and ken he will make as fine a laird as his grandda is now and his da will be. Please, Lord. Hear ma prayer. Amen.

Greer hastily made the sign of the cross before she opened her eyes. She knew others had noticed her praying, but no one appeared to pay her any attention, for which she was grateful. A more peaceful sense enveloped her, and she possessed more confidence than she had only minutes ago. That calm remained with her until it was time for her to turn southeast to Dunbeath. Dread and fear unlike anything she'd experienced even during the most horrific moments of her past sank their talons into her as her course no longer followed Thor's.

CHAPTER 20

Thor watched every man he could see, which was only a quarter of the ones who'd captured Dominic and him. His friend kept his head facing forward, but Thor he knew was scanning their surroundings too. The Gunns who pulled him from his horse took his sword and as many dirks as they could find. They'd even lifted his plaid to take the ones strapped to his thighs. MacDonnells did the same to Dominic. They'd bound their wrists and forced Thor and Dominic back onto their horses.

Scouts spotted the Mackays and Sinclairs riding toward them, so Wallace ordered several of his men to ride with Thor and Dominic, forcing them east. Matthew sent half a dozen Gunn warriors with them, and Thor learned they headed to Gunn Castle. It reassured him when the other Gunns, MacDonnells, and MacDonalds joined the advance party. He heard that his uncle and cousins learned of his predicament. It didn't alarm him that none of his family went on a vengeful rampage to free him. He knew it wasn't the right time, and he knew no one would kill him until they at least reached Castle Gunn.

The thing that terrified him the most was no one

stated whether Greer rode with Tristan and the others. No one mentioned her when the groups joined. He told himself over and over that Wee Liam, Alec, and Hamish must be with her and were protecting her, not allowing her to get close enough for their enemy to grab her too. He had to repeat that to himself on a loop lest the fear consume him or turn him into a raving beast.

Their progress was slow until they reached the end of the bogland and could turn north. It didn't take them long to change course toward the coastal road, but he wondered why they chose that path, knowing they would likely pass more Sinclairs and meet Keiths, too. They'd traveled for only five minutes when he understood why his captors believed they'd have safe passage. Ahead of them on the path were a dozen men in Keith plaids. Drew sat at the head of the party. The man's smug expression told Thor everything. He'd been the one to point the Gunns and their allies in the right direction.

Marcus swore Drew would be loyal and the best scout for them if Thor had taken Greer to Dunbeath directly. Instead, Thor was certain Drew had tracked them on the Gunns' behalf. The other Keiths were men Thor didn't expect. It shocked him to see a few of the faces since they'd all appeared devoted to Blaine. Some were even men who'd traveled to Dunrobin with Blaine, then fought alongside the Sinclairs against the Gunns. It made no sense to Thor. From the way Dominic shifted in his saddle, Thor knew he thought the same thing: why would these men betray Blaine?

Thor could only assume Douglan had a larger following than Blaine knew, and they resented Rose marrying into the clan. It made him wonder if these men supported Marcus becoming the Keiths' next laird rather than Blaine. It also made him wonder if Marcus aspired to become the next Laird Gunn. That was his father's intention, but Marcus made it seem like he didn't enjoy acting as Blaine's tánaiste while Blaine stood in for his father as laird. Had he been duplicitous this entire time, fooling Blaine?

He didn't like the way Marcus allowed his men to behave, and Thor's current predicament spoke to that. But he'd concluded Marcus was thoroughly loyal to Blaine. The men who sat atop their mounts acted independently from Marcus.

"Where's the whore?" Drew demanded as his gaze swept the approaching riders. "Ye promised me a turn before she married the auld bastard."

Thor controlled his temper, not allowing it to get the better of him. An impulsive response allowed Keenan and Greer time to escape, but another one would get him killed. Wallace's amputated arm still bled and would until they could make a campfire and someone cauterized it. One of the MacDonnells bound it tightly enough to staunch much of the blood, but the man now rode double with one of his warriors. They'd tied them to together to keep the slumped-over laird from falling from the animal.

"Ye said ye wanted a turn," Matthew replied. "But we never agreed to it. Ye assumed that because I didna tell ye nay that I agreed. I did nae."

"Ye lying—"

"I've lied aboot many things, *lad*, but nae that. Nay one touches her now that she belongs to Laird MacDonnell."

Thor's fingers flexed every time someone spoke about Greer as though she were an object to pass from one set of hands to another. While the Gunns and MacDonnells might agree that Greer belonged to Wallace now, Thor didn't believe men in either clan believed she was off limits. He doubted the MacDonnells or MacDonalds knew even half of Greer's torture, but they'd easily deduced plenty from the comments. He wondered what Dominic thought.

As if his friend could read his mind, Dominic spoke under his breath. "Aught I learn goes to the grave with me."

"Thank ye."

Drew wouldn't be deterred and nudged his horse forward. "Where is she, anyway? Did ye lose the bluidy bitch?" He looked at Thor as he spoke, trying to antagonize him. Thor returned his stare until Drew blinked first.

"How much did they pay ye, Drew?" Thor wondered what the man valued his own life to be worth. He sacrificed his life for those coins.

"That doesnae concern ye."

"So nae nearly enough to make up for ye dying." Thor shook his head and tsked.

"Ye'll be dead long before I am, Sinclair."

"Ye daft sod. I'll live because there isnae a clan alive that wishes to be slaughtered, which is exactly what will happen if I dinna return to Dunbeath as hale as I am now. But now that ye've tracked me, ye've served yer purpose. Ye willna be left to live. None of ye will be. The Gunns dinna need ye now, and the MacDonnells and MacDonalds never gave a shite aboot ye. They willna let ye live to tell the tale. They'll kill ye and take their coin back." Thor figured if the leaders of the three clans hadn't already planned that, he'd given them a good idea that would allow Thor to gain the revenge he wanted without having to worry that he couldn't do it himself.

"They will do nay such—"

An arrow protruded from Drew's throat. Thor recognized the MacDonald fletching that vibrated as blood spurted around the arrowhead. The archer severed the man's jugular. The other Keiths sat in stunned silence before they scrambled to turn their horses. While they weren't as close to the larger group of riders as Drew had been, they were still within firing range. With the round of arrows, Thor recognized the MacDonalds' and MacDonnells' feather patterns on the end of the shafts.

"Nae just a bonnie face. He has a bit of brains to him."

Thor didn't recognize the voice, but it belonged to a man Thor assumed he was a leader. It shocked him to catch sight of the Macnaughten plaid. The man wasn't a chieftain or laird Thor knew, but he was from Greer's mother's clan. Why would he ride with these men when his own ally, John Gallda MacDougall, petitioned King Edward for Greer's hand? Thor would observe him before he drew any conclusions or gave away any information that might bring the English to his family's door.

"Enough clishmaclavering," Wallace croaked. "We ride."

No one paid him any attention. Matthew looked back at the MacDonalds and their distant brethren, the MacDonnells. "Do something with these bodies. Even if ye pull yer arrows from them, it's still obvious they're Keiths. We'll already have them breathing down our bluidy necks because they're allied with the Sinclairs now. We dinna need to make it worse."

"Since when are ye worried aboot keeping the peace with the Keiths?" Wallace demanded, his voice weak.

"We dinna need to deal with all the world's problems at once. First, we get ourselves back to Gunn Castle. Then, ye can sort out yer second for the single combat."

Single combat? Against whom? Me, I suppose. I've already drawn first blood. I'm certain that piece of shite intends it to be to the death, but he canna fight me now. He's likely to die before we even make camp for the night. If only I should be so lucky. He canna do aught to Greer if he's dead. And I willna have to fight him. I dinna fear losing to him or whoever he'd force into fighting me. But I dinna want to waste the time. I need to get to Dunbeath. Ma cousins are most likely taking Greer there. They willna bring her anywhere near these men or Gunn Castle. Uncle Tristan will come for me.

Thor watched seven MacDonalds break off from the group and ride to the slain Keiths. They tossed the dead men over their horses' backs and led the horses back to the MacDonalds' mounts. Thor knew they would ride to the coast, which was only a few miles away, and dump the bodies. Then these men would ride for Gunn Castle. If they were smart, they would don the Keith plaids, then just keep their distance from that clan as they passed along the Keith and Sinclair border. He wouldn't give them any suggestions, but he doubted they would think to do that.

"Thor," Dominic muttered. He looked at his friend and realized the others were on the move. He urged Gaisgeach to follow the other horses as they rode across the bogland. There were parts that threatened to suck man and beast under. The MacDonnells and MacDonalds weren't as experienced with the landscape, so their animals tried to rebel, not liking the uncertainty they faced with each step. It took the riders' full concentration, while the Gunns, Thor, and Dominic easily picked their way across the hidden ponds and sodden peat.

They progressed nowhere near as far as they would without the Highlanders who weren't from Caithness. They'd barely made it to reliably solid ground before dusk. The men who'd broken off and dealt with the dead Keiths were already waiting for them. Many men, including Gunns, grumbled that they should have cut through the woods too and found the road like they'd planned but opted not to at the Macnaughten leader's insistence. Thor wouldn't disagree. But once they allowed him off his horse, his mind moved to what he and Dominic could do to escape. The two Sinclair men stood together.

"I still have the *sgian dubh* at the back of ma belt." Thor's leine billowed over his belt and easily hid the short knife's handle. The blade was far shorter than any of his other dirks, except for the *sgian dubhs* he usually wore in his boots, but it was sharper than the longer blades. It was deadly with little effort.

"Same. If I can get to yers, I can cut yer ropes, then ye can do the same for me."

"Aye. We'll have to wait till dark. As much as I'd love to kill them all in their sleep, we must run the moment we can. Even if we havenae freed our hands, we have to take the chance if it comes."

"We dinna have our swords, but they arenae doing aught to secure them. Look." Dominic jutted his chin toward where a Gunn rested them both near a tree."

"When the time comes, ye get the swords, and I'll get the horses." Gaisgeach wouldn't go with anyone but Thor. At least, not without making a fuss. Dominic's warhorse was more tolerant of people leading him places, but he would refuse to move if anyone but Dominic attempted to ride him. Thor often teased Dominic that his horse was more stubborn than a four-year-old who didn't want to nap. Dominic would tell him that Gaisgeach was a cantankerous old man, just like his owner.

"Sounds good. Which—" Dominic snapped his mouth shut as men commanded them to take their horses to the loch where they would make camp. Neither reacted to taking orders from the Gunns, but it rankled. Once their horses were watered and they ensured they'd picked a spot with plenty of grass for the beasts, the two men found spots to lean against a tree. They would sit back-to-back if they had to, but they wouldn't leave their backs voluntarily unprotected.

Night fell and morning came with no chance for escape. They'd been bound to the tree, and Gunns stood watch over them all night. Emmanuel assigned two men to each of them, clearly trusting them not all. They mounted at dawn and continued to ride east until they crossed onto Gunn land during the late afternoon. When the clan's keep appeared in the distance, Thor's rage burst back to the surface. The mere sight of where they tortured Greer for years threatened to steal any of Thor's common sense.

The urge to rampage and kill anyone within reach threatened to rob him of his sanity. He breathed through it, and he knew Dominic was prepared to stop him. Only thinking about how vulnerable his actions would leave Greer kept him from acting. She'd been right when she asked what would become of her if he died. His family would take care of her and allow her to remain since she'd become family the moment they married by consent. But it wouldn't be the same. He didn't want to do that to her. He wouldn't intentionally or carelessly make her a widow.

He knew she should make it to Dunbeath before nightfall the next day since the weather remained sound. He also knew his Mackay family wasn't far behind them. He'd heard Mackay scouts calling to one another, and he'd even heard a Sinclair. Neither he nor Dominic could respond, but they'd exchanged glances each time. It reassured them both that their clansmen and the Mackays continued to follow them, and some even road apace with them while they still kept their distance. He hadn't doubted Tristan followed him, but it was easy to forget and despair when he couldn't see them.

The first man he spied when he passed beneath the portcullis and into the Gunns' bailey was Albert. His eyes widened to saucers when he recognized Thor, then he scanned the group to find Greer. When he couldn't spot his daughter, he looked back at Thor. The younger man realized the older warrior took Thor's grim expression to mean Greer was dead. Albert's distress was visible even from a distance. Thor softened his mouth to a half smile and nodded when he caught Albert's gaze again. The man placed his fist over his heart and rubbed. Thor feared he'd almost given Greer's true father a heart attack.

When men pulled Thor from Gaisgeach's back, Matthew came to stand before him. Thor knew that man would never forgive him for thwarting the councilman's plans. He expected to find his accommodations in the dungeon, but Matthew had a different way of punishing Thor. "Lock him in Lady Greer's chamber."

Men separated Thor and Dominic, the latter going to the dungeon. Thor fought against men as they wrangled him through the keep's front door and toward the stairs. Despite his hands still being bound, he fought many of them off. He wrapped one hand around the other and made a mighty fist that he swung sideways, forwards, and down depending on how he could reach an opponent. He kicked and rammed his shoulders, even snapping his teeth and catching a man's triceps. He wouldn't willingly go into that chamber where he would find reminders of Greer's past. It wasn't until something struck his temple, making him go limp, that he gave up his fight.

HIGHLAND STRENGTH

"Thor, wake up. Wake up."

Thor was certain he dreamed as Greer's voice filled his mind. He rolled over and reached for her, disoriented when he wrapped his hand around an ankle instead. His brow furrowed as pain ricocheted through his head. He fought to open his eyes.

"Thor." The voice belonged to a hand that shook his shoulder. He groaned as he rolled over. His eyes fluttered open to torchlight that made him wince. Strong arms that couldn't belong to Greer's voice yanked him onto his feet.

"Bluidy hell. Nay more meat pies for ye."

"Hamish?"

"Aye, ye bluidy boulder. Can ye stand on yer own?"

"What—" Thor swayed backward as he raised his hand to his temple.

"St. Columba's bones. Ye werenae kidding. He's like propping up a mountain."

"Wee Liam?"

"Aye."

"Greer? Where's ma wife?" Thor tried to turn, but two sets of hands held him in place.

"Wheest, *mo dhuine*. I'm here."

"Yer mon? More like *mo dhaimh*."

"Alec, dinna call ma husband an ox." To Thor's ear, Greer sounded truly offended on his behalf. But he couldn't understand why any of them were there or how. "Thor, can ye walk? The tunnels willna make it easy to carry ye."

"Is that how ye got in, wee one?" Thor's senses were coming back to him.

"Aye. I can explain everything to ye, but we must hurry. We have a birlinn, but the tide's going to change soon. We have to go."

Thor reached for Greer and pulled her against his chest. She barely handed her torch to Alec in time not to burn Thor. Her arms encircled his neck as their mouths fused. The three brothers' deep voices cleared more than once, but the couple ignored them until they were breathless.

"Can ye walk on yer own, Thor?" Greer slid her hand into his as she took the torch back from Alec.

"Aye. Ma head's pounding, but I can think clearly now. Once we are in that birlinn, ye are going to explain to me what the bluidy hell ye were thinking, sneaking back into this keep. Then ma cousins are going to explain to me how they can be such eejits as to let ye come back here."

"Hauld yer wheest. Yer cousins are brave, so dinna call them names. And ye ken why I came here. Dinna ye be the daft one. I love ye. There's yer explanation. Now be quiet." Greer pressed a hidden latch in the wall beside her former bed. The door sprang open, and she pushed it wide enough for the four enormous warriors to pass through. Wee Liam shut it once they were all in the tunnel. She held up her torch for the others' sake. She could traverse the warren in the dark. She'd done it many times. No one spoke until they emerged into the same cave Thor once swam into.

At the mouth of the inlet, a birlinn bounced in the waves. Greer boarded far more gracefully than Thor, who more fell than stepped. Once Greer tossed the torch into the sea, he opened his arms to her again. She clung to him as much as he clung to her while Alec, Hamish, and Wee Liam set the boat on a course south to Dunbeath.

"How'd ye get here? I figured Uncle Tristan would have sent ye and ma cousins to Dunbeath."

"He did, but when we crossed into Gunn territory, I insisted we meet up with yer uncle again. I kenned we could sail in and use the tunnels to get directly to ma chamber. Yer uncle and some men must have already gotten Dominic out of the dungeon because the other birlinn is already gone."

"Dominic. I just wondered aboot him. I thought I would wind up in the dungeon with him. I'm glad Uncle Tristan went for him. I confess I wasna thinking aboot him when I came round."

"That's all right."

"How'd ye ken where I would be?"

"Because I ken Matthew. He's more spiteful than an auld crone. I kenned he would wish to punish ye, and the dungeon wouldnae be bad enough. He kenned forcing ye into ma chamber would be far worse."

"Aye, but someone knocked me out while I fought to stay away. I hadnae woken yet. I didna ken where I was because I was out the entire time."

"Good." Greer's whisper barely reached Thor's ear.

"Wee one, I wish ye'd never gone back inside that place. I'm so sorry ye had to rescue me. I never wanted that."

"Thor, ye ken I would live a lifetime in that chamber again if it kept ye safe. We didna linger, and I didna look around."

"Matthew was right. Kenning where they were sending me was worse than telling me I would die in an oubliette."

"That's why I kenned where ye would be. These are Gunn birlinns that we borrowed. I ken the two families. They're good people, and they depend on these boats for their livelihood. We canna keep them. If all worked out, Albert got Gaisgeach and Dominic's horse out. He'll meet us at the coast."

"I ken what I want, wee one. What do ye want?"

"Let's go home, Thor."

CHAPTER 21

Thor always loved spying Dunbeath perched on the promontory. It meant he was finally home, and he loved no place better. But never had he been more grateful than at that moment. Greer rode in front of him on his steed, and he'd been content throughout the next day as they made their way south after a night hiding from Gunn patrols. It hadn't taken long for someone to notice Thor and Dominic were missing. They'd spent hours evading their pursuers who didn't desist once it grew dark. Everyone in their party, Sinclairs and Mackays, were exhausted, but he knew they were just as relieved to see Dunbeath as he was.

The only person who seemed more on edge as they drew closer was Greer. Thor hadn't let her out of arm's reach except for when they both needed a moment of privacy. Otherwise, they'd held hands, embraced, or he'd kept an arm around her shoulders or waist. He refused to let go lest they get separated again. She hadn't complained, but now he sensed she wished she were anywhere else.

"Wee one?" Thor kept his voice low as his lips brushed her ear.

"I'm scared. The last time I arrived, all I could think aboot was warning yer family. It's vera different now."

"Aye. Ye're ma wife." Thor squeezed her and kissed her cheek.

"And what if ye're the only one who's happy aboot that?"

"Are ye nae happy aboot it anymore?"

Greer heard the ounce of hurt and uncertainty that Thor's humor couldn't hide. "I've never been happier aboot aught else. But that doesnae mean people will accept me."

"Uncle Tristan and ma cousins accepted ye without a second thought."

"They dinna ken what Keenan and Dominic ken."

"Lass, they will take what they've heard to the grave. Nae only have they both told me that, but I already kenned. They've been ma friend since we were weans. They wouldnae do that to me as a friend. But they also wouldnae do it to me as a fellow warrior and their future laird. They ken how unwise it would be to cross me when it comes to the woman I love. They're nae foolish men. That's why I agreed to them riding with us, and I'm glad they did."

"But what if they let it slip accidentally? What if people hear some other way? They'll brand me a whore. They'll believe I'll always be that way. They'll question any bairn I bear ye. What if they question whether a son is really yer heir? What if—"

Thor's forefinger and thumb turned her head toward his. He silenced her with a kiss that left her clutching a handful of his leine and pulling him back to her when he tried to lean away.

"What if they complain to yer grandda? What if they shun me? What if—"

"Since kissing ye didna calm ye, mayhap I should do something else." Thor had wrapped the extra length of plaid from his *breacan feile* around Greer to keep her warm against the coastal wind. Now it afforded him privacy to slip his hand beneath her mound. "If I pull yer skirts out of the way, will I find ye ready for me?"

"Ye ken ye always will. But there are people around us. I'm worried aboot people calling me a whore, and ye wish to ravish me in public."

"I wish to settle yer nerves and let ye relax. Lean back against me, Wife."

"Are ye commanding me to let ye pleasure me, Husband?"

"Aye."

"I am forever yer obedient wife."

Thor snorted. "Hardly. But ye can be for right now." He helped her pull her skirts out of the way without making it obvious what she was doing beneath the plaid. "We only have five minutes until we're at the gate."

"I only need one. Last night behind the tree wasna enough."

They'd sneaked away from where the Sinclairs and Mackays intended to make camp. Thor's fingers had just brought her to release, and they were pushing his plaid out of the way, when a guard sounded the warning. They'd scrambled to adjust their clothes and get to their horses. When Greer grew too tired to ride on her own at dawn, Thor lifted her onto his horse where she napped.

Now he slid his fingers between her thighs and into her slick heat. Her breath caught as his thumb brushed her pearl. The rocking motion from the horse's gait helped him caress the smooth skin of her sheath. She fought not to writhe as her desire urged her to move on his hand.

"Thor," she whispered.

"Aye. I'll get ye there. I promise."

"I ken, but all of me aches for ye. I wish ye could touch me everywhere. I want to touch ye." Her hand rested on his thigh, but her fist bunched his plaid when Gaisgeach's next step pressed her weight forward against Thor's hand and the firm saddle. He redoubled his efforts, rubbing her nub until she released his plaid, and her nails raked up his thigh. Her breath caught before she slumped backward against her husband's expansive chest. Her head lolled back against his shoulder. She realized too late that if anyone looked at them, it wouldn't be difficult for them to guess what they'd been doing. She moved to sit straighter, but Thor's arm wrapped around her, unwilling to let her move even a hair's breadth.

"Keep rubbing yer arse against me, Greer. I'm close." Thor had pushed his sporran to the side when he pulled her onto his horse. His *breacan feile* covered it even though it was closer to his hip. Every step his horse took was sweet agony with Greer's bottom rubbing against his rod. He'd been hard since the moment she grazed it as she adjusted her skirts. Now she pressed her hips back, letting the horse's gait help her roll her hips and brush against him. "I dinna care who comes to our gates. I'm locking us in our chamber for a sennight. If ye even think aboot putting a stitch of clothing on, I will burn it all."

Greer giggled until he pinched her nipple. It didn't hurt. It set off another round of longing. She would burn her husband's clothes if he thought to get dressed during their sequestered week. Thor shifted, then Greer felt him tense. His groan was for her ears only. He pressed a quick, hard kiss to her neck before they both turned their attention to the men riding toward them.

"Thor!"

Thor recognized his father without hearing him call

out to him. He nudged his horse forward along with everyone else's. Magnus, Alex, and Tavish accompanied their brother as they raced toward the party. He didn't understand why his father gestured for them to turn back. When he and the others didn't immediately turn around, all four Sinclair brothers made the same gesture. But it was too late. Thor spotted the royal standard as five men passed beneath the portcullis.

"Now we ken where they went," Greer whispered.

"Wee Liam, Alec, and Hamish, ye ride with us." Thor let the other riders pass them before he spun Gaisgeach to face south. It wasn't ideal that Greer rode double with him, but at least he knew they wouldn't get separated. He would have to be careful not to exhaust Gaisgeach, though.

"Dunrobin." It wasn't a question. Alec stated what they all knew. It was less than a day's ride to their Sutherland family. They all knew the route well enough to ride through the night. Even their horses could traverse the distance in their sleep. It was dangerous to travel in the dark, but they remained confident they could.

However, they made it less than a hundred yards before men surrounded them. These knights only wore their hose and doublets, much like Sir Richard and his men had when they came to Ackergill. But even without their panoply, or full suit of armor, Thor knew they were too great a threat to face with Greer in front of him.

"We canna outrun them. We go home. Grandda will already ken what to do. Out here, we're unprotected." Thor and the others knew it was the truth. They'd had a slim chance, and it hadn't worked out. Now he would rely on the might of his clan and his family to protect them. If they had to be anywhere with King Edward's men buzzing around them, he was glad to be home.

"We tried. Mayhap if we'd understood Uncle Callum's intention sooner." Alec shrugged. If the entire party had time to turn and ride south, they might have made it. But slipping away with only four horses hadn't worked. The English camped at the southern side of Dunbeath, which none of them could see from where they approached. They'd inadvertently ridden straight toward their enemy.

"We'll go with ye without a fight. Stay away from ma wife, and none of us will draw our weapons," Thor announced to the Englishmen who tightened their circle. Thor, Alec, Hamish, and Wee Liam walked their horses in a small semi-circle rather than whirling them around. They cantered to the gate with their unwelcome chaperones.

Tristan, Callum, Alex, Tavish, Magnus, and Liam waited for them alongside the man with the English king's standard.

"Fucking hell," Greer murmured. She knew who'd they'd find, but it didn't make her any less angry. Beside the flag bearer sat Sir Richard. His smug expression made her want to drive her fist through his face, but she knew she would never succeed.

"Ye have quite the choice phrase, wee one."

"I ken."

They all remained silent as they reined in their horses in front of the older Sinclairs, Tristan, and Sir Richard. Callum leaned forward and grinned, setting Thor more at ease.

"Felicitations, lad. I hear I have another daughter. Lady Greer, I ken ye have a father, but mayhap one day ye will see me as one too. Ye are as much *mo nighean* as Rose and Shona." My daughter. While they spoke English for Sir Richard's sake, Callum emphasized his welcome with the Gaelic phrase.

"Thank ye. May I call ye Father?"

"I'd prefer Da. But if Father is what ye're comfortable with, then I will gladly answer."

"Silence!" Sir Richard barked.

"Lad, that is the last time ye will give any orders in ma home. I've warned ye twice. I willna do it thrice." Liam continued to beam as his newest granddaughter, but his voice held such a chill that Greer wondered how the Sassenach hadn't frozen in place.

"I—"

"Breathe because I allow it. Dinna misunderstand ma hospitality. Ye arenae in the dungeon because it doesnae suit ma purposes. Wear out yer welcome, and I willna even bother giving ye that comfort. I will toss ye into the sea and let the sharks do as they wish with ye." Liam's tone hadn't warmed. Sir Richard snapped his mouth shut, but he shot Liam a resentful glare.

"Someone ought to smack ye across the head and see if that look sticks," Tavish taunted. He leaned forward to look around Magnus and at Sir Richard. "It's bad enough ye're English. But ye've been here nae even an hour, and ma da is already letting ye ken how we'll kill ye. He usually lets Sassenachs have a last meal before they wind up in the drink."

Tavish resembled Liam the most in build since they were both barrel chested. His posture on his horse made him a replica of his father, even if Alex's face resembled Liam's the most. Greer glanced at Thor's cousins, then Tristan. It amazed her how strong the resemblances were in each family. Thor's strawberry-blond hair made it easier to miss how much he looked like his father at first glance, but his face was a copy of Callum's. She found something immensely reassuring about this. While there were other Sinclair and Mackay warriors with them, knowing Thor and his family also surrounded her gave her a greater sense of peace than she'd had in years. She knew that no matter what happened, her new family would never back down or give in to someone who threatened any of them.

"Enough nashgabbing. I wish to say hello to ma son and daughter. Move, Englishmon, or I will move ye maself." A female voice came from above them.

Greer looked up to the battlements beside the portcullis. Wild strawberry-blonde hair blew in the wind as a woman stood with her arms crossed. Greer couldn't see through the bricks, but she imagined Siùsan's legs were hip-width apart.

"Shut your—"

"Say another word to ma wife, and I will kill ye now. Ye dinna seem to understand, Sassenach, that ye are alive because we let ye live. We dinna give a sow's fart that ye represent yer weak-kneed imposter king. Yer position at a royal court we dinna even recognize means naught to us. Ye are much too far into the Highlands for anyone to side with ye. The moment our curiosity ends, so does yer life. Speak ill of a woman in this clan, and we willna care why ye're here."

"As I said, I wish to see ma son and daughter." Everyone's gaze followed the arrow that swished through the tail of Sir Richard's horse. The animal whinnied and sidestepped, unsure of what happened to it but certain it didn't like it. Siùsan now aimed her bow at Sir Richard's head.

Thor nudged his mount forward, grinning at Sir Richard as he approached his family and the gate. Greer lifted her chin and looked down her nose at the royal messenger. Her heart raced, but she would show none of her fear. She drew strength from her new family, who appeared unfazed by their unwanted guests. She watched Siùsan walk down the steps from the wall walk as they passed beneath the portcullis. Her lips twitched a smile at Greer as she gave her a quick nod. Greer realized Siùsan hadn't feigned her threat, but she wanted Greer to feel confident about her arrival and to distract from the growing tension outside the gate.

Thor dismounted before helping Greer from the horse. Siùsan swooped in and wrapped her arms around both of them. Greer hugged her new mother-by-marriage and Thor. They shifted her into the center, protecting her from anyone unwelcome who might come too close.

"Och, lass. I'm so glad ye and ma bairn made it here safely. The men returned from Ackergill by birlinn and told us what happened. I've been so afraid for ye both." Siùsan kissed Greer's cheek before she gazed up as Thor. "Lad, I love ye. When ye have weans one day, ye will understand how relieved I am to have ye back in ma arms. If ye didna have a wife now, I might never let ye go."

"Ye say that every time I come home, Mama."

"And I meant it the first time and every time since then. Lean down." Siùsan still had to stretch to kiss her son's cheek, but Thor smiled and twisted his head to buss a kiss on his mother's cheek in return.

"Ye said they just got here."

"Aye. He nearly lost a hand when he thrust a scroll in yer grandda's face. These English believe they rule the world like the second coming of the Romans. Except the Romans kenned to leave us alone. The English arenae that smart."

Greer walked between Thor and Siùsan as everyone made their way into the Great Hall. Thor tried to guide her to the stairs, but Sir Richard's voice filled the Great Hall.

"For Lady Greer's disobedience and perfidy to the Crown, I sentence her to hang."

There was utter silence for a heartbeat before the Great Hall erupted into Bedlam. Sinclairs—men and women—surged forward, dirks drawn. Greer's gaze swept the gathered people, uncertain if they were defending her or merely angered by the English presence. She leaned toward believing the latter. Her eyes were so wide she feared they might fall from her head. She didn't notice how she pressed closer to Thor's side as Liam stepped forward.

"I would see yer king's writ," the distinguished and intimidating laird demanded, even though his voice was low and even. Authority drilled into him from a young age and the experience of more than two score years in leadership lent an air of supreme control to the man who barely had half a head of gray hair.

Sir Richard smirked and raised his chin, but Liam continued before the English knight could speak.

"As I thought. Ye smug, bastard. Ye havenae aught from yer king to say ye have the duty to arrest ma granddaughter. Yer ego is wounded, and so ye wish to punish her and ma grandson because ye didna get what ye wanted by squawking like a magpie. Leave ma home, and dinna return until ye have something enforceable." It slipped no one's attention that he added no qualifier. Greer was his granddaughter, not his granddaughter-by-marriage. He would put no distance between her and the rest of his family.

Liam glared at the blustering man half his age. The laird's most comfortable stance showed forearms that rippled with muscle as they rested, crossed, against his still-lean abdomen. Legs like tree trunks braced him hip-width apart. His father had preferred to stand with his arms akimbo, but it had created the same ominous aura. Now Liam's four replicas stood the same way, and those men's sons adopted the stance, too. His son-by-marriage had taken to it immediately when he married into the family, and Tristan's three sons stood just like their relatives. Only Thor stood differently, one arm wrapped around Greer's shoulders and the other hand on his hip.

"King Edward granted me the right to do whatever is necessary to convey Lady Greer to her betrothed, John Gallda MacDougall. If that means she arrives in shackles, so be it."

"Ye dinna ken much aboot us, do ye?" Liam took a step forward, and he could tell it was sheer willpower that kept Sir Richard from taking two steps back.

"I know all I need to about you heathenish Highlanders. These marriages Lady Greer and her lover claim are illegitimate and do not withstand any scrutiny."

"Do ye realize that I have ten score warriors? I have the five-score who live within these walls, and I have another five-score living in the surrounding village. Ye might have wanted to learn that even the Sinclair farmers learn to wield a sword. They may toil in the fields by day, but they've all learned how to defend our clan. Do ye have two hundred men with ye? I saw nay army from ma battlements."

"There aren't two hundred—not even one hundred—warriors in here. You're just trying to intimidate me, and it will not work."

"Ye forget the ones in the barracks who're sleeping because they have night duty and the ones on the wall walk with arrows pointed at yer camp. Ye forget the ones who patrol just beyond those arrows' reach. Do ye ken that our nearest relatives are less than a day's ride? I ken ye've already visited the Keiths, but did ye ken that ma wife was a Sutherland? Hamish has ten-score men too. He could easily send five-score, and he wouldnae notice them gone. Mayhap it's a good time for a family reunion. Naught like shedding blood to bring family together."

"The king will only send more men if I don't return

with Lady Greer."

"And how will those men get all the way north when every clan between the border and here learns there are English knights trekking across our land? They willna make it past the River Dee."

"I challenge you, old man. Not your sons or grandsons. Not your warriors. You. I challenge you to single combat to the death, not first blood."

Everyone in the Great Hall took and held a collective breath. This had—inevitably—escalated rapidly. Every Sinclair present knew it would come to a fight of some sort since the English would never back down. It was no more in their nature to admit defeat to a Scotsman than it was for a Highlander to run from a battle.

Five baritone voices rang out. "I'll be yer second, Da."

In their youth, Robert the Bruce once named the Sinclair brothers collectively as cherubim. They acted as one with four faces—an ox, an eagle, a lion, and a man. Nothing had changed in twenty years except to add Tristan, who answered with the four brothers. Instead, there were merely more of them. Thormud, Tate, Wiley, Blake, Torquil, Wee Liam, Alec, and Hamish, along with Kirk Hartley and his father, Ric, stepped forward.

Seven more voices spoke in unison, "I will be yer second." The words "Grandda" and "ma laird" clashing at the end.

"Go and stand with Mama," Thor whispered to Greer.

"Nay, dinna do it. Please dinna leave me."

"Wheest, wee one. This must end. Grandda will be the one to fight, but I must be the one to stand beside him. It's ma right and duty as yer husband and as the second in line to nay only a lairdship but an earldom. I must. I love ye. Now, please, go stand with Mama." Thor kissed the top of Greer's head before she stepped back. She knew immediately that the kind arms she stepped into were Siùsan's.

"Grandda, I will be yer second." Thor walked to Liam's right side. Without thinking because it was the Sinclair men's most natural pose, Thor crossed his arms and stood with his feet hip-width apart.

"I accept, Thor." Liam clapped his grandson on the shoulder before turning back to look at Sir Richard. "Dawn. Dinna be late. Ye're dismissed."

Sir Richard's mouth flapped like a beached fish before his left eye twitched. Liam and Thor wore matching grins. Thor leaned forward with a conspiratorial whisper.

"I'd leave now while ye can get a good night's sleep. Ye shall need it. If ye dinna, we can make yer accommodations in the oubliette. I dinna think ye'll come to the fight in yer best form." Thor straightened and cocked an eyebrow. Liam stifled his laughter as he thought about the toddler who'd once hung from his arms and stood on his feet while Liam pretended to be a sea monster. That toddler had grown into a man for whom Liam held immense pride. He didn't doubt that his clan would one day be in good hands.

Liam whispered to Thor, "It's a good thing I dinna have a bonnie bride to keep me awake all night. Try to get some sleep just in case." No one had shared a bed with Liam since the day Kyla died. He hadn't touched another woman since none could ever interest him.

"Aye, Grandda. But are we meeting in yer solar?"

"Gather yer cousins, and I'll gather ma sons and daughters. It shall be a tight fit." *Good thing ma daughters dinna mind sitting on their husbands' laps. Nae that ma sons would ever turn them away. As bad as I bluidy well was with ma Kyla.*

CHAPTER 22

Greer stood in front of Thor with his arms wrapped around her waist. Liam, his sons, and the additional members of the clan council sat around the table. Wives perched on knees, and sons and daughters stood behind their fathers. Blake's wife, Cerys, stood in front of her husband in the same position as Greer. Tristan had a seat at the table while his sons stood behind him, too. Normally, only the clan council members would be present, and often the wives joined, but this was hardly a typical meeting.

"Our scouts say there are two-score and ten riding with him. We need to encircle them, so none can escape and carry word to Edward." Magnus rested one arm on the table as he leaned forward to see everyone.

"Aye. Tate and Wiley, ye take a dozen men each and spread out from the coast inland," Tavish instructed his sons. He looked at his only younger brother. "Blake and Tor, ye ride with yer da and block the road. Ye three are the biggest of all of us. They'll think a mountain grew overnight."

"Ric and Kirk can each take a dozen men and ride with me to the south while Tristan and his lads wrap around to the west." Alex was the only brother to have no sons, but he wouldn't trade his three daughters for all the money in Christendom. Tristan nodded in silence. The Sinclairs always encouraged his opinions, but he had nothing to add.

Liam shook his head. "We need two of the lads on the wall walks. I say Kirk and Wiley. They're our best archers." Liam looked at his grandson and raised his eyebrows.

"If that's where ye want me, Grandda, then there's where I go." Wiley grinned and interlaced his fingers, pushing his palms out as his knuckles cracked.

"Try to be more patient than yer da," Ceit whispered none too quietly to her younger son.

"I have the patience of a saint, *seillean beag*." Little bee. Tavish had called Ceit that since they courted, since he said she liked nothing more than to buzz around him like an angry bee, but there was never a sweeter honey than his wife's—kisses. Ceit rolled her eyes and shook her head. Tavish whispered something in her ear.

"Promise?" Ceit answered with cocked eyebrow.

"Ahem, little brother." Alex elbowed Tavish, who loathed the supposed endearment. Not only was he just over a year younger than Alex, he was half a hair's breadth shorter than his three brothers.

"Uncle Tavish, Uncle Alex." Thor notched up his chin but glanced down at Greer. He normally enjoyed his family's banter, and it always eased scary and tense situations. But they were discussing Liam's life and Greer's future. He found no humor in either. He could also tell that Greer's endurance was running out, but neither he nor Greer wanted to leave the meeting.

"All right, lad." Tavish nodded. "Wiley and Kirk go up to the battlements. I dinna think we have to worry too much aboot nae having enough men along the coast since we havenae seen any hint of ships. They arrived on horseback. Callum and his men will face the British and guard the path to the gates."

"We allow the eejit in with his second, his standard bearer, and four witnesses. Be prepared for the Sassenachs to either scatter or charge the keep once they discover I've killed their leader." Liam spoke with confidence despite being at least twenty years older than his opponent. It wouldn't be his first single combat, though he'd thought his last had been over decades ago. "Thor, ye stand at the ready. Dinna watch us, watch his second."

"Aye, Grandda."

No one trusted that the English knight's stand-in wouldn't break the rules and charge into the fight at first blood.

"There's naught more to settle until morning. We ride out before dawn. We should all get some sleep." Callum finally spoke. He'd been silent while he watched his son. Just as with any battle, fear and pride warred within. He had only one son. He couldn't imagine what Tavish and Magnus went through with their two sons apiece or his brother-by-marriage, Tristan, who had three. He had an appreciation for his father's sacrifice with four sons who fought toward the end of the War of Scottish Independence. No clan skirmish since had been as violent as those battles, and Liam had ridden into them with all four of his lads, leaving Mairghread alone after Kyla died.

"May I ask something?" Greer swallowed and tried to relax when Thor pressed his chest more firmly against her back.

"Of course, lass." Liam smiled encouragingly.

"I dinna doubt ye'll be victorious. I truly dinna ken why he would challenge ye unless he doesnae see well. But what happens afterward? Willna the king send more men to take me? Will the MacDougalls or Macnaughtens send men?"

"If the Macnaughtens send men, it'll be with the Gunns." Thor spoke from behind her. She twisted to look back at him. "I recognized their plaid among the men with the Gunns, MacDonnells, and MacDonalds. I dinna ken if they're playing both sides or if they've aligned with the Gunns, but I ken some were there."

Greer looked at the floor before meeting Thor's gaze. "I didna ken their plaid well enough to recognize any of them." Her mother had been a kind woman who'd done her best to raise Greer despite her violent husband. It embarrassed Greer that she couldn't even recognize her mother's plaid. She couldn't recall them at Highland Gatherings, and she'd definitely never been introduced to any.

"I understand the Gunns and their allies are still a threat, but I worry aboot the English just as much. They may nae send enough men here to defeat ye, but what aboot all the other threats? Yer land, yer coin, yer titles. What of those? What if Edward is of a mind to strip ye of those things?"

"Ye've clearly learned to lead, lass." Liam's voice held approval. "It's good that ye think of those things. But there is nay one in the Highlands who would take our land except for the Gunns, and we already ken how things work out for them when they try to take aught that is ours. As for the titles, aye, they give me authority and power, but I've also earned those in ma own right. Callum has done the same. Nay one will think less of him or fear him less if he doesnae hold the title of earl. The English certainly arenae sending any of their own up here to take our land, and even if one of them bears the title, the people of Caithness ken who rules this land."

"What aboot yer coin? They could levy heavy taxes

against ye. Isnae going to pay taxes and fines for fighting how Magnus found Deirdre at court?" Greer knew the various couples' stories from Rose.

"We barter as much as we sell things. If nay coin exchanges hand, that doesnae mean we canna still get what we need. I dinna want ye to fash over this until there is a reason to, Greer. Ma clan and I have survived three Edwards, all as arrogant and daft as the other. We've had contingency plans for more than thirty years."

Greer nodded, only somewhat reassured. She didn't think herself important enough to fear being an entire clan's ruination. But she did fear causing them so much trouble that they would banish her. She looked at Siùsan as her hand to came to rest on Greer's forearm.

"We willna send ye away, so ye can cease worrying aboot that. We dinna abandon any of our family." Siùsan's fierce gaze and tone froze Greer, so she didn't dare argue with her mother-by-marriage. The woman was decisive, and it was clear to Greer that Siùsan had already made up her mind that Greer was her third daughter. Her voice softened as she continued. "Now that ye're ma daughter, I canna imagine nae having ye here. I've missed ye dreadfully."

"I've missed ye, too," Greer whispered. That didn't entirely allay all her fears, but they weren't screaming for her to run anymore.

"There's naught more to be done for now, so we may as well enjoy our evening meal. Callum, ye and Alex will brief the men before ye retire." Liam turned to Thor. "Lady Greer, ye look a wee fatigued. Mayhap ye and Thor would like an early evening after the meal."

Thor gritted his teeth before he nodded, realizing Liam didn't slight him by not having Thor brief the men with his father. Liam was giving him an excuse not to leave Greer's side, which he realized was far better than what he'd originally wanted.

"Thank ye, ma laird." Greer offered a wan smile. Her fatigue slammed into her when Liam mentioned it. She wondered if she could make it through the meal.

"Liam or Grandda, lass."

"Thank ye, Grandda." It amazed Greer how that one word, affirming her place in the family more assuredly than anything anyone else could offer, perked up her drooping energy.

"Get settled, then join us belowstairs," Siùsan said, embracing Greer as those who sat rose. Everyone filed out of the solar, each with their own duties. Thor led Greer to the chamber they would now share. Before she could step over the threshold, Thor scooped her into his arms and carried her across, kicking the door shut.

"I'm knackered. I canna imagine how ye feel. Do ye wish to rest? Or would ye like a bath?" Thor eased his petite bride onto the bed. He still worried that she would fall ill since she'd lost so much weight.

"A bath and a nap sound marvelous."

It wasn't long before servants brought an enormous wood and copper tub accompanied by an army of buckets containing steaming water. Greer had never seen a bath as large as the one that now sat in the middle of the chamber. She looked at Thor, who grinned wickedly. She considered how tall and broad he was, and he didn't differ from the other men in his family.

"I'm certain the blacksmith already kens to speak to the cooper again."

"Why?"

"Because every time one of us gets married, we end up needing another tub."

Greer's brow furrowed until her eyebrows shot up

to her hairline. She stared at the tub before glancing at Thor then down at herself. She realized that if she sat on Thor's lap, she could fit in the tub as well.

"Do ye mean all the couples bathe together?"

"Mayhap nae for every bath, but aye, the husbands and wives often leave their chamber at the same time, both with wet hair."

"And ye would like to share a bath with me?"

"Only if that's something ye're comfortable with. Greer, just because we've started making love again doesnae mean that I expect aught from ye. If this isnae something ye want, then ye will always have privacy for yer toilette."

"I didna ken taking a bath together was a thing couples do. But I dinna see how it's any different from us coupling in the loch. I—I'd like to try." Greer walked across the room to Thor, who'd moved a couple buckets closer to the fire to keep the water warm. She turned her back to him and waited for him to pull the laces loose. "I shall never need a lady's maid, Husband. Ye do too fine a job."

"Aye, well, I prefer the undressing to the dressing, but I'll always gladly lend a hand." Thor kissed her neck as Greer pushed her sleeves down. They undressed together before Thor stepped into the tub, ensuring the temperature was comfortable. He helped Greer in and sat, then he guided her to straddle his thighs. He knew she wanted to talk.

"Thor, what happens tomorrow? I can guess ye'd rather I be inside, but I dinna think I can stay in the keep and nae ken what's happening to ye."

"Naught is happening to me, wee one. I ken ye've never seen Grandda train, but he's more like a mon half his age than some auld and graying grandfather. He doesnae ride into battle every time there's trouble, but he doesnae shy away from it either. He's ridden to Blake and Magnus Óg's side."

Saoirse, Alex and Brighde's oldest daughter, also married a man named Magnus. For everyone's sake, they knew her husband, Magnus Mackenzie, as Óg, or the lesser, while the older Magnus Sinclair was called Mòr, or the greater.

"He traveled all the way to France to fight alongside Blake. Watching Grandda, ma da, and ma uncles is like watching the Devil and the Four Horsemen of the Apocalypse riding into battle. Any foe with a peck of sense runs. Those who dinna have the sense God gave an ant soon learn nae to cross the Sinclairs."

"I feel guilty that yer clan—"

"Our clan, Greer. Our." Thor wrapped his arms around her hips loosely and rested his hands on her backside.

"I feel guilty our clan is riding into any battle because of me. The English wouldnae have come here if it werenae for me. Grandda wouldnae be swinging a sword tomorrow."

"What day is tomorrow? Wednesday, I think. Aye, he would. He goes to the lists on Mondays, Wednesdays, and Thursdays. Just a typical day for him."

"Dinna tease, Thor. I dinna find this funny. I'm scared. If aught happens to Grandda, then it's all ma fault."

"Nay, it's nae. Grandda has been a warrior since he was auld enough to lift a steel sword. He got his first wooden sword when he was five. He rode into battle for the first time at three-and-ten. If he wasna confident aboot the outcome, he would have found another solution. It's nae that he's immortal, despite what all of us want to believe, but there are few people with his experience. With that experience comes the knowledge of how to read his opponents and always be a few steps ahead. I ken ye wish to be outside, and I willna stop ye. I dinna want ye sneaking out if I forbid it. Please, just promise me that ye'll stay with Da, Mama, and Shona. Ye may have to help ma parents to keep Shona from joining the fight." Thor grinned, only half kidding. It wouldn't surprise him if his impatient sister put an arrow between Sir Richard's eyes.

"But what if—"

"Greer, I've trained ma entire life to become tánaiste and eventually laird. I dinna want to take that first role any time soon. But I've always kenned it will come one day. Ma family already has plans in place for that inevitability. Grandda will probably die a vera auld mon in his sleep. Or he could die on a battlefield. Either way, we all ken what to do."

"But I dinna want to speed that day along."

"*Mo ghaol*, I ken ye dinna come from a loving family like mine. I ken ye havenae experienced the love I have or felt like ye belong the way I have ma entire life. But ye are ma wife now, and ye will have a place in this family and clan that ye should have claimed eight years ago. The one I should have made sure ye had. Ye are a Sinclair. It's just that simple. We will love and protect ye and welcome ye the same as if ye were born into this family. Ask Cerys if ye doubt it. She was a Kerr, and we havenae gotten along with her clan since Auntie Brighde came to Dunbeath, on the run from her father. Nay one doubted how much Cerys and Blake love each other, and nay one will doubt how ye and I feel aboot each other. They accepted her just as they will accept ye."

"Her clan doesnae live a stone's throw from here and hasnae been harassing ye." Greer knew she should let the matter go and not worry until she had a reason to, but she couldn't help it. Guilt was an oppressive weight on her shoulders and chest, making them ache.

Fear threatened to steal her breath. When Thor pressed her to lean against his chest, she gladly sank against him. He simply held her, and that was all she needed until neither could ignore the desire that grew from being so close. Careful not to slosh water over the sides, they made love before moving to the bed for a nap. The evening meal was subdued, and it was soon time for them to retire for the night. They didn't let go of each other throughout the night, waking to make love with a desperation that each time might be their last. The predawn hours arrived far too soon.

CHAPTER 23

"Look, Da." Tate pointed toward shadows approaching from the north.

"Gunns from the looks of it," Tavish responded.

"They're still riding with the MacDonnells and MacDonalds. According to Thor, they ken all aboot the English insisting upon taking Greer. Have they come to fight them and us?"

"Who the bluidy hell kens with that lot? That daft MacDonnell challenged Thor, but he lost his hand before they even came to fight. I dinna ken how he plans to beat Thor with nay way to hold his sword. I ken for a fact he canna swing it with his left. He might have planned for his single combat to be to the death, but Thor seems to have won by first blood."

Thor had explained everything that happened to his family, and Tristan filled in the parts where he'd met with the rival clans. The younger man knew it displeased his father to learn Thor amputated the MacDonnell's arm, but Callum would never fault his son for protecting his wife. Callum simply wished Thor had knocked the man from his horse instead.

"Do ye want me to tell Grandda?"

"Aye and find Thor. He's going to have to face them, too."

Tate hurried down the battlement steps and across the bailey toward the armory. He noticed Liam sharpening his sword with a whetstone. He'd learned how to take care of his own sword by watching Liam and practicing with his grandfather long before Tavish gifted him with the sword strapped to his back.

"Grandda, the Gunns, MacDonnells, and MacDonalds are riding toward us. They'll be here within a half an hour. What do ye want us to do?"

Liam cast a speculative gaze in the Gunns' direction, even though he couldn't see them through the wall. His eyes shifted to each of his sons, their expressions as studiously blank as his. But he knew what they were thinking as though they were his own thoughts. Tate and Thor stood together, watching the older generation and their grandfather.

"What do ye thinking they're planning?" Tate whispered.

"I dinna ken for sure. But if I were Grandda, I would take the Gunns' arrival as a Godsend." Thor grinned at Tate, who nodded, certain he and Thor shared the same suspicions. Tate headed back to the battlements while Thor went to find Greer. He entered the keep and spied her at the dais. He'd kissed her goodbye almost two hours earlier. His cousins rode out while the stars were still overhead. His father and uncles would be through the postern gate by now, barely more than the shadows Tate spied.

"What's happening?" Greer whispered as Thor took his seat beside her. He'd already had an apple and four strips of dried beef to break his fast, so he declined when a servant offered him a bowl of porridge.

"Everyone is moving into place." He debated whether to tell Greer about the newest arrivals. "Riders approach from the north. Tate and Uncle Tavish spotted them."

"Gunns?"

"With MacDonnells and MacDonalds."

"Will someone else challenge ye? Will ye stand as Grandda's second only to turn around and fight yer own battle?"

"If all happens as I think, nay Sinclair will fight today."

"What do ye mean?"

"I didna understand why there were Macnaughtens riding with the others. I assumed it meant they nay longer sided with the MacDougalls, but I dinna think that's the case. It wouldnae surprise me if it werenae the Macnaughten leader who urged them to ride here. I think he is delivering them."

"Delivering them? To us or the English?"

"Either. Both. Mayhap he thinks the English will be indebted to him if he helps rid the English of their competition. Mayhap he thinks we'll be indebted to him for being rid of the Gunns. I dinna ken, but—"

Bells rang, alerting people to the new arrivals. Greer gripped Thor's arm, but he eased her hand off, forcing her to let go of his leine.

"Wee one, that isnae the alarm for an attack. It will alert the English, though. They willna ken what's happening and will think it's an attack."

"Oh ma. Is the goal to have the English fight the Gunns rather than either of them fighting us?"

"Aye."

"Is it safe to go to the bailey right now? I want to ken what's happening. I want to ken if I need to—"

"Ye willna run without me. If I say we must go, then it's together. Ye dinna leave ma side."

"I'm too scared to go anywhere without ye." Greer stood as Thor helped pull out her chair. His mother and aunts followed them off the dais along with his sister and female cousins. "Will they trap the villagers in the middle?"

"Nay, *piuthar*." Sister. Shona looped her arm through Greer's. "We usually have a full Great Hall, but there are far more women and children here than usual. They came in from the village an hour ago. The men have stayed to defend their homes. It willna come to that, but Grandda, Da, and our uncles like to be cautious."

"Sister?" Greer heard the rest of what Shona said, but only that word registered.

"Of course. The balance is back. I have two sisters instead of one sister and two brothers. Now we outnumber them." Shona grinned and squeezed Greer's arm. She knew the younger woman was trying to ease Greer's anxiety, and it worked.

"Dinna get ma wife in trouble with Mama. I already canna defend ye, Shona. I dinna need Mama angry at me because I canna control both of ye."

"Control me?" Greer and Shona spoke together.

"St. Columba's bones." Thor shook his head and wished to swallow his tongue. "Ye ken what I meant. Come on."

The trio followed the others out to the bailey. The portcullis was still down, and it would normally remain that way until at least sunrise. With two sets of enemy combatants outside the wall, it wouldn't open until any fighting ended. Thor and the others stopped at the base of the keep's steps.

"I'm going up to stand with Wiley and Kirk. I dinna want ye up there with me, Greer. Ye'll be too easy a target. Stay with the others until I come back. If a single arrow comes over that wall, ye go to our chamber and barricade yerself into it."

"Nay. She goes with Shona to yer da and ma chamber. Ye lasses shut yerselves in there. Ye dinna open the door unless it's yer da, Thor, or me."

"Aye, Mama." Shona nodded and wrapped her arm around Greer's waist as Thor kissed his wife's cheek and hurried across the bailey. Greer watched as he bounded up the steps and came to stand between Wiley, with the Sinclairs' chestnut hair, and Kirk, with his mother Isabella's white-blond hair. His shock of strawberry-blond hair made the trio an impressive sight with their height and warrior builds.

Greer heard the soft murmur of women's voices around her, but her attention shifted to looking out through the front gate. She couldn't see much, but she caught glimpses of the Gunns and their allies approaching. Her eyes widened as a volley of arrows soared through the sky toward the unwanted Highlanders.

"What's happening? Are the English attacking?" Greer spun to look at Siùsan.

"That's what it would look like." Siùsan grinned, and at first, Greer couldn't understand the woman's good cheer.

"Those arenae English arrows, are they?"

"Nay. But they came from the English side, and that's all the Gunns and those shites need to ken."

Greer looked up at Thor, worried that he would suddenly become a target when the Gunns, MacDonnells, and MacDonalds fired arrows back at their newest enemy. It took Greer a moment to realize that the first wave from each side didn't send many projectiles toward the enemy. It was the second and third wave that announced the beginning of a battle. She longed to stand on the wall walk with Thor and see what was happening. She shifted anxiously, and her hands clutched her skirts.

The sound of pounding horses' hooves filled the air

before the melee began in earnest. The women watched a hoard of Highlanders surge forward, recognizing three different plaids. Swords clashed as metal ground against metal, and pain-filled screams rent the air. Greer shifted her gaze and shielded her eyes as the earliest rays of sun reflected off of suits of armor racing toward her former clansmen.

"Were those Sinclair arrows?" Greer asked anyone who would answer.

"Aye, and likely some Mackays, too." Ceit shifted to stand on Greer's other side. Shona's arm remained around Greer's waist, and Ceit wrapped hers around her newest niece's shoulders. "The plan must have changed once our men spotted them arriving. Da and the others kenned they could instigate the fight by making the Gunns think the English attacked. Now they're letting them fight each other while our clan stays out of the way."

"Then why havenae they come back? Do they nae dare open the postern gate?"

"There's that," Deirdre answered a few feet away. "But they'll also widen their circle to now enclose the Gunns and their allies. Neither side will be able to run. They'll tighten the net until it forces the English to fight our other enemies. The arrows have stopped flying because they're too close to each other. The Highlanders will unseat the knights, and they'll have the advantage once both sides are fighting on foot. Look."

Greer's gaze followed where Deirdre pointed through the gate. Her brow furrowed as she tried to understand what she saw. There were Highlanders facing in both directions, and it appeared like half of them fought amongst themselves. She didn't recognize a single blue Sinclair plaid amongst the fray.

"Are those Macnaughtens? Is that who's attacking

the MacDonalds and MacDonnells?" Greer could see the Gunns were too entrenched in their fight against the English to notice what happened behind them. Half of the two southern Highland clans fought alongside the Gunns against the English, but the other half tried to defend themselves against the Macnaughtens.

"Aye. They must still side with the English," Brighde answered. "Ma guess is they convinced the Gunns they would be allies together for auld time's sake, or the Gunns asked them to fight alongside them in exchange for giving them back whatever was yer mother's contribution to yer dowry. The Macnaughtens agreed, but they lied. They believe the English are their better bet in this fight. Now they've turned on their fellow Highlanders and defend the Sassenachs. Whatever their reasoning, they're killing each other and keeping our men's hands clean."

Thor watched from the battlements alongside his cousin and their childhood friend. They pointed out the flaws in the English knights' strategies. While all three had ridden into battle alongside their fathers within the last couple years as the Second War of Scottish Independence continued, none of them had fought nearly as many English knights as they had other Highlanders. However, Kirk's father, Dedric, had been a young boy when the English stole him from his Lowland clan and forced him to appear before King Edward I.

The English saw Ric's father as a traitor for marrying a Scotswoman and making his home along the border. They murdered both his parents while they lived among his mother's people, the MacLellans, before the English kidnapped their young son. Raised at the English royal court, Ric became a knight. But as soon as his tenure ended, he returned to Scotland. Within weeks, he'd fallen in love with Lowlander Lady Isabella Dunbar. It didn't take the couple long to realize moving to the Highlands was far safer than continuing to live so close to the border. Kirk and his twin, Kiera, along with their younger sister, Sarah, were born at Dunbeath. The Hartleys were really Sinclairs, just with a different surname.

Ric's training as a knight had been invaluable to the Sinclairs over the past two decades. Now the young men noticed the weaknesses for which Ric taught all the Sinclairs, Mackays, and Sutherlands to watch. They took turns predicting which warrior would win as the Highlanders and knights fought a violent battle at their feet.

"This willna take long at this rate," Kirk noted. "But what happens after? I dinna want to be the one out there digging graves for the bastards." Kirk, Keira, and Sarah all sounded like Highlanders. Their mother sounded like the Lowlander she was, and their father sounded like the Englishman King Edward I forced him to become. Listening to the family still amused Thor, and he could tell it confused Greer.

"Nay. Bluidy hell." Wiley pointed to the south. "Look. Those men are trying to break past Uncle Magnus, Blake, and Tor and their men. Now our family is in the fight."

They watched in frustration as the Englishmen in the rear tried to escape the battle and ended up engaging part of the Sinclairs' force. As the men abandoned their goal to flee south, they turned to the west, which drew Tavish and Tristan, along with their sons and men, into the fight. Wiley's knuckles turned white as he gripped the top of the wall, watching his father and brother fight back-to-back. Alec and Wee Liam

HIGHLAND STRENGTH

partnered, while Tristan and Hamish fought together, keeping their laird and their heir separate.

With the Macnaughtens pushing the Gunns, MacDonnells, and MacDonalds forward as they began firing their arrows into their supposed allies, and the English scattering, the battle descended into chaos. It rapidly forced the Sinclairs and Mackays to press inward to keep the attention away from the castle and to keep most of the fight between the Sinclairs' adversaries. The ring surrounding the two sides tightened.

"Thormud!"

Thor spun around when he heard Liam call up to him. He hurried back down the steps and dashed across the bailey to where his grandfather stood near the armory. He glanced at Greer as he ran past the keep's steps. It relieved him to see she remained with his mother and sister. The other women in his family clustered together, too.

"Aye, Grandda."

"The Macnaughtens are doing a fine job picking off our enemies, but they'll soon be the only ones left. They'll try to claim Greer next. If they werenae interested in her for their own purposes, they wouldnae have joined this fight. We need them gone, too. Wiley and Kirk must position their men to cover ye, me, and the warriors who ride out with us. We need to get behind the Macnaughtens and squeeze them into the fight. There are still more Gunns, MacDonnells, and MacDonalds fighting the English than the Macnaughtens. There willna be enough English to finish the duplicitous pricks. Get our horses saddled and organize the men. I'll speak to Wiley and Kirk. The portcullis only rises high enough for us to ride under. Then it closes again. There's nay coming back for anyone until this is done. Go kiss yer wife and mother, lad."

"Aye, Grandda."

Liam turned toward the battlement steps but paused. He wrapped his massive paw around the back of Thor's neck and drew their foreheads together. "Lad, ye are the mon we all kenned ye would become. I'm in nay hurry to leave this world, but I'm as confident riding out with ye as I am any of ma lads. If aught happens to me, ken that I dinna greet yer grandmama with any doubts aboot ye becoming our tánaiste."

"Grandda, ye've never said aught like this before. Is something wrong? Should I worry? Should ye stay here?"

"Naught like that. I just dinna want to miss the chance to tell ye. I love ye, Thor."

"I love ye, Grandda. And dinna frighten me like that again. I still have too much to learn from ye." Thor grinned as he embraced Liam. They went their separate ways, and Thor took the steps two at a time until he reached the stoop and pulled Greer, Siùsan, and Shona into his arms.

"Are ye riding out?" Greer whispered.

"I must. We're going to make sure this ends with nay one left to challenge us." Thor kissed Shona's and Siùsan's cheeks before drawing Greer away. "Wee one, I have too much to live for to leave ye. I'm coming back and locking us in our chamber for a sennight. If aught goes wrong before then, listen to Mama. She kens exactly what to do. I love ye."

"I love ye. I ken ye canna promise me, Thor. But be careful." Greer wrapped her arms around his neck as he lifted her off her feet. Just as he'd seen his parents do countless times, he kissed Greer with all the love and passion he possessed. When he placed her back on her feet, they exchanged a peck, then he was leaping down the steps and vaulting into the saddle a moment later.

CHAPTER 24

Thor rode alongside Liam as they led their men out of the portcullis and turned right. They skirted the ongoing battle before wrapping around to the left. Liam drew his mount to a stop, but Thor continued on until their men were in line between them. Each had his bow and quiver full of arrows. He'd once asked Callum if there was honor in this tactic, attacking an enemy from the rear and shooting them in the back. Thor would never forget his response.

"It's nae our duty to watch their backs for them. They should ken better, and that's why all Sinclairs fight back-to-back with a partner. Together, they see in all directions."

He knew not every man they rode past could have missed their approach. None sounded the alarm until the first round of arrows soared through the air, picking off the enemies closest to Thor and his warriors. As those men fell, a second wave crested, then imbedded into the unsuspecting enemy. This one came from the men closer to Liam. All of them inched their horses closer as some of the Macnaughtens registered the newest threat. Shouts went up as they tried to fight the encroaching Sinclairs along with the men they'd already betrayed. They were unprepared to be sandwiched instead of remaining on the outside.

Those on foot continued to battle the Gunns and their partners, while the mounted Macnaughtens charged the Sinclairs. All on horseback, Thor and his men drew their swords. Liam gave the signal, and they hurtled forward, their swords swiping from right to left and back again. They unseated some and cut through others. Sweat dripped from Thor's brow, but he didn't dare take a moment to wipe it from his eyes, instead blinking it away as it stung. He spied the man who'd been with the Gunns when they captured Dominic and him. He pointed his sword toward the man as his next opponent smirked. He squeezed Gaisgeach's flanks and gripped the reins. His steed knew what to do. He lunged forward, barreling toward the opposing horse.

Thor was certain Gaisgeach knew the moment the Macnaughten's horse spooked. Gaisgeach snapped his teeth toward the other animal, and Thor laughed when his opponent's mount whinnied and tried to rear. Instead, it sashayed away, but it brought the man within Thor's long reach.

"Why?" Thor demanded as his sword sliced through the man's left arm.

"Why nae? It's the right time now that Edgar is gone. It's just a pity the MacDonnells and Gunns realized that at the same time as John MacDougall did. Ma clan paid a steep dowry for the lass's mother to marry into the Gunns. We got naught in return. We've waited long enough to collect." The man panted every few words, already winded from fighting.

"That was yer own fool fault for allying with them in the first place. It's been more than forty years since the last time the Gunns were a respectable clan anyone would want to stand beside. That was long before Lady

Greer's mother married Edgar." Thor spoke steadily, his voice even. He'd learned to control his breathing, so he could talk clearly enough to give orders during battle. It was a struggle to say so much now, but he managed.

"It wasna ma decision, but I'm here to defend it." The Macnaughten swung his sword at Thor's head, but he maneuvered away. It gave him the chance to slice the man's left thigh.

"Daft sod. Ye've led yer men to death. For what? Naught. She's already married. And even if she werenae, besides her, what do ye have to offer the MacDougalls? What are ye getting from them?"

"King Edward may nae be the great strategist his grandfather was, but he's king now. Our future is better secured with him and his lot nae targeting us. We ken which side our bread is buttered on."

"Ye willna be alive to butter aught. This was a fool's errand. Ye had to ken the moment ye saw Lady Greer with me that ye wouldnae succeed. The moment Uncle Tristan rode up to ye, it confirmed it. Fighting outside ma door sealed yer fate. Did ye wake this morn planning to die? Ye couldnae have thought to do aught else if ye showed up here."

"Ye clishmaclaver too much!" The man whose name Thor still didn't know released his reins and wrapped both hands around his claymore's handle. He lifted it over his shoulder, ready to swipe downward and cleave Thor in half. But in the few moments it took for him to raise his arms, Thor nudged his horse forward and thrust his sword through the man's chest. He barely yanked his weapon back before Gaisgeach reared and struck the other horse with his powerful hooves. The Macnaughten fell sideways, but his foot caught in the saddle as his steed bolted. The beast dragged the dead man farther into the fray before figuring out how to escape.

Thor would have liked to learn more from the man, but he supposed there wasn't much else to hear. He set his sights on his next opponent, then the next, cutting through one man after another until he and the other Sinclairs came even with the Mackays. They'd maintained the western perimeter. Thor glanced to his left as Liam approached, and they walked their horses to Tristan and his sons.

"Bluidy hell! I've ripped ma leine. Mairghread's going to skelp me. She made this for ma saint's day this year."

Thor grinned, picturing his aunt, who was a foot shorter than her husband, taking Tristan to task. But when he noticed the hint of blood on the back of the leine, he pointed to it. "How bad is it, Uncle?"

"A little more than a wee scratch. It'll take a few stitches." Tristan grimaced as he shifted in his saddle. "Burns like the devil, though."

"Hide yer leine until Elene can mend it. It's the only way Mama will kiss ye better." Wee Liam snickered at his father as he suggested his own wife would come to Tristan's rescue.

"I liked ye better before ye learned to talk." Tristan winked at his oldest son.

The battle was winding down, with only a handful of enemy Highlanders and Englishmen still standing. The Highlanders who remained on their feet struggled against the Sinclair men, who pushed them toward the portcullis. They would go directly to the dungeon. If their clans paid a ransom, they would return home. If not, they would rot.

"Where is that Sassenach maggot?" Thor stood in his stirrups as he tried to recognize the English bane amongst the few fully armored knights. They stood with their backs together as Callum and his men surrounded them. Thor wondered if he'd survived. There were plenty of arrows sticking out from the gaps in the knights' armor. Some laid in pools of their own blood, trapped beneath their slain mounts.

"Da! Thor!" Callum bellowed. Liam and his family members trotted to where Callum stood with a man at sword point. Sinclair and Mackay warriors systematically walked among those on the ground, killing any enemies who still breathed. Injured Sinclairs and Mackays made their way to the keep, either over another man's shoulder or propped up by a clansman.

Thor dismounted when he reached his father, his sword still in hand. He surveyed the man in the tin can standing in front of him. "Remove yer helm."

First the visor flipped up, then the warrior lifted his helmet off. Sweat drenched Sir Richard, his face an alarming shade of red. He appeared dazed and uncertain of his surroundings. Thor snapped his fingers as Liam handed off his reins to a clansman. He crossed his arms as Thor continued to try to get the man to focus.

"Do ye wish for a few drams of whiskey before we fight?" Liam offered congenially.

"Fight?" Sir Richard shifted his bloodshot gaze to the older man.

"Aye. Ye challenged me to single combat. Since ye and I survived the battle, it's our turn to fight. Do ye need a little liquid fortification first?"

"You wish to fight me to the death?"

"Of course, I dinna wish to fight ye to the death. But since ye're already on its doorstep, I dinna see why nae. Ye challenged me, nae the other way around. If ye arenae up to it, and ye canna keep yer word, then ye can go to the oubliette." Liam shrugged casually, as though he were trying to choose between two fruit tarts rather than whether he would battle to the first man's death.

"You didn't fight as I did," Sir Richard argued.

"I dinna see how that's ma concern. Ye issued the challenge. A battle got in the way, but we're here now. I'll give ye a third choice. Ye fight me, ye go to the oubliette, or I kill ye now and put ye out of yer misery. What say ye?"

Richard shook his head and blinked several times, as if that would clear the battle haze from his mind. His eyes swept over Liam, who'd fought in his *breacan feile* and leine. Richard had spied him more than once and silently marveled at the man's endurance. Now he rued the arrogance that had made him certain he could defeat the more experienced bear of a man. He sighed as he accepted he would die whether it was from starvation in the pit or by losing the single combat. If he surrendered, he might die with some dignity rather than in a pile of his own pish and shite in the oubliette or mangled with a crowd cheering on his executioner. He dropped his helm, spread his arms out from his hips, and sank to his knees.

"Tell me the truth," Thor demanded. "Why Lady Greer?"

"I don't know for sure. I wasn't privy to any conversations between MacDougall and the king. I am merely the messenger and her would-be jailor for the journey back to England. I can only surmise from what I've learned about the lady. MacDougall is an ambitious man. If he can't marry a well-connected English or Scottish woman, then he'd settle for a woman from a clan his family had already successfully manipulated. Lady Greer would have sounded perfect given her past. He assumed she would be weak and timid, already broken to a man's will. It's likely he would have regained what land he could from the Crown and taken what he wanted from the Macnaughtens. Then he would have killed Lady Greer. He will always look for the next best match. It's said that he's secretly trying to ingratiate himself with your exiled king behind His Majesty's back. He plays a dangerous game against King Edward."

It disturbed Thor that anyone outside of the Highlands knew about Greer. He didn't shift his gaze from Sir Richard, but he wished to see his father's and grandfather's expressions. Neither he nor Greer had shared any of her past. Now all of his uncles and cousins, along with his father and grandfather, had heard the man say Greer was already broken to a man's will. He prayed his relatives believed it meant Edgar had accustomed her to dictatorial leadership.

"Ye arenae returning to England, and neither are any of yer men. When will the arse licker demand yer imposter king send more men?"

"It wouldn't surprise me if more are already on the way. My men and I have already been away nearly two moons."

Thor canted his head as he considered the man's response. "Did ye ride the entire length of the isle, or did ye sail and come ashore somewhere like Dornoch Firth and ride north?"

"We sailed. We knew it would be assured death to ride the length of Scotland. From there, it wasn't difficult to pay enough coin to get directions and learn where Lady Greer was."

"So, more men will come by ship?" Thor pressed. He had a solution. He just needed to be sure he implemented it in the right place.

"Yes."

"I am going to kill ye. If ye have aught more to share, then I will listen and make yer death swift. Lie to me now and tell me naught, I will drag this out for days." Thor had no idea if there was anything else for Sir Richard to share, but he would test him.

"After meeting the Gunns at Ackergill Tower, but before the MacDonnells and MacDonalds joined them, their leader tried to sell Lady Greer to us. Matthew said for the right price, he would end Lady Greer's betrothal to Wallace MacDonnell."

"Why would he do that? The MacDonalds and Mac-Dougalls dinna get along. If the Gunns allied with the MacDougalls, he'd anger the MacDonalds. The Mac-Dougalls arenae in a position to defend the Gunns against such a large clan with so many branches. Besides, how did Matthew ken the MacDougall would agree if he's all the way in England?"

"I don't know that part. I don't think he had any intention of ever letting the lady come with us. I believe he was going to try to get more coin from the Mac-Donnells and assert himself as an equal to the Mac-Donalds rather than their toady. Whatever his plan, it was far too intricate and ambitious for him to pull off. That's why he and his men are dead, and the MacDonnells and MacDonalds who survived are headed to your dungeon."

"Aught else?" Thor asked.

"No."

Thor's blade drove through Sir Richard's neck just below his Adam's apple. A moment of shock froze on the knight's face as blood erupted from him. Everyone took a collective step back before Thor withdrew his blade.

"We dinna dig them any graves, and we dinna send their bodies back just yet." Thor looked at Liam. "We send birlinns down to Dornoch to see if the English have arrived. It willna take them more than a day to sail back and forth. If they have, then we work our way toward the firth. If they havenae, then we send men and horses there. From the coast inland and to the north, we put each knight's body on a pike up their arse along the road. Let the English follow that all the way here."

Thor glanced toward the keep, recognizing several heads of uniquely colored long hair. As though they might hear him, he lowered his voice.

"Dinna tell Mama or Greer this because it'll scandalize them, and dinna tell any of the lasses because half of them are likely to demand they join us. But we behead them all, then tie their heads to their hips, their faces toward their cocks. I canna think of a louder message to send."

The younger men among the group grinned and chuckled. The older men pretended a disapproval none felt. All eyes turned toward Liam, whose lips were tucked between his teeth. He nodded. A wave of deep laughter drifted on the wind up to the women looking down at them from the wall walk.

"Coming, *mo ghaol*" and "Coming, Mama" filled the air as the men hurried toward the keep. Once inside the bailey, Thor tossed his reins to a stable boy and leaped from his horse. He'd already glanced down at himself and knew blood covered him. He'd run his hand over his chest and back as he rode to the keep, ensuring none was his own that he hadn't noticed. He watched as Greer's eyes welled with tears as she rushed down the battlement's steps. She hurried so much that Thor feared she'd trip and roll to her death. He ran to her and ensnared her waist, carrying her down the last half.

"None of it is mine, wee one. I'm hale. I promise."

"But there's so much of it, Thor. Are ye sure ye arenae hurt and just nae feeling it yet?"

"I'll be sore in the morning, but I'm nae injured."

Greer cupped his face and kissed him, not caring who might see them. With her eyes closed, she didn't realize every other husband and wife was doing the same thing as the warriors continued to filter into the bailey. She wrapped her arms around his neck and clung to him, unwilling to end the kiss. Thor was more than happy to oblige. It was the first time he'd returned to a wife after battle. He'd seen the relief his parents always shared, but he hadn't understood it on an elemental level until that moment. He felt it in his bones and his soul. Life only mattered when he was with Greer. Life only mattered to be with Greer.

"I love ye so much, Thor."

"I love ye too. Ye have two-and-a-half days."

"Until what?" Greer's brow furrowed.

"Until I marry ye on the kirk's steps. It's just enough time for Rose to get here. I'm marrying ye the minute ma sister arrives." Thor couldn't imagine the ceremony without his twin there. He regretted Auntie Mairghread wouldn't be there, but he could survive that. He would regret it until his last breath if Rose weren't there. "Then ye and I are disappearing into our chamber for a sennight."

"Promise?"

"Aye." Thor eased Greer to her feet, reluctant to mention the next part of his plan. "I have to ride out in the morn."

"Why? Where are ye going?" Greer couldn't help the panic in her voice. She'd watched the battle end, but she wasn't confident that the threat was gone.

"We are going to make sure the English understand what awaits them if they persist. Grandda already has men sailing to Dornoch Firth to see if the Sassenachs have come ashore. If—"

"Wait. There are more coming?" Greer looked toward the North Sea, and Thor felt her tremble.

"It's likely, but we dinna ken for sure. Whether they're here already or nae, we will make sure that any who arrive understand their fate if they come here."

HIGHLAND STRENGTH

"What are ye going to do?"

Thor glanced around. "We're taking the bodies with us. We'll put them on pikes as markers along the road. We'll cluster a few by the shore, then spread them out aboot a mile apart all the way here."

"So, the new arrivals can find the dead ones staring at them as they ride to us."

Thor paused for a moment before he nodded.

"Thor? Tell me. What am I missing?"

Thor debated what to say, but he wouldn't start keeping secrets from his wife. One day they would lead together, so she would need to know everything that happened within the clan once she became its lady. He wanted her to trust him now, so they would have as strong a relationship as his parents did. Despite suggesting that none of the men tell the women the second half of his plan, he knew no husband would keep it from his wife. He wouldn't be the only one.

"We will behead them and tie their heads around their hips, so their mouths are against their own cocks."

Greer stifled her laugh. "I ken I shouldnae find that funny, but it is. I'd say do away with their hose first."

"Greer!" Thor stared, open mouthed, at his bride. He'd feared his idea would scandalize her and even disappoint her in his behavior. He never imagined she'd have a dirtier imagination than him.

"Thor, I spent a lot of years plotting many men's demises in the most painful or humiliating ways I could conceive. Believe me, what ye suggested is naught compared to a few I came up with." Greer leaned forward and whispered in Thor's ear. "If ye really wish to make a statement, take a different mon's head and tie it to an arse. Pull their tongues out now and keep their mouths open before their bodies go rigid. Then it'll look like they really are arse lickers. Or tie them to look like they're sucking each other's..." Greer leaned back and shrugged.

Thor could only blink dumbly as he pictured what Greer suggested. Then his chest burned, and tears pricked the back of his eyes when he realized what she'd said at the beginning. She'd spent years plotting. Eight years all because he hadn't believed her. It was his fault that she'd ever had a single one of those thoughts.

"Thor, stop." Greer kept her voice soft. "It's nae yer fault. Whether ye believed me or nae, Edgar chose what happened. Ye didna."

"Ye would have been here and safe if I'd believed ye. He never would have touched ye."

"He could have married me off to someone else. Locked me in the dungeon to die. He could have pushed me off a cliff. There were plenty of other ways he could have dealt with me. He chose what happened, and nay one forced him. Ye didna do it. He did. Dinna put this obstacle back in front of us. Neither of us will forget what happened or pretend like it didna. But dinna make it the center of our lives. I willna let him destroy us again."

Thor pulled Greer against him, burying his nose in her clean hair as they clung to each other. "Ye're right. I willna let him destroy us again, and it willna be an obstacle all the time. But I canna promise there willna be times when ma guilt overwhelms me. I dinna think it will ever go away completely. I'll try nae to worry ye with it."

"Nay. Dinna hide it from me. That willna solve aught. We deal with yer guilt and ma memories together."

"Always together, wee one."

"Always."

Greer and Thor walked arm-in-arm to their family, and Thor accepted Siùsan's embrace, receiving a different type of succor from his mother than he did from Greer. But it was just as fortifying. The couples made their way to their chambers, and the unwed men headed to the loch. The warriors would bathe, then the family would plan what came next—retribution and a wedding.

CHAPTER 25

◈

Thor and his cousins watched from the crest of a hill as the English reached the twentieth body on a pike. They'd seen the men come ashore and chuckled at the knights' horror when they found the first five bodies, including Sir Richard's, on the posts. Thor and the others placed them where they knew the English would begin their journey on the road north. They'd remained a few miles ahead of them as the shocked Englishmen rode toward Dunbeath. Now they were halfway home, and Thor couldn't stop grinning.

The knights stopped at each body, and the Sinclairs could tell they argued each time. Many gestured wildly in the direction whence they came. Their leader insisted they push forward, but with each mile, even that man's resolve floundered.

"I say they turn back after the next body." Wee Liam sat with his arms crossed casually over his saddle's pummel. He jerked his chin. "That one's already thrown up three times."

"I dinna even think they're that gruesome," Tate mused. "I mean, it's nae like we brought their shite with them. We left that on the battlefield. The grass'll be nice and tall by autumn."

"We ken they've seen us. I think Wee Liam's right. They willna last beyond one more body. Between us watching them and what they've found, they're ready to run." Thor turned his mount and nudged him forward once he saw the Englishmen steering their steeds back onto the road. He and his cousins continued north for another ten minutes before they came to the next corpse. He twisted in the saddle but could barely see their shadows since they were on a flat stretch. "This time we stay close enough that they can tell us apart, but we dinna engage."

The nine young men trotted their horses half a league, then stopped once more. At almost two miles away from those they taunted, the Highlanders fanned out once more. They rode with a score of Sinclair warriors and a dozen Mackays. As the knights came into view, Thor drew his sword. The others followed suit before adjusting their targes on their left forearms. Thor began the steady cadence as he banged his sword's hilt against his shield. The noise filled the air and surely carried to the unnerved knights.

"Look at that one." Blake nudged his chin forward. "If he shakes his head any harder, it will tumble from his neck. We could tie it to that corpse's groin. Then it could have a tongue up its arse and on its cock."

Thor had hesitated to admit it was Greer's idea to attach some of the severed heads to the corpse's arses, but it didn't take him long to realize his cousins had yet another newfound layer of respect for his wife. The men didn't think twice to embrace the suggestion, having more than one laugh as they positioned their dead victims.

"They're turning back," Wiley observed. He moved his sword to his left hand and waved before giving them an obscene gesture. Some of the other men whistled and cheered, while at least one Sinclair called out the clan's ancient battle cry, "*Girnigoe! Girnigoe!*" Not to be outdone, Hamish bellowed, "*Bratach bhan chlann aoidh!*" The white banner of Mackay!

If they hadn't known better, they would have thought they had an entire army with them as their calls and shouts carried on the wind. It was enough to persuade the knights to turn back, certain an entire band of Highland demons would soon descend upon them. The Sinclairs and Mackays watched as the English horses kicked up clouds of dirt as they galloped back to the coast and the ships that awaited them.

"I canna believe that's all it took," Tor mused.

"Aye, well, I think our reputations may have had a wee influence. Between the displays and our name, I think they realized it wasna wise to carry on." Thor shrugged, but he wore the same mischievous grin he'd had as a child when he and his cousins found just enough trouble to make their fathers punish them without their mothers actually skelping them within an inch of their lives like the women threatened. It was no secret that Thor and all his cousins—male and female—feared their mothers and aunts far more than their fathers and uncles. The women didn't need size. They just needed *the* look.

"Let's head back. I'm starving," Alec complained.

"Rose and Blaine should be there by now. Henry promised to ride late and rise early. I ken Rose will have been on a horse and waiting for Blaine before her poor husband could give Marcus a fare-thee-well and any instructions." Thor might jest about his sister, but he couldn't wait to see her. It had only been a few days, but it felt like a lifetime. He prayed his sister and brother-by-marriage would remain at Dunbeath long enough for Thor and Greer to have a brief honeymoon in their chamber and still get to visit with his twin.

Kirk Hartley nudged his horse to ride alongside

Thor. He'd remained quiet while his friends bantered. He was a keen observer and a man of few words most of the time. It made him the best strategist of his generation of warriors. Not the best in the clan, since his twin could claim that as the undefeated chess player, but the best of the men.

"I dinna ken how ye can do it." Kirk kept his voice low. "Ma hope is Keira marries a Sinclair."

"I've kenned ma entire life that ma sisters will leave Dunbeath since they're the tánaiste's daughters and must marry well. But it doesnae make it any easier to let them go. I ken ye understand. It's like losing a limb but still feeling as though it's there."

"That's why I dinna ken how ye manage. When we fostered, we kenned we'd be back. Now..." Kirk shrugged.

"Truth be told, I havenae had much time to think aboot it since leaving Ackergill. Ma mind has been filled worrying aboot keeping Greer safe. But now that there arenae any English or Highlanders after us, I'm feeling anxious and sad. I want Rose to be happy, and I ken she is. It's just hard."

"Well, she may nae be yer twin, but if ye need *a* twin to drive ye barmy, I'll lend ye Keira."

"I shall tell her ye said that." Tor leaned forward to see past Blake and Thor to Kirk.

"Stay away from ma sister. Ye dinna need to be telling her aught." Kirk glowered at Tor, who offered him just as dark an expression in return.

"Dinna let me find ye walking with Maisie again." Tor notched up his chin. While no true animosity existed between the two men, things had become strained at times since it was clear a fondness existed between both pairs.

"Do ye ken who I'd like to be walking with?" Tate

asked, lightening the mood. "Did ye see little Adeline Grant at the last Gathering?"

"Aye. She's nae so wee anymore," Alec noted. "Ye nearly lost an eye when Fingal spotted ye ogling his lass. He isnae a da to test."

"I was just looking. I didna touch." *Yet.* Tate would keep that last thought to himself. For all he knew, she might be married by the following summer when the clans met for the next Highland Gathering. But if she wasn't…

"I'm still hungry. Can we be off?" Alec spurred his horse into a canter, and the others followed. It was after dusk when they returned to Dunbeath, but Thor recognized the horses in the stables when he brushed down his steed. He knew the laird's table would overflow that evening.

Greer covered her face with her hand, fearful wine would shoot from her nose as she choked on her mirth. Her sides ached from laughing throughout the evening meal. It hardly felt like she'd watched her husband ride into battle the day before or had spent four days on a mad dash back and forth across the northernmost Highlands. It felt like she'd always belonged at Dunbeath, surrounded by a loving and accepting family.

"Swallow." Thor thumped her on the back.

"I was trying." Greer spluttered and took a sip of wine to wash down the last poorly timed gulp. "I canna believe yer aunt just said that."

"Auntie Mairghread has always had a colorful sense of humor. She's ever the lady when she isnae with her brothers. When she is…" Thor shook his head. "She's a horrible influence on Shona and Ainsley."

"Her daughter is exactly like her. It's uncanny."

"Now ye can see why Wee Liam, Alec, and Hamish all have as much gray hair as Uncle Tristan."

None of the Mackay men had a single gray hair Greer could spy, but the four men all wore the same aggrieved expression when mother and daughter turned their teasing toward Tristan and his sons. They were merciless.

With nearly forty people in Liam's immediate family, there was no room to add any of their visitors to the dais. Servants had moved the tables off the raised platform and added four more to the enormous rectangle. When the Sinclair and Mackay men, plus Kirk, returned, they not only found Rose and Blaine already at Dunbeath, they discovered Mairghread and Elene had arrived with Elene's younger brother and sister, and Wee Liam and her two children.

They'd journeyed with the MacLeods of Assynt, who'd stopped at Varrich to rest along the way. When a man returned to Varrich, informing Mairghread of what happened and how Tristan and their sons were chasing after Thor, she decided she, Elene, and the children would join the MacLeods on the way to Dunbeath.

"Which brother is which?" Greer whispered. "I ken Michail is married to Isabella's sister, Blythe. But which one is Edward, and which one is Aidan?"

"Edward—he prefers Ward—is the one with the shorter hair. He's the youngest of the three."

"I canna believe how much Isabella and Blythe look alike even though Isabella's so much aulder. Ye canna tell which one is the baby of the family." Greer watched the two women, their white-blonde heads together as they chatted.

"It's Blythe. Their middle sister, Emilie, is married to Dominic Campbell, the laird's brother. Michail,

Ward, and Aidan are ma cousins through Mama. Torrian is her uncle through ma grandmama."

"Aye. If I'd truly been Edgar's daughter, Catriona would have been some sort of cousin to me. She was Edgar's father's cousin. She's the only Gunn besides ma real da who I wish I was related to. She and Torrian look as perfectly matched as yer parents." The older woman reminded Greer of her mother. Catriona favored the same scent Greer's mother had, and it brought back a flood of happy memories when they embraced as Liam introduced their guests.

"They are. Just like Blythe and Michail are, too. I dinna ken Aidan's or Ward's wives vera well, but they're kind women. I ken Blythe because she's come to visit so many times."

"Why do ye think they're here? They couldnae have kenned aboot our wedding. I understand why Mairghread and Elene would want to come since they worried aboot their men. But why did Torrian and Catriona bring their entire family?"

"I dinna ken. It surprised me to recognize the horses when I entered the stables earlier. I'm certain we'll ken soon enough." Thor pushed more food onto Greer's half of their shared trencher. "Eat up, wee one. Ye shall need yer strength."

"I could say the same to ye. I ken ye're still a growing lad." Greer's hand slid up Thor's thigh beneath his plaid. He made a strangled sound as he snagged her wrist and pulled it away from his groin. He wanted his wife to touch him there and anywhere, but he didn't wish to embarrass himself by climaxing at the family table.

"Wheest, lass. Ye're killing me."

"I ken." Greer pressed a quick kiss to his cheek before turning to talk to Shona.

"I canna believe how things worked out for ye two."

Rose wrapped her arms around Thor's. "I'm happy for ye."

"Are ye still angry that I didna tell ye all those years ago?"

Rose inhaled and held her breath for a moment as she considered her answer. "Nae really. I dinna love that either of us kept any secrets, but we both did it because we thought we were protecting Greer. I also understand how ye wouldnae want to admit to marrying a woman ye thought betrayed ye."

"I'm still sorry for hurting ye by nae telling ye the truth and trapping ye between us, Rosie."

"I ken the truth now, and that's what matters, Thorny."

"*Rosie.*" Thor snatched the kertch from his sister's head and tossed it across the table to Wee Liam, who flung it down the bench to Tate. Thor tugged a lock of his sister's matching hair. "Ouch! Ye dinna need to use yer nails!"

Rose pinched him, making sure it smarted as she narrowed her eyes at Tate. Her cousin shook his head and handed the piece of white fabric across the table to Wiley.

"Give it back to her. I dinna want to sleep with one eye open, and I dinna want to find snails in ma boots in the morning."

"If ye lot dinna stop causing trouble at the table, ye'll be mucking out stalls for a moon of Sundays."

"Aye, Auntie Ceit," Thor and Wee Liam responded while Tate muttered, "Aye, Mama."

Rose smirked at Thor but stopped when she caught Siùsan's eye. She ducked her chin, hiding her smile. Thor elbowed her. "See. Mama's told ye nae to call me names."

"Are ye five? Ye sound like it with yer whinging." Rose's knee knocked against Thor's. She leaned past her twin to look at Greer, who watched the spectacle wide-eyed. "See what ye've married into?"

"Aye. I couldnae be any luckier." Greer leaned against Thor as he wrapped his arm around her. She rested her head on his chest and savored the comfort he offered and the warmth she felt as the family continued to laugh and tease around her. *So, this is what it's like to have a family.*

Thor and Greer retired to their chamber after hours of dancing and merriment. They heard other doors closing as they undressed. The unmarried male cousins would sleep in the barracks to make room for the newly arrived couples. An image flashed through her mind. She felt certain the other couples were all about to do what she and Thor would. She gladly stepped into her husband's arms once they both stood bare. She'd gotten used to the feel of his hands caressing her back, and now she found it soothing when it had initially mortified her.

She ran her hands over his chest's defined planes before tunneling her hands into his hair. Their mouths came together slowly, each teasing the other before their impatience got the better of them. Their kiss threatened to consume them; the dueling tongues were not nearly enough contact. Thor wrapped his hands around her bottom and lifted her, so her legs wrapped around his waist. His sword nudged her sheath as he turned toward the bed. She marveled at how her enormous warrior husband was so gentle as he laid her on the mattress. She didn't release his waist, but he pulled back. He shot her the wolfish expression she knew forewarned hours of passion and pleasure.

Thor eased down the bed, but Greer sat up. She

caught his arms and shook her head. "Ye always make sure I find ma release first. I want ye to experience pleasure before me. Let me taste ye."

"If I let ye go first, everything will be over in a flash." Thor dipped his chin ruefully. "I willna last long enough to have ma turn at the feast then join our bodies."

Greer bit the corner of her lower lip. She looked at Thor's cock before glancing at her mound. Her question embarrassed her enough to whisper, but she found the courage to ask. "Is there a way we could both enjoy it at the same time? We wouldnae be looking each other in the eye, I suppose. But can it work?"

Thor slowly nodded. His bride's innocent questions reminded him that her experiences were limited in some ways that he hadn't considered. Nothing from her past had been about her enjoyment. He remembered how she said no other man had ever put his mouth on her mound. It embarrassed him that he knew the answers to her questions because of his own experience. Guilt and shame dampened his mood, but he wouldn't ruin it for Greer.

"Thor, I asked ye because I kenned ye'd have the answer. I dinna fault ye for having done this before. One of us should ken what to do."

He shifted upward, so he rested on his forearms beside her shoulders. He brushed hair from her forehead before pressing a soft kiss to her plump lips. "Did ye ken ye're the bonniest lass in the world?"

"If ye say so," Greer whispered.

"Did ye ken ye're the bravest woman in the world?"

"If ye say so."

"Did ye ken I love ye more than aught in this life or the next?"

"Aye."

Thor brought their mouths together, fusing them as

he rolled them, so he was on his back. When they pulled apart, he explained. "Turn around and press yer hips back to me."

Greer eagerly followed his directions, quickly understanding the logistics. It was as she'd imagined. She'd worried they might have to lie on their sides, and that seemed beyond awkward. A moment of doubt flashed through her mind when she realized Thor would have a clear view of her back while she could see very little else of him than his cock. But all thought vanished when she felt his tongue swipe her seam. She lowered her head and licked him from stem to stern. His groan spurred her on to swirl her tongue around the bulbous head, and she sighed when his tongue dipped inside her.

They went back and forth, taking turns with small motions that drove them both to the edge. Thor's hands massaged her bottom as she cupped and rolled his bollocks. When one hand wrapped around her thigh to tease her nub as his tongue thrust in and out, she inched toward her release. She sucked in a noisy breath when his hand swept up and down her back, but her worry soon passed, finding the sensation erotic. Her core tightened before the spasm shot pleasure outward to the tips of her fingers and toes.

"Greer, turn around." Thor's voice sounded strained and desperate to his own ears. He held on by the last thread of his willpower. He breathed easier when she sat up, and he helped her move toward him. He didn't expect her to shift and lie on her back, stretching her arms over her head. It arched her back, lifting her breasts toward him. He kneaded one as he suckled the other, settling between her legs. As he thrust into her, she drew his hand away from her perky nipple that he teased. She brought it up to the wrist that remained above her head, wrapping it around her before sliding her other hand beneath theirs. "Greer?"

"I trust ye completely, Thor. I love that ye're bigger than me, stronger than me. I always feel safe with ye. I never feel threatened when we're lying like this because we're making love. Even when we dinna take our time, I never fear ye hurting me because it's rougher than like this. I dinna feel out of control with ye. Instead, I enjoy letting ye lead sometimes. I dinna mind ye holding ma wrists, making me wonder what ye'll do next. When I ken I'm at yer mercy, I ken it's only a question of what pleasure ye will give me next."

Thor tightened his hold just enough to capture and keep her hands in place, but she could easily break loose. He kissed her neck and behind her ear as he thrust into her over and over. She pressed her feet into the bed, her hips meeting each surge with their own.

"More... Aye... Merciful saints. Aye, right there... Like that... Oh!" Greer struggled to keep her eyes open as the sensations overwhelmed her.

"Ye're perfect, wee one. Ye feel so good. I canna wait much longer."

"Dinna. I'm so close."

Thor thrust into her, circling his hips before withdrawing. He thrust again, his pubic bone rubbing against her pearl. He felt Greer's core tighten around him, clamping him in place as they rocked together, his seed filling her. He released her arms, and they wrapped each other in a tight embrace, sharing soft, breathless kisses. They remained joined, panting and staring into one another's eyes. This was bliss.

CHAPTER 26

Thor watched his grandfather take a seat at the head of the oblong table in the laird's solar. To Liam's right sat Thor's father, then his mother. Thor sat to Liam's left, a seat he'd never occupied before. Alex had always sat there. It shocked him when his uncle pointed to the chair and told him it was now his. Greer sat to her husband's left, uncertain why she'd been called into the meeting. Alex, Tavish, Magnus, and Tristan stood behind their wives, who sat beside each other. Torrian and Catriona sat at the far end of the table with Michail to his father's right, and Blythe on his other side. Ward and Aidan stood behind their wives.

"I invited the MacLeods to visit because we're in the midst of an important shift in our part of the Highlands. Tristan and Mairghread are here nay only as ma son and daughter but as neighboring laird and lady. Greer, I asked ye and Thor to join us because this is aboot the Gunns."

Greer had suspected as much, but she didn't understand why the MacLeods were involved. They were related to the Gunns through Catriona, but their land didn't border the Gunns like the Sinclairs' and Mackays' did. She watched Liam, then shifted her gaze to everyone else. But before Liam could say more, someone pounded on the door. Without waiting for an invitation to enter, the door swung open. Hamish Sutherland held it open for his wife as Amelia passed through.

"Aboot bluidy time ye arrived." Liam stood with a broad smile as he strode over to embrace Amelia, then Hamish. "We have a wedding in a few hours, so we couldnae wait much longer to start this meeting."

"It's nae like ye gave us much warning," Hamish grumbled as he pulled out one of two remaining chairs. He stepped aside for Amelia to take it as another couple entered behind them. Greer recognized them as Hamish and Amelia's son, Lachlan, and his wife, Arabella.

Now Greer was thoroughly confused. The Sutherlands also bordered the Gunns, but to the south instead of to the north. She supposed they might be there for the wedding; however, they'd come to the meeting too. She remained silent as the Sinclairs, Mackays, and MacLeods greeted the newest arrivals. She smiled and dipped her chin when both couples looked in her direction as Liam spoke again.

"When it became clear matters were simply untenable with Edgar, I sent a missive to King David. Inevitably, Edgar would die, and while I urged the Gunns to accept Greer as their laird, I kenned it was improbable. In ma missive, I suggested an alternative, so Gunn blood might still flow through the next laird, but the mon I named would be intelligent, fair, and levelheaded. Those are traits that have long been missing from the Gunn lairds over the past three generations. As soon as King David's response arrived, I dispatched a messenger to the MacLeods, asking them to come here."

Liam leaned forward to see Greer and reached out his hand. She slid hers into his before he gave it a gentle squeeze.

"Greer, ye sacrificed much for yer clan, always trying to protect them. We all ken the truth: if ye'd been a mon, ye'd be laird right now. It's nae fair. But the clan of yer birth needs a leader now. King David has granted the title of Laird of Clan Gunn to Edward." Liam looked at Ward. "Much like me with Callum, Torrian has handed over almost all the duties of laird to Michail. Michail and Blythe's son is still too young to be yer clan's tánaiste, so Aidan still fills that role. One day he willna, but that is a long time to come. He'll always play an important role in yer clan. As the third son, Ward, ye would too. But I believe ye can lead as well as either of yer brothers and being the youngest brother shouldnae keep ye from that. While the Gunns' land is within ma earldom, Assynt lies in a unique position, as part of it is in the Earldom of Sutherland and part is in the Earldom of Caithness. As such, Hamish and I both wish to confer the lairdship upon ye. Edward MacLeod, do ye accept?"

Greer froze as she watched Ward. It was clear he already knew why Liam summoned his family and him. This was a technicality. She glanced down at Liam's hand, which still held hers before looking up at Thor. He appeared as stunned as she felt. He hadn't known either. She supposed he hadn't been around enough to hear any of the discussions or for Liam to inform him of his plan. Emotions warred within. Hurt that her former clan would never acknowledge her for how she'd led them for most of her life conflicted with the disdain she felt for them. Fear for the good people of Clan Gunn made her worry about whether Ward would be as fair a leader as Liam believed. Relief that she was no longer responsible for her clan lifted a weight from her shoulders.

When Thor wrapped his arm around her and drew her against him, Liam released her hand. She looked around and noticed everyone watched her. She'd expected cheers and congratulations for Ward. Instead, she shifted uncomfortably, disliking being the center of attention yet again. Her brow furrowed when Ward left his spot behind his wife and walked around the table to her. He offered her his hand, palm up. She hesitated for a moment before resting her hand in his. She didn't know what to think when he bowed over it.

"Lady Greer, I ken what a surprise this must be for ye since it nearly shocked me out of ma boots when Da told me. I never imagined I'd be a laird, even though I've kenned the role since I was a wean. I watched everything ma brothers did, wishing to be just like them. I ken I'm ready to lead. Yer life is here at Dunbeath, and I can understand why ye may nae want to visit yer clan of birth, but ye will always be welcome at ma table. If ye're willing, I'd like to meet with ye and get yer advice on many things, so I can prepare. The Gunns have much to do before they earn back anyone's trust and respect, but I hope one day ma new clan can earn yers."

"Thank ye." That was all Greer could manage along with a weak smile. She wished Liam told her in private rather than in front of a full chamber. But she supposed she was fortunate to be involved in any conversation about the Gunns' future. Ward nodded and walked back to where he'd stood before speaking to her.

"Do ye wish to retire?" Thor whispered. "I dinna like how pale ye look."

"I'm all right." She reminded herself of the role she'd played for so many years. She could hide her thoughts and emotions better than anyone else she knew. With a fortifying inhale, she eased into a warmer smile, appearing as though she was accepting the news and feeling better about her former clan's future. She noticed how relieved many appeared, and that only made pretending feel worse.

Thor didn't care for how wan Greer appeared, and he sensed how troubled the news made her. He shot a reproving look at his grandfather, annoyed that Liam placed Greer in a position of scrutiny. What could she say? She had no choice but to be gracious about this news, even if it hurt her or she disagreed. He pushed back his chair and guided Greer to her feet.

"Congratulations, Ward. Ye shall make a fine Laird Gunn. If everyone would please excuse us, ma wife and I have much to do before our wedding this evening." Thor didn't wait for anyone's response, his arm wrapped around Greer's waist as he guided her to the door. But Greer stopped and turned toward everyone.

"This surprised me. Part of me is relieved to ken that I have nay responsibilities or ties left to them. It's nae that I dinna think Ward will make an excellent laird. I just canna find it in me to care what happens to them anymore. The only piece of advice I'll offer is that Albert is the only one ye can completely trust. He's ma real father and sacrificed almost everything to keep me alive while I sacrificed almost everything to serve that clan. I wish ye the best, and I appreciate yer offer to dine at yer table. But I will never go to Gunn Castle again. I suggest ye burn everything that was in the chamber I once used. Naught but evil existed there."

Greer turned back to the door and left with Thor. She didn't care what people made of her final words. They could do as they pleased. As the couple made their way outside to the gardens, a place they both preferred when they wanted privacy outside their chamber, Greer's emotions settled into one overwhelming feeling. Peace.

"Before they leave, can ye meet with Ward and tell him everything? I canna do it, Thor. But he should ken the truth before he arrives and before anyone poisons his ear. I dinna care what he thinks aboot me, but ye're family and ye're an ally. I dinna want him to question yer decision to marry me and whether that makes ye a sound future leader."

"Wee one, Ward has kenned me ma entire life. He kens the mon I am, and I believe he understands how I fell in love with the most wonderful lass in Scotland. But I will speak to him if that's what ye want."

"Aye. Tell yer grandfather, parents, and aunts and uncles at the same time. That way it's done, and nay one needs to speculate anymore."

"If that's what ye want. But they'll all respect yer privacy and nae expect ye to share."

"I ken, and that's why I'm asking ye to do it for me. I ken they dinna expect it, but they should ken too."

"I'll do it after the wedding and before everyone leaves."

"Nay. Please do it now. While everyone is there and before I officially enter the family. I would do so with a clear conscience." Greer sighed.

Thor wanted to refuse, but he sensed how important this was to Greer. He relented and kissed her before she went through the garden gate, and he left her to return to Liam's solar. He didn't worry about Greer's safety, but he disliked leaving her alone after such a surprise. When he reached his grandfather's solar, he steeled himself for the imminent conversation. He knocked and waited to be bade entry.

He moved back to his chair, but he remained standing for a moment, then decided it would appear better if he sat. He gathered his thoughts as everyone watched him. He clasped his hands on the table and leaned forward.

"What I say now never leaves this chamber. If anyone who isnae here right now says aught aboot this subject, I will ken it came from someone in here. I willna forgive that. Greer asked me to come back and speak on her behalf. I dinna want to, but I will do aught to protect ma wife, and she believes ye should ken aboot her past."

Thor looked at his mother as he began, her smile encouraging and knowing. It made him wonder what she'd deduced over the past few months and what she might have known from all those years ago.

"Greer and I met at the same loch where Great-uncle Daniel met Ceana Gunn. Our story is far too much like theirs. We met there nearly every sennight for nine moons. I arranged hunting trips and patrols so I could see her. After six moons, we handfasted. I should have brought her here, but we were worried aboot what would happen if we told anyone we married. Greer feared leaving her people in Edgar's hands, and I feared our clan would reject her. We thought we'd have more time to work it all out. We had a horrible misunderstanding—one that was entirely ma fault—during that battle when Jamie died. I thought she'd betrayed me, and I left her, saying horrible things aboot the life I thought she deserved."

Thor paused and breathed through the tightness in his chest. He closed his eyes as he gathered his courage to go on.

"After that battle, Edgar kenned we'd handfasted. He had men watching Greer, and they figured it out. He beat her so badly that she lost a bairn we didna ken she was carrying. She'd kenned since she was a young lass that Edgar wasna really her father. He used that truth and her nay longer being an innocent to justify assaulting her repeatedly over the past eight years. Her clan members didna ken what he did to her in private, but they kenned what he allowed his men to do to her. When she said naught but evil existed in that chamber, she didna lie. They restrained her for days at a time while men—"

Thor thought he might be ill. He swallowed several times.

"She bears visible and invisible scars from the torture she survived. She did it because she feared what would happen to her people if she left Edgar unchecked. If I'd kenned even a hint of what was happening, I would have brought her here. But she didna tell Rose or me what was happening. I've loved Greer since we were five-and-ten. We spent years believing in a betrayal that could have been avoided if I'd kenned how to deal with ma emotions after ma first battle and after Jamie's death. I will never stop feeling like I caused what happened to ma wife, even if she doesnae blame me. When ye go to the Gunns, ye will learn aboot this. Marcus Keith's father was one of the men, and he spread rumors aboot Greer that some of the Keiths still believe. Apparently, word of what happened to her even reached John MacDougall in England. But it isnae aught I want to be common knowledge here or anywhere. This goes to yer grave, or I'll leave and take Greer somewhere she can be safe. I ken ma duty to this clan, and she would never agree to me leaving, but I canna endanger her again."

The ensuing silence made Thor's heart race faster than telling his family about Greer's past. He feared the lack of reaction, uncertain what that meant for Greer and for him. He turned to Callum when his father spoke.

"Greer is ma daughter now. Ye willna forsake yer duty to this clan or yer birthright to protect her. There will never be a reason to need to. I will love her just as I do Rose and Shona. I canna think of a mon fool enough to speak against one of ma weans to me or yer mother. God help the fool who does. There willna be a scrap left to them after yer mama is done."

"And if there is, it's ours," Deirdre pointed to her sisters- and brothers-by-marriage. "Nay one comes after one of us without getting all of us. *Familia prima.*"

"*Semper familia*," every Sinclair plus Tristan responded. Family first and always family. It was the family creed; the one ingrained into each of them and their strongest belief. It was all they needed to say to prove they accepted Greer as one of their own.

Greer peered down at the gown she wore. It was magnificent and a complete surprise from Siùsan that afternoon. Her mother-by-marriage slipped into Greer and Thor's chamber while Rose kept her company as she bathed. The other lasses begged to be part of the wedding preparations, but the older generation refused, knowing it would traumatize Greer. Instead, they sent Rose to help her bathe and get ready. Siùsan explained she'd begun working on the gown when Greer arrived at Dunbeath the first time. The moment she'd seen how Thor reacted, she knew something special existed between them. She'd prayed and had faith that they would reconcile, so she'd created a wedding gown for Greer.

"Are ye ready, lass?" Callum whispered beside her.

"So vera ready, Da." Greer beamed up at him, seeing a face so recognizable to her. She knew from Callum how Thor would look as they aged together. She knew he would only grow more handsome with the passing years, and she looked forward to the life they would make together.

Callum led her across the bailey to the kirk, the clans members stepping aside to allow them to pass. The moment she had a clear view of the kirk's steps, her gaze locked with Thor's. He took her breath away. He wore a saffron leine, denoting his position in his clan. His plaid appeared brand new. The hilts of his sword and dirks gleamed, and his hair shone in the waning sunlight. She barely noticed anyone around them, only registering later that Rose stood beside her twin throughout the ceremony. The couple only had eyes for each other. Every moment during the exchange of vows would stick with them both, even if the wedding Mass passed in a blur.

"Are ye happy, wee one?" Thor asked as he handed her their chalice during the wedding feast.

"I couldnae be happier, *mo ghaol*. Ye've given me so much, and I finally feel whole again. I'm as happy as I was when we were younger and all we worried aboot when we were together was whether we'd be rained on. Ma heart hasnae felt this light since then. Are ye happy?"

"Beyond belief. I've considered ye ma wife again since we talked in yer chamber that day. I kenned then that I would never let ye go again. We've wed by consent, by handfast, and by a priest. There canna be any doubt to anyone what we've always kenned. The Lord meant us to be together, Greer. Naught will keep us apart again."

"There is nay mon better than ye. I dinna care what any other wife in here believes. She's wrong. Ye are the best."

"I love ye, wee one."

"I love ye."

"Shall we retire and see if we can make a real wee one?" Thor waggled his eyebrows.

"Mayhap we already have."

Thor froze, his eyes widening. "Have we?"

"I dinna ken yet. It's far too soon. And ye ken I—" Greer couldn't finish.

"If we dinna have any bairns, that simply means I dinna have to share yer attention. I always shared everything with Rose. I dinna mind having something that is only mine." Thor winked.

"Ye're an overgrown wean." Greer giggled.

"I'll show ye something that's grown. Come here, lass."

"Catch me first!" Greer pushed back her chair and gathered her skirts, racing to the end of the dais, uncaring that people watched her. Thor snagged her around the waist, tossed her in the air, then slung her over his shoulder.

"I always will."

The couple disappeared abovestairs for the sennight Thor promised. When they returned to the land of the living, their love and happiness radiated from them. It took no time for the clan to love Greer just as they loved each bride who married into the Clan Sinclair. Some whispered things they heard at markets and Gatherings, but no one dared say it where any member of the laird's family might hear. None wished to die for the sake of gossip.

A moon after they arrived at Dunbeath, Greer took Thor to the loch where they'd first met. They made sure they remained on the Sinclair portion of the land surrounding the water. "*Mo ghràidh*, do ye remember this tree?" she asked.

"Of course, I do. It's where I asked for our first kiss. It's where I asked ye to handfast with me. It's where we made love for the first time."

HIGHLAND STRENGTH

"We had many firsts here, but they were never destined to be our lasts. Remind me again of what it's like to make love on a plaid beneath an oak tree." Greer tugged at her laces as she kicked off her slippers. A moment later, they sank down onto the plaid they'd spread for their picnic. Time slipped away, and they were once again the besotted adolescents they'd been eight years earlier. Hours passed as they coupled and swam.

They'd begun their life together under that tree, and just as it had the strength to withstand the harshness of life in the Highlands, Thor and Greer had the strength to keep their love strong despite life's harshness.

EPILOGUE

"Would ye stop? We shall be late." Greer pretended—not too hard—to shoo Thor away as he plucked at her kirtle's laces as she attempted to tie them.

"We have five minutes."

"Since when do ye only take five minutes? We'll be here for at least an hour."

"Lass, it's still a battle of wills to nae finish in five minutes. However, that would be a good thing today." Thor pressed a kiss to Greer's neck as his hands gripped her backside. He felt her sigh as his kisses trailed along her jaw until their mouths fused. He gathered her skirts and drew them upward, but the moment the cooler air hit her legs, she danced away.

"Yer parents and everyone else in the clan will ken why we're late. I canna face all of them like that. Cease, ye randy auld mon."

"Auld? I wouldnae let Da or Grandda hear ye calling me that. What does that make them? They'll be in the lists in the morning proving ye wrong."

Ten years into their marriage and into his seventh decade, Liam retired the lairdship entirely. While he still held the title of Earl of Caithness, Callum had officially become Laird Sinclair. He'd spent five decades as laird, but he'd already handed over all his duties to Callum shortly after Thor and Greer married. It had elevated Thor to tánaiste.

Now fifteen years after the day Callum became laird in his own right, he was retiring his title. Everyone knew he and Siùsan looked forward to more time together without the constant demands pulling them apart. Liam's voice remained strong, but he struggled to get around now that he was in his nineties.

"Can I trust ye to finish tying this?" Greer turned her back to Thor and pointed. "Since ye still willna let me have a lady's maid."

"Ye dinna need one. Ye have me." With an aggrieved sigh, Thor stepped behind her, kissing her nape before he finished where Greer left off. He slid his arms around her waist when he was done. "Are ye ready, wee one? I ken ye've been helping Mama since ye arrived, but it'll be different once ye hold the title Lady Sinclair."

"I'm ready. Mama and our aunts have been the best teachers, and I ken they will all continue to help, but they've earned the right to quieter days."

"Aye, quieter days," Thor snorted. "As though ma uncles dinna already chase their wives around this keep enough. They shall just be underfoot now that they and Da dinna go to the lists every day."

"As though they'll be under yer feet while ye and yer cousins hide in the lists." Greer rolled her eyes as she turned to face Thor. It was more likely they would only see the older couples at meals. They would disappear into their chambers, or off to the loch and beach. She smoothed her hands over Thor's new saffron leine. She'd sewn it for this occasion. Her gaze swept over her husband, still in awe of the braw man she'd married.

"Dinna keep looking at me like that, wee one. It

willna be ma fault that we're late." Thor pressed a quick kiss to Greer's lips before moving to open the door. "Nay lass has ever been bonnier in our clan's plaid. I'll never tire of kenning ye're a Sinclair and ma bride."

"Bride? We've been wed five-and-twenty years."

"It doesnae feel like it's been that long. It's gone so fast." Thor wrapped his arm around Greer's waist. It wasn't as trim as it had been when they were a newlywed couple. Within months of living at Dunbeath, she'd gained the weight she'd lost after Edgar's attack. Now, her body reflected the four children she'd birthed.

"I ken. How are our weans so auld when we're still so young?" Greer leaned against Thor as they entered the Great Hall. It still amazed her how large their family had grown. At times, she was certain there were more members of the laird's family than the rest of the clan. All of Thor's cousins had married and become parents. That day, everyone gathered at Dunbeath. The female cousins who'd married into other clans had returned with their husbands and children, and the male cousins who remained at Dunbeath were there with their wives and weans. There were over five score people there, including all their Mackay and Sutherland relatives.

"I canna believe Uncle Hamish and Auntie Amelia came too. It's nae an easy journey for them these days." Thor pointed to where the older couple sat with Liam on the dais. All of his father's cousins were there with their families. He swept his gaze across the crowd and spied his mother's half-brothers. His uncle was still Laird Mackenzie, but he suspected the lairdship would soon pass to Thor's oldest cousin.

"Are ye ready, lad?"

Thor and Greer turned toward Callum as he came to stand beside them. Greer let go of Thor as she turned to embrace Siùsan while Callum embraced Thor. The older warrior's hair was now mostly gray, and Siùsan's hair was nearly perfectly white, but nothing else spoke of their age.

"Aye, Da. Are ye ready?"

"Vera. Yer mama and I are so proud of ye both. The clan trusts ye, and I ken this is the right choice." Callum released Thor and moved to embrace Greer while Siùsan embraced her son. The two couples took their places on the dais along with Thor and Greer's four children. Not only would Thor become Laird Sinclair and Greer would become Lady Sinclair, their oldest son assumed the role of tánaiste, taking over Tate's position. As Thor's next oldest male relative, Tate received the official title, but all the cousins now filled the roles that once belonged to the older generation.

Greer stood beside Thor as he swore his oath to lead the Clan Sinclair, rededicating his life to his people. They beamed with pride as their son recited a similar pledge before Thor sat in the laird's chair and Greer took her place in the lady's seat as the entire clan processed forward to promise their fealty to the newest Laird Sinclair. At the end of the ceremony, four generations mingled, passing around jugs of whisky.

"Wee one, I couldnae do this without ye. Thank ye for being ma wife." Thor whispered.

"I canna imagine a better life than the one we've made together. Ye gave me a family and a home when I never thought I'd have either. Thank ye for being ma husband."

"I love ye," they said together as a cheer and well wishes passed through the crowd.

turned to embrace Susan while Callum embraced Thor. The older warrior's hair was now mostly gray and Susan's, too, was nearly perfectly white, but nothing else spoke of their age.

"Aye, Da. Are ye ready?"

"Aye, Katriona and I are so proud of ye both. The clan trusts ye, and I hop this is the right choice," Callum released. Thor said and so did, too, embrace. Greer and Susan embraced his son. The two couples took their places on the dais alows with Thor and Greer's four children. Her only wo ful Thor become Laird Sinclair and Greer would become Lady Sinclair, their place so assumed the role of transits taking over Kate's position as Thor's next oldest male relative. Thor received the Laird title but all the cousins now filled the role that once belonged to the older generation.

Greer stood beside Thor as he swore his oath to lead the Clan Sinclair, rededicating his life to his people. They behind with pride as the two recited a similar pledge before Thor said, in the clan's cheer and Greer took her place as the lady's seat as the entire clan processed forward to promise their fealty to the newest Laird and Sinclair. At the end of the ceremony, four generations mingled, passing around hugs of visits.

"Wee one, I could not do this without ye. Thank ye for being ma wife," Thor whispered.

"I canna imagine a better life than the one we've made together. Ye gave me a family and a home when I never thought I'd have either. Thank ye for being ma husband."

"I love ye," they said together as a cheer and well wishes passed through the crowd.

THANK YOU FOR READING HIGHLAND STRENGTH

Celeste Barclay, a nom de plume, lives near the Southern California coast with her husband and sons. Growing up in the Midwest, Celeste enjoyed spending as much time in and on the water as she could. Now she lives near the beach. She's an avid swimmer, a hopeful future surfer, and a former rower. When she's not writing, she's working or being a mom.

Subscribe to Celeste's bimonthly newsletter to receive exclusive insider perks.
Subscribe Now

www.celestebarclay.com

Join the fun and get exclusive insider giveaways, sneak peeks, and new release announcements in
Celeste Barclay's Facebook Ladies of Yore Group

THE CLAN SINCLAIR LEGACY

Highland Lion
Highland Bear
Highland Jewel
Highland Rose
Highland Strength

THE CLAN SINCLAIR

His Highland Lass **BOOK 1 SNEAK PEEK**

She entered the great hall like a strong spring storm in the northern most Highlands. Tristan Mackay felt like he had been blown hither and yon. As the storm settled, she left him with the sweet scents of heather and lavender wafting towards him as she approached. She was not a classic beauty, tall and willowy like the women at court. Her face and form were not what legends were made of. But she held a unique appeal unlike any he had seen before. He could not take his eyes off of her long chestnut hair that had strands of fire and burnt copper running through them. Unlike the waves or curls he was used to, her hair was unusually straight and fine. It looked like a waterfall cascading down her back. While she was not tall, neither was she short. She had a figure that was meant for a man to grasp and hold onto, whether from the front or from behind. She had an aura of confidence and charm, but not arrogance or conceit like many good looking women he had met. She did not seem to know her own appeal. He could tell that she was many things, but one thing she was not was his.

His Bonnie Highland Temptation **BOOK 2**

His Highland Prize **BOOK 3**

His Highland Pledge **BOOK 4**

His Highland Surprise **BOOK 5**

Their Highland Beginning **BOOK 6**

THE HIGHLAND LADIES

A Spinster at the Highland Court
BOOK 1 SNEAK PEEK

Elizabeth Fraser looked around the royal chapel within Stirling Castle. The ornate candlestick holders on the altar glistened and reflected the light from the ones in the wall sconces as the priest intoned the holy prayers of the Advent season. Elizabeth kept her head bowed as though in prayer, but her green eyes swept the congregation. She watched the other ladies-in-waiting, many of whom were doing the same thing. She caught the eye of Allyson Elliott. Elizabeth raised one eyebrow as Allyson's lips twitched. Both women had been there enough times to accept they'd be kneeling for at least the next hour as the Latin service carried on. Elizabeth understood the Mass thanks to her cousin Deirdre Fraser, or rather now Deirdre Sinclair. Elizabeth's mind flashed to the recent struggle her cousin faced as she reunited with her husband Magnus after a seven-year separation. Her aunt and uncle's choice to keep Deirdre hidden from her husband simply because they didn't think the Sinclairs were an advantageous enough match, and the resulting scandal, still humiliated the other Fraser clan members at court. She admired Deirdre's husband Magnus's pledge to remain faithful despite not knowing if he'd ever see Deirdre again.

Elizabeth suddenly snapped her attention; while everyone else intoned the twelfth—or was it thirteenth—amen of the Mass, the hairs on the back of her neck stood up. She had the strongest feeling that someone was watching her. Her eyes scanned to her right, where her parents sat further down the pew. Her mother and father had their heads bowed and eyes closed. While she was convinced her mother was in devout prayer, she wondered if her father had fallen asleep during the Mass. Again. With nothing seeming out of the ordinary and no one visibly paying attention to her, her eyes swung to the left. She took in the king and queen as they kneeled together at their prie-dieu. The queen's lips moved as she recited the liturgy in silence. The king was as still as a statue. Years of leading warriors showed, both in his stature and his ability to control his body into absolute stillness. Elizabeth peered past the royal couple and found herself looking into the astute hazel eyes of Edward Bruce, Lord of Badenoch and Lochaber. His gaze gave her the sense that he peered into her thoughts, as though he were assessing her. She tried to keep her face neutral as heat surged up her neck. She prayed her face didn't redden as much as her neck must have, but at a twenty-one, she still hadn't mastered how to control her blushing. Her nape burned like it was on fire. She canted her head slightly before looking up at the crucifix hanging over the altar. She closed her eyes and tried to invoke the image of the Lord that usually centered her when her mind wandered during Mass.

Elizabeth sensed Edward's gaze remained on her. She didn't understand how she was so sure that he was looking at her. She didn't have any special gifts of perception or sight, but her intuition screamed that he was still looking.

A Spy at the Highland Court **BOOK 2**

A Wallflower at the Highland Court **BOOK 3**

A Rogue at the Highland Court **BOOK 4**

A Rake at the Highland Court **BOOK 5**

An Enemy at the Highland Court **BOOK 6**

A Saint at the Highland Court **BOOK 7**

A Beauty at the Highland Court **BOOK 8**

A Sinner at the Highland Court **BOOK 9**

A Hellion at the Highland Court **BOOK 10**

An Angel at the Highland Court **BOOK 11**

A Harlot at the Highland Court **BOOK 12**

A Friend at the Highland Court **BOOK 13**

An Outsider at the Highland Court **BOOK 14**

A Devil at the Highland Court **BOOK 15**

PIRATES OF THE ISLES

The Blond Devil of the Sea **BOOK 1 SNEAK PEEK**

Caragh lifted her torch into the air as she made her way down the precarious Cornish cliffside. She made out the hulking shape of a ship, but the dead of night made it impossible to see who was there. She and the fishermen of Bedruthan Steps weren't expecting any shipments that night. But her younger brother Eddie, who stood watch at the entrance to their hiding place, had spotted the ship and signaled up to the village watchman, who alerted Caragh.

As her boot slid along the dirt and sand, she cursed having to carry the torch and wished she could have sunlight to guide her. She knew these cliffs well, and it was for that reason it was better that she moved slowly than stop moving once and for all. Caragh feared the light from her torch would carry out to the boat. Despite her efforts to keep the flame small, the solitary light would be a beacon.

When Caragh came to the final twist in the path before the sand, she snuffed out her torch and started to run to the cave where the main source of the village's income lay in hiding. She heard movement along the trail above her head and knew the local fishermen would soon join her on the beach. These men, both young and old, were strong from days spent pulling in the full trawling nets and hoisting the larger catches onto their boats. However, these men weren't well-trained swordsmen, and the fear of pirate raids was ever-present. Caragh feared that was who the villagers would face that night.

The Dark Heart of the Sea **BOOK 2**
The Red Drifter of the Sea **BOOK 3**
The Scarlet Blade of the Sea **BOOK 4**

VIKING GLORY

Leif **BOOK 1 SNEAK PEEK**

Leif looked around his chambers within his father's longhouse and breathed a sigh of relief. He noticed the large fur rugs spread throughout the chamber. His two favorites placed strategically before the fire and the bedside he preferred. He looked at his shield that hung on the wall near the door in a symbolic position but waiting at the ready. The chests that held his clothes and some of his finer acquisitions from voyages near and far sat beside his bed and along the far wall. And in the center was his most favorite possession. His oversized bed was one of the few that could accommodate his long and broad frame. He shook his head at his longing to climb under the pile of furs and on the stuffed mattress that beckoned him. He took in the chair placed before the fire where he longed to sit now with a cup of warm mead. It had been two months since he slept in his own bed, and he looked forward to nothing more than pulling the furs over his head and sleeping until he could no longer ignore his hunger. Alas, he would not be crawling into his bed again for several more hours. A feast awaited him to celebrate his and his crew's return from their latest expedition to explore the isle of Britannia. He bathed and wore fresh clothes, so he had no excuse for lingering other than a bone weariness that set in during the last storm at sea. He was eager to spend time at home no matter how much he loved sailing. Their last expedition had been profitable with several raids of monasteries that yielded jewels and both silver and gold, but he was ready for respite.

Leif left his chambers and knocked on the door next to his. He heard movement on the other side, but it was only moments before his sister, Freya, opened her door. She, too, looked tired but clean. A few pieces of jewelry she confiscated from the holy houses that allegedly swore to a life of poverty and deprivation adorned her trim frame.

"That armband suits you well. It compliments your muscles," Leif smirked and dodged a strike from one of those muscular arms.

Only a year younger than he, his sister was a well-known and feared shield maiden. Her lithe form was strong and agile making her a ferocious and competent opponent to any man. Freya's beauty was stunning, but Leif had taken every opportunity since they were children to tease her about her unusual strength even among the female warriors.

"At least one of us inherited our father's prowess. Such a shame it wasn't you."

Freya **BOOK 2**

Tyra & Bjorn **BOOK 3**

Strian **VIKING GLORY BOOK 4**

Lena & Ivar **VIKING GLORY BOOK 5**

CPSIA information can be obtained
at www.ICGtesting.com
Printed in the USA
LVHW091506070223
738880LV00018B/1343

9 781648 393730